MY NAME IS
EMILIA DEL VALLE

ISABEL ALLENDE

MY NAME IS EMILIA DEL VALLE

a novel

TRANSLATED FROM THE SPANISH
BY FRANCES RIDDLE

BALLANTINE BOOKS · NEW YORK

Published in the United States by Ballantine Books, an imprint of Random House, a division of Penguin Random House LLC, 1745 Broadway, New York, NY 10019.

BALLANTINE BOOKS & colophon are registered trademarks of Penguin Random House LLC.

Published in the United Kingdom by Bloomsbury Publishing, London.

Hardback ISBN 978-0-593-97509-1
Ebook ISBN 978-0-593-97510-7
International edition ISBN 978-0-593-98356-0

Printed in the United States of America on acid-free paper

randomhousebooks.com
penguinrandomhouse.com

2 4 6 8 9 7 5 3 1

First U.S. Edition

Translated by Frances Riddle

Book design by Jo Anne Metsch

The authorized representative in the EU for product safety and compliance is Penguin Random House Ireland, Morrison Chambers, 32 Nassau Street, Dublin D02 YH68, Ireland, https://eu-contact.penguin.ie.

To Johanna Castillo, my dear agent,
and Jennifer Hershey, my wise editor,
who support me unconditionally in
this solitary craft of writing

PART ONE

———————

1

THE DAY I TURNED SEVEN YEARS OLD, APRIL 14, 1873, my mother, Molly Walsh, dressed me in my Sunday best and brought me to Union Square to have my portrait taken. The only existing photograph of my childhood depicts me standing beside a harp with the terrified expression of a man on the gallows, a result of the long minutes spent staring into the black box of the camera, holding my breath, followed by the startle of the flashbulb. I should clarify that I do not know how to play any instrument; the harp was merely one of the dusty theatrical props crowded into the photography studio alongside cardboard columns, Chinese vases, and a stuffed horse.

The photographer was a small mustachioed Dutchman who had made a good living at his trade since the times of the gold rush when the miners came down from the mountains to deposit their nuggets in the banks and have their portraits taken to send home to their all-but-forgotten families. Gold fever soon died down, but San Francisco's upper-class patrons still frequented the studio to pose for posterity. My family didn't fall into that category, but my mother had her own reasons for wanting a photo of her daughter. She haggled on the price of the portrait, more on principle than out of real necessity; I've never known her to purchase anything without attempting to obtain a discount.

"While we're here, we'll go and see the head of Joaquín Murieta," she told me as we left the Dutchman's studio.

At the opposite end of the square, near the entrance to Chinatown, she bought me a cinnamon roll and led me to the door of an unsanitary tavern. We paid the entrance fee and traversed a long hallway to the rear of the locale. There, a scary thug lifted a heavy curtain and we entered a room hung with lugubrious draperies and lit with altar candles like some ghastly church. There was a table shrouded in black cloth at one end of the space and atop it sat two large glass jars. I cannot recall any further details of the décor because I was paralyzed by fright. My mother seemed euphoric even as I quaked with fear, both hands clutching at her skirts. The first jar held a human hand floating in a yellowish liquid. The second, a man's decapitated head with the eyelids sewn shut, lips pulled back, teeth barred, and hair standing on end.

"Joaquín Murieta was a bandit. A reprobate, like your father. This is how bandits usually end up," my mother explained.

It goes without saying that I suffered horrible nightmares that night. I was even feverish, but my mother was of the opinion that unless a person was bleeding, there was no need to intervene. The following day, wearing the same dress and the same cursed lace-up boots that pinched terribly, since I had been forcing my feet into them for the past two years, we picked up my portrait and walked to the wealthy part of town, a neighborhood I had never set foot in before. Cobbled streets wended their way up the hills flanked by stately homes overlooking rose gardens and tidily trimmed hedges, coach houses stocked with glossy horses, not a single beggar in sight.

Up to that point, my entire existence had transpired within the confines of the Mission District, that multicolored, polyglot multitude of emigrants from Germany, Ireland, and Italy; Mexicans who had always lived in California; and a considerable cohort of Chileans who came with the gold rush in 1848 and, several decades later, were still as poor as when they had first arrived. They never saw any gold. If they did find anything in the mines, it was snatched from them by the whites who arrived a year later. Many returned to their homeland with nothing more than fabulous tales to tell. Others stayed because the return trip was long and costly. The Mission District was bursting with factories, workshops, piles of rubbish, stray dogs, skinny mules, clotheslines, and doors thrown open wide because there was nothing of value to steal.

That pilgrimage with my mother to the restricted universe of the upper class was my first hint that we were poor. We were far from hungry and plagued by rodents, like my maternal grandparents in Ireland, but we led a modest lifestyle like everyone else around us, who lived hand to mouth. I had never paid any mind to people of greater means before because I had never had any contact with them. I had seen them from afar when I went downtown with my parents, but that seldom happened. The coaches pulled by lustrous horses; ladies in exaggerated Victorian fashions festooned with ruffles, fringe, and rosettes; gentlemen with their top hats and canes; and children dressed in sailor suits were creatures of another species. Our working-class neighborhood was filled with barefoot children, eternally pregnant women, and drunken men working odd jobs to scrape together enough money for bread. Compared to our neighbors, my small family was fortunate. My honorable stepfather always said that as long as we had work, love, and dignity, we should want for nothing. We also had a decent little home, and we were not indebted to anyone.

I didn't dare ask my mother where we were going. I followed her up and down the hills, enduring the blisters on my feet. At that time, Molly Walsh was a young woman with an angelic face, that is to say, with the beatific expression of church martyrs, and the crystal clear voice of a mockingbird, which she still retains. That voice is deceptive, however, because my mother is actually quite forceful and bossy. On the rare occasion that she has cause to mention my father, her voice changes and her singsong tone becomes halting as she spits out her words. She hadn't said it, but I guessed that this torturous walk to the wealthy area of town was somehow related to him.

Finally, we reached the top of Nob Hill, panting from the effort, and took in the panoramic view of the city and San Francisco Bay. We came to a stop in front of the most imposing mansion on the street, with a marvelous garden hemmed in by a monumental iron fence. Through the bars, I glimpsed a statue of a fish shooting water from its mouth into a stone fountain. At the end of the garden an enormous butter-colored house rose up with a columned porch and a heavy wooden door flanked by two stone lions. My mother said it was a nouveau riche eyesore, but my mouth hung agape; this must be what a fairy-tale palace looked like. We stood before the iron gate for a few minutes catching our breath, as my mother dabbed sweat from her brow and straightened her hat. Before she could pull the cord to ring the bell, a man stepped out from a side door, dressed in a black suit with a starched collar. He crossed the vast expanse of garden and stopped before us. He did not open the gate. A mere glance was all it took for him to accurately size us up despite the care my mother had taken with our appearance.

"How may I help you, madam?" he asked in a haughty British accent, his lips so tight we could hardly understand him.

"I am here to speak with Mr. Gonzalo Andrés del Valle," my mother declared, trying to imitate the man's petulant tone.

"Do you have an appointment with Mr. del Valle?"

"No, but he'll see me."

"I am afraid he is traveling at the moment, madam."

"When will he return?" my mother asked, somewhat deflated.

"I couldn't say, madam."

The man stared at us for a moment and finally opened the gate, but he did not invite us in. I suppose he had reached the conclusion that we did not pose any real threat or major nuisance, because he took on a slightly more friendly tone.

"Mr. del Valle visits San Francisco from time to time, but he resides in Chile," the Englishman explained before adding that the family did not accept visitors without previous appointments.

"Could you provide an address where I can send him a letter? It's a very important matter," my mother said.

"You can leave it with me, Mrs. . . . ."

"Molly Walsh," she replied, without mentioning her married name, Claro.

"I will personally see that it reaches him, Mrs. Walsh," he assured her.

She then handed the man an envelope containing my photograph and a note introducing Gonzalo Andrés del Valle to his daughter, Emilia. This was not the last letter she would write to him, nor was it the first.

I GREW UP being told that my father was a very wealthy Chilean and that I had a claim to a certain inheritance. Destiny had stolen my birthright from me but God, in His infinite mercy, would place it in my path in due time. Our present economic hardship was merely a test handed down from heaven to teach me humility; the future would hold great rewards as long as I remained obedient and virtuous, something measured in virginity and modesty, because nothing offends God more than a brazen woman. At mass and in my nightly prayers kneeling before my bed, my mother had me ask God to soften the hearts of those indebted to us and to pardon them to the extent that they repaid their debts. It would be several years before I understood that this Byzantine prayer was a reference to my father.

In truth, my childhood was perfect. My mother fussed over me, but she was very busy and couldn't watch me too closely. My stepfather believed his perfect princess to be utterly incapable of misbehavior and he left me to my own devices as well. He was right. I was an introverted child, an avid reader, solitary and sensitive by nature and content to entertain myself. I was never a nuisance at all, that is until the strong gale of adolescence churned me up into a true harpy. Fortunately, that phase did not last long. The economic hardship my mother referred to in our nightly prayers was irrelevant to me, because no one around us had more abundance than we did. As for my hypothetical inheritance, I saw it for what it was—a fairy tale—and I was careful never to mention it to anyone we knew because they would have found it laughable. More than anything, I was terrified by the thought that my mysterious Chilean father, a bandit like Joaquín Murieta, might one day appear to claim me as his daughter and whisk me away to some far-off land. I couldn't bear the thought of being separated from my mother and Francisco Claro, who was and always will be my only father, even if we do not share the same blood.

But I had better tell the story in its proper order, to avoid confusion. I shall start with my mother, because, to explain who I am, I have to go back to her and my stepfather, whom I have always called Papo.

Molly Walsh, my mother, was born in New York, daughter of Irish immigrants who came to America fleeing the potato famine. In 1849, when her father heard that the streets of California were paved with gold, he joined the caravan of prospectors crossing the continent from east to west with hopes of striking it rich. One of his four children died along the way and was left behind in a small unmarked grave. A few months after arriving in the nascent, chaotic city of San Francisco, his wife died of consumption. That woman, my grandmother, heroically endured the long, terrible months of travel, trudging onward for the sake of her remaining children, but her strength and courage were not enough to prolong her existence once they reached California, land of crude, opportunistic people. One day, during a violent fit of bloody coughing, her heart stopped.

Her widower, my grandfather, suddenly found himself alone with three children in an inhospitable city, and he understood that he could not care for them properly if he aimed to fulfill his dream of finding gold. He took the oldest son, who was twelve, with him into the hills, placed the second as an indentured servant, and left Molly, age four, at an orphanage founded by three Mexican nuns, with the promise that he would return for her as soon as he obtained the fortune he was after. That never happened.

AS A YOUNG girl, Molly was submissive and pious, seeming to delight in sacrifice and suffering. This is what Papo has told me anyway, but it is hard to imagine it seeing the warrior woman she is today, capable of leading street protests and, armed with her rolling pin, facing down any drunk, bandit, cop, or other scoundrel making trouble in our neighborhood. Little Molly spent so many hours on her knees, fasted with such fervor, and accepted the mockery of her peers with such resignation that she was dubbed "Saint Molly" by the other orphans. The two younger nuns, simple women, favored her over all the other girls, moved by the thought of a budding saint in their midst. At first, Mother Rosario, the leader of that tiny religious order, paid no attention to Molly's exaggerated devotion and the other nuns' desperate hopes; her pupils, all orphaned or abandoned girls, often displayed strange conduct. The mother superior was forced to intervene, however, when, at age eleven, young Molly began to have visions and hear voices. That was taking it a step too far. Mother Rosario felt that saintliness was fine for women of leisure but it had no place there, where a love of God was demonstrated through hard work. She believed there to be a very fine line between celestial communion and mental illness and so set about curing Molly's miracles through baths of cold water and geranium oil. She forced my mother to eat three meals daily, closely guarded to ensure she swallowed every bite and kept it down. She put her to work in the garden with a shovel and hoe, at the washing troughs and the bread oven, had her scrub the floor with bleach. Between the daily dishes of beans and rice and the sweat of hard work, the girl sailed through the difficult years of puberty with a certain normalcy, but she always maintained her inclination toward melodrama. Her father and brothers never returned for her or even sent news and so she eventually accepted that those three good sisters were her only family. She was now too busy to find creative ways of imitating the martyrs from the calendar of saints, but her religious fervor remained unwavering and at age fifteen she begged to be accepted as a novice.

And that is how Molly Walsh was blessed enough to don the rough white habit of the novice nuns. Her hair was shorn off like an inmate and she joined the small circle of women who had raised her, prepared to give herself over, body and soul, to charity. She would've preferred to enter a cloistered convent, some austere, medieval fortress made of icy stone where spiked belts were employed to punish the flesh, sleeping on the hard ground with a log for a pillow and fasting to the point of collapse. Instead, she had to make do with a more agreeable existence in the large adobe house of the orphanage, where the bunk beds had horsehair mattresses and the food was simple but plentiful. The mother superior, whose healthy appetite manifested in the contours of her hips and the rolls on her waist that her loose habit was unable to dissimulate, was of the belief that the body should be well nourished in order to better serve the Lord in strength and good health.

BY AGE SEVENTEEN, Molly was ready to exercise the calling she'd been trained for: serving and educating. There was much work to be done at the orphanage, but Mother Rosario thought it best for her pupil to move down out of the clouds and into the real world so that she could acquire a bit of common sense and put her calling to the test. She suspected that the girl had a bonfire raging inside, so fierce that no religious habit would be able to contain it.

The world that the mother superior was referring to was limited to the Mission District, which took its name from the first Franciscan mission founded in the eighteenth century. San Francisco's large Mexican population was concentrated here. Mere days after the discovery of gold, the shameful Treaty of Guadalupe Hidalgo was signed, putting an end to the war and ceding more than half of the Mexican territory, including California, to the United States. The better part of the old Mexican haciendas were expropriated and the campesinos, who had lived on the land for generations, were expelled from their homes. Some futilely chased the illusion of gold, others became bandits, and the rest got by the best they could. Growing up there, we knew that certain neighbors earned their living as highwaymen, robbing travelers on the roads, but as long as they respected the people of the Mission District, no one would turn them in. More than once the neighbors had hidden them during a police raid because they knew they would be later compensated with favors or an interest-free loan in a time of need. No one trusted the bankers, who were the true thieves.

Molly Walsh got a job as a teacher in a little school by the pompous name of Aztec Pride. It consisted of a one-room adobe schoolhouse with a thatched roof where the students, all boys between the ages of six and seventeen, crowded in. The lessons were dictated in Spanish, but there were two Irish kids and one black boy, the grandson of slaves whose family had escaped the Civil War in Alabama. All three learned Spanish quickly. The modest space included two long tables flanked by mismatched stools and chairs donated from the neighborhood, a wood-burning stove in one corner to combat the damp fog and to fry eggs, a cupboard for school supplies, and a latrine outside in the yard. There was also a henhouse that provided the eggs for the boys' lunch, because many of them were sent to school on an empty stomach. There were still some powerful Mexican families in California, but their sons were educated in Catholic schools far from the Mission District. The students of Aztec Pride were all poor.

The school's founder, director, and only teacher until Molly's arrival was a mestizo man from Chihuahua named Francisco Claro, known by everyone as don Pancho. He was a true scholar, a man who had dedicated his life to his studies with the lofty ambition of being able to fathom the universe, life, and death. Nothing escaped his passionate curiosity or his formidable memory. His desire to awaken a thirst for knowledge in his students crashed up against hard reality, because as soon as they had learned the rudiments of reading, writing, and arithmetic, the boys left school to start work. Rarely did a student stay on for more than a year or two. Even the youngest had to contribute to the family and earn his sustenance.

Don Pancho took in the young novice nun with respectful appreciation. He needed her. With her assistance, he could now separate the students into groups. He divided the one-room schoolhouse using a paper screen painted with scenes of cranes and emperors, purchased in Chinatown, and he dedicated his time to the older boys while she taught the younger ones. He also assigned Molly the unpleasant task of raising funds to support the school through donations from the few Mexicans of good fortune and the wealthy whites eager to appease the guilt that so often accompanies unchecked greed. With her angelic face, soft manners, and novice's habit, her request for charity was hard to deny. Just as Mother Rosario, who was a full-blooded mestiza, had always said, Molly's translucent skin and blue eyes could open many doors that were closed to people of color.

FROM THE START, both Molly's and don Pancho's lives were changed as she saw unexpected horizons open before her and he was able to share his passion for knowledge and education. They worked side by side, arriving at dawn to clean the yard, latrine, and henhouse; at midday they prepared a lunch of tortillas and scrambled eggs for the class; they taught until five in the afternoon and then, after their pupils left, Molly stayed on to study under the maestro's tutelage. That is how she learned of the vast animal world, endless galaxies, the customs of remote cultures, the infallibility of mathematics, and everything else that her professor considered essential. As far as the evils of the world were concerned, however, she remained as ignorant as she had been among the nuns.

Don Pancho had never had a disciple so eager to learn. He saw Molly as malleable, a smooth blank canvas on which he could leave his mark; he never suspected that beneath her apparent naïveté lay an indestructible willpower. Perhaps she herself did not yet realize it. They very quickly fell into a comfortable working routine and developed an innocent master-apprentice relationship. This made Mother Rosario breathe easy at leaving the novice to spend so much time alone in the company of a man. The director of Aztec Pride was not known to be given to the vices of alcohol, gambling, fighting, or women, and he didn't seem to like men either. In fact, it was rumored that he'd lost his balls in the Battle of Chapultepec, where he had fought at age twenty-one, not out of patriotic fervor, as he himself admitted, but because he was recruited into Santa Anna's army at the tip of a bayonet. He believed that only murderous madmen went to war voluntarily.

The religious habit that covered Molly from head to toe concealed the shape of her body, but it did not cover her pretty face. My mother has the type of skin, luminous in youth, that blushes with any emotion but does not stand up to the passage of time. She has the straight nose of a classical statue, a small mouth, childlike dimples, a cleft chin, and eyes of an intense lapis lazuli, which have not faded with age. Not a single strand of her hair was visible under her tight headpiece, but from the color of her skin and eyes one would've guessed that she was blond. She wasn't. Under her veil, my mother's black hair was regularly shorn off with scissors. If don Pancho was ever tempted to admire her feminine attributes, he immediately discarded the notion. Her habit was a carapace; Molly Walsh was untouchable. Even though he considered himself a bitter enemy of all religion, he exalted the young novice nun, as sacred as the Virgen de Guadalupe.

Three years went by in this way, the two of them enjoying scholarship, hard work, and camaraderie as the day when Molly would take her vows and become a nun drew near. Mother Rosario had decreed that the ceremony would take place in December, when they would be blessed by a visit from a Mexican bishop who was making the rounds to all the churches and parishes of California. It would be a solemn occasion celebrated within the orphanage's dignified poverty.

MOLLY WALSH NEVER became a nun, however. Any illusions of sainthood she might've harbored in her youth were dashed in a few days' time by a young Chilean gentleman of considerable fortune, striking good looks, and scant scruples. His name was Gonzalo Andrés del Valle. He was my father, or so I've been told. The man set his sights on the novice nun, enchanted by her beautiful face and graceful stride, deducing that under that horrendous habit lay an appealing figure. I don't know where they met; maybe she was knocking on the doors of the Nob Hill mansions with her little basket asking for donations and he saw her there. Whatever the case, the Chilean man, accustomed to satisfying his every whim, decided he would have her. The nun's habit, far from dissuading him, was an incentive.

I'll never know how he managed to seduce that devout zealot of a girl who viewed almost everything as an unspeakable sin and lived in fear of God's implacable wrath, but the fact is that she fell into his trap like a hypnotized rabbit. Maybe he did not even need to employ any complex persuasion tactics; it was enough to simply awaken the desire for love that she bore within her like a slumbering volcano. I don't know where they committed the act that gave rise to my existence. And I refer to it in the singular because I imagine that, after his successful conquest, del Valle immediately lost interest.

Of course, none of this was relayed to me by my mother, but it's easy enough to imagine since I know her so well. Stripped of her habit, Molly was even more beautiful than the Chilean had imagined, despite the fact that her shaven skull gave her the appearance of a lunatic, but she was prudish to an extreme, overemotional, and melodramatic. The girl was unwilling to participate in any erotic play, the encounter was barely consensual, and the fleeting pleasure of the act soon left him with the bitter taste of guilt over having deceived that bride of Christ. The girl's innocence complicated matters immensely; the last thing he wanted was a hysterical woman who gave herself over to him rigid as a corpse, muttering the Lord's Prayer while bathed in tears, begging God to forgive her as he put his pants back on. He had to be free of her and the most compassionate way to do it was to cut the relationship short in a single blow, like decapitating a chicken. That would quickly convert her passionate love to bitter anger and the girl would soon get over him. His solution was to avoid her at all costs.

Molly Walsh might have been oblivious to the more mundane aspects of existence, but she wasn't stupid and quickly realized that she'd been used and tossed out like an old rag. Through severe fasting, gravel in her shoes, and other mortifications, she tried to atone for her sins and rip that illusion of love out by the roots. She refused to let herself even think of her fugitive lover ever again, and she might have achieved it if I hadn't come into existence.

Several weeks after that rushed carnal tryst, she discovered that she was with child. She took it as a divine punishment, something she always reminded me of whenever I misbehaved: I was not the fruit of love, nor even pleasure, I was a punishment from God. But I never believed her, even as a child, and now that I'm an adult it makes me laugh. Luckily, I had my Papo, who gave me the confidence to march out into the world; according to him I was a gift sent down from heaven. But why waste words on this matter that never really affected me?

Gonzalo Andrés del Valle did not respond to the desperate missives that Molly sent to the mansion on Nob Hill, but she finally managed to corner him outside Sacred Heart Cathedral, where the wealthier Catholics attended Sunday mass decked out in their finest, to see and be seen. From the back of the nave, she saw him exit the confessional, take communion, and kneel down to pray with theatrical devotion. She waited for him outside, gripped him by the coat, and began rebuking him, red with shame. Several people stopped to gawk at the spectacle; nothing juicier than a scandal among the aristocracy, although, in truth, the del Valles were anything but aristocratic. They were new money, like almost all the wealthy citizens of San Francisco, city of adventurers. He wasn't a native English speaker or a Protestant, he hailed from a land hardly anyone could locate on a map, and therefore he couldn't even aspire to being accepted by the upper crust in the United Sates.

The origin of the del Valle fortune, amassed during the gold rush, was the curious enterprise of shipping food products from Chile to California. Paulina del Valle, the visionary matriarch of the family, had the inspired notion of lining the hull of a ship with chunks of glacier from southern Chile, adding a layer of salt and sawdust, and filling the hold with vegetables, fruit, eggs, smoked meats, sausages, cheeses, and other delicacies. The merchandise then made the two-month journey from Valparaíso to San Francisco, perfectly preserved, and retailed at a price comparable to gold. The leftover ice was later sold in Panama on the way home. This process was repeated over and over with immense profits until other, quicker ships began to compete. Unfortunately, none of doña Paulina's descendants had inherited her enterprising spirit, which soon disappeared from the family line. If I refer to her here, it is because our paths would one day cross. Gonzalo Andrés, her nephew and godson, turned out to be just as lazy and dim-witted as the rest of her cousins and siblings.

That day at the church, Gonzalo Andrés took Molly by the arm, pulling her gruffly away from the exiting flock of parishioners, and accused her of trying to saddle him with a child that did not belong to him. What proof did she have that he was the father? It's true, she had been a virgin when they lay together—and let's remember that she did so more than willingly—but two months had passed since then, and in that time, she could've had any number of other lovers. If her nun's habit had not kept her from lying with him, why would it impede her from doing the same with other men, he spat in a harsh whisper so that the ever-growing crowd of curious onlookers would not overhear. In an inexplicable impulse, given her fainthearted and submissive nature up to that point, Molly Walsh brusquely wiped the tears from her face and threatened the spineless Chilean with a terrifying, oracular intensity. "No woman will ever love you. You will not be able to bear other children, and you will be thrown headfirst into hell!"

In that moment, the true Molly Walsh, bold and brave, blossomed from beneath the folds of her habit. The young seducer met the sinister prophecy with a mocking laugh, turned his back, and walked away. But, in time, Gonzalo Andrés del Valle would live to see those words cut deep to the bone. He was never able to forget them.

MY MOTHER HID her pregnancy until December came. Then, instead of preparing for the ceremony before the bishop, she had to reveal her condition to Mother Rosario. She was no longer a bride of Christ, but a future single mother, an immoral sinner, another whore of Babylon. The mother superior responded that California was far from Babylon and that they should face the situation with calm. She felt somewhat responsible, having sent the innocent girl out into the world, and she didn't have the heart to reprimand her too harshly. Molly had been abandoned and seen her honor stripped away, may God now take pity on her. She offered the girl some money from the alms box, and from among the clothes that had been donated for the poor she gave her a black skirt and severe white blouse with long sleeves and high collar. Molly bid farewell to the nuns with a promise to lead an irreproachable life and educate her future son or daughter in the Catholic church. Then she went to seek comfort from her only friend, the director of Aztec Pride.

Don Pancho Claro had loved Molly from the moment he met her, but he transformed his initial attraction into companionship. He did not feel worthy of that young woman, half his age, destined for the church. Even though he'd seen her every day for three years, he hadn't noticed the recent changes in Molly's appearance because she was very thin and the novice's robes easily concealed her growing belly. It took him a moment to recognize her when she appeared dressed as an ordinary young woman, at that unexpected hour, and he did not notice her waistline until she confessed to him her situation.

"Death would be preferable! There is no place in this world for me now. What am I going to do?" Molly sobbed tragically.

"For the moment, nothing. Waiting is all you can do, Molly," don Pancho responded.

"How am I supposed to do that? I cannot return to the orphanage to offend the good sisters with this proof of my sin. I am out on the street!"

"Come live with me. My house is small, but there is a spare room for you. Things often have a way of working themselves out," he offered.

"Live with you? What would people say?"

"People will talk anyway, Molly. Unless, that is, you would do me the immense honor of marrying me." Don Pancho muttered the words so shyly that she thought she had misheard him, and the poor man had to repeat his proposal.

"Marry you, don Pancho? But I don't love you . . ."

"We have respect and affection for each other—that's a good start. Although I don't deserve you, maybe in time you might get to love me a little. I will not bother you with marital demands. We can help and accompany each other; being alone is very hard, Molly."

"And what about this?" she said, gesturing dramatically to her belly.

"I shall take responsibility for the child, you needn't worry about that."

"The person responsible is named Gonzalo Andrés del Valle and this baby will bear his name," she declared.

"Whatever for? That man has washed his hands of the situation," the professor argued.

"Because this baby has a claim to his fortune," she returned.

"That shan't be necessary, Molly. I may not have a fortune, but I can assure you that this baby boy or girl will want for nothing."

The couple was married the following week. Molly suggested that the ceremony be held in strict privacy, given the shame of her condition, but don Pancho thought it best to face the gossip head-on; a wedding without a celebration would be an affront to the community. He'd lived in that neighborhood for many years, he knew everyone there, had educated many of the children, was considered an arbiter of disputes and counselor in hard times. No one would ever forgive him for marrying in secret.

The neighbors cordoned off the street, hung multicolored banners, and prepared mounds of food. There was a thirty-ingredient mole, stuffed chiles, roasted baby goat, carnitas, enchiladas and tacos, pork pozole, piles of tortillas, both flour and corn. The entire neighborhood attended the celebration. The nuns, led by Mother Rosario, filed in bearing trays of cakes. There was horchata and fruit punch for the children and, for the adults, an unlimited supply of sotol, a Chihuahuan liquor that contains 50 percent alcohol, so strong it can be used to kill cockroaches and to numb the pain of surgery. The musicians played lively rancheras, jaranas, waltzes, and popular songs as the Mexicans and emigrants from other lands all danced joyously. After the festivities had ended, the street was strewn with rubbish and drunken revelers. Even the good sisters stumbled as they made their way back to the orphanage.

·   ·   ·

IN DUE TIME, Molly Walsh gave birth to a baby girl—me—and no one celebrated the event more joyfully than don Pancho Claro. "She's just like me!" they say he exclaimed when he saw me for the first time, and he wasn't wrong, because although physically we look nothing alike, we have many other things in common. I was christened with the name Emilia del Valle Claro in the local Mission District church. My mother insisted on including del Valle, but don Pancho wanted Claro to be my last name, because I wasn't just another bastard, I was the daughter he always wanted.

I never lamented the fact that my biological father abandoned me before I was born, because I had an excellent father, but that slippery Chilean man hovered in the air of my childhood like a pesky blowfly. Without my stepfather's cheerful sweetness, my mother would've surely poisoned my soul, unable as she was to get over the deception she'd endured, with my presence an all-too-frequent reminder. Even though she remained soft-spoken, with her childlike voice and her God-fearing scruples, she had hardened inside. I believe that she had always carried that iron core inside her but it had only manifested with the disillusion of that first betrayal. My mother is a very sensitive woman who takes everything personally, down to the wind and the rain, and over the years she has become sickly. She doesn't suffer from any real illness, but instead acquires symptoms of every disease she hears mentioned. This is how she has managed to pass unscathed through dysentery, cholera, and malaria, which does not exist in California, but which she read about as having decimated the British colonists in India.

One day when a spider bite left a red welt on her skin, I could not resist teasing her. "What you have is leprosy, Mama," I said to her.

"May God serve as witness that my own daughter mocks me! I shall sit in this chair and wait for all of Job's suffering to rain down upon me!" she exclaimed with a certain underlying sarcasm.

Since then, we remind her of Job whenever she becomes overly dramatic and that generally quiets her down. She suffers from migraines, which are not imaginary, and she has a delicate stomach due to the extreme fasting of her youth, but it does not diminish her energy and willingness to work. My mother never rests. She wears dark, simple clothing, never adorning herself with accessories or applying rouge to her cheeks, as current fashion dictates; if it were not for the care she dedicates to her hair, she would look just like the nun she always wanted to be. Living with don Pancho, the agnostic anarchist, has somewhat attenuated her Catholic fanaticism, but he has not been able to cure her of it entirely.

At that time, Aztec Pride was the only school with classes in Spanish and it was the heart of the neighborhood; in some ways, it still is. Molly shared her husband's responsibilities when it came to teaching and charity, in addition to taking care of the domestic chores, because don Pancho is a wise man who feeds on ideas and can't be bothered with prosaic matters, as she says. The true reason is that he doesn't have a hint of practical sense. When tasked with frying two eggs, don Pancho will waste ten minutes over the frying pan musing aloud on the clichéd philosophical question of which came first, the chicken or the egg. Molly does not have the patience for that.

ALTHOUGH I WILL never know the details of my mother and her husband's intimacy, because that's one of the few topics that I would not dare touch with them, I am guessing they were chaste for a long time. At the beginning, Molly's trauma, her pregnancy, and motherhood came between them. During the first five years of my life, I slept in my mother's bed in the main bedroom while my Papo used a cot in the little room. I think they didn't have a normal marriage, although they cared dearly for each other; people commented that they were an ideal couple. He has always been very kind, indulgent, and generous with my mother, and she reserved her coquetry and her jesting only for him. This woman, so serious in public, becomes a playful girl when she is alone with her husband. He had always been in love with her, and in due time the affection that she felt for him evolved naturally into love and maybe passion.

One day they announced that I was old enough to sleep alone and without much ado they moved me to the room that had belonged to my stepfather. In turn, he took my place in my mother's bed. I am sure that all that waiting was worthwhile. In spite of their many differences, don Pancho and Molly have remained in love like newlyweds. As was to be expected, our family grew and I soon had three brothers.

Before having her other children, my mother visited the elderly, sat with the sick, helped abandoned women and widows. She still gets up every day at dawn to bake bread for the beggars and attend the first morning mass before moving on to all her other obligations. Don Pancho's small house, built on the same lot as the school, initially consisted of three half-empty rooms, which Molly quickly transformed into a cozy home. She climbed up on a ladder to paint the house inside and out, knitted blankets and sewed curtains, then planted a flower garden and several fruit trees. She has always been the one who raised money to fund the school and the natural administrator of all the family finances. Since her husband is better at giving money away, she has him on a monthly allowance that barely covers his cigarettes. Scrimping and saving, Molly was able to buy furniture and add on to the house, building a kitchen, a living room, and a covered porch to sit on in the evenings.

Despite my mother's taxing nature, her real and imagined maladies, her quickness to judge, her tendency toward tragedy, and her sullen silences, her husband adores her and still considers himself fortunate that she conceded to marry him. In his eyes, Molly will always be the beautiful youth of seventeen who came to teach at Aztec Pride; she has never changed. Even though she is almost twenty years his junior, the difference is hardly noticeable because she has aged prematurely while, for him, the clock seems to have stopped. I can verify this because I have seen their wedding photo and now, more than twenty years later, Papo looks no different, his teeth stained from tobacco, a full head of hair, black mustache, and the same mischievous smile. From him I get my optimistic nature. I inherited very little, however, from my mother, not her glossy black hair, her pearly skin, or her lapis lazuli eyes, only her height, which has served to keep anyone from ever being able to look down on me. I have dark eyes and brown hair.

I have always known that Francisco Claro is not my father, but that is a minor, abstract detail, because he has been the best father I could've wished for. No one has ever loved me as much as that short, mustachioed teacher, my Papo. He had three sons with my mother, but I was raised as an only child for eight years before my brothers were born. In that time, I received all of his attention and love. I have always been his favorite—the apple of his eye, as he calls me when he gets sentimental, something that happens often. According to him, he can spoil me like a princess because I am his little girl, whereas the boys must be raised with a firm hand to ensure that they shall grow into good men. He never let my mother hit me, but he has accepted corporal punishment as the most effective means of keeping my brothers in line.

"You spoil Emilia rotten! The little brat believes we are here to wait on her hand and foot, incapable of doing anything for herself. I pray she contracts scabies, so she may learn to scratch her own self, at least," my mother often said.

2

WHILE SPANISH WAS THE LANGUAGE OF MY EARLY YEARS, most people born in the United States end up speaking English. I was educated at Aztec Pride, like many of the boys in my neighborhood, but my culture and my self-assurance were inculcated in me by don Pancho Claro during every moment of our life together. He also gave me my insatiable curiosity, which has been my driving force since very early on. According to my mother—from whom I inherited strength and tenacity—curiosity is a liability in a woman: It leads to misfortune. She often said that curiosity kills the mouse, and if I ever got in trouble, my stepfather was to blame. This characteristic of mine has taken many forms over the years, but in essence it has kept me always looking around the next corner or over the horizon.

Whereas other kids played ball or jumped rope, I entertained myself by absorbing anything and everything my Papo felt like teaching me, from the contents of the dictionary and his scientific texts to cards and dancing, which he said were good ways to make friends. To this day, now that I'm a grown woman with my own life, we are close friends, I tell him my secrets; we share books and magazines; comment on the news, which is always bad; go walking in nature to identify plants and birds; visit museums, the theater, and, sometimes, when a touring company visits from New York or Europe, go to the opera. My mother, always busy with her younger children, her chores, and her charity work, rarely participates in our activities, except when it comes to plotting crimes.

While it's true that my Papo doesn't indulge in any of the common vices, he has one weakness that I share as well: dime novels. Everyone is familiar with these little books, popularized during the Civil War, around ninety to a hundred pages in length, pocket-sized, printed on cheap paper with hastily written stories about cowboys and Indians, adventurers, and soldiers, easy to read and entertaining. Critics consider them garbage for the semi-illiterate, but in reality, they fill a space in the life of many ordinary people, especially men and boys, since most women don't have the time to read and the upper-class ladies of leisure prefer poetry and romance. My Papo collects these novels and I've devoured every single one in his library. At age seventeen I got the idea to contribute to the collection.

"What do you think of me writing dime novels, Papo?" I suggested one day.

"How do you plan to do that, princess?"

"It's easy. Murder, jealousy, cruelty, ambition, hatred . . . you know, Papo, the same as in the Bible or the opera."

"You're quite young for all that."

"I won't lose anything by trying. Will you help me?" I asked.

I had been working with him at the school for a few years by that point, because my mother was too busy with my brothers, but, although I wanted to help ease my Papo's workload, I don't have the talent for teaching; I'm too impatient. He accepted my help gratefully, but suggested I develop another skill. He said I needed a profession that would allow me to support myself and do whatever I pleased, without depending on a husband or anyone else. My mother believed that any woman who worked to make a living would end up in poverty, since we were paid so little, and she added that Papo wanted me to become an old maid so that I would never leave him. She was almost certainly right.

If it was a diploma I was after, she suggested nursing, whereas Papo insisted I should become a doctor. There were already a few women in the field of medicine, graduates from the University of California. But pain and blood, wounds and death, things I've put to such good use in my dime novels, don't interest me in real life. I couldn't imagine at that point that destiny had reserved a healthy dose of them for me.

THAT'S HOW I began my career in letters, if I can call my work by that name. In the dime novels I found an outlet for my desire to explore beyond my limited reality. Through writing I could go anywhere and do anything I wanted. My Papo tried to help me, but, curiously, it was my mother who imagined the plot of my first book: A young woman is ravaged by a band of heartless criminals who end up paying for the misdeed with their lives. Nothing too original, except that the vengeance isn't dealt out by a hero with a chiseled jawline and perfect aim, but by the girl herself, who dresses up as a man to kill the four evildoers, one by one, in the most brutal way.

We'd never seen my mother so excited about anything; the gorier and bloodier the details, the happier she seemed. Melodrama fits my mother like a glove. I think that sending those four felons down into hell was her way of vicariously punishing her one-time seducer, Gonzalo Andrés del Valle. She even suggested that the damsel castrate her rapists before murdering them, but I worried that might be too much for my potential male readers. Men are very squeamish when it comes to their private parts.

My Papo polished up the manuscript for me, I translated it into English, and then he personally took it to an editor, because I would have been ignored completely. *The Damsel's Revenge* was published under the name Brandon J. Price simultaneously in English and in Spanish, to compete with the novels that came in from Mexico.

The excitement over seeing my first book in print was indescribable; I've never felt that way about any book I've published since. Upon opening the brown paper package to find the ten copies sent by the editor, I began crying like a little girl. My Papo wanted to invite the entire neighborhood to celebrate, but I reminded him that we couldn't reveal Brandon J. Price's true identity. We'd spent hours coming up with the most macho name we could think of before finally landing on my pseudonym, which was a secret that my brothers, all under age nine, would have to keep. Unable to throw a party, Papo decided to mark the occasion with special gifts for my mother and me. He bought his wife a pair of gold filigree-and-garnet earrings and for me a gold medallion with the image of the Virgen de Guadalupe, both pieces of jewelry in the purest Mexican style.

That summer they sold nine thousand copies of the book in English across the country and twenty-nine hundred Spanish copies in Texas and California. When the publishing house asked for another novel, I already had one ready, thanks to my enthusiasm for writing and my mother's morbid imagination. The second book was called *A Bad Woman* and the protagonist was the same defiled damsel from the first novel, now devoted to avenging other wronged women. Many more dime novels followed, along with weekly serials in the newspapers, as Brandon J. Price made a name for himself. I tried to expand my repertoire to romances for the female readership, but in this genre I was unsuccessful. The formula was simple enough, consisting of variations on the theme of love laden with obstacles between a good, poor girl and a rich, noble boy disenchanted with love. But since the editors demanded that virtue and morality triumph in the end, I was never able to get sufficiently inspired. My mother also had trouble coming up with convincing plot lines, always more inclined toward tragedy than romance.

.   .   .

THE "BAD WOMAN" from my book's title was a joke within our family. My mother raised me with the strict Catholic morals that the nuns had instilled in her: sins, contrition, guilt, heaven, purgatory, hell, and when her husband would intervene in my favor to soften the rules, she would cut him off with the argument that they should be trying to shape me into a good woman. That would put an end to the discussion. She never clarified what being a good woman consisted of exactly, but it seemed to be the traditional idiot who submits to rules imposed by others. One day, in the midst of a tantrum, I shouted that I wanted to be a bad woman. I was six years old at the time. It's the only real mutiny that I remember from childhood; my true acts of rebellion came later, when the two protuberances appeared above my ribs and the hair between my legs. My mother invoked God as her witness and raised a sandal in the air, but my Papo managed to hold her back. My dear stepfather used that scene to mock the notion of a "good woman" and he did so with such eloquence that my mother had to admit that on certain occasions it was better to be a bad woman, while never making a fuss, of course, no need to cause a commotion.

The revenue from my literary ventures, which have always been successful, served to contribute to the household income and to my savings, which my mother considers sacred. "Given that you don't have a husband, and at the rate you're going I doubt you ever will, you must save for your future," she often says to me.

She and I support the family, me with my books and other writings, she with her common sense, thrifty nature, and hard work. The bread for the poor, which Molly Walsh had been baking out of charity for many years, eventually became a domestic industry. She had two brick ovens built in the patio to bake bread of all kinds, both salty and sweet, first on her own and then with the help of a couple of girls from the neighborhood. Every morning, even Sundays, there's a line of customers waiting for her baked goods. And every morning I wake up to the comforting vision of my mother and her two assistants kneading dough and the incomparable smell of fresh-baked bread steaming beneath white towels as it cools on the wooden countertop. What she doesn't sell in the morning, she gives away to the poor, who have dubbed her Saint Molly, never suspecting that this was her childhood nickname.

My mother maintains that it's not enough to earn money, you have to know how to manage it, especially in the case of a woman, because people will always try to fool us, pay us less, or rob us, and if we get married, everything passes into our husband's hands. She doesn't have that problem, because my Papo would never even think to ask her for the money that she earns or question how she manages it. He knows that if it weren't for his wife's efforts and good sense, we'd be much poorer. He isn't interested in what I earn either; it's my mother who keeps our accounts.

At the time of this writing, my Papo still works at the school, even though he's a few years shy of seventy and at his age most men are either dead or nodding off in a wicker rocker chewing at the air. He spends his time studying, reading, and thinking, unconcerned with more mundane matters. He never asks for anything, as long as he has his cigarettes. My mother says that his grasshopper personality keeps him young, whereas she's more like the ant in the story, always working and saving, which is why she has wrinkles and gray hair.

BETWEEN HELPING MY Papo at the school and writing novels filled with action and blood, the years slipped by. I was about to turn twenty-three when I began working as a columnist for a newspaper. *The Daily Examiner* was the new name of a paper that had previously supported slavery and had therefore been prohibited in don Pancho's home. After President Lincoln's assassination, the newspaper office was attacked by a furious mob that destroyed the building. Since then, its political inclinations have changed along with its name.

It was then acquired by a mining magnate who gave it its current name; it is said that he won it in a game of poker. When I found out that the newspaper had passed into the hands of that impresario's son, a young man named William Randolph Hearst, I got up the nerve to request a meeting with him, because he was known for his modern ideas and he was hiring illustrators and writers my Papo and I read, such as Jack London, Ambrose Bierce, and Mark Twain. Hearst was an ambitious man who dreamed of creating a press empire, a chain of newspapers across the most important cities in the country.

I figured that somewhere in that empire, there might be a place for me. I was beginning to grow bored with classes at the Aztec Pride and dime novels; I wanted to open myself up to the real world and all that it actually held, instead of only dreaming up stories about it.

I wasn't able to speak with Hearst himself, of course, but after much insistence, clarifying that I didn't want a job as a typist but as a journalist, the editor in chief agreed to meet with me.

A glass wall divided his office from the newsroom, where a dozen reporters worked in a haze of cigarette smoke to a thundering concert of typewriters, telephones, telegraphs, and voices. Mr. Chamberlain was a man with a long career in journalism, energetic and impatient, who had granted me exactly ten minutes, the receptionist informed me. He remained standing, prepared to dismiss me in five, but we are the same height and as we stood there face-to-face he found it difficult to intimidate me. My Papo had instilled in me great self-confidence from a young age. "Remember that you're more intelligent than everybody else," he would tell me often. Also, I'd spent several years publishing books and had a good deal more writing experience than most of those boys mashing at the keyboards out in the newsroom.

"We don't have any female reporters," Chamberlain announced by way of greeting.

"That's why I'm here, sir. Your newspaper needs me," I answered.

"What experience do you have in journalism?" he asked, taken aback by my audacity.

"None, but I know how to write."

"Prove it. I'll give you fifteen minutes to present me with a page on the San Francisco Flower Show," he told me. He pointed to an empty desk on the other side of the window separating us from the newsroom.

"I can't do that, sir. Flowers bore me. But if you like I could write two pages on the murder of Arnold Cole. In twenty minutes."

The editor fixed his gaze on me for several eternal seconds, his brow furrowed, and finally gestured toward a chair, sat down behind his desk, and slowly lit a cigar as he observed me with curiosity. I could tell he was sizing me up and I took the opportunity to do the same. I was twenty-two but I looked young for my age, despite the fact that I'd tried to dress in matronly attire for the interview, a dark blue velvet blazer with puffy sleeves and a hat in the same color adorned with a feathered bird, something my mother reserved for special occasions.

"Let's see, Miss . . . what did you say your name was?" the editor finally asked me.

"My name is Emilia del Valle Claro, but for obvious reasons, I have been writing under my pen name, Brandon J. Price."

"Pen name? How's that?"

"I write dime novels and adventure series for newspapers and magazines. They sell very well. My editors don't know me personally; I send them my work by messenger or mail. They believe the author to be a man," I explained, pulling a couple of copies from my bag.

The editor shot them a disgusted look, like someone forced to rummage through the trash. The crude illustrations on the covers were gruesome, with dismembered or decapitated bodies, knives, revolvers, pools of blood.

"You wrote these?" he asked, picking them up with his fingertips.

"Everyone likes crime, don't you agree?"

"I suppose you're right. But I have several seasoned reporters already covering crime. And the subject matter is not befitting of a girl. I can try you out in the ladies' section, the social pages; I hope you will not disappoint me, miss."

I stood up and smoothed my skirt. "I'm sorry, sir. Goodbye."

Chamberlain stopped me in the doorway. He wasn't accustomed to negotiating with women. "What can you write about Cole's murder that I don't already know?" he asked.

"That depends. Based on what came out in the press today, I could certainly rehash the same information with much more flair, but if you'll give me a few days to investigate, I can bring you something new," I told him.

"I'll give you eighteen hours. But I have to warn you that I have Eric Whelan on the case and he's our best reporter. Write me a column on it. Don't send it with a messenger, bring it to me in person."

"If you publish it, will it be under my name?" I asked.

"No one would take it seriously under a woman's name. I can run it using your pen name. What did you say it was? Brandon J. Price?"

IN SAN FRANCISCO, like almost everywhere else, humanity is divided into social classes. According to my Papo, in some countries, such as England or France, it requires generations of aristocratic names or a noble title to be accepted as a member of the upper class. In San Francisco, a frontier town that only forty years back was a Mormon settlement called Yerba Buena, all it takes is money, generally made not from the gold rush but from business deals, banks, and industry, as well as corruption and crime. Wealthy men hold the political and economic power, whereas their wives jealously control access to high society. For these people, among them the unfortunate Arnold Cole, the world of the working class, immigrants, and the poor would always be a foreign land. I doubt that any of them had ever set foot in my neighborhood, the Mission District, where my family, friends, and many of my readers lived. We, on the other hand, those of us on the bottom, can slip into their lives undetected. We are invisible to them.

As soon as the Cole drama had come to light, just one day prior, a wave of rumors began to wash through the Mission District. My mother came home from the market with vegetables for supper and juicy details about the crime, passed on by word of mouth. Everyone was urged not to say a word, in order to protect the innocent neighbor who had provided the information. Luckily for me, not a single one of us could keep a secret.

When Mr. Chamberlain gave me the Cole assignment, the first thing I thought was to access the rumor mill in my neighborhood, because I did not yet have the contacts in the police force that I do now. In a few short hours, aided by my parents, I had discovered the source of the gossip and located Josefa Palomar, the unassuming woman who knew more than anyone else about Senator Cole's private life and whose anonymity the gossips had been unable to protect.

Arnold Cole was a California politician, born in Delaware, known for his fiery speeches. He initially spoke in favor of slavery but when that rhetoric fell out of fashion, he turned his attention to the defense of the white race and the Protestant religion. He had sowed hatred with his diatribes against Catholics and Jews, both groups that he felt threatened the nation's moral and racial equilibrium, and the Chinese, who didn't mix with the broader population but according to him were still a problem. America is a white, Protestant country, he alleged, and we had to stop the invasion of inferior people of color who came to take advantage of the benefits we have here and impose their backward customs on us. He claimed that black people had come over as emigrants from Africa, that they had been civilized under the protection of the whites, and that the best thing for them was to be repatriated to their tribes. Behind his back it was whispered that he had a marriage of convenience. His wealthy wife was eight years his elder and took little care of her appearance; she was considerably overweight, whereas he had a reputation as a dandy, thanks to his athletic build, tailored suits, and Thoroughbred horses. His wife's money financed his fancies and guaranteed him an advantageous position in society. The racehorses earned him a certain amount of fame, with his portrait appearing on collectible cards of the kind that come in boxes of tobacco and cigarettes. It was said he wore so much cologne that plants withered as he walked by.

Just like any politician, he had as many supporters as he had detractors, but none who took him seriously enough to want to kill him. He was forty-seven years old when he died of a bullet to the head, delivered so cleanly that it left only a hole the size of a half-dollar at the base of his skull. Someone had snuck up on him from behind; he might not have even realized what was happening as he died instantly, then slumped to the ground. The police were keeping silent as they conducted their investigation, but the press was having a field day with speculations.

JOSEFA PALOMAR WAS born and raised on one of the old Mexican haciendas that had been confiscated and divided up in the middle of the century. She was an older woman, I guessed fiftysomething. As far as she was concerned, the concept of America did not exist, she still lived on Mexican soil. She spoke very little English because she didn't need to; her entire existence was carried out in Spanish, though she worked for the whites. She knew my Papo well, because her sons had attended Aztec Pride when they were little, which is why she agreed to speak with me. I turned up at the little house she shared with her daughter, her son-in-law, and three young grandchildren. She offered me coffee and we sat on the patio, far removed from the hubbub of the family.

"Tell me what you know about Mr. Cole, doña Josefa. I promise to protect your identity," I said.

"They didn't kill him on the street, niña Emilia, that's all I can tell you."

"You worked for him, is that right?"

"Just cleaning, that's all. An apartment he has on Fillmore Street," she replied.

"So, you knew him well . . ."

"I hardly ever saw him; he would leave my payment on the table and by the time I got there he was already gone. Boys visited him there," she explained.

"What's that?"

"I never saw any women. Men, yes. Young ones. Making messes that I had to clean up," she went on.

"Why do you say they didn't kill him on the street?"

"He did not arrive on that street corner of his own free will, niña Emilia. Someone dragged him there. I know for certain because they found him yesterday, which was Wednesday, but I saw him dead on Tuesday with my own two eyes, lying on the floor of his apartment. Naked, he was, the poor man, with all his shame right out in the open, may God forgive him," she said, making the sign of the cross.

"What did you do?"

"The Christian thing would've been to put some underwear on him, at least, but I was too scared. I ran right out of there. I didn't tell anyone, only my daughter, but you see how word gets around," she replied with a sigh.

"You should notify the police, señora Josefa."

"How could you think such a thing, child! I don't want trouble with their kind, those white men are the worst bandits out there," she exclaimed.

"Sooner or later, they'll find out about the apartment and the fact that you cleaned it. They'll surely come to interrogate you," I told her.

"What will they do to me?"

"If no one saw you go in or out on Tuesday, I suppose you have no reason to tell them what you saw."

"Then what do I say?" she asked me.

"Play dumb, you don't know anything, you haven't been there since last week. Based on what you're telling me, someone dressed the body and took it out onto the street to make it look like he'd been robbed," I said.

"It was some quarrel among queers, child . . ."

My Papo, who knew people everywhere, spoke with a custodian in the morgue and to the woman who delivered food to the police officers at the station. They offered up more details. That night I wrote my column using only some of the information we'd obtained, without mentioning Josefa Palomar. It would've been the perfect topic for my next novel, as my mother pointed out, but I had to turn it in to the *Examiner*.

IN THE SECOND interview, I didn't have to wait in reception, Mr. Chamberlain received me immediately. He gestured to the chair I'd sat in before and he stood at the window to read my two pages. Then he leaned out of the doorway and asked his secretary to call in Eric Whelan.

"Would you like a coffee or a chamomile tea, miss?" he offered, opening a cabinet full of bottles and serving himself a large glass.

"Brandy, please," I answered, in an attempt to shock him.

He poured it and handed it to me, surprised.

At that moment Eric Whelan entered. He was tall and disheveled, freckled with red hair like an Irishman of the kind that abounds in San Francisco, especially among the police force. His shirt and two of his fingers were stained with ink, his wrinkled pants were held up with suspenders, his nose looked as if it had been broken, and he had a short beard and mustache that were not red but brown. He did not fit the image I had of a journalist, his appearance more in line with a low-class boxer. He looked to be in his early thirties and, I can't deny it, I was attracted to him, even though he wasn't my type; I usually prefer dark-haired Italian men. Chamberlain handed him my two pages and looked down at the street as Whelan read. Meanwhile, I discreetly dumped my brandy into a spittoon beside the desk.

Whelan finished reading with a long whistle. "Where did you get this? Who is Brandon J. Price?" he asked his boss.

"It's the name used by a dime novel writer. Sitting right there," Chamberlain replied, gesturing toward me with his chin.

"I don't understand," said the redheaded man.

"That's me. Emilia del Valle Claro, at your service," I informed him.

"You? I suppose this is a work of fiction . . ." said the Irishman, shaking my pages.

"Exactly which part of my column seems fictitious to you?"

FRIDAY, FEBRUARY 15, 1889
AN EXEMPLARY MAN
By Brandon J. Price

Day dawns on San Francisco. The city sleeps, swathed in a thick veil of fog. Only a mule cart and a few early morning workers venture onto the silent streets. Among them, a German baker, stooped, his hat damp, the collar of his coat raised, his steps hurried. It is Karl Josef Meyer, owner of the Vienna Bakery and Pastry Shop on the corner of Fillmore and Lombard. He's two blocks from his destination and he cannot yet view the nearby bay as the pale winter light filters dimly through the thick fog coming off the Pacific.

Karl trips and curses. A man is lying on the sidewalk, another drunk from the local tavern, he thinks. He's about to continue on his way, but he notices the man's unusual posture, one leg bent at an impossible angle. He leans over, shakes the man, strikes a match, observes him more closely in the trembling glare of the flame, and sees with a start that the man is dead. His first reaction is to ignore the problem, the poor soul is none of his business, he has to light the ovens, open up shop; he hesitates, takes a few steps, stops, and finally decides to fulfill his duty as a good citizen. The baker sounds the voice of alarm.

People soon gather and day has broken by the time the police arrive. The corpse is barefoot and wears no coat. They turn him over and someone who collects tobacco cards recognizes him. It's Arnold Cole, the politician. A heart attack, one of the officers surmises, but then another notices spots of blood on his shirt and they follow them up to a hole in the back of his head.

At this moment, as you read these lines, the body of Arnold Cole lies on a metal table in the morgue. An initial autopsy determined that the death occurred between twenty-four and thirty-six hours before the body was found. The bullet embedded in the man's skull came from a derringer pistol that was likely fired at point-blank range. This is all the information that has been leaked to the press.

What was this well-known gentleman doing at that hour so far from his home and office? It seems impossible that his body could've lain for so many hours on a busy corner without being discovered; he doubtless died, or more accurately was killed, at some other location and was moved under the cloak of fog.

I ask myself: Was it a surprise attack? Or maybe he knew the murderer—or murderess—someone he turned his back on, trustingly? Where was Arnold Cole that fateful night and who was he with? No traces of a struggle or robbery have been found; it seems more like a clean execution, a vendetta. His wife has stated that he did not return home Tuesday night; this was not uncommon because Cole often traveled to Sacramento to attend to government matters or worked late. But no one saw him in Sacramento and there is no register of him at any hotel. A love nest, perhaps, where he could enjoy unspeakable diversions? A garçonnière? The police will surely get to the bottom of it, but whether the truth comes to light is another matter. In this city, the truth is often as slippery as soap and there are many ways to cover up a scandal, as we well know.

The press has published laudatory obituaries and statements from the governor and other of Arnold Cole's colleagues lamenting the tragic end met by this exemplary man, a family man, a public servant respected by everyone, even his political adversaries, a victim of the rampant crime the honorable citizens of San Francisco are forced to endure as our streets are overrun with delinquency. However, those of us who were born here know that these streets have never been safe. Ours is a city founded by adventurers, criminals, sailors, preachers, and renegades drawn in by gold; it is a city where morality is negotiable.

What secrets was this exemplary man hiding? Why was he murdered? Was his morality, like San Francisco's, perhaps up for negotiation?

Eric Whelan was of the opinion that my column equated to baselessly accusing the dead man of leading an immoral double life. The family would surely file a complaint, the public reaction would be negative, the *Examiner* could not be turned into a tabloid rag, he said.

"The apartment exists," I assured him.

"How do you know?" asked Mr. Chamberlain, who up to that point had remained silent.

"I can't reveal my sources, Mr. Chamberlain."

"Did he have a mistress?" Whelan asked.

"No. He brought boys there . . ." I responded, blushing.

"Are you telling me that Cole was homosexual?"

I'd never heard that term uttered aloud; it was more common to speak of "masculine love" or other euphemisms, but it wasn't typically a topic of conversation in polite company, and I suddenly felt unable to tell them what I'd heard. I was still very ignorant and prudish when it came to these kinds of matters, and I could not even conceive of the dirty deeds that Josefa Palomar had mentioned. Now, even as a more experienced woman, the truth is that I still don't quite know what she was referring to. I nodded, my eyes fixed on the floor.

"Your column is pure speculation, but I like it, miss," said the editor.

"Thank you. Are you going to publish it?"

"One of the newspaper's lawyers will have to go over it first to make sure we won't have any possible legal trouble. I'm going to put you both on the Cole story and I expect you to work together."

"I've always worked alone," said Whelan, clearly annoyed.

"You'll continue to report the news, Eric, and the young lady will come on as a columnist."

"What's the difference?" I asked.

The editor explained that journalism was based in concrete facts and aimed to objectively inform the public, which is what Eric Whelan would do. But a columnist could be more subjective, providing an interpretation of the events through the personal perspective of the author, in this case Brandon J. Price. He liked the tone of my piece and insisted that the mark of a good columnist was to have a unique voice easily identifiable by the readers. The use of first-person narrative and present tense had been clever. He added that the two of us would have to share all the information we obtained: Whelan would speak to the authorities and the public, and I would have to use my own sources, the ones I did not wish to reveal, and write in my own style.

"Understood?"

"Understood. Shall I call you Brandon or Mr. Price?" the Irishman said with a mocking wink.

"Miss del Valle Claro will be fine," I answered.

"Pleased to meet you, Miss del Valle Claro. Call me Eric," he said, stretching out his hand.

. . .

SO THAT'S HOW I began publishing my regular column in the *Examiner*. This form of journalism opened the world for me: I was interested in everything that happened in the city, and there was never a lack of stories to investigate. I got information for my second piece through that friend of my Papo, the custodian at the morgue. Eric Whelan had visited the morgue on the Wednesday that the crime was discovered, and on that following Saturday he was present for the autopsy as he interviewed the medical examiner and his assistant. Among other details, he discovered that Senator Cole registered high levels of alcohol and also morphine. His widow tearfully confirmed to Eric that her late husband had suffered from inexplicable pains, alleviated only by injections.

They did not allow me to witness the autopsy; it would be a gory scene not fit for a young lady's eyes and would surely induce a fainting spell, the medical examiner informed me, and I was unable to persuade him otherwise. I am certain, however, that I would have withstood the autopsy better than Whelan, who got quite queasy. In the end it was the custodian who provided the most useful information. He told me that in his twentysomething years working at the morgue he'd seen a lot of things, because San Francisco was not lacking in crimes of all sorts—from women murdered by their lovers or husband, to Chinese immigrants stabbed to death over gambling debts. But he had been struck by the fact that the politician was found in his shirtsleeves and bare feet out on the street in winter, something that the press had already reported.

"But when we undressed him, he wasn't wearing underwear or an undershirt either," he told me.

Out of loyalty to Josefa Palomar, I couldn't write that Arnold Cole had been naked when he was murdered, but that information from the custodian allowed me to pose it as a theory. No matter how rushed or drunk Cole might've been, he was a very meticulous dresser and he would not have forgotten to put on underwear. More likely, someone had hastily dressed him after his death. And if he was underdressed or naked when he was attacked, he must've been in a place he felt safe, a room or apartment he used when he didn't go home, a place he could rest—or entertain himself—discreetly.

After leaving the morgue, pale and shaky, Eric Whelan invited me for a drink at the bar of the dazzling Palace Hotel, the tallest and most luxurious building in the city, which, in its few years of existence, had established itself as the heart of the local social scene. We passed groups of friends who had arranged to meet in front of the huge clock in the foyer, as was the custom, and found seats.

"You were right, Miss del Valle Claro."

"In private you can call me Emilia," I interrupted.

"Well then, Emilia, Cole was married and had a daughter, but he preferred men. I'm not going to tell you how I know."

"I think he was naked when they killed him. Might he have been with a lover?" I suggested.

"More than one, perhaps. It's not easy to dress a body and drag it out onto the street," he said.

"They only moved him a short distance. Tell your officer friends to look for Cole's garçonnière on Fillmore, near the corner of Lombard. It shouldn't be hard to find."

"You know exactly where it is but you aren't going to tell me, are you? That's considered a cover-up, you know," the redheaded man said accusingly.

"Don't ask me to betray my sources, Eric. I'm giving you a scoop, making you look good. You know the inspector and the chief of police, both just as Irish as you are, I take it. You can access places I can't," I told him.

"Can I ask what your next column will be about, Emilia? I should warn you that we cannot publish what I told you about Cole without proof. And even if we had evidence we wouldn't run the story anyway, out of respect for his family and their social status."

"I'm planning to write about the impunity extended to the wealthy and well-connected, the manipulation of truth, the partiality of justice, and the secrets of honorable men. I won't name any names; it won't be necessary," I replied.

OVER THE YEARS that I've worked with the *Examiner* I have not been the only woman; there are a few ladies who cover the society section and fashion, the flower shows, the formal balls and galas, and domestic topics, but I am the only one who had to hide behind a male pseudonym. I was not considered a journalist by my editor, who kept reminding me that I was a columnist and my success depended on how original and personal my chronicles were. According to Eric Whelan, I had a unique perspective that the readers liked. However, I was not part of the regular staff and I did not receive a monthly salary; they paid me a ridiculously low wage that not even a hermit could live on, but I felt proud to be published. The fact that women were always paid so much less than men infuriated my Papo and me as well, but I did not have enough seniority at the *Examiner* to argue with Chamberlain about my wages. I first had to prove myself indispensable.

I considered myself more experienced than most of the reporters at the newspaper, because I was doubly published, writing my columns as well as my dime novels, which supported me and contributed the better part of the household expenses. I gave my mother a percentage of what I earned, which was only right, because while she kneaded dough or swept the patio, she would come up with juicy plots for hair-raising crimes and fatal passions. My Papo would buy tabloids to gather ideas as well, but Molly Walsh didn't need any help to get inspired. I've often asked myself what kind of person my mother would've been if she hadn't been raised by the nuns. Those good sisters were not able to tame her gruesome imagination, but they instilled in her great respect for the traditional norms of good behavior, which she always applied rigorously to her own life and whenever possible to the lives of her husband and children, especially mine.

As my mother always said, if I only made an effort with my appearance, I could catch a wealthy husband and write just for the fun of it, since novelist was no proper profession for a young lady, as teacher or nurse would've been. This was a typical argument between my parents:

"Who's ever even heard of a female journalist?" my mother asked.

"Well, for example, there's Fanny Fern, who rose to become the highest-paid newspaper columnist in the country," my Papo replied.

"If her name comes to mind so readily it is because she is the only one. Anyway, she's dead."

"People are in the unfortunate habit of dying, Molly," Papo pointed out.

"How many lady writers are there? More or less five, right? And they're all dead, too; several of them committed suicide. Emilia would have to be a hundred times more capable than any man to compete on the same playing field," my mother said.

"She *is* a hundred times more capable. If she doesn't let herself be looked down on by anyone, she will achieve anything she sets out to," my Papo asserted.

And what was it that I wanted to achieve? I still wasn't sure, but I secretly dreamed of publishing a real novel, something more than ninety pages long that sold for more than ten cents. Under my own name, of course. There were several female fiction writers who could serve as role models, despite the fact that the critics considered their literature to be inferior, claiming that we women didn't have the same experience of the world as men, that our minds were not as rational. If we did write, we should stick to matters of the heart since any incursion into other areas might offend our fathers or husbands.

"How ridiculous!" my Papo would respond to that notion. "Mary

Shelley was just eighteen when she started writing *Frankenstein*. Let's see any man imagine something like that!"

My mother read that book in two days and determined that the best character in the story was the poor monster, so sad and solitary. His creator's mistake was in bestowing him with awareness and feelings, which were what condemned him to suffering. Her reading of *Frankenstein* inspired another Brandon J. Price novel, in which a deformed circus freak, caged, hungry, and humiliated, escapes with the help of a female trapeze artist. Together they commit multiple misdeeds in order to survive, pursued by the evil ringmaster, who desires the girl. I can't remember all the details, only that the villain kills the monster. Then the trapeze artist, heartbroken, sets fire to the circus tent and the bad guys are charred to a crisp. Of course I made sure she set all the circus animals free before lighting the match.

FOR MY COLUMN in the *Examiner* I had to limit my topics to the Bay Area, which, fortunately, was extensive and quite perverse. I wrote about crimes, which were always of interest to the readers, but I wasn't able to continue investigating the death of Arnold Cole. Political pressure and threats from his widow kept the dead man's sexual preferences from coming to light, along with his extensive gambling debt and the apartment on Fillmore. It was concluded that he'd been killed in a robbery, but the police knew that, just as Josefa Palomar had intimated, it was in truth a murder involving male lovers who dragged his corpse out to the street afterward. Through the information Eric provided them, the police were able to find his apartment and uncover unmistakable evidence of what had occurred.

Whenever acts of delinquency were scarce, I had to opt for more banal topics and give them a newsworthy angle: communities and neighborhoods, all as different as small independent nations, the dockworkers' strike at the port, the garbage collectors, the mistreatment of horses and mules used for transportation, new waves of immigration, the insane asylum, the coyotes that came out at night to eat hens and pets, the invasion of rats in the city.

Eric Whelan became my mentor and best friend. He introduced me to his pals in the police force, investigators and informers; he taught me how to catch the reader's attention in the first few sentences, how to structure a piece from beginning to end, how to check the information I gathered. I thought I knew how to research, but he showed me how to conduct an interview in depth and he made sure that I always used more than one source. According to him, I was a very good writer, but that didn't make me a good journalist. I had a lot to learn from him and he was always willing to share his knowledge and experience. I never perceived a hint of condescension or romantic intent in him; we treated each other as comrades, which suited me perfectly.

There was always new material for my chronicles but there came a time when I wanted to step out of my bubble and venture farther, and Eric encouraged me to do so; it was his idea that I should try my wings away from San Francisco. After I'd been writing for the paper for more than a year, I announced to Mr. Chamberlain that I was going to take a trip to New York, and I pitched him the idea of a travel column. We agreed on a price for each piece and a budget for expenses and accommodations. He gave me a period of one month in which to write ten columns, which I would send to him by train, given that the telegraph was reserved for breaking news.

My mother worried that the trip would provoke a chorus of rumors, that people would say I was an adventurer. Who had ever heard of a young lady taking off on her own across the continent without any real need to do so, three thousand miles of danger and temptation? I pointed out that San Francisco was home to the very same dangers and temptations.

"If you play with fire you're bound to get burned, Emilia. Why tempt the Devil? I pray every day that my only daughter won't suffer the same fate as me!" she exclaimed in one of her fits of melodrama.

"Are you referring to what happened to you when you were a novice nun? You see how that kind of thing can happen anywhere, Mama, there's no need to go all the way to New York. When are you going to forgive and forget that Chilean man anyway? You've been highly fortunate. Thanks to him you have me as well as the best husband in the world," I argued.

My Papo was against my travels as well; for once they were in agreement on something. But I reminded him that, from the cradle, he had instilled in me a desire to see the world. They could not stop me.

3

THE TRANSCONTINENTAL EXPRESS, INAUGURATED IN 1876, traverses the route from San Francisco to New York City in eighty-three hours, a journey that would have previously taken a month by stagecoach. That train connecting two oceans is one of the most spectacular technological advances to come out of our marvelous century of inventions. It was no longer a novelty by the time I climbed aboard, but it was a transformative experience for me nonetheless. I traveled to New York in a heated cabin with upholstered seats that reclined for sleeping, personalized attention, delicious foods served on porcelain dinnerware, and wine in crystal glasses. I had never before seen such luxury, and the first thing I did when I arrived was send a telegram to Mr. Chamberlain thanking him for the first-class ticket.

Since much had already been written about the famous train, I decided to focus my first travel chronicles on the workers who all but abandoned their families to keep the train running: the invisible laborers, almost exclusively Chinese, who laid out the tracks and maintained them; the sweaty, soot-smudged men who fed the steel beast with tons of coal; the waiters who slept sitting upright; the shocking variety of people and landscapes I encountered along the rails.

In fewer than four days I reached New York City, rested and happy to be there. I declined to check in to the residency for young ladies that had been recommended to me because the rules were as strict as my mother's. I hadn't come all the way to Sodom and Gomorrah, as the preachers often called that city, just to lock myself away inside at eight o'clock each night.

New York was more fascinating than I ever could've imagined, with something surprising around every corner; San Francisco was a tiny hamlet by comparison. To extend my budget, I found a boardinghouse for poorer immigrants, a hodgepodge of races in furious, incessant activity, and took a room. There, the clamor of the traffic, workshops, and factories competed with the cacophony of multiple languages; at no time of day, not even at midnight, did the streets go silent. The smell of fried food and garbage permeated the air. Necessity is cruel, leaving no room for compassion. Ragged children played, fought, and worked in the streets, stole coal from the carts, often at risk to their own lives, and were chased by the police with their clubs. I once watched as laborers, laying tar, heated pennies to the point that they glowed red and then tossed them at the children, so desperate to pick them up that they burned their tiny fingers as the men doubled over with laughter. My hotel stood among ruined buildings mired in a poverty quite different from that of our neighborhood in the Mission, where we at least had space, we could breathe the air without coughing, and we were not forced to live in a state of desperation. The hotel had illusions of respectability; when they handed me the key, they proudly informed me that the mattresses were free of bedbugs.

ERIC WHELAN HAD given me the address of one of his brothers, Owen, considerably older than he, so that he could show me around and look out for me, as he said. I assured him that I could get by just fine on my own, but Eric sent me with a box of cigars as a gift for his brother. That's how we met.

I lost my virginity to Owen Whelan. It's hard to explain how it happened so quickly. From the moment we met, I felt drawn to him magnetically, unable to resist the attraction. For the first time in my life, a man made me feel like I was interesting and pretty. He was much older than me, but his masculine energy pulled me in like an inescapable whirlwind. Owen did not look at all similar to Eric; the elder brother was dark-haired with an intense gaze, like the Italian men that I like so much. I did not have any experience with romance and so I gave myself over to him with the passionate innocence of first love, never sparing any thought for the possible consequences. He simply offered to take me back to my hotel and I agreed.

Female guests staying alone were not allowed to receive visitors in their rooms, only in the foyer, as indicated by a sign tacked to the wall of the establishment, but in practice the rule was not enforced. Out of precaution, however, Owen presented himself at the front desk as my husband and was issued a key.

I prefer to keep the things I experienced in that room to myself, because some people I love dearly may one day read these pages—despite the fact that I will take every measure to keep them from doing so—and I prefer to spare them the details. It is enough to say that with a little practice I managed to overcome my shyness and clumsiness and I spent many a happy hour of my monthlong stay in bed with Owen.

I still devoted time, of course, to the travel chronicles I had promised the newspaper. In New York City, where the unexpected was the norm, it was easy to find stories with the human interest angle that Mr. Chamberlain wanted to see.

FROM OUR FIRST kiss, Owen Whelan warned me that I should not harbor any illusions of romance, because he was offering only pleasure, pure and simple. He never suspected that I was a virgin, and by the time he found out there was no turning back. So he set about teaching me the fundamentals, principally how to have a good time without falling pregnant. He explained that condoms could be acquired at any pharmacy or tavern, but they could not be sold to women and no respectable female would ever try to obtain them anyhow. Although the consequences were much more dire for me, the most efficient precaution was beyond my reach. The next day Owen took me to see a doctor, a compatriot of his with the large eggplant nose of an inveterate alcoholic. The supposed physician sold me an ingenious apparatus made of rubber called a diaphragm, which was shaped like half a lemon. He informed me that this was considered more effective than sponges, washes, or other common methods of protection. Needless to say, no single woman could obtain any of these items without an obliging doctor. Owen wanted me to get used to them.

"Condoms can also help avoid infections, which is why I find them more convenient. You don't have to worry with me, but you should always be careful in the future. No intelligent woman can trust that any man will protect her," he warned.

I was offended deep to my core at the mere suggestion that there could ever be other men in my life, but I hid my hurt feelings behind the iron will I'd inherited from my mother. Owen had been very clear with respect to his intentions: We would have a good time for a few weeks, without worrying about the future; there would be no talk of love on his end. But I secretly believed I could change his mind. My love was enough for the both of us.

In the end I cannot complain. I learned a great deal from Owen Whelan and I was very happy during the brief month we spent together. I enjoyed the things he taught me so thoroughly, in fact, that once I finally overcame the extreme heartbreak of losing him, I began to take advantage of certain opportunities to have similar experiences. This is no easy feat for a woman who aims to maintain a good reputation. Virtue and decency are priceless and one moment of weakness is enough to lose all trace of respectability. And that disgrace is a fate worse than death, according to my mother.

With this first lover, I learned that in order to duly enjoy the festival of the senses one must go into it with patience, good humor, and tenderness. This initial stage is essential for me and perhaps for all women, but I suspect that the majority of men skip over it; desire turns them blind and deaf. For Owen, on the other hand, my pleasure was more important than his. This was his secret as a great seducer, something he had learned in adolescence through his first romantic encounter with a woman of dubious reputation, several years his senior. That woman taught him the basics and the rest he learned by asking, because what may pleasure one person could be repugnant to another. He took pride in the fact that he had never forced himself on any woman, paid for sexual services, or tried to lure someone into bed with lies and false promises.

Owen gave me a feminist pamphlet written by Victoria Woodhull, the psychic, activist, and first woman to run for president, who, before she found religion and began to abhor her past, was a proponent of free love. *Yes, I am a Free Lover. I have an inalienable, constitutional and natural right to love whom I may, to love as long or as short a period as I can; to change that love every day if I please, and with that right neither you nor any law you can frame have any right to interfere.*

Since then, I have espoused this notion, dogma of faith for most men and prohibited for us women. I suppose that meant I had officially become a bad woman.

OWEN PROVIDED ME with a list of places and persons that could be useful for my travel chronicles and he occasionally accompanied me on my outings. We went, for example, to see a freak show with five people exhibited to the public as "horrible pygmies," but they were neither horrible nor pygmies, just very short. I interviewed them and they were very pleasant people, all from the same family: two sisters, a brother, and two cousins, who had come over on tour from Switzerland. Susana, the tallest, was three feet tall and weighed forty pounds; Julius was two point eight feet tall and weighed twenty-six pounds; and the other three all weighed less than him. Their tiny statures had helped them make a living; they were proud of being different and proud of their fame.

I also managed to get invited to a séance led by Cora Hatch, who was in New York City giving demonstrations of her psychic powers. The woman began her career as a spiritualist at a young age; she had married four times and had tens of thousands of devotees. I attended a session held at a mansion belonging to one of her admirers, armed with the healthy dose of skepticism that my Papo had instilled in me from childhood.

At fifty years old, Cora was as charismatic and beautiful as in her youth. A few minutes into the session, she fell into a trance and began to speak haltingly in a masculine voice that the owner of the house recognized as that of his son who'd died at age eighteen in Gettysburg, the bloodiest battle of the Civil War. The spirit of the dead son answered questions that, according to the father, no one else could have known the answers to. It wasn't my place to reveal any possible charlatanism, but I wrote about what I saw with the irony it merited.

Several of my chronicles were inspired by things I encountered by chance out strolling the streets. I once got swept up in a suffragist march that turned into a stampede when the police charged at us on horseback. Another time, I observed a strike organized by female workers at a match factory denouncing their inhuman working conditions: sixteen hours on foot daily, poverty wages, toxic fumes that burned their skin, caused vomiting, and even led to premature death. I visited several of those women in their miserable housing and met their children, many of them severely malnourished, but I wasn't able to speak to the bosses or foremen of the factory. Mr. Chamberlain wasn't overly interested in the issue, since it occurred so far from San

Francisco, on another planet. But he loved the piece I wrote about a scantily clad exotic dancer. This was considered newsworthy to our readers in California, who could dream about seeing her in person someday.

DECEMBER 1890, NEW YORK
THE DIVINE ODALISQUE
By Brandon J. Price

Omene causes a sensation in the vaudeville houses of New York and Chicago, great urban centers where almost nothing surprises the exacting audiences. The reason for the furor is her exotic belly dance. She is dubbed by the press "the divine odalisque," and we know her from the Virginia Brights and Sweet Caporal cigarette ads. Her likeness appears on no less than thirteen of the different cards included with the packets of tobacco, but only two of them depict her in her exotic dancer attire, the others showing her demurely covered from head to toe. Adding to her fame is her long list of reported lovers and the rumor that more than one man has committed suicide over her. Armed with this background information, I set out to interview her.

The variety hall, a second- or third-rate venue with ninety seats, is packed to capacity. The spectators, entirely male, whistle and shout obscene jokes as they wait for the show, emboldened by the alcohol sold in the foyer. The opening acts consist of a musical number, a ventriloquist, and a magician to fill the time before the main attraction of the evening; they are unilaterally received with boos and jeering from the audience.

When the curtain opens on the final act, Omene is greeted with a collective sigh as she sways curvaceously onto the stage, enveloped in golden silk. She saunters around to the rhythm of sitars, lutes, and flutes. Moments later, two supposed eunuchs glide from the wings costumed in turbans and harem pants, with scimitars at their hips, only to rip the tunic and sandals from the body of the beauty, leaving her barely shrouded in thin veils as she continues to execute her voluptuous harem dance. Confronted now with the odalisque's bare belly, which dips in and out like a ferret, the audience bursts into enthusiastic applause, cheers, and whistles, as some men even try to rush the stage. The dance is less scandalous than it would seem based on the riotous reaction it incites in the spectators, who behave like animals in heat.

After the show, I slip backstage and knock on the door of the starlet's dressing room. Omene's initial impulse is to slam the door in my face, but I introduce myself as a columnist for an important newspaper in California and her mood immediately lifts. She agrees to speak with me, for all notoriety is welcome in her profession.

Up close, the divine odalisque is less attractive than she appears onstage, where the veils, the eunuchs, the lighting, and the music work to build the illusion that we are in the presence of Cleopatra herself. In person, the woman is short and somewhat stout, but well proportioned, with light skin and dark eyes made larger by makeup. Her grace and coquettishness, which she projects so naturally whilst she dances, are replaced by hostility in the intimacy of the dressing room. She is in a hurry.

"What do you think of the suffragettes?" she asks out of nowhere.

"I think women should have the right to vote . . ." I answer.

"Whatever for?" she interrupts. "The vote certainly hasn't done men much good."

"Democracy . . ." I stammer, disconcerted by the direction the interview has taken.

"Oh, that's all rigged by a group of crooks," she interrupts again. "The only thing women can do is try to manage those crooks."

As she rubs cold cream into her face to remove her thick makeup, she tells me of her early life in Turkey, where her mother taught her to belly dance at age eight. By twelve, she was married to a much older man, who abandoned her, and then she ran away to London, where she began to earn a living at her extravagant art. Eventually, she met an American man who presented her to an eager public in the United States.

"Before I brought it to the West, belly dance had never been heard of here, all that existed was a crude imitation," she informs me.

When asked about the rumors of suicidal lovers, she clarifies that so far only one man has died for her, an unfortunate poet. I pose questions about Istanbul and the history of the traditional art of belly dance, but she evades response, more interested in telling me about her brilliant and romantic rise to fame. Among her plans for the future are a possible trip to California, where I assure her that she will be warmly welcomed.

In sum, seated before the divine odalisque, I find myself in the presence of a true businesswoman, first and foremost, whose talent lies not only in dance, but in a determined drive to reach legendary status and make some money along the way. Seeing her, I understand that beauty does not have to come naturally, it can also be fabricated through guile and nerve. If Omene had the face of a gorilla, we might not notice, bewitched as we are by her poses or entranced by her kohl-lined eyes. But I for one was more impressed by her forceful ambition and open lack of scruples, two characteristics that so often launch men to the apex of success. These traits are thought to lead to ruin in women, unless, that is, they are as savvy as Omene, who flouts all conventions and excels in using men's weaknesses to her outstanding advantage.

WHEN MY TIME in New York was up, Owen Whelan and I enjoyed one last night together drinking white wine and nibbling Italian charcuterie in my hotel room, naked. I expect I will always feel a wistful nostalgia when I look back on those hours spent in gluttonous lust, unhurriedly exploring each other's bodies, laughing hysterically over foolish nonsense. That man was refreshingly uncomplicated; he enjoyed boxing above all else and never read anything, not even the newspaper, so different from his brother Eric. My Papo never would have understood how his little princess could frolic for long hours in a hotel room with a man who had never even heard of Frederick Douglass or Charles Darwin.

The next day, Owen saw me off at the train station and we said goodbye with a firm handshake, given that we were in public. Neither of us expressed any intention of remaining in contact, as had been agreed upon from the outset, but I have to confess that I felt hurt. I had fallen hopelessly in love and wished more than anything for a passionate kiss and a promise of returned sentiment. Reason should guide our actions, my Papo has always maintained, but the heart laughs in the face of logic and does whatever it pleases.

For the return journey to San Francisco I traveled in a third-class car, because I had already ridden in first class and I was looking for new experiences to write about for my chronicles. The steel car was hot, with terrible ventilation and narrow wooden benches where we had to sleep sitting up. Not even drinking water was made available to us. I purchased all my meals from the women who sold food at the stations or climbed aboard with their baskets of meats, bread, and apples. The nights were cold and the stale air was filled with the smells of body odor and dirty clothes. The conditions were a torture at first, but I soon got used to them and began to feel grateful for the proximity that invited conversation and led to several stories for Chamberlain. The distraction of work made it possible to repress my immense desire to mail passionate love letters to Owen Whelan from every train station along the route.

Most of the passengers were young men traveling in search of work or adventure out West, but there were also families of immigrants, mostly Italians and Russian Jews. The four-day journey was extended to nine days, because the third-class car was unhooked from the train on several occasions to make room for cargo or first-class cars, which had priority. Each time we were forced to wait patiently for as long as a day or two until they could hook us to another locomotive and recommence our route.

By the second day I could no longer bear my corset and managed to discreetly slip out of it. I realized then that I could dispense entirely with that armor under my dress, because I am slim and still fairly young. My mother believes a corset to be necessary for keeping our flesh in its proper place and the back duly straight, since good posture is what distinguishes a disciplined and elegant woman. Soon thereafter I also freed myself from my hairpins, which seemed to drill into my brain, and twisted my hair into a braid, like several of the other women traveling alongside me. This enabled me to better blend in with the rest of the third-class passengers; I'd surely stood out as quite pretentious in my corset, jacket, gloves, and hat.

Those endless days of discomfort allowed each person's true character to shine through. Food was scarce, but some were willing to share what little they had. The men passed the time playing hands of cards, which sometimes ended in insults, especially when they drank gin and whiskey, but everyone respected the tacit agreement to refrain from blandishing the weapons that almost all of them carried. The mothers, busy with their families, bore the inconveniences of the train without complaint, as they tried to distract the children or rock them to sleep. A large Greek man with few teeth and long lashes played the accordion in the evenings, captivating us with the music of his homeland.

I was asked often about my constant writing and several people requested I read my traveling chronicles aloud, but I did not have any copies of my column, only my most recent notes. I was able to entertain my fellow travelers, however, by narrating the plots of my dime novels. The damsel's dishonor pulled tears from more than one traveler and everyone applauded when she finally exacted her revenge. The Greek man and several others were unable to understand a word, since they did not speak English, but they clapped just the same, out of courtesy.

BEFORE REACHING SAN Francisco, I tried to clean myself up as best I could to spare my parents from seeing me in such disarray when I walked into the house, but it was impossible to mask my foul odor, oily hair, and stained clothes. Waiting for me at the station when I arrived was Eric Whelan. I had not been expecting him and I tried to slip away, embarrassed at my appearance, but he trapped me. At least he had the courtesy to hide his shock over the state I was in. He carried with him a paper bag of sweet rolls and a canteen of coffee, which felt like a small miracle after that nine-day odyssey in third class.

"How did you know I was coming?" I asked him.

"Owen sent me a telegram. My brother was very impressed with you."

"And I by him. You look different—I almost didn't recognize you," I said.

"I got a haircut and a fresh shave. You've never seen me without a beard," he explained.

"Oh, that's it! Well, if you were trying to surprise me, you've achieved it. You look so clean and handsome."

"Thanks. I'm sorry I cannot say the same about you," he answered, laughing.

We sat on a bench in the square outside the station to attend to the coffee and sweet rolls. I gave him the broad strokes of my impressions of New York, many of which he'd read about in my travel chronicles, and he brought me up to speed on the most relevant news published by the *Examiner* in my absence.

Seated on that bench drinking lukewarm coffee and tossing crumbs to the birds, I learned that Owen Whelan was married. All those weeks of such intense intimacy in which I bared myself body and soul I'd been convinced that he was doing the same; he had never once mentioned his wife and four kids. And, naïve as I was, I had never even thought to ask him, simply taking it for granted that he was an eligible bachelor. The possibility of adultery never entered my limited knowledge of the world.

Eric mentioned his brother's family in passing, never suspecting what a blow it would be to me. I felt like I was on fire from head to toe, as my heart drummed wildly and I struggled to breathe. Eric asked, confused, if I was all right. I told him that I was simply exhausted from my journey and that I needed to have a bath and a nap at once. He hailed a hansom cab but I did not allow him to escort me home, not wanting him to know where I lived or with whom.

Once home, I thought over and over about what had transpired between Owen and myself. I was quite relieved that I had not sent him foolish love letters from the train. I vowed never to send that type of sentimental missive; sooner or later love ends and the ridiculous confessions remain in another's possession.

It is true that I was not responsible for Owen's actions; he was the one who would have to answer to his wife, to his confessor—he was Catholic—and to his conscience, if in fact he felt any guilt over his infidelity, but the experience taught me to be more cautious.

My Papo, who does not believe in sin or divine punishment, follows one very simple rule: Do unto others as you would have them do unto you. I would suffer greatly if another woman took the man I loved, even if it was only a meaningless tryst. Perhaps Owen's wife never suspected what went on between the two of us, or perhaps she is aware that her husband is a womanizer and she looks the other way because the pleasure he is able to offer her makes up for his faults. Whatever the case, I will never again take part in any betrayal. I decided from that moment onward that I would only accept the company of a man who had no other commitment. Fortunately, there are many such men in the world.

. . .

ERIC WHELAN HAS always been the best of friends to me. According to my mother, friendship between a man and a woman is impossible; there is always an undercurrent of seduction that could end badly. Or it might end well; it depends. She is correct, in part, because despite the fact that we are colleagues and he talks to me like I'm one of his drinking buddies, and despite the fact that I don't like unkempt redheads, I found myself, on more than one occasion, imagining what it would be like to kiss him. I expected he would probably taste like tobacco and beer. I also could not help but wonder if he was as skilled a lover as his brother, in which case I could perhaps overlook his carrot-colored hair.

The closer we became, the more I learned about him. He had been born in a mining town in Ireland, the youngest of a ridiculous number of children: seventeen, all from the same forlorn, fertile woman. They were poor, just like everyone else around them, but theirs was a more dignified and less desperate poverty because the father was not an alcoholic and he worked with the resigned fortitude of an ox. The children also worked from around the age of puberty, the boys in the mines and the girls as servants. Owen, who was tall, strong, and quick with his fists, was tasked with caring for his little brother Eric, seven years his junior. Eric was shy and enjoyed reading, unlike the rest of the large Whelan brood, all quite brutish, according to Owen. There wasn't a single intellectual or artist among them going back several generations. Eric was the only exception.

Owen took his role as protector quite seriously, willing to resort to kicks and blows with anyone, even double his size, while Eric took refuge in any book or magazine he was able to get his hands on at school. The family considered reading a fine activity for ladies of leisure, but not for a man who would have to survive in this world. So Owen marched his little brother to the local boxing ring and shoved him through the ropes so that the boy could learn to defend himself.

Eric owes his broken nose to one of these teachings. Faced with any conflict outside the ring, however, Owen would push his brother aside and defend him with a suicidal determination. Eric felt an admiration bordering on idolatry for his older brother, and when Owen decided at age twenty-one to immigrate to America, Eric had gripped his suitcase and didn't let go until they disembarked together on Ellis Island. The Whelan brothers traveled to New York inside the hull of an English ship along with dozens of other immigrants, all equally full of hope.

At first Owen and Eric got by with the help of a distant relative who provided them with a place to sleep in the basement of his fish shop in exchange for long hours of work. They survived on old fish that couldn't be sold, and the nauseating smell was fixed forever in their minds to the extent that neither one ever so much as tasted seafood again after they were able to strike out on their own. Owen took work wherever he could get it and used his iron fists to supplement his meager income through underground boxing matches held in shady venues. Meanwhile Eric submitted to every ad contest he could. By age fifteen he was composing amusing rhymes and persuasive phrases to sell ladies' undergarments, laxative tablets, hats, and everything else under the sun. As soon as an announcement for a new contest was posted, Eric sent half a dozen ideas and invariably hit the mark with one or more.

According to what Owen had told me during our brief bacchanal, Eric never again sullied his hands with manual labor after their time in the fish shop, managing always to sell his words instead. He'd joked that Eric, the only redhead of his numerous siblings and so full of ideas, must've been engendered by another father. I did not take it seriously, of course, since a mother of sixteen couldn't possibly have the time or energy to stray from her husband and give birth to a bastard.

I had initially considered Eric to be a cynical man of the world but upon getting to know him better I realized he was more of a reluctant romantic whose true nature only surfaced after several drinks. I have been able to verify that, like any good Irishman, Eric knows many Gaelic songs, which bring tears of nostalgia to his eyes even though he came to America at a young age and has never again set foot in his motherland. I once saw him get into a fistfight with men who were mistreating a mule; the brawl landed him in the hospital. He is the best journalist in California and has been for many years now, something I can confidently assert without fear of hyperbolizing.

BRANDON J. PRICE, who had already made a name for himself as a writer of adventure novels, was now gaining notoriety in the more prestigious sphere of editorial journalism. His traveling chronicles were very well received by the newspaper's readership. The fictitious columnist received abundant correspondence at the *Examiner* and was often invited to give lectures; he was even offered a multicity tour as a guest speaker. But he could not take advantage of any of these opportunities without revealing his true identity. He had a reputation for being a mysterious man, a loner. Not even Mark Twain had been able to meet him in person because each time the celebrated Southern author had visited San Francisco, Brandon J. Price was out exploring the Wild West or combing Chicago's seedy underbelly in search of inspiration for his novels and chronicles.

Apart from Eric Whelan; William Randolph Hearst, the owner of the *Examiner;* Chamberlain, my editor; and my immediate family, no one knew that Brandon J. Price was me. I told Mr. Chamberlain on more than one occasion that I did not plan to remain in anonymity forever. His response was always the same: "That'll happen over my dead body, miss."

Fortunately, that was not necessary. In 1891 I was presented with the opportunity I'd been waiting for.

4

DESPITE THE INCURABLE BITTERNESS MY MOTHER HAR-
bored toward the Chilean seducer who engendered me, I never had
much curiosity about that man or the place he hailed from and I never
bought into the ludicrous fantasy about the inheritance that was owed
to me. I could hardly pinpoint Chile on a map when Mr. Chamberlain
asked me to write something about the country. He didn't give the
story to me exclusively, assigning Eric Whelan as well. He explained
that there was some kind of revolution or a civil war going on down
there—he wasn't sure which—and that some rebels were attempting
to acquire weapons and ammunition in New York and then ship them
to Chile via a Californian port.

"Purchasing weapons is perfectly legal in this country," Eric
pointed out.

"Yes, but the United States supports the Chilean government. We
cannot be seen selling weapons to the enemies of the legitimate president."

"What does our government care about what happens there?"
Eric asked.

"The official story is the defense of democracy, but the real truth lies in the Chilean mineral deposits, controlled by the Brits," Chamberlain replied.

"I don't expect that would be of much interest to our readers," Eric insisted.

"Well, that all depends on how you write it," I interrupted, immediately seeing the opportunity for adventure. I could perhaps even track down my father. "The weapons are just a starting point. It would be more interesting if we could follow their trail all the way to Chile and cover how they are used in the civil war there."

"That is actually a good idea, Miss Emilia. Chile's arrogance could be of interest to our readers. It sounds ridiculous, but that tiny nation aims to compete with the United States for influence and control of the Pacific coast. Are you willing to travel all that way, Whelan?" the editor asked.

"I'll go," I interrupted again. "I speak Spanish and I have a connection to the country. My father is Chilean."

This was the first time I had ever admitted, outside the confines of my home, that I had any other father besides Francisco Claro. Chamberlain and Whelan gawped at me incredulously, but I assured them that I had family in Chile and I knew everything there was to know about the nation's current political turmoil. Fortunately, they did not ask me to prove it.

"How could you even think I would send *you* as a war correspondent, young lady?" the editor exclaimed.

"Why not? Being a woman means I shall be safer because no one will pay me any mind. I would not be surprised if there were several female journalists there already," I said.

"All right," Chamberlain finally agreed after a long pause. "You can both go as correspondents, but you will have to split up to cover more ground. You, Eric, will cover the war and the political situation. You, Emilia, will send me human interest stories."

"What does that mean? You don't believe I can write about the same topics as Eric?" I demanded, turning red.

"Be thankful I am even offering you this opportunity before I think the better of it. You will have to find ways to provide our readers with a broader image of that country. The war too, yes, but from the human perspective, do you understand? You will not be lacking for material, I am certain," he replied.

"Yes, I understand, but I need to have it in writing, Mr. Chamberlain. Everything I write will be published under my real name, Emilia del Valle Claro. Brandon J. Price is dead."

"How do you expect me to publish war chronicles written by a woman?"

"It would be an amazing publicity stunt, Mr. Chamberlain! Everyone would be talking about it," Eric interrupted, always looking out for me.

"Emilia del Valle is enough of a mouthful, let's leave it at that," Chamberlain decreed after some consideration.

"What's wrong with Claro?" I returned.

"Nothing, but long names don't stick, much less a Mexican name," he replied.

We spent the next half hour discussing the best way to cover the story. Eric would go immediately to New York to report on the weapons acquired by the Chilean rebels and their transportation to the Pacific coast by train. I would find out precisely how the men planned to ship everything to Chile.

I refused to leave the office without a contract, which consisted of two handwritten sentences on the newspaper's letterhead signed by the editor and Eric as witness indicating that my future work would bear my real name. Being a woman is a serious inconvenience to success in general and particularly in a profession dominated by men. Omene, the divine odalisque, had taught me that docility and eagerness to please, celebrated qualities in a woman, were grave obstacles to moving up in the world. Spurred on by sheer insolence, I managed to get my way with Chamberlain.

·　　　·　　　·

I RUSHED HOME from the newspaper to tell my parents that I was going to Chile. My mother, who had been so opposed to my traveling alone to New York, was ecstatic to learn that her only daughter was heading off to a cruel war at the tail end of the world.

"What a stroke of luck, Emilia! You will finally receive your inheritance and the trip is all expenses paid, to boot. What a shame I can't go with you," she said, wiping her doughy hands on her flour-dusted apron.

"We are talking about war here, Molly. I don't like it one bit. What if something terrible happens to the girl . . ." my Papo said.

"Don't be so dramatic, Pancho. Most people survive war," my mother replied.

Seeing that he would not be able to dissuade me, my Papo agreed to help me learn everything I could about Chile from the basic information that had been published about the conflict there. The good man has a habit of cutting out newspaper articles that he feels worthy of being remembered, another consequence of his insatiable thirst for knowledge. In this instance, it served me well. His large archive contains all the relevant occurrences of the universe organized into an order of his own invention that only he understands. When he dies, we shall have to burn it all because no one else could possibly make any sense of it.

I suppose that he'd saved the news on Chile thinking that his wife might be interested, but she was connected to that remote country by bitterness alone. There was enough information in my Papo's files to get an idea of the mess I was getting myself into. He filled in the missing pieces with information gathered at the San Francisco Free Library, which had been founded a few years prior as a space for male readers only. He found it odd that the *Examiner* would send not one but two journalists to cover the Chilean conflict.

"In case one of us dies, they shall have the other one there on re-serve," I joked.

"I only hope you're not the one to die," he replied gravely.

"I imagine there will be numerous correspondents there. England, France, and the United States all have economic interests in the Chilean mines."

I should clarify that, in spite of my many outward displays of self-sufficiency, I still lived at home with my parents, just like any respectable unmarried woman from a middle-class family. Although we weren't exactly middle-class, my mother was implacable when it came to matters of reputation. For the past ten years, I had slept in the same little bedroom that my Papo built for me when I turned fifteen. By then my three younger brothers had been born and we'd out-grown the limited space of our small house. I did not wish to live anywhere else. That little house in the backyard of Aztec Pride was my safe harbor: I could sail the world with the confidence that the compass would guide me back to those shores. Eric Whelan believed me to be a liberated woman. He would've laughed if he had discovered that the ambitious journalist and suffragette I presented myself as was still dependent on her parents.

Our neighbors in the Mission District wondered when I was going to marry and start my own family; they had already labeled me as an old maid. There must be something wrong with that girl if she hasn't been able to find a husband yet, by age twenty-five, they said. Too tall, too skinny, too plucky, unfeminine, that's what she gets for trying to be an intellectual, the men don't want a woman who knows more than them and doesn't even try to hide it, they whispered. My mother told me everything they said behind my back, angrier with me than with the idle gossips.

In spite of my deficiencies, I wasn't completely lacking in prospects, including one very rash suitor who had asked for my hand. But marriage and motherhood did not interest me. I supposed that, some-time in the distant future, I might change my mind, but at that moment I was much more attracted to war than any possible husband. I was grateful to Owen Whelan for having broken my heart, which made it easier for me to be free.

ERIC WHELAN LEFT immediately for New York, where he had managed to contact the person responsible for purchasing the weapons on behalf of the Chileans, while I researched the circumstances that had led to their revolution. Eric and I had decided that each of us should focus on one side of the conflict, flipping a coin to determine which: Eric would follow the insurgents and I would cover the government, led by President José Manuel Balmaceda. In general, we would try to respect the division of labor that Chamberlain had ordered, but we weren't going to let that limit us. Eric could do human interest interviews if the story called for it, and I could get close to the conflict if the opportunity presented itself. While waiting for the weaponry to reach California, I wrote a series of pieces informing our readers of the situation. Grudgingly, Chamberlain published them with my name.

APRIL 1891, SAN FRANCISCO
CHILE, WARRIOR COUNTRY
By Emilia del Valle

At the southern tip of the American continent lies Chile, a long, remote, and proud nation, isolated from the world by the Andes Mountains to the east and the Pacific Ocean to the west, some four thousand miles of abrupt coastline. It is inhabited by a blend of two warrior races: the fierce Araucanos, quelled by three hundred years of struggle but never defeated, and the no less tenacious Spanish conquistadors and European settlers. Throughout this century, the people of this nation have never been long without weapons in their hands and have walked away victorious in each conflict, justifying their feelings of superiority and their aims for territorial expansion.

The recent War of the Pacific saw Peru and Bolivia defeated as Chile annexed extensive northern provinces holding valuable mineral deposits. Nevertheless, the nation's immense wealth does not benefit the entire population; the majority of the 2.5 million Chileans live in poverty. Chile is still a rural, hierarchical society with little popular representation. Despite the emerging middle class, economic and political power have always remained concentrated in the hands of the landholding oligarchy of European descent. The right to vote is but a farce in this nation, as presidents are handpicked from the political aristocracy.

President Benjamin Harrison has his eye on it, to be certain, since we need Chilean nitrate (also known as saltpeter), as do other foreign powers, such as Great Britain. The United States aspires to control the natural resources in Latin America and cannot allow this small southern nation, motivated by patriotic fury, to manifest imperialist pretensions.

In September of 1886, José Manuel Balmaceda, of the Liberal Party, assumed the presidency of Chile a few years after the war with Peru and Bolivia. His ambitious program aims to utilize the income from nitrate for public works, education, health, and industrialization, but his government has been characterized by successive political and social crises. The opposition accuses him of exerting dictatorial powers. His reforms threaten the interests of the large landholders, the aristocracy, and wealthy impresarios who argue that if the country is doing well, what need is there for change? The popular support that Balmaceda enjoyed at the start of his presidency has largely deteriorated.

At the end of last year, the Chilean Congress, with a majority opposed to the president and supported by England, refused to approve the presidential budget for 1891. The president therefore decided to apply the budget from the preceding year. Congress declared this action to fall outside the scope of presidential power, to which the president responded by dissolving Congress.

In January of the present year, the Chilean Navy revolted in support of the rebel congressmen. The army, however, remains loyal to the president. With the nation's armed forces divided, a civil war began to brew. The insurgent congressional faction now controls the northern seas of Chile, where they have established a provisional government of their own, called the Revolutionary Junta, at the port city of Iquique. This strategic location allows for easy control of the nitrate mines and the recruitment of miners into the rebels' ranks.

President Balmaceda's army lacks the means to travel to the north, and the rebel forces are too small in number for successful combat. The government needs ships, which they have requested from Europe, and Congress needs weapons and men. In the meantime, both factions must wait, separated from each other by the most inhospitable landscape on the planet: the Atacama Desert.

Great Britain has already pledged its support for the insurgent congressmen whilst the United States has promised to back Balmaceda's legitimate government. Each nation is motivated by the same objective: nitrate, used in both fertilizers and explosives. No empire can do without gunpowder.

The editor accepted my column, but he reminded me that the political issues fell to Eric, who was still in New York. In my subsequent columns I described Chile, without ever having been there, based on the information available to me from newspapers and what my Papo found in books, maps, and magazines, as well as long conversations with some Chilean immigrants who had been drawn to America in the gold rush and still yearned for the mythic homeland that they hadn't seen in over forty years. These immigrants were congregated in an area of the Mission District called Little Chile, where they flew the flag of their native land and patriotic nostalgia was kept alive through empanadas and sentimental songs. Weeks later, when I finally arrived in Chile and began to familiarize myself with the land and its people, I was able to verify that what I'd written had been fairly accurate.

Meanwhile Eric sent information from New York by telegraph and letters to me by mail, which arrived by train in a few days' time. He became friendly with a lawyer by the last name of Trumbull, who, seasoned in this type of negotiation, had been tasked with acquiring weapons for the revolutionary congressmen. Eric explained that the arms purchase was top secret, since the insurgents did not have the support of our government, but that he was able to get some details out of Trumbull after several glasses of whiskey at the bar of the luxurious Fifth Avenue Hotel. The rebels had obtained five thousand Remington rifles and two thousand cases of ammunition. I concluded that if a Californian journalist knew about it, it could not be a very well-kept secret.

As Eric and I flooded the newspaper with reports on the situation in Chile, Chamberlain became so interested in that distant conflict, which at first had bored him, that it became something of an obsession. When Eric received a cable saying that the crates of weapons had been loaded onto a train and were making their way to California, the editor sent me to the port of Los Angeles to find out which ship would receive the cargo. I planned to set out for Los Angeles knowing it would be but my first stop on the way to Chile. I would never have a better opportunity to learn about my origins.

WHEN IT CAME time to say goodbye, my mother pulled me into the schoolhouse, which was empty at that hour, and she handed me a letter addressed to Gonzalo Andrés del Valle. Her behavior seemed suspicious, and I refused to serve as messenger without knowing the contents of the envelope. In the end she showed me the letter, first informing me that it was confidential, and I could not tell my Papo.

Reading it, I was ashamed of my mother. Saint Molly, the exemplary woman adored by her husband and respected by everyone, who gave to charity and attended daily mass, was capable of intense rage and pettiness. The letter was a laundry list of reproaches: that he had never fulfilled his duty to support or educate his daughter, fruit of his sin; that God was witness to his neglect; and that nothing would escape the smiting of His justice and there would be no absolution without penance and reparation, which consisted of legally recognizing his daughter and restoring to her everything she was rightfully owed.

I understood why my mother did not want Papo to read the letter; he would've destroyed it, as ashamed as I was. I made no attempt to reason with her, however, because experience had taught me that it was futile. Molly Walsh had been hoarding resentment for years and nothing I could say would purge her heart. She asked me to kneel in front of the crucifix that hung on the wall and solemnly swear that I would deliver the letter to my father. I did it only to appease her, because I could see she was on the verge of one of her nervous breakdowns.

My Papo, for his part, also took me aside to tell me that this trip made him very nervous. "I'm concerned that something might happen to you, princess. War is no joke," he said.

"Is there something else bothering you, Papo?" I asked, because I know him well.

"Well . . . I also fear that you will meet that Mr. del Valle and forget all about me," he confessed.

"Have you gone insane, Papo? That man may have engendered me, but he is not my true father and never will be. No one, not even the Pope, if he had seduced my mother, could ever replace you," I added. We both laughed like children imagining that possibility.

.   .   .

I TRAVELED TO Los Angeles by train, armed with credentials that proved I was a citizen of the United States and a correspondent for the *Examiner*. By then the United States government was trying to stop the weapons from being shipped to Chile, after it had been reported in several newspapers that they were in transit. Trumbull's purchase had not even made it to California and the secret was already out.

I had packed clothes suited to the Chilean climate, which was similar to California's but with opposite seasons, as my Papo learned through the published journals of Charles Darwin, one of his favorite authors. He'd also studied Darwin's book on the origin of the species, published in 1859, which provoked heated debates between himself and my mother, who maintained that Darwin was nothing but a devilish atheist who denied the divine creation of the universe. I would set out in a California summer and arrive in Chile at the start of winter. Fashion had changed that year and the extravagant hats and enormous skirts with rear ends adorned like theater curtains had been reduced and simplified. I'd chosen comfortable skirts in blue and black, white blouses without any frills, a short jacket and another long one, a cape, and a taffeta evening gown in a moss color, which did not suit me, but hid stains well.

New shoes proved more of a challenge since I am accustomed to walking everywhere and I have strong legs and large feet unsuited to the leather slippers or party shoes that mark an elegant lady, according to my mother. For my journey to Chile I purchased the most indestructible boots I could find. My luggage amounted to a trunk, a suitcase, and a hat box. I was envious of Eric Whelan, who traveled to New York with nothing but a single suit and often wore the same shirt for two weeks straight. In his case, the world cared very little about his appearance. In my case, looks were of the utmost importance, even if we were headed into war.

.　　　.　　　.

MY PRESS CREDENTIALS from the *Examiner* enabled me to meet a federal sheriff by the last name of Gard. This was the man tasked with impeding the American weapons from being loaded onto the Chilean ship that had come to get them. I surmised that he would be staying at the Sportsmen's Lodge, the only decent hotel in Los Angeles, that flat, dusty, sprawling city of fifty thousand. I booked myself a room and prepared to corner Sheriff Gard.

Eric Whelan had taught me that a direct frontal attack was the best strategy for obtaining an interview. I marched up to the table where the man sat having his breakfast with his nose stuck inside a copy of the *Examiner* and announced that I was a reporter for those very pages. He peered at me distrustingly over his half-moon spectacles, but I placed my press credentials in front of him and he seemed to relax. Taking advantage of his momentary hesitation, I sat down at his table without being invited and struck up a conversation. In just a few minutes I had managed to completely lower his defenses. Gard was one of those men who enjoy impressing women with their knowledge and experience— the dumber my question, the more time he spent explaining. Without much effort on my part at all, I was able to ascertain that the Chilean rebels would have to load their weapons onto the ship on the open ocean.

"They won't be able to do it any other way, because they will have serious problems at any American port. They plan to transfer the weapons from a schooner to a ship called *Itata* but I will not allow it. I am here to personally ensure that they do not succeed in carrying out their plan."

Gard went on to explain that the weapons had been acquired legally, but the United States could stop the arms from being exported through any domestic port, given that the shipment of that cargo would constitute a hostile act against an allied nation. He added that the Chilean president had obtained the support of the president of the United States through diplomacy and economic promises.

"Fascinating! What I wouldn't give to accompany you on that ad-venture, Sheriff Gard!" I exclaimed.

"Oh, no, certainly not, my dear. It would not be at all appropriate for a pretty young lady like yourself," he answered with a benevolent smile and a few fatherly pats on the back of the hand.

"Whyever not?" I asked.

"Very dangerous. This is a military matter."

"I am a correspondent for the *Examiner*. I will soon be traveling to Chile to cover the conflict there," I informed him.

"I do not approve of the press sniffing around my operation . . ." he replied.

IN ACCORDANCE WITH the division of assignments that Eric and I had agreed on, he would travel to Chile with the Congressionalist faction aboard the *Itata*, which would take him directly to the port of Iquique, where the rebels had established their base of operations. I, on the other hand, would travel on a cargo ship where I would have to share the cabin with three other passengers. With luck I'd arrive within three or four weeks at Valparaíso, Chile's largest port, where the troops loyal to the government were quartered. From there I'd have to travel to Santiago, the capital, and find a way to gain access to the president, his ministers, and generals.

A message from Eric Whelan reached me that afternoon with the news that the weapons had already been secretly loaded onto a schoo-ner, one that he had been allowed to board as well. They had used a small vessel authorized for local navigation only, meaning that it was not submitted to the rigorous regulations imposed on ships of inter-national provenance. This boat did not have to declare its cargo or register with the port authority. The Chileans' plan was to navigate their schooner to a rendezvous with the *Itata* on a small island where, free from customs protocols and American law, they could openly transfer the weapons to their ship.

The Chileans' plan was foiled, however, when the *Itata,* before receiving its shipment, stopped to resupply with coal at the port of San Diego, near Los Angeles. The Chilean ship had immediately drawn the attention of port authorities because the crew consisted almost entirely of soldiers.

SHERIFF GARD TRAVELED to the port of San Diego and I was hot on his heels, but try as I might, I was not able to board the *Itata* alongside him. What I know of these events was relayed to me much later by Eric Whelan. The incident was amplified by the press across the entire country as the public was bombarded with headlines announcing that "Chilean pirates" were violating U.S. laws. Gard, however, did not find any weapons aboard the *Itata* and therefore had no reason to impede the captain from making his ship ready to launch.

Gard and his lieutenant had been received warmly by the crew of the *Itata;* the captain assured the sheriff that he would obey all orders, and also show the men their famous Chilean hospitality. That evening, he served the American authorities a delicious dinner of fresh seafood, washed down with the best Chilean wine and enough French cognac to lower the defenses of even the most incorruptible man, but not Sheriff Gard, who remained alert, sober, and attentive to his duties. The next day, the sheriff set off in a rented boat to intercept the schooner containing the weapons, which had been sighted in the surrounding area, leaving his lieutenant to guard the Chilean ship. Gard's rented boat, however, was unable to stop the schooner, which slipped away into open ocean.

Meanwhile, the captain of the *Itata* gave the order to raise anchor and flee the port at full steam. The federal lieutenant was playing cards and drinking below deck, so absorbed in his game that he did not notice. The *Itata* met the schooner near a small island. There, the captain loaded the weapons and unceremoniously dumped the federal lieutenant.

. . .

ON MAY 7, while Eric Whelan traveled south with the *Itata*, I did the same aboard the USS *Charleston*, an American battleship that took off in pursuit of the Chilean steamer. It goes without saying that I was the only woman aboard the *Charleston* among thirty-four officers, two hundred and ninety-six sailors, and thirty marines. My passage aboard the ship would have been entirely impossible without direct intervention from a senator who was Chamberlain's friend. The commander and officers greeted me with cold courtesy, and the crew avoided me like a leper due to the deep-seated belief that a woman aboard a battleship brings bad luck. Their attitudes slowly changed over the course of the following weeks as they warmed to me. According to my Papo, hostility often vanishes once people get to know one another. My voyage on the *Charleston* seemed to prove him right.

THE VOYAGE TO Chile lasted three weeks and the most enduring memory I have of the journey is the relentless seasickness I experienced for the first three days. I had fortunately been assigned a small individual berth where I could suffer in peace. The mere thought of enduring that experience in a cabin shared with three other people makes my stomach turn. The ship's doctor, a jolly old man who looked ill-suited for a military mission, cared for me until I was able to stand, dehydrated and aching from head to toe. The ship's captain, a serious man with sad eyes, checked in on me several times. On one occasion, believing me to be asleep or unconscious, I heard him say to the doctor, "This is what we get for bringing a woman aboard." I later learned from Eric Whelan that he was equally nauseous for the first days, despite the fact that he's a man. I have to admit, however, that once I was able to leave my cabin, with a greenish tinge to my skin and dark circles under my eyes, the captain treated me more sympathetically, as did the other officers. I had earned their respect for having survived my baptism at sea.

I've never been a flirt and I did not make even the slightest effort to seduce any of the sailors, but a woman alone on a ship full of men certainly stands out and I was not without propositions, some delicate and others more direct. I had a few worthy candidates to choose from, something I was unaccustomed to, and I ultimately selected the first officer below deck, bolder than the rest and able to visit me without being seen. He was handsome and he was unattached, he assured me when I asked him before our first kiss, determined to avoid intimacy with any more married men. I won't reveal his name, because it could cause problems for him, but I'll say that he was from Kansas, the son of a welder and a schoolteacher, and grew up obsessed with the idea of the ocean. At seventeen he enlisted in the Marines as a cabin boy and had since had an impressive military career. I have no doubt he'll one day reach the rank of admiral because his most notable traits were his tenacity and ambition. Compared to Owen Whelan, he was extremely lacking in the practice of giving pleasure—as were the other two lovers I'd had up to that point. I endured his rushed embraces and long descriptions of maritime charts and ocean currents for a few nights, and then found excuses to stop seeing him. For the rest of the voyage I avoided any solo encounter with the officer and locked the door to my cabin every night.

I spent my time interviewing the sailors I was able to catch in their scarce free moments; those men never rested. I also passed the time playing cards with the officers. Gambling with money was strictly prohibited, so we used matchsticks. I lost several boxes at first and the other players took me for a dopey girl to be easily swindled. But I soon caught on to the rhythm of the game, learned to remember cards and decipher the men's expressions, since they did not make an effort to conceal their emotions in front of me, and soon I started winning, angering some of the men. Unfortunately, it was only matches, otherwise I would've disembarked with a small fortune.

Being faster, the *Charleston* bypassed its target on the water, and never spotted it. I was sorry to miss the chance to witness a maritime battle, as a result. I had not yet seen war up close, or I would have known better.

PART TWO

5

IN EARLY JUNE WE ARRIVED AT IQUIQUE, THE MAIN PORT
for Chilean nitrate exportation, where we were met by several ships
under different international flags. It was there that we learned that
we had left the *Itata* behind on the high seas.

In Iquique, the insurgents had established a provisional government and set up their center of military operations. Being a port city,
it had a milder climate than locations farther inland, where the driest
desert in the world imposed its harsh reality. This was a region of
bald plains and distant mountains painted extraordinary colors by the
rich minerals below their surface, hot by day and freezing by night, a
rough, inhospitable terrain. The sparse vegetation was concentrated
along the coast and in the gardens cultivated with enormous effort by
the foreign settlers who aimed to replicate the lifestyle enjoyed in
other latitudes. This illusion came to an abrupt halt on the outskirts of
town.

My first impression was one of order and prosperity, a main avenue with smaller streets running parallel and perpendicular, wooden
houses and buildings, the occasional palatial mansion built by the
owners of the nitrate mines. As soon as I ventured into other areas of
town, however, I saw that the comfort of the upper classes clashed

violently with the abject poverty of the laborers, miners, and beggars, who were everywhere and were referred to indiscriminately as *rotos*, the broken ones.

That contrast between the people of means and the masses was also visible in their semblance: Those in power, who controlled politics, commerce, banks, and, of course, the war, looked to be of European descent. The rest of the population looked to have indigenous heritage but were often mestizo, mixing various races, or newly arrived immigrants with nothing to their name; they would do the heavy lifting and be sent to die in the war. I quickly learned that Chilean surnames positioned each family within a complex social hierarchy and that the color of a person's skin determined their destiny. I was surprised to discover that my last name, del Valle, represented one of the more prominent clans. For the first time in my life, I was happy that my good mother had insisted on giving me that name at birth and that Mr. Chamberlain had chosen it to publish my column. The appellation would serve me well in Chile, where the father's last name comes first, as the family name, and the mother's comes second.

A few days after our arrival, the *Itata* finally appeared on the horizon, loaded down with the "Chilean pirates" that the *Examiner* had reported on. My adventure in Chile had officially begun.

JUNE 1891, NORTHERN CHILE
WHITE GOLD
By Emilia del Valle

I am in Iquique, Chile's main port for nitrate exportation, chasing the story of a civil war. Here I manage to persuade the manager of a mine to authorize a visit and even send a coach for me. With the excuse of avoiding accidents, they limit my visit to the mine office and whatever else the foreman deems worthy of showing me. I accept the conditions without any intention of adhering to them. I prefer to ask for forgiveness than for permission. Nitrate is at the center of this conflict.

We set out at dawn. The journey is hot, dusty, and exhausting, but it provides me with the opportunity to converse with the coachman, a Mr. Amador Troncoso, on our stops along the way. I offer to share my food with him and in exchange he holds out his canteen of aguardiente, which burns my insides as it goes down. He is a well-read man, like many in this region—more newspapers circulate here than in San Francisco.

"What do you think of the president?" I ask him.

"Well, I'll speak frankly, young lady, if I may. He claims to defend the people, but he's betrayed us. Last year we had the largest workers' strike the country has ever seen; it started with the dock workers and spread everywhere. There were thousands of us. We were asking for fairer salaries and better working conditions."

"What happened after the strike?"

"The government sent in the troops to repress us and they killed many people. The same thing happened with the nitrate miners' strike back in February. The miners were asking for food, because they were going hungry, and to be paid with money instead of vouchers and company chips," he tells me.

"How does that work?"

"That's how they pay the miners, not in pesos but with chips that can only be used in the company store where the company controls the prices. Without any coins in their pockets, how can they save? But the government sent in their army to gun them down."

"The civil war began in January. The rebel forces were in control of Iquique in February, not the government," I point out.

"Yes, but part of Balmaceda's army is still here. Bloody men seasoned in the Peruvian war."

"What do you believe will happen with this revolution?" I ask.

"Nothing much, I reckon. This is a war between the *futres*," he replies.

"Futres?" I repeat.

"All from the same upper class, who own this country. The people have no power to decide anything and nothing to gain. We simply work, fight, and die."

Amador has received instructions to take me to the mine offices, where I am met by an administrator, a large Scottish man who has lived here so long that he speaks English with a Chilean accent. As soon as I arrive, he offers me tea with bread and cheese. He wants to explain the mineral extraction process, displayed on drawings and photographs that cover the walls of his office, but I persuade him to take me to see the mining site.

Nitrate lies on the surface of this infinitely lonely desert landscape strewn with rocks and more rocks. I watch as workers burst them open with a dynamite blast that shakes the ground like a geological catastrophe. After the dust settles, the miners move in to attack all that remains with shovels and picks. These are iron men, hardened by work under the blazing sun, all bare chests, bulging biceps, and defiant stares. They load mounds of stone onto carts pulled by miserable mules who ferry the cargo to a waiting train and from there to the processing plant.

The installations are formidable. The stones are moved by conveyor belt into machines that mill them like grain. From there they pass to tubs where water separates out the nitrate; once dry it will become the valuable powder that nations battle over, the magic dust that has made fortunes for the very few and misery for so many more. White gold. I visit only one of the fortysomething nitrate mines in the region and I see thousands of men, like ants, laboring on the force of sheer muscle in that calcined desolation.

Before saying goodbye, the Scottish administrator once again offers me tea, which I drink as fast as I can, because Mr. Amador Troncoso has agreed to introduce me to some of the miners and their wives. This falls outside of the official agenda for my visit.

The miners' camp was a grouping of long, narrow alleyways with shacks on both sides made from sandy desert material and wood. Some housed entire families but most were dormitories for men alone. Children, dogs, and women worn down by the effort of surviving. Public latrines, a dusty plaza, a chapel, and the company store. The benefits of white gold had not touched the camp.

Amador found four women who agreed to speak with me inside one of their homes. A few minutes later more women arrived, drawn in by the news of a foreign woman visitor. Half-naked children ran around and a baby was latched to his mother's breast. The house consisted of a single room, four walls, a dirt floor, and minimal furnishings of rough-hewn wood and clothes hung on nails. Among the women was a prostitute who openly introduced herself as such and who looked no different from the other mothers; all of them appeared greatly aged by the dusty desert patina and all of them projected a quiet strength and dignity. These women struggled alongside their men, encouraged their husbands to stand up to the bosses, participated in protests and strikes, children in tow, and sometimes were shot at or trampled by soldiers on horseback. When there was no coal, firewood, or food, they turned out en masse to block transportation or shut down the mining machines. They were combative, decisive, immune to fear.

The women offered me mate, an infusion of green yerba, bitter and aromatic, slurped through a metal straw from a hollowed gourd that passed from hand to hand and mouth to mouth. In the very brief time I had been in Chile I had learned that it was unacceptable to visit a home, humble as it may be, without accepting something to eat or drink, even if sometimes this was only water. They told me about the failed strikes, the children who died young, the pain in their bodies, the dirty water, the bone-grinding work, the alcohol that turned the men violent, the feverish rage over their irredeemable poverty. They read newspapers, some clandestine, and political pamphlets that circulated discreetly. They were not ignorant of what went on beyond the confines of the camp and the broader province, country, even the world; they had heard of many modern-day inventions, the ways other people lived, the incalculable fortunes of mining companies. They commented sarcastically on the revolt of the congress, echoing Troncoso's opinion: a *futres* war.

"What good does the right to vote do men, miss? Nothing changes for us. We don't want poverty wages, we don't want credit and tokens. We want school for our little ones, medical attention, some trees in the plaza, more latrines, clean water," they told me.

AMADOR TRONCOSO DROVE me back to the city. We stopped to give the horses a rest and as we waited in the incandescent desert light, seated on the rocky ground barely shielded from the sun by the minimal shade of the coach, the man told me about his life. He had been a soldier in the war against Bolivia and Peru, fighting for this very land we stood on.

"I have scars everywhere, miss. Hand-to-hand combat, fixed bayonets and knives, we really gave it to those *cholos*. The death count was tremendous."

"Who are the *cholos*?" I asked him.

"Well, they're the enemy. Peruvians, Bolivians . . . the *cholos* aren't like us, they are ignorant Indians, uncivilized. After the war I worked for a year in the nitrate mines."

He explained that he did maintenance for the locomotives in the camps, a mechanic by trade, until he got a job as a coach driver for the Iquique offices. He said that he had a better hand with horses than machines because animals were like people, they just needed love. That new job changed his life as, finally paid in pesos, he was able to save a little and settle down with his family.

"We're together now. I never wanted to take them with me to the mining camp. That's no place for a woman, much less children," he told me.

"The truth is that it didn't seem like a good place for anyone, Mr.

Troncoso," I replied. "But the women I met seemed as strong as the most seasoned man."

"Mark my words, miss, one day the workers of this country are going to band together, with the women in the lead. And then we'll have a true revolution," he said.

WHEN THE *ITATA* arrived, Eric Whelan found me waiting for him on the dock as he disembarked. I threw my arms around his neck and planted a couple of kisses on his cheeks. This left him disconcerted; in the years of our close friendship we had always avoided physical demonstrations of affection. I caught him in a moment of weakness, his knees wobbly from the voyage, and he wasn't able to fend me off.

As soon as he could walk in a straight line I took him to have a cup of tea, one of the many rituals that well-to-do Chileans observed religiously. On the way Eric confessed that he too had vomited his guts out from seasickness during his first few days aboard the ship.

In the end it was not necessary for the United States to make a display of its naval force to resolve the problem of the *Itata*. All it took was a little diplomacy. Before the ship even docked, the commanders of the *Charleston* and other American ships had come to an agreement with the Chilean rebels, who wanted to avoid a skirmish with the colossus from the north at all costs. They willingly turned over their weapons and ammunition without any resistance as a gesture of goodwill. That was the official version anyway. The true reason for their seeming surrender was that they had received a shipment of more modern weapons of German fabrication and they no longer needed the guns aboard the *Itata*.

The presence of Great Britain was felt everywhere in Iquique. Eric and I sat on the hotel terrace decorated with Victorian furniture and potted plants defending themselves tooth and nail against the dry desert heat. I brought my friend up to speed, explaining that the king of nitrate was John Thomas North, son of an English coal miner, who had amassed an incalculable fortune with his unchecked greed. There was no corner of the country that his power did not reach. His deep coffers provided the funds for electoral corruption and bribes; he had effectively purchased an entire social class, blinded as they were by gold. President Balmaceda considered North personally responsible for having corrupted the Chileans' most noble characteristic: austerity. He had set out to reduce the mining magnate's power, but Congress had defended the man.

A tuxedoed waiter served us tea on fine porcelain with warm rolls and an orange marmalade imported from Harrods in London. Practically any English product could be obtained in Iquique.

"I see you really do speak the language," Eric commented, impressed at how well I was able to communicate with the hotel staff.

In reality, at that time, newly arrived in the country, I only understood about half of what was said. The Chilean accent was nothing like the Spanish spoken in my neighborhood back home in the Mission. The Chileans seemed to swallow their words, as if they were speaking around a rag stuffed in their mouths. They also sprinkled in terms that were not Spanish at all, taken from indigenous languages, I believe, and they used so many euphemisms that it was often impossible to know what the devil they were talking about.

"I don't know how you're going to manage here," I said to Eric.

"I suppose there are people who speak English," he replied.

"Why do you think that? English is not a universal language."

We refined the details of our plan for Eric to stay in the north covering the rebels and me to go south to cover the president. We mapped out a method for remaining in contact during the time that we would be separated. Communication within Chile was difficult even under normal circumstances, and the mess the war had made of things presented further obstacles. Corresponding about military matters was dangerous, as it could raise suspicions of espionage if the letters were intercepted. We needed a code, but we didn't know any. I had the idea to use sentimental language, like in romantic novels. Eric hadn't read any such book and I was no expert either, crime novels being my forte, but we spent a few hours doubled over with laughter as we drafted an inventory of terms expressing passionate love and their translation to matters of war.

"How are you planning to get to Santiago?" he asked me.

"There's no train and the roads are in a disastrous state. I have booked myself passage on a ship leaving in a few days' time for Valparaíso; from there I can take a train," I explained.

"The war is being waged at sea. Both sides have sunk several ships," he warned me.

"It is an unavoidable risk, Eric."

"I do not even want to think about all the things that could happen to you, Emilia. You are drawn to risk like a magnet. You would be safer with me."

"There is no such thing as safety for anyone in war."

I WAS FORTUNATE on my voyage to Valparaíso and we did not cross paths with any enemy vessels.

We reached Valparaíso at dawn and had to wait a couple of hours before we were able to disembark onto dry land. In the gentle light of that cloudy morning, the city was sketched on the sky like a pale watercolor painting, a mishmash of colorful ramshackle houses hung on the hills framed by purple mountains in the distance. Hundreds of barges and other vessels rocked in the wild, inky ocean as it thrashed and frothed against the rocks. Thousands of pelicans and shrieking seagulls disappeared behind the sullied white sails as they dove sharply into the water in urgent hunger. The fishermen's boats, returning from a night of casting nets, were loaded down with live conger eel and tuna. Valparaíso was the largest port on the Pacific, only comparable to San Francisco. The storehouses held Chilean products for export to the world including metals, leather, wool, wood, and grain.

From early in the morning, the port simmered with the incessant coming and going of miners, stevedores, peddlers, coachmen, and people of all classes, from ladies and gentlemen of fashion to beggars dressed in rags. I have never in my life seen so many dogs and mules in one spot. Or so many soldiers. Valparaíso and the surrounding area had become a military base, but it was lacking the euphoric crusading atmosphere that I had observed in the north.

The head of the United States Foreign Consulate, a Mr. Patrick Egan, was waiting for our steamship when it docked in Valparaíso. There were several other Americans on board, most of them with their families, including some delegates from the State Department. I'd learned from them that Egan originally hailed from Ireland, where he'd begun a political career that was always marked by a rashness and readiness to fight. My compatriots from the steamship made the introduction between me and Egan, and I explained to him that I was a correspondent for the *Examiner*.

"They sent a woman?" he asked.

"You're not the first one to notice it, sir."

Egan turned out to be a fascinating man. His short stature did not in any way reduce his imposing presence. He was fifty-four years old, with gray hair and mustache and a fervent way of speaking that left no room for dialogue. He was rash and quick to anger, more akin to a revolutionary than a diplomat. In spite of his years as an activist against the British and his vertiginous political career, he'd somehow found time to father fourteen children, of which nine had survived. I felt sorry for his wife.

As with almost every man I met, he was dismissive of me as a journalist. Instead, he took a paternal interest in me, clearly deciding that he could not leave me to my own devices, insisting I travel in his train car with him the rest of the way to Santiago. There, he said, his wife would be delighted to present me to polite society.

6

THE CITY OF SANTIAGO SPREADS OUT OVER A FERTILE
valley surrounded by foothills and mountains. They say that from
every corner of Chile one can feel the majestic presence of the Andes
Mountains and their telluric energy that defines the proud, serious,
and stoic nature of the Chilean people. Santiago's city center repli-
cates the typical Spanish colonial style, with a cathedral, main plaza,
and government headquarters, just as I'd seen in my Papo's books.
From there, streets run off perpendicular and parallel, laid out on a
grid.

The day I arrived in Santiago the air was filled with the smell of
ash and the feeling of rage. I soon learned that the political crisis had
been so dire that President Balmaceda had suspended telephone service to keep it from being used by the opposing faction. But when a
fire started accidentally the previous day, the lack of telephone service meant that the firemen were not called into action until a good
while later, when the smoke began to sting their eyes. It took them an
hour to arrive on foot, because the horses for their carts had been
requisitioned by the army to aid the war effort. An entire city block
burned to the ground, including the new Catholic University. Many

people blamed Balmaceda, some even asserting he'd told his ruffians to start the fire to target the office of the opposition press.

Unlike in Iquique, where it seemed that the majority of the population were working-class laborers, the capital had a large middle class. The streets were teeming with public and private employees, tradesmen and professionals, monks and nuns, mounted guards, and poor beggars as well, of course, the *rotos*. Dogs everywhere—this was the land of strays. There was a large variety of stagecoaches, mule carts, and once in a while a piled-high buggy pulled by oxen. The working-class men wore sandals, ponchos, and conical hats like the Chinese, the middle class wore formal suits and top hats, and all the women on the street were wrapped in black shawls. My cape was long and dark and looked a good deal like the Chilean shawls so that I would not have stood out at all if it weren't for my height; the people there were of shorter stature.

Aside from the fire, everyday life did not seem to have been disrupted by the war, save for the presence of uniformed soldiers and the curfew, which prohibited circulating through the streets after dark. Businesses were open, nannies pushed strollers through the parks, people hurriedly came and went to and from their offices. Street vendors sold fried fish, toasted peanuts, empanadas, sweets, and roasted chestnuts. The whinnying and clomping of the horses could be heard along with the shouts of peddlers selling newspapers or offering services such as knife sharpening, mattress and wool combing, unclogging of sewers, and extermination of rats. There seemed to be a church on every city block, a notary public on every corner.

I set myself up at the residency for young ladies because it was cheaper than a hotel. The boardinghouse was owned by two spinster sisters of French ancestry. Their home was a bastion of hygiene and cleanliness in a city where manure piled up on the corners and the open gutters ran with the unholy filth of human waste. They charged me one week up front and handed me a list of the strict house rules written out on a card in flowery calligraphy. My room was simple, but much larger and better furnished than my bedroom back home. It had a metal bed with a thick wool mattress, two chairs, a dresser with three drawers, a speckled but fully functional mirror, a table that served as a desk, and two kerosene lamps. The room also included a pitcher and washbasin, and I was allowed to use the bathtub in the basement beside the washtubs once a week. Breakfast was served at eight o'clock every morning in the dining room, laid out on starched tablecloths with linen napkins, and consisted of tea or mate, bread and butter, cheese, and quince paste; on Sundays they offered eggs with sausage from the same German butcher that supplied the presidential palace. The severe French spinsters and the two indigenous women they employed, both silent as little mice, maintained a rigorous cleaning regimen; no fly would dare to venture in through the window.

The next morning, I went out to purchase all the printed press material I could get my hands on, from the oldest and most important newspaper, which was in the service of the rebels, to the multiple satirical publications with grotesque illustrations of the men in power, including Balmaceda. There were also workers' newspapers—almost all socialist or anarchist-leaning—which denounced poverty, poor working conditions, and employer abuses. I read everything I could find, and spent the following days talking to people: waiters, street peddlers, and cart drivers, even some public functionaries that I caught in passing.

The invitation from the American diplomat, Mr. Egan, and his wife was not long in coming. The soirée would begin at five o'clock in the evening and he offered to send his carriage to drive me to his residence. I ironed my moss-colored dress, which I'd worn only once, on the last night aboard the *Charleston*, and in lieu of jewelry, since I don't own anything of value besides the Virgen de Guadalupe medallion that I always wear pinned to my brassiere, I tied a red velvet ribbon around my neck, as was the style in San Francisco. Inspecting myself in the mirror, I looked like my throat had been slit with a knife.

I couldn't repress a shiver; it felt like a forewarning.

THE EGAN MANSION had beautiful architecture and French-inspired furnishings, all curved legs, fragile tables, brocade sofas, teardrop chandeliers with dozens of candles, porcelain vases, paintings of Olympian gods, and fireplaces burning in every room. I would soon discover that all this was far from typical in a Chilean home, where cold air currents were considered healthy, luxury was suspect, and decoration was superfluous. The house was designed for many children, but half of them no longer lived there, causing a strange sense of emptiness, as if the rooms were waiting for someone. Despite the early hour, the guests had dressed with the elegance usually reserved for a dinner party, the men in tuxedos and the women in velvet, silk, and lace in dark tones and with very discreet jewelry. My dress did not stand out too terribly.

The guests in attendance that evening were some of the few people of rank who remained loyal to Balmaceda. There were several military officers, a young journalist named Rodolfo León, and a priest with a corpselike appearance, Father Restrepo, who was introduced to me as "the conscience of Chile." He served as confessor and spiritual guide to the upper class, and on more than one occasion had acted as intermediary between the government and the rebels. Despite the fact that Balmaceda had a tense relationship with the church, this robed man had direct access to the president.

"Miss Emilia del Valle Claro," Egan introduced me.

"Del Valle? Are you any relation to Paulina del Valle?" a gray-haired woman asked me with an insolent tone that reminded me of a cockatoo. Paulina del Valle was the Chilean woman who had made a fortune shipping delicacies to San Francisco on ice during the gold rush.

"Yes, but I have not yet had occasion to meet her. I arrived in Chile only recently," I told her.

"Claro . . . Which Claros are those?" the woman wanted to know.

"The Claros out of Chihuahua," I answered with such firmness that she did not probe any further.

Egan then quietly explained that, in Chile, political and economic power was held by a handful of families, landed gentry who owned the large haciendas and managed them like feudal lords. Whippings and the stockade were common punishments for tenants, who were often sold along with the lands they worked. This did not constitute slavery, he said, because the campesinos were free to leave, but in reality, they had nowhere else to go. No one else would hire them and they would end up as beggars and vagabonds on the roads and in the cities.

The upper-class families used the surnames of both father and mother to locate a person's place in the social hierarchy and within the intricate web of relatives. Del Valle was a high-ranking surname, according to Egan, but no one had heard of Claro from Chihuahua.

PATRICK EGAN'S WIFE was a small, robust woman, deformed by motherhood. She'd lost five children and others had died in her womb; of the nine that had survived only three lived in Chile. The pain of her deceased and absent children was visible in her clouded gaze and her sad expression, but the trials she'd borne had not broken her. I learned that she was an observant Catholic but had openly expressed support for reforms, which had garnered more than one incendiary reprimand from Father Restrepo. The woman could control her indomitable husband with the mere raise of an eyebrow, as I witnessed when the diplomat launched into a diatribe on women with the nerve to intrude upon a man's professional field. He was referring here to Chile's first female doctor, but I felt that he was hinting at me as well, since I was the only woman among those gathered there who worked for a living. His wife's eyebrows stopped him cold.

"Pardon me, Miss del Valle, I was not referring to you," Egan added quickly.

"If we had access to the same education as men, we would be able to occupy the same professions," I said.

"Some women are fairly intelligent," Father Restrepo interrupted. "But if God wanted them to be professionals, He would have made them men, don't you agree? The Lord, in His infinite wisdom, has assigned women the sacred duty of raising children. The weaker sex is . . ."

Mrs. Egan stopped him there. "With due respect, Father, our sex is not weak. It is time now to move into the music room. We have arranged a small diversion."

We were regaled with a brief concert on the harp and piano, followed by an endless poetry recitation. Two young women wearing plissé tunics and golden tiaras, like ancient vestals, took turns reciting poetry by the Nicaraguan poet Rubén Darío.

JUST AS I was beginning to detest Rubén Darío and my stomach was rumbling with hunger, the vestals finally took their bows and we moved on to dinner: oysters, creamed mushrooms, partridges stuffed with walnuts and dried fig, filet mignon with cauliflower in truffle sauce, several salads, cheeses, fruits, and cake decorated with two marzipan flags, one for the United States and one for Chile, all washed down with French champagne and Cousiño red wine.

"The Chilean wines are as good as the French ones, don't you agree, Miss del Valle?" Egan asked me.

"I couldn't say, Ambassador. I don't know anything about wine," I replied.

"How could she know, if these Americans only drink beer!" said the cockatoo.

"I am no expert on beer, either, ma'am," I told her. She perhaps disliked my tone, because she fell silent.

Father Restrepo was served only a clear broth, and as the rest of us filled our bellies with that lavish banquet, he touted the purifying effects of fasting and self-flagellation.

In the few moments I was able to converse with the journalist, Rodolfo León, we compared the press and culture of our two countries, spoke about my role as a war correspondent, and discovered we shared common interests. We agreed to meet the next day.

Over dinner that evening, we discussed politics, the conversation led by Egan with his characteristic passion. Hounded by questions from several of his guests, he admitted that Balmaceda was losing the battle where foreign propaganda was concerned, given that the rebels' position garnered more sympathy than the government's.

"Journalists like yourself, Miss del Valle, have the duty to inform the public of Balmaceda's truly extraordinary accomplishments and his modern vision. Those who would call themselves revolutionaries are wholly opposed to change," he added.

"How is that, Ambassador?" I asked.

"They want to concentrate all power in Congress, which they control, of course. If it were up to them, there would be no progress at all."

"Excuse my ignorance. It seems I was quite mistaken, but I believed that the rebels did want change—free elections, for example," I said.

"We have elections, miss. Adult males can vote, as long as they know how to read and write. Traditionally the president appoints his successor," Rodolfo León interrupted.

"And the candidate always belongs to the oligarchy, correct?" I asked.

"Yes, because in general they're the best prepared for the task, but a candidate's social status is not a determining factor," he responded.

"So then you could have a working-class or middle-class president?"

"Of course. That has never happened, but it will, one day," he assured me.

"In the United States, our presidents also come from the political and social elite," Patrick Egan pointed out.

"But they are elected by the citizens, not appointed," I said.

"But which citizens? The blacks? The poor? The immigrants? There is as much corruption in the electoral system there as there is here," Egan replied emphatically.

"I have a lot of questions, Ambassador. It would be a great help to interview the president," I said.

"Then I shall see to it. Give me a few days to set it up," he said.

The evening concluded with the women sipping liqueur out of tiny Venetian crystal glasses in the sitting room while the men retired to the library to enjoy cognac and cigars. The female circle made little effort to include me in their conversation and I inferred that these ladies were scandalized by a foreigner criticizing their country.

Between sips of sweetish liqueur, I learned that Paulina del Valle, the unquestionable leader of her extensive clan, along with the rest of the del Valle family, was on the side of the rebels, like the majority of the Chilean aristocracy. I did not dare mention Gonzalo Andrés del Valle, but I now had a plan for how to locate my father.

I returned to the boardinghouse with my stomach roiling just before the nightly curfew went into effect. The silent streets echoed with the clomping of hooves of the horses pulling the Security Force's fearsome wagons.

RODOLFO LEÓN WAS a vastly cultured, earnest, and generous man. Before our meeting, I took it upon myself to find out a bit about his career. In Chile, it was considered bad taste to speak of one's personal achievements; they found American arrogance quite jarring. I learned that Rodolfo was a doctor, that he had served as a field surgeon in the Peruvian war and had been decorated for his valor. In recent years, he had founded a newspaper, and he told me that his mission was to defend Balmaceda's agenda and attack his political enemies.

"You don't believe in the impartiality of the press?" I asked.

"Frankly, miss, I don't believe it exists," he replied.

We met in a tearoom and pastry shop in the city center, where office workers lunched at midday, all dressed alike down to the same vest and hat as if it were some uniform, a contingent of men in gray and black. I arrived first, sat at one of the little tables, and soon noticed that the other patrons were openly staring at me. Just then the journalist arrived.

"I must apologize for the delay, Miss Emilia. I am terribly sorry to have kept you waiting," he said.

"Do not concern yourself with it, it was only a moment."

"It is unacceptable here for a lady to occupy a table alone. In general, ladies should be accompanied in public places."

"Now I understand why everyone was staring at me before you arrived," I said.

"In some ways, we are still stuck in colonial times, whereas in other areas we are the most progressive country in the region. And, I must add, we're the most stable nation on this continent of revolutionaries."

"That's the first thing I learned about Chile," I admitted.

"I hope from the bottom of my heart that this conflict is only a brief lapse in our solid democratic tradition," he added.

Rodolfo León went on to explain that the rebellion had nothing to do with defending Congress; it was founded instead on the greed of those who owned the mines, the land, and industry. They were opposed to Balmaceda's laws in defense of workers. He added that the true enemy was the aristocracy—asserting the interests of a wealthy few above all else—and all we could hope for was that the two sides came to an agreement before more blood was spilled.

He told me also of his years as a military surgeon, the battles he'd witnessed, and how history is written by the victorious; atrocities committed in the name of patriotism are often conveniently omitted. "In war, there's no honor or mercy, no one is ever right, Miss Emilia. Everyone behaves like bloodthirsty beasts."

Up to that moment I had not been able to measure the gravity of the conflict. The troops in the north and in the south were all in a holding pattern and the civil population clung tightly to a fictitious sense of normalcy.

He explained that, for the moment, the rebels dominated the seas, but the president had two state-of-the art torpedo bombers. In April, Balmaceda's torpedo bombers had flanked the rebel navy's most powerful battleship, which had sunk in a matter of minutes.

"It was a tremendous blow for the rebels," Rodolfo informed me.

"I gather that the rebellion is not concentrated solely in the north. There is also opposition to Balmaceda right here in the capital and in Valparaíso," I said.

"It has become fashionable to declare oneself in opposition to the government," he replied. Rodolfo told me of a group called the Revolutionary Committee of Santiago, formed mainly by young men from prominent families. While in hiding, they plotted against the government as if all this military fervor were a game or diverting pastime.

"They believe themselves to be above the law, but they will be stopped," he told me.

As a reporter, it was not my job to form an opinion about who occupied the higher moral ground in this conflict—I knew that when I traveled to Chile—but now that I was in the thick of it, I could not ignore the feelings in my gut. I believed that Balmaceda was fighting for the rights of the common man, trying to break the iron grip of the aristocracy. And yet I had heard that he did so with a shocking brutality, and that his motives were not pure. I didn't know what to think. What was the truth? I imagined that Eric would be conducting his interviews with professional neutrality, but maybe it was inevitable that his sympathy would be with the rebels among whom he was embedded. Could he remain impartial? Or was he full of doubts, as I was?

IN THE END I did not have to wait for Ambassador Egan to introduce me to the president. A few days after my meeting with Rodolfo León, the Chilean journalist arranged an interview for me. Like all men of his clan, Balmaceda descended from the oldest oligarchical bloodlines and owned vast lands that included an entire province complete with train stations, towns, and hundreds and hundreds of campesinos. He had a reputation for being brilliant and of incorruptible honesty. He was authoritarian, to be certain, accustomed to leading, but he believed in the institution of democracy and had respected the constitution. Until, that is, he decided to interpret it in his own way. And now the profits from nitrate were in play. Chile was a wealthy country.

That Thursday at three in the afternoon, I entered the government palace alongside Rodolfo. We passed through several semi-darkened rooms with antique furnishings and epic paintings and walked up to the second floor. In spite of the climate of hatred and violence the country was mired in, the presidential palace had a calm atmosphere more befitting a museum. No one demanded that we identify ourselves or even asked where we were going.

At the antechamber to the president's office, a secretary gestured for us to take seats in a row of high-backed velvet chairs. A few minutes later the hinges of a heavy dark-wood door creaked open and out stepped a military man. He was bearded and sallow, with his uniform hanging from his skeletal frame.

"That is General Barbosa," Rodolfo informed me in a low voice. "He fought in the campaign against the Araucanía Indians, the war with Peru and Bolivia, and is now head of the army. He is ailing but he remains at his post, directing the fight against the rebels."

I did not think that the general's decrepit appearance boded well for his troops.

The secretary informed me that it was time for my audience with the country's leader. My new friend wished me good luck, and an instant later I found myself face-to-face with the president of Chile.

JULY 18, 1891
THE PRESIDENT
By Emilia del Valle

Chile's presidential palace has an appearance more in keeping with a colonial fort; it is a square, two-story building with iron bars on the windows and an interior patio. A couple of guards, mounted on black purebred horses, fulfill a more decorative function. Pedestrians appear perfectly at home as they stroll across the patio.

President José Manuel Balmaceda is a man of fifty-one, tall, thin, with large dark eyes, high forehead, thick hair, and a dense mustache. Charismatic, intelligent, he projects a calm assuredness. This is the refined product of several generations of distinguished lineage; his surnames date back to the dawn of the colonial period in the seventeenth century and his family boasts extensive landholdings that span mountains and coastline. He stands to greet me with a kiss on the hand.

"Wouldn't you like a little cup of coffee?" he offers.

In Chile, questions are often formulated in the negative—*wouldn't you like*—and the diminutive form—*a little cup of coffee*—is used for almost everything. This tendency to minimize, which would seem to convey humility or modesty, stands in contrast to the superiority that the Chileans feel: best race, most solid republic, strongest economy, most disciplined army, the star country of South America.

Since first arriving in Chile, I have been told that Balmaceda wields his power like a tyrant; that he has mercilessly repressed his people through arrests, raids, tortures, and executions; that his army recruits young men by force, paralyzing agriculture and industry with a dearth of workers; and that his henchmen's prepotency and brutality is out of control. His political adversaries are persecuted and imprisoned, forced into exile, or have taken refuge in foreign consulates. He is accused of arrogance and vanity, of not listening to criticism and ignoring the opposition press, of manipulating elections, flouting the law, and overriding Congress.

It is hard to reconcile what is said about him with the impression of extreme equanimity that Balmaceda transmits, and the impressive list of public works that his government has accomplished. The iron fist with which he wields his power is understandable given the context of the country's civil war, but the repression began before that. At my question over the newspapers he has shut down, he replies that the opposition press lies and incites violence, that it represents the interests of the social elite, that it is an enemy of the government.

"They say that I have betrayed my class. They will not forgive me for representing the emerging social classes. But *they* are the future of Chile. Progress is measured by an educated populace paid just wages," he tells me.

"Yet, last year, your government brutally repressed striking workers demanding better salaries. Your army left hundreds dead. And just months ago something similar happened with the strikers at the nitrate mines," I point out.

"The government must maintain order," he replies in a biting tone.

Turning to the topic of the church, he informs me that the clergy blame him for the secular laws and the project of separation of church and state, but that these changes date back to his predecessor. And the church has always aligned itself with the aristocracy. The president refuses to call these men revolutionaries, because they are fighting to conserve the status quo, mainly their immense privileges.

"My government is revolutionary; they are counterrevolutionary," he tells me. "They fear change. A parliamentary regime, like the one they aimed to impose, would be fatal to the country. I will not allow my nation to fall to a dictatorship, whether it is run by Congress or even by myself. Public powers should be free and independent," he adds.

He declaims with conviction and eloquence, but without raising his voice, always measured. In the same tone, he mentions his plan to nationalize the nitrate industry, to the detriment of the British mining companies and wealthy local investors, many of whom are senators and congressmen. This explains why Great Britain supports the rebels, who have guaranteed British control of the mines.

"Nitrate is a limited resource, it will not last forever. This is our moment and we must take advantage of it," he explains. "The victory in the war against Peru has provided us with more than enough to build a great nation. Let's do it."

After my interview with the president I was trying hard to hold all the contradictions of this place in my head. I was a stranger in Chile and could not aspire to understand it, but the country was pulling me, as if in a mysterious way I belonged in this land. Sitting in my room at the boardinghouse, I thought of my stepfather with infinite gratitude. I had traveled from my home to another hemisphere—borne largely on his confidence in me—and had found my way through a foreign country, one where a single female was deeply suspect. And now I had accessed the highest office in the land. Don Pancho would be proud of me.

7

PAULINA DEL VALLE LIVED IN AN IMPRESSIVE NEOCLAS-
sical mansion on Avenida Ejército Libertador, in the sector favored
by the aristocracy. It loomed up on the corner of two main streets like
a small palace, with its entrance framed by columns, huge windows
on the first and second floors, and smaller ones on the third story and
turret. As soon as the civil war had begun in January, the del Valle
family, all sworn enemies of the government, disappeared from the
Santiago social scene. Some fled to their lands outside the city or left
the country entirely, others joined the rebels in the north or sought
asylum to avoid repression.

Paulina, however, had not budged from her residence. Her friendship with President Balmaceda's mother, which was somehow sus-
tained despite her loyalty to his enemies, afforded her immunity; no
one would dare to touch her. As the boarded-up mansions in the area
were vandalized with threats and insults, she made a display of leaving all the lamps burning in her windows well past curfew.

After living for many years in San Francisco, where she'd made
her fortune, the del Valle matriarch had returned to Chile—now widowed and remarried to a second husband whom she'd seemed to pull

out of her hat like some illusionist—and had settled in with a level of luxury unprecedented for that somber society. Her displays of wealth caused as much talk as her handsome husband, an Englishman of mysterious origins, considerably younger, who had been quickly assimilated into the upper crust of Santiago. It was said that the man was British royalty but, out of inexplicable modesty, he did not use his title. It was also speculated, however, in whispers, that he had been Paulina's butler back in San Francisco. In any case, it was clear that he had married her for her money; there could be no other motivation, the gossips asserted. Paulina was well aware of the talk, which caused her great delight. She understood the classism of Chilean society and knew that those people would shut down all suspicions in order to avoid the shame of having been made fools of. The notion of having accepted a servant as one of their own was intolerable, and worse still was having confused him for an aristocrat.

The news that someone from California bearing the del Valle name had arrived in Santiago had piqued the matriarch's curiosity. News traveled fast in that tight social circle, but, just in case, I made sure that Paulina learned of my existence through Ambassador Egan's wife, who played cards with her every Thursday. Cards were the official excuse to gather, anyway—in truth it seems that they held séances. Paulina wished to invoke Feliciano, the first husband with whom she'd had epic fights and passionate reconciliations, as she herself admitted so often that it was no secret. Mrs. Egan wished to communicate with her deceased children. She soon relayed Paulina's invitation to me.

I dressed the best I could for the visit, bought a box of fine chocolates because I had heard that Paulina loved sweets, and arrived half an hour late, which was considered polite among Chileans. The interior of the mansion was crowded with extravagant decorations, fringed drapery, and uncomfortable furniture, not at all in keeping with the neoclassical architecture. Paulina del Valle received me in a glassed sunroom that looked out over an interior courtyard. Surrounded by bird cages and tropical plants that stoically bore the climate, she sat in a high-backed wicker chair with a wooly dog stationed on her lap. At her feet, a girl of around ten or eleven was busily drawing in a notebook.

"Come in, señorita. Excuse me for not standing, I am suffering a touch of gout. Have a seat," she said, gesturing toward another wicker chair. "This is my granddaughter Aurora. Come now, kid! Greet our guest!"

The girl stood up, stretched out her skirt, and made a small curtsy, then sat back down at her grandmother's feet.

Paulina was a woman of around seventy, although it was hard to calculate her exact age because although she was extremely overweight, her face was young, with rosy cheeks and sparkling eyes, and her hands were as white and delicate as a damsel's. She wore a satin dress in black, which seemed to be the preferred color in those parts, and she was adorned with an extensive collection of necklaces, rings, bracelets, and earrings, like some Asian idol. As I've noted, extravagance was considered terrible taste in Chile, and I suspected that she enjoyed clashing with the prim and proper locals.

She opened the box of chocolates, popped one into her mouth, and rang a small silver bell. Instantly, as if she had been waiting behind the potted ferns, a woman in a white apron and starched hat appeared carrying a tray.

"Wouldn't you like a little cup of hot chocolate?" Paulina asked me.

I soon found myself balancing a cup of thick chocolate in my hands and a plate of cake with dulce de leche and meringue on my lap. Chilean pastries are limited almost exclusively to these two ingredients, which combined contain lethal doses of sugar.

"Which of the del Valles do you belong to?" the imposing lady asked.

"I am the daughter of Gonzalo Andrés del Valle, ma'am."

"Can you prove it? It does not take much to attribute paternity to someone," she spat.

"It is not possible for anyone to prove paternity, ma'am. The mother is a fact, the father is a matter of opinion," I answered.

She received my words with a start, followed by a girlish giggle that seemed incongruous with a person of her volume. "Well said!" she exclaimed.

"I have traveled from San Francisco to meet him," I explained.

"Aren't you a journalist? That is no proper profession for a woman . . . but then almost nothing I have done in my life has ever been proper. That has never stopped me from doing just as I please. I was told that you traveled here because of this absurd civil war," she replied.

"I came to cover the war and also to meet my progenitor. I have little interest myself, but my mother made me promise I would return with news of him."

"Whatever for? If Gonzalo Andrés is your father, as you say, your mother would do better to forget him. She will never get anything out of him. He is quite slippery. I care for him; I have no choice, since he is my nephew and also my godson, but I am not blind." She said this in the aggressive tone that seemed to be her habitual manner of speaking.

"All the same, I should like to meet him, ma'am," I told her.

"I do not know that he will agree to see you. He has never mentioned a daughter."

"Please, ma'am, if you would just ask him. He may decide not to see me, and if so, I will accept his decision. It is quite possible that he does not remember my mother or the fact that he left a daughter behind in San Francisco."

Paulina del Valle deliberated for a few seconds, petting her little wooly dog and sipping her second cup of hot chocolate.

"He is in hiding," she finally informed me. "No one is after him since he plays no role in this upheaval, but he is very cautious, if not to say cowardly. He could stay with me, no one would bother him here, but I am not an easy person to live with. Isn't that right, Aurora?"

"Yes, Grandmother," the girl answered without looking up from her drawing.

"I shall send a note to my nephew to advise him that you wish to meet. Let it be clear: I am not doing this for you, but because it will be entertaining to see how this whole mess turns out," she told me.

"Thank you. What else can you tell me about him, besides the fact that he is slippery and cowardly?" I asked.

Paulina laughed again, so heartily that she choked on her cake. The girl set her notebook aside and gave her grandmother a few pats on the back.

"Why bother dancing around it? You are a *huacha*, isn't that right?" Paulina said, once she had caught her breath.

I had already heard this term, used to describe illegitimate children. President Balmaceda had been born before his parents were married, which is why he had been nicknamed El Huacho.

"The law and the church discriminate against *huachos*, but the world is full of them. There is nothing to be ashamed of, señorita. It is not your fault. It is the fault of your parents: your mother for letting herself be taken in like a fool and your father for being an irresponsible fornicator."

I was startled to hear her openly use that term, but then I remembered that Paulina was famously foulmouthed.

"Sometimes people change. What is your nephew like now?" I asked, somewhat disheartened by the portrait she had painted.

"He has become a sanctimonious Catholic. He has crushed his lungs beating his chest in church. I liked him better before, when he was a rake," she replied without hesitation.

PAULINA DEL VALLE launched into a diatribe against the government repression, how Balmaceda had closed universities, schools, and political centers, filled the prisons, jailing and torturing his detractors. There was no semblance of a judicial system left, the dictator having shuttered the courthouses and dismantled the Supreme Court for allowing political prisoners to walk free. Those judges, who were simply adhering to the law, were replaced by military tribunals who found any excuse to seize assets and lands from the wealthy.

"Write about that for your newspaper, señorita. My family and all of my friends are in hiding or have fled far away. There are only a few crazy young men left here risking their hides, plotting against Balmaceda."

In that moment a large dog trotted in with muddy paws and shook itself dry on the rug. He was followed by a tall man in a hunting coat with gray hair, thick sideburns, and a mustache with waxed tips. The wooly lapdog jumped to the floor and the two animals ran around in circles barking and smelling each other's rear ends.

"What have you been up to?" Paulina del Valle scolded the man.

"Taking the pulse of the situation outside, my dear. I do not like what I see. There is so much violence in the air it could explode at the slightest spark. The government is in a state of red alert," the man responded in a well-educated British accent.

"I hope the boys of the Committee do not provoke Balmaceda with any more of their foolishness," Paulina said in English with terrible pronunciation. I remembered that Rodolfo León had mentioned the Committee—a group of young aristocratic men who stirred up trouble.

"It is best you don't go out, Paulina," he warned her.

"Where would I go with this gout?" she replied. "This is Fredrick Williams, my husband," she said, introducing us. "Miss Emilia del Valle. This young lady claims to be the daughter of Gonzalo Andrés and I suppose she has come all this way to settle up with the family."

I did not have time to react to this rude comment, because her gallant husband, who looked young enough to be her son, greeted me with an old-fashioned kiss on the hand. I had the impression that I had seen him before, but that was impossible.

"I am sorry, miss," the man said, and I did not know if he was apologizing for his wife's tone or the bad luck of my paternity.

"I am too, Mr. Williams. I would prefer to be the daughter of Francisco Claro, my stepfather, but one cannot choose their family," I responded.

"If you are Gonzalo Andrés's daughter, that makes my wife your great-aunt," he said.

"Just a moment, Fredrick! I do not count anyone as a relation until they can offer proof!" Paulina exclaimed.

I reckoned then that it was time for me to take my leave. I thanked the lady, gave her the address of my boardinghouse so she could send me word of my father's response to my suggestion to meet, as promised. After that, I bid her farewell. Her husband and little Aurora walked me to the front door, trailed by the large dog.

"I hope you are able to meet Gonzalo Andrés and clear up your situation," the Englishman said.

"Thank you, Mr. Williams."

"Paulina often forgets her good manners and can come across as quite hostile. She is accustomed to getting her way, but she has a good heart. She has nothing against you, I can assure you, Miss Emilia. Out of necessity, my wife has learned to be wary when it comes to strangers; many people have tried to take advantage of her generosity."

"Please inform Mrs. Paulina that I do not need anything from her or her nephew. I only wish to fulfill my mother's orders to meet him," I responded, ears burning with anger.

"Pardon me, I did not mean to offend you; nothing was further from my intention, miss. I am happy to hear that you do not expect anything from Gonzalo Andrés, because he has nothing to offer besides debt. You shall see for yourself that he is not well."

"He is ill?" I asked.

"He has been preparing to die for some time now; he even has the funeral planned, if you can imagine. He has taken it upon himself to write his own obituary and purchase a coffin, a mahogany monstrosity with silver rivets that he has asked us to store in the basement. The servants are convinced that it will bring bad luck, that we are calling down death. I believe Gonzalo Andrés has fallen under the influence of Father Restrepo, who tortures him with detailed descriptions of the horrors of hell. Do you fear the inferno, miss?" he asked me wryly.

"Yes. I fear the inferno of *this* world," I replied.

"Oh! You are quite refreshing! I must confess that I prefer depraved San Francisco to the Catholic prudishness of Santiago," he told me.

This brief conversation proved to my mind that Fredrick Williams could not possibly be a member of the British royal family. Those people are incredibly stiff and none of them ever would have spoken openly about family matters, money, or religion, much less with a plebeian like myself. I suspect that Paulina del Valle's handsome husband truly had been her butler in San Francisco, as they said. I believe, however, that he married her not for her money but for the sheer irony of it. How that man must be laughing at those Chilean aristocrats who imitated and envied him!

PAULINA DEL VALLE fulfilled her promise and alerted her nephew to my existence. Three days later, a letter arrived for me at the French sisters' residence, an elegant card bearing the shield of Argentina in gold relief. In it, his Supreme Excellence Ambassador José Evaristo Uriburu cordially invited me to pay a visit. Though I did not yet know how this related to my father, I accepted.

The exterior of the Argentine consulate was as grandiose as the United States diplomatic headquarters, but, inside, disorder reigned. All of the rooms were occupied by political refugees, their bundles and suitcases lining the hallways. The majority of those seeking asylum were well-known in the political or business spheres, accustomed to special treatment; under these circumstances, however, their usual privileges mattered little. It was then that I realized that my father must be among the people living here.

The foreign ambassador, around sixty with a beard and thin mustache that seemed to mar his otherwise austere face, was a seasoned diplomat who had served in several countries, but who had never faced a situation like the one he had experienced during the past months in Chile. He counted himself a friend to President Balmaceda, but, out of diplomatic duty, he was required to offer political protection to the man's enemies. He received me in the library, a stately room with Persian rugs, English furnishings, floor-to-ceiling bookcases, and a large fireplace with a fire blazing inside.

"This is the only room in the residence I have been able to reserve for myself, señorita. We have been invaded, with new guests arriving each day," he told me.

"How do you expect this revolution will turn out, Ambassador?" I asked.

"Victory for some, defeat for others, but bad for Chile. Hate, violence, killing, revenge . . . that's all that comes of a civil war. Only God knows what will happen here!"

Apparently, all Paulina had told the ambassador was that I wanted to meet Mr. Gonzalo Andrés del Valle; she had not explained why. He inquired after the reason for my visit, and I said that we were related and that I brought news from my mother, but I did not confess that the man was my father. I deduced that if Paulina del Valle had not proffered that information, it was best to omit it.

The ambassador informed me that Mr. del Valle had been staying at the residence for two months. He had arrived suffering from a cough and chest pains, as well as a melancholic nature, made worse by the tragic moment the country was facing. The two men were friends, having met years prior in Argentina, and in light of del Valle's condition, the ambassador had assigned a servant to look after him. He pulled on a thick velvet rope and soon a small mestiza woman with the upright, dignified posture of an admiral appeared.

"Rufina, Miss Emilia has come to call on Mr. del Valle," the ambassador informed her.

"Father Restrepo has just left and Mr. del Valle is praying. I cannot interrupt him," she replied.

"I can wait . . ." I offered.

"Come with me, señorita," the woman told me.

She led me into one of the salons filled with refugees, some entertaining themselves over board games or cards, others reading, writing, or napping on the sofas, almost all men, save for two women who sat embroidering in a corner.

I have lived my entire life in the Mission District surrounded by women like Rufina, with whom I feel an easy comradery. From the moment I began to practice the peculiar profession of journalism, these women have always proven invaluable. I would not have been able to write my first column for the *Examiner* without the information provided by Josefa Palomar, and I learned through her that when it comes to uncovering what is hidden below the surface, it is best to turn to women in service.

"Excuse me, Rufina, but there are so many men smoking in here that it is hard to breathe. I would love the chance to speak somewhere, in private," I told her.

"You want to speak with me, señorita?" she asked, surprised.

"Yes. I am new to Chile, I live very far away, in the United States. I came here to meet my father."

Intrigued, the good woman led me through a long hallway, down a flight of stairs, into the entrails of the building, past the kitchens, pantries, cellars, and washrooms that serviced the crowd of lodgers. The ironing room was not occupied.

"Wouldn't you like a little cup of tea?" she offered.

And so I told Rufina, in a few words, the story of Molly Walsh, my mother, the beautiful novice who was seduced, and also about don Pancho Claro, my true father, and his infinite wisdom. I described for her my home, my neighborhood, my childhood, my uncertain origins, and my supposed progenitor.

Why did I feel the need to confide in her? I do not know, but I had an instant connection with her, as if she were one of the blessed women who baked bread for the poor with my mother. She listened silently as I bared my secrets, blowing on her tea between sips. Outside, it was raining, but the room was warm and smelled of clean laundry and the hot coals used to heat the irons. It was the first time since I'd left my parents in San Francisco that I felt I could let my guard down with someone, and I was suddenly overwhelmed by tension, fatigue, and uncertainty. I would have liked to have rested my head on Rufina's shoulder. I did not even notice that my cheeks were stained with tears.

Rufina, for her part, told me how she had worked in the Argentine consulate since adolescence, becoming part of the inventory; the diplomats came and went, the governments changed, but she remained at her post. She knew every corner of the building and every detail of the complex domestic organization. She had recently had to double the staff in order to meet the needs of all the refugees. She was in charge of training the new employees and seeing that they fulfilled their required duties, and in recent weeks, she had been personally caring for Gonzalo Andrés del Valle.

"The doctors say that his lungs are bad, but I believe it is the worm of regret eating him up from the inside out," she told me.

"Why is that, Rufina?" I asked.

"Once that little worm gets inside your guts, there is no rest. Mr. del Valle is a good man, but he does not know it, that's what I say, señorita. He spends his days with a rosary in his hands, in fear of hell. He has me pray with him, which takes up a lot of my time. May God and the Virgin forgive me for speaking ill of the clergy, but all those visits from the priest only make him suffer more. Confessing every day may be a fine activity for the bishops, but not for a mere mortal like that man. What terrible sins must he have on his conscience if he cannot even leave his room, I wonder?"

WE SPENT OVER an hour sharing confidences, until Rufina estimated that Gonzalo Andrés del Valle would have finished with his prayers. Then she led me to his room on the second floor. While many of those seeking asylum at the Argentine consulate were forced to share a room or resigned themselves to sleeping on cots in the hallways, Gonzalo Andrés, thanks to his friendship with the ambassador and his poor health, had been assigned a small private bedchamber. Crossing the threshold, I was hit with the smell of urine and medication, the stench of old age and illness. It took my eyes a moment to adjust to the semidarkness. The curtains were drawn and the only light in the room came from a single dim lamp beside a chair.

What did I feel meeting my father for the first time? Nothing special. Since I had hardly ever thought of him, I had no preconceived notions or expectations. Seeing him face-to-face, I felt a mixture of vague curiosity and indifference, as if I were viewing the portrait of a stranger. I'd estimated that he must be somewhere around fifty years old, because he was a young man when he met my mother, but instead I found seated in the room's only chair an elderly man in a wool cap with a shawl over his legs. He looked up when Rufina announced the arrival of Miss Emilia del Valle, and proceeded to examine me for a long while with his crusty red eyes, then he gestured for Rufina to leave us.

"Come closer and let me get a better look at you, girl," he said.

I obeyed, silently, examining him in turn for some shared trait, but I did not find any. Up close, he appeared younger than I had initially believed but he was aged by his papery skin and defeated posture.

"My aunt Paulina has written. I understand you presume me to be your father?" he asked.

"That is what my mother, Molly Walsh, says."

Another eternal pause followed at the mention of my mother's name. I stood waiting before the chair, uncomfortable during that prolonged silence, thinking that the man must be lost to dementia or sadness.

"You do not look like her," he finally said.

"No. I do not look like you, either."

"You look like me when I was young. It's the Spanish blood. What have you come for? What do you want from me?"

"Nothing. If it were up to me, I would not have come at all, Mr. del Valle, but I promised my mother that I would. She was very insistent," I explained.

"Well, now you've seen me."

"Indeed. I shall not bother you again. Do you have any message for her?"

The man fell silent once more, his head tilted downward, his hands trembling, reduced to the size of a shivering child. My mother's hate-filled missive weighed down my handbag like a chunk of granite. How could I give it to this poor soul?

I was about to leave when I realized that he was silently sobbing. My indifference gave way to compassion, and I saw him as he was in that moment—a sick man—not the villain my mother so detested, that arrogant young buck who had engendered me on a whim. I approached him timidly, without knowing what to do or say to console him. He took my hand and pressed it between his, racked with sobs, and we remained that way for several minutes, united by some strange complicity, until he collected himself.

I had always mocked my mother's bitterness, believing it to be hers and hers alone. But, now, holding my father's hand, I understood that this sentiment had infected my heart more than I knew, and I carried it like a stone. While he sat shaking with sobs, I finally felt that craggy bitterness dissolve into gravel, into sand, into nothing.

My father asked me to fetch for him a box that he kept in a dresser drawer, and from it he extracted a yellowed envelope. He opened it and handed me a piece of paper and a portrait. He explained that this was the last letter he'd received from Molly Walsh, the only one he still possessed, and that the girl in the photograph was me. I remembered well the day when I accompanied my mother to the photography studio in San Francisco, how my shoes had pinched.

"I am dying of sadness over a wasted life, over my frivolity and selfishness. How shall I ever present myself before my Creator? I have nothing to show him, no wife, no children, no works of charity, nothing that might redeem me. And of all my many sins, the most grave was the one I committed with your mother. She was preparing to take her vows and become a nun. She was the bride of Christ and I ripped her away from Him, our Redeemer. That was my ultimate sacrilege . . ." he blubbered, mournful.

"Love is never a sacrilege," I answered.

"She loved me. The sin is all mine; I used her and abandoned her. I will pay for it in hell."

"According to who?" I exclaimed.

"According to Molly Walsh, your mother. And Father Restrepo," he responded.

"Do not listen to them. No one has the right to judge another person's soul. There is no key to hell or passport to heaven. Rufina is right, you are being eaten up by the worm of regret."

"Who is Rufina?" he asked.

"She is the woman who has been taking care of you for the past two months. It is high time you learned her name."

OVER THE COURSE of that afternoon, my father and I got to know each other. We talked about his life, marked by waste and loneliness. In his endless pursuit of ephemeral pleasures, he had spent more than he owned. He had never cultivated love and had now ended up alone—he repeated this over and over. He would have to pay for his sins as a carouser and gambler, for squandering his family's money and betraying his friends. In the brief moments I managed to distract him from his regrets, he seemed rejuvenated, and we were able to talk about other matters, such as the civil war, a topic that obsessed him. He referred to President Balmaceda as a tyrant for punishing decent people.

"Whippings and the stocks should be reserved for *rotos* and *siúti-cos*," he declared.

I had never heard that term before, and he explained that *siúticos* were the middle-class upstarts who aspired to elevate their social status, as if that were possible. The oligarchy could not simply be accessed through money or merit, it was one's birthright, according to him.

"And as if that were not enough, hija, some of his henchmen who dole out whippings are resentful *rotos* themselves, out for vengeance. A cousin of mine was almost murdered by a despicable man who, with every lash, sought to exact revenge for what my cousin had done to his father. Apparently, before joining the army, the crude man had grown up as a tenant on my cousin's land and had watched as his father was whipped on more than one occasion."

"An eye for an eye, as the saying goes. There's a certain justice in that reciprocity, don't you think?" I asked him.

"Justice? No! It is simply hatred borne by the ignorant, filthy masses, envious of those who have more than them because we have worked to obtain it."

"Or perhaps you have more because you inherited it, or were born into a privileged position. I don't believe that people of your class do much work. Nor do I think everybody has the same opportunities," I told him.

"You are quite mistaken. In this country, any man who is willing to work will get ahead," my father insisted.

"Can you give me an example?" I asked.

"You sound like some kind of anarchist!" he declared.

Though he scorned the lower class for their supposed unwillingness to work, he was scandalized by the fact that I worked, since no decent woman would ever do such a thing, much less a member of the del Valle clan. He was ashamed that he could not support me the way a proper young lady deserved, and he said that he would speak to his aunt Paulina about giving me an allowance that would permit me to live well. He insisted that it was unacceptable for me to risk my reputation and my life out walking the streets and writing about war, and did not understand how I could have gotten such a notion into my head, taking a man's job when I should be safe at home with his aunt, never setting foot outside.

I assured him that I did not need anyone's charity and that I knew how to take care of myself, having done so for years. To change the subject and shock him a bit more, I told him about the divine odalisque, the belly dancer I had interviewed in New York, who had taught me the advantages of being a bad woman instead of a respectable young lady. He laughed at the story, which surprised me, because I had supposed so much guilt and fear would have dried up any humor he had left.

He asked many questions about my mother; he believed he had ruined her life when he ripped her away from God. I explained that he was mistaken, that Molly Walsh was happy, had married a marvelous man, my Papo, that they loved each other very much, they were the heart and soul of our community, and that she went to mass and practiced charity. He asked me for more details, her fate being of great interest to him. I described my mother's best qualities, exaggerating them a bit, to be certain, and I omitted her defects. Why would I tell him that in her bursts of hysteria my mother begged the heavens to purge her only daughter—me—of the debauchery and lust she had inherited from her father? Instead, I assured him that Molly Walsh valued and respected him, that she recalled with nostalgia the immense love she had felt for him, that she had forgotten the heartbreak of losing him and was grateful for the daughter he had given her. I also added that she was thankful to him for having saved her from the convent, because she was not cut out to be a nun.

"She taught me to pray. When I was a little girl, every night we would ask God to protect you, wherever you may be, and to grant you peace and happiness," I lied.

"Your words are like a soothing balm for my soul, Emilia. You are the angel of my salvation," he said, choking up.

We said goodbye with an embrace, and I assured him that I would return to visit as soon as my work as a correspondent permitted.

That night I burned my mother's letter. Some promises should not be kept.

OVER THE WEEKS that followed I visited my father several times, at first out of pity for his hopeless terror of death and divine justice. Soon, however, I grew to enjoy his company; like any good rake, he had stupendous stories to tell. His class snobbery was appalling, but I could set that aside for a chance to know him. I owed Gonzalo Andrés del Valle much of my physical aspect, and probably also much of my character. I assumed that my desire to see the world and experience everything intensely was his legacy. That's how he had conducted his life. I thought that if I was as adventurous as him, I had to be careful not to make his mistakes and not to waste my life in frivolous pursuits.

I admitted to myself that I seemed more like this man whom I had only recently met than like my mother. Chilean blood weighed more in me than Irish blood. Maybe that explained my feeling that I had roots in Chile. I often found myself studying him discreetly, trying to imagine what he had been like as a young man, or searching for some similarity between us.

He coughed frequently, spitting up blood, and breathed with a death rattle that sometimes made it seem like he was on the verge of losing his soul, but then Rufina would come in with an infusion of ginger and honey or a camphor poultice to warm his chest. The good woman would ask me to pray with her until the sick man's symptoms eased. That always soothed him.

Gonzalo Andrés, like almost all the members of the ancient del Valle clan, had been born into fortune and social status. His father had died at age forty-nine in a mysterious hunting accident that, like so many things in that family, was hushed up. This only fed the rumor mill—there was suspicion that the death had in fact been a suicide over debts or revenge exacted by a wronged husband. The man had been a renowned womanizer, a trait that his son inherited, evident from the time the boy entered adolescence.

My father was the eldest of five, two boys and three girls, but his only brother had suffered from a congenital defect and died in infancy. At age twenty-two, Gonzalo Andrés found himself managing the plentiful assets that his father had left behind and supporting his widowed mother and sisters. Unfortunately, he did not have the head for such responsibilities. Money had been treated as a distasteful topic that was never discussed in his home, and due to that, and the fact that it had never seemed to be lacking, he grew up with the notion that it came in endless supply and reproduced spontaneously in the bank. As soon as he got his hands on the family fortune, he immediately set about squandering it. He left vast landholdings in the hands of unscrupulous overseers, surrounded himself with unsavory characters, lost important sums in horse races and card games, and sold his father's now-ruined lands for a song.

Although he did not confess as much to me, I suspected that there had also been some clever women who had taken advantage of him. When I mentioned the divine Omene, for example, it turned out that he had met her in New York. How well did he know her? If it was in the biblical sense, it must have cost him a pretty penny. His travels had kept him away from Chile, where his mother and sisters lived on scarce resources in the family mansion, now deteriorating due to lack of maintenance. As termites, leaks, and time ate away at his family home, he toured Europe with luggage fit for a duke, venturing to Egypt to see the pyramids, spending entire seasons in Paris, and making sporadic visits to his godmother, Paulina, in California.

The aunt and nephew got along famously because, as she maintained, they were a pair of rogues. It was on one of these trips to California that he had discovered Molly Walsh. By that time, he had already squandered his fortune; he was a pauper, but he continued to live as if he were a prince. He paid little mind as the debts began to pile up, believing that everything would work itself out given time. But the creditors soon seized his assets, and his mother and sisters were saved only by the charity of Paulina del Valle and the rest of the clan, which in times like these closed ranks around the fallen to prevent any further dishonor.

"Did you think of me often when you were a little girl?" he once asked me.

"Oh, yes," I lied. I knew that the true answer would be hurtful.

"How did you picture me?"

"Like Joaquín Murieta," I said.

"Who is that?"

"A bandit. His head was cut off in 1853 and is still on display floating in a jar of tequila in San Francisco," I explained.

"My God, girl! You certainly have a morbid imagination," he replied, shocked.

As he told me about his life, I continued to spin the tale of a nicer version of Molly Walsh, sprinkling in details of her true story. I told him, for example, of her ritual of baking bread every morning, her strong hands kneading the flour, water, and yeast, the dough resting on the rough wooden counter covered in white cloths that had been washed a thousand times, the miracle of the loaves rising in sighs as she toiled before the mud oven amidst the delicious aroma of fresh-baked bread. I described her dutifully sewing in the last rays of evening light or praying beside the bed of a sick pauper. Saint Molly. On a few occasions, my father and I were even able to laugh about his forbidden romance with the bride of Christ.

8

AS I CONTINUED IN MY EFFORTS TO COVER THE WAR, RO-dolfo León, the journalist who had become my friend and guide, traveled with me to Valparaíso, where the bulk of the army was quartered and thus much of the press was as well. Rodolfo knew many of the local reporters and all of the foreign correspondents covering the conflict in Chile, and he also had access to government leaders. He continued to have faith in the president's patriotic plan and political vision.

Rodolfo found it ironic that the navy had revolted to join the rebels, because Balmaceda, aware that Chile's power lay on the sea, had granted it vast resources. In the pages of his newspaper, Rodolfo lent his unshakeable support to Balmaceda, but in private, he was ashamed by the government repression, especially the retaliations against the working class. Rodolfo believed that workers had the right to unify and protest the deplorable conditions they were forced to endure, and that it was the government's duty to consider their demands instead of sending troops in to silence them.

My new friend was one of those intransigent men of true honor, rare in this world, who often end up crushed by a cruelty unimaginable to them. He was young, just over thirty, thin, with boyish good looks. I think that he was not completely indifferent to me, but if any momentary romantic illusions ever crossed my mind, I immediately discarded them because he was a married man and father of a child.

Rodolfo agreed to arrange a meeting with General Barbosa, the leader of the government's armed forces—the emaciated man whom I'd seen briefly at the presidential palace. He received me in the foyer of the best hotel in Valparaíso; the place had become something of a makeshift operations center, where the general was temporarily quartered along with General Alcérreca and other top army officials, while the bulk of the troops were stationed on the outskirts of town. Barbosa granted me exactly three minutes of his time, out of respect for Rodolfo and because I was the only woman in the group of journalists and photographers who were also staying at the hotel. President Balmaceda had given Barbosa express orders to treat the press with consideration, since public opinion of the government, both locally and abroad, depended on us, but the general had much more important matters to attend to than serving as nanny to a bunch of reporters.

Up close, I confirmed the first impression I'd had of Barbosa: The general was in terrible health, so worn down that the outline of his teeth was visible beneath his skin. He was practically a bearded skeleton. Rodolfo told me that the general could barely keep himself upright on horseback, but in battle he always charged with the vanguard to set an example of courage. In the three minutes that the interview lasted, I managed to obtain a letter of safe conduct that would allow me to travel through all national territory, speak to the soldiers, and access the telegraph system.

Barbosa also wanted to assign a young officer to serve as my bodyguard, but I assured him that I would not have any trouble. Rodolfo then intervened and offered to escort me, since he knew the top brass and had been to the military encampments several times in his capacity as journalist.

It was said that the insurgents in the north would arrive by sea, and Rodolfo was concerned that Balmaceda's generals had not yet come to an agreement over an effective strategy. He also believed that they underestimated the enemy and that this oversight might cost them very dearly. The rebels were better trained and organized than the army imagined.

"When do you think they might arrive?" I asked.

"It could be as soon as August, but I am not sure how much we can trust the spies. The reports are often contradictory," he replied.

As promised, Rodolfo escorted me to one of the nearby military encampments, explaining that they were all similar. Thousands of men. Lines of identical tents separated by narrow alleyways, larger tents for the command, hospital, kitchens, and other services. The latrines were holes in the ground with a board atop them to squat on. Corralled at one end of the camp were the exhausted horses, oxen, and mules that transported everything from cannons to provisions. Stabled separately were the officers' steeds, handpicked specimens of purebred Chilean horses, a harmonious combination of local equine and Arabian stud, small, strong, and intrepid. Most of those noble animals would die. There was also no shortage of stray dogs wandering in packs sniffing for scraps among the refuse. Those always survived.

We were high in the hills, in the middle of winter, with rain and icy wind coming off the sea, the ground turned to mud. The officers kept the men busy with a strict, disciplined regimen; free time was considered dangerous since an idle mind could nourish doubts and eat away at courage. The soldiers marched in circles, trained, cleaned their weapons, dug trenches, bailed buckets of mud, carried water, looked after the animals. The day began at dawn and ended at nightfall.

AUGUST 1891
THE CANTEEN GIRLS
By Emilia del Valle

Chile is again at war—another of several in this century alone—but this time it sees Chileans pitted against Chileans. In the north, the navy, in revolt, prepares to attack the army, loyal to the government of President Balmaceda. Everyone waits. The tension in the air is palpable. The days pass and uncertainty mounts.

A portion of the army is camped near the port of Valparaíso with the rest spread out across other provinces. I visit the sector of the camp reserved for the women, called canteen girls, who during battle carry water to the combatants. Angelita Ayalef is the most seasoned among them, something that gives her a certain authority over the other women. She gives orders and they obey. She is not sure how old she is; somewhere around forty would be my guess, but it could be that so much hard work has aged her beyond her years. Short in stature, wide-hipped, with two braids down her back and a long scar across her cheek, brusque manners. She does credit to her name: Her job is to be an angel. Like all Chilean soldiers, she carries a corvo, a curved, double-edged blade, both mortal weapon and multipurpose tool. She also wears a small canvas bag tied at her waist. I ask her what it contains, but she simply shrugs her shoulders in response. I later find out that it holds instruments used to perform surgery—a medic gifted it to her after teaching her to extract bullets, cauterize wounds, and sew stitches.

Angelita introduces me to the others, who greet me warmly and dub me *gringa*, a term reserved for English-speaking foreigners. These strong, austere, brave women approach me with curiosity; I am a *gringa* who speaks Spanish with an accent they find comical. My clothes are impractical for this environment, and they offer to lend me the uniform of a woman who recently gave birth and had to leave the camp with her newborn. The red-and-blue attire consists of trousers beneath a short skirt, a jacket, a white blouse, a hat, and a scarf tied at the neck. A small wooden barrel of water is meant to be carried over the shoulder. The women live in a permanent state of activity; there is much work to be done, but they move unhurriedly, singing as they cook, smoking while they sew, joking, arguing and making amends.

The army once attempted to eliminate the canteen girls, but quickly found their work to be indispensable: They cook, wash, sew, convey messages and food, and, when necessary, serve as nurses. They also aid the men in battle, treating the wounded, holding the dying, and sometimes even taking up the weapons of fallen soldiers to fight in their stead, exposed to gunfire and the terror of defeat. Military regulations state that the canteen girls have the right to use the regimental uniform and receive the same pay as a soldier. They are supposed to be unmarried women of proven virtue, but in practice, they are wives, mothers, girlfriends, and sisters who march in the rear guard to support their men, and no one would dare to question their virtue.

In previous wars, some of these women who fought shoulder to shoulder with the men were captured, raped, tortured, and mutilated before being executed. I ask myself if, in this civil war, any of them may suffer the same fate.

I shadow Angelita Ayalef as she milks the goats, trailed closely by the regiment's unofficial mascot, a caramel-colored mutt. The cuisine in camp is basic: beans, soup with strips of beef or pork, potatoes and pork rinds, hardtack, raw onion, horsemeat jerky, and, sometimes, sweetened chicory coffee. The women keep goats and chickens for additional food. Later on, as I help peel mountains of potatoes, I am asked to butcher a string of rabbits that someone brought in. I have never skinned or eviscerated an animal before, but I try to hide my repugnance and follow Angelita's instructions. Today there is no washing being done as it rains at regular intervals, but they expect that tomorrow will bring clear skies. We sit in a circle around a brazier, the mate passing from hand to hand, savoring the aromatic green tea as we mend uniforms, darn socks, reattach buttons, and converse. I ask them to tell me about their lives, they laugh, saying they hold no mysteries, that every life is a story and all stories are alike.

Dusk settles in, the temperature drops, my clothes are damp with mud up to my knees, and the skin of my hands is red and cracking. I am exhausted and freezing but content, my head and my heart full. A sergeant comes to escort me from the camp with a horse for me to ride. I bid the canteen girls a fond farewell, kissing them each on the cheek one by one.

"Come back to see us, *gringa,* before all the commotion begins," Angelita tells me.

In the time I had been in Chile, I had sent the *Examiner* an average of two or three columns per week. Not all of them were human interest pieces, as my editor had ordered, because politics and the war were inescapable. For his part, Eric Whelan had bombarded the newspaper with fairly biased reports based on the rebels' version of events. He had described Balmaceda in very unflattering terms, without ever having met him. Eric's reports were published not only in San Francisco but in newspapers across several other cities, and they were also sent abroad by cable. In the United States, the result was that readers had lost all sympathy for Balmaceda's cause, even if the White House still supported him.

I, on the other hand, moved in circles loyal to the president, except for the del Valle family, who detested him, and I was able to write from the government's perspective. Unlike my colleague, who let himself be seduced by the northern insurgents' rhetoric and hospitality, I was determined to remain objective, aware of the mistakes and abuses that had been committed on both sides. I was annoyed by my editor, who censored several of my chronicles, whereas everything Eric sent in was published without question.

In my effort to remain impartial, I wrote about the mood on the street and the opinions of the troops at the front line, which were not as favorable to the president as he believed. My friend Rodolfo León grudgingly admitted that popular support was waning, but he still insisted that the army would nonetheless squash the rebellion. He anxiously awaited the arrival of the navy fleet, eager for the conflict to be over with once and for all, he said.

IT WAS NOT just Rodolfo, everyone waited, anticipating the navy's arrival with uncertainty. Time seemed to stretch out and contract inside the clocks, hours felt like days, and then all of a sudden an entire morning could be gone in a sigh.

My intention had been to stay with Barbosa's troops under Angelita Ayalef's wing with the other canteen girls, but one evening, I received a message from Fredrick Williams calling me back to Santiago. This took me by surprise, as I had not had any contact with Paulina del Valle's husband since our brief initial encounter. The Englishman's message indicated that he wished to speak to me about a matter concerning Gonzalo Andrés del Valle, requesting I meet him at the same tearoom where I had often sat with Rodolfo León.

I took the morning train to Santiago and arrived just in time for tea.

More than likely, Fredrick Williams had no aristocratic blood to speak of, but he imitated it to perfection. He sat waiting for me at one of the tearoom's little round tables, dressed casually in a derby hat and tweed coat as if he had just come from a sports club, in stark contrast to the dark frock coats, vests, and top hats preferred by the wealthier Chileans. He was elegant without affectation, his posture was straight without being rigid, and, it must be said, he was fairly attractive for a man his age. His stained teeth and fingers belied his affection for tobacco, but he did not smoke in front of me.

"Forgive me for being so bold, Miss Emilia, but I do not think you should return to Valparaíso. The political situation is quite dire. What were you doing there?" he asked me.

"I came to Chile to report on the war, Mr. Williams," I explained.

"It's a shame; you are sure to come away with a bad impression of this country. The current conflict is an aberration. In normal times, life is quite pleasant, people are agreeable. It is an orderly society, with everyone in their place, as it should be."

"Are you referring to the class stratification? A democratic republic should allow for upward mobility," I said, repeating something my Papo often said.

"The popular vote is a conceptual error. Chile would be much better off with a monarchy."

I supposed that the Englishman's impeccable manners kept him from getting straight to the point, as anyone in the United States would have done, so I waited patiently as the waiter served the tea, describing each and every pastry on the tray in detail. Fredrick Williams took his time to choose, and as he did so, he explained the vulgar impracticality of democracy, which did not account for humanity's chaotic nature, something that demanded hierarchy and authority. I realized that he was not joking, so there was no point in trying to convince him of the advantages of democracy. I hardly knew him, but I really liked him.

Finally, after twenty-five minutes had been lost to that topic and others, Mr. Williams confessed that he had contacted me without consulting his wife, who was opposed on principle to anything that could place her family's good name in jeopardy. He was of the opinion, however, that since this was a delicate matter that affected me directly, he should take the liberty.

"As I mentioned, Miss Emilia, it is about Gonzalo Andrés del Valle," he said.

"I am his *huacha*," I responded.

"That is a vulgar term, young lady. Do not use it. But that is precisely what I wanted to talk to you about. Apparently, don Gonzalo

Andrés is on his deathbed, and he wishes to deal with a few earthly matters before he leaves this world. At least this is what Father Restrepo, his confessor, has told us."

"I am so sorry to hear it, Mr. Williams! I visited him less than two weeks ago and his health seemed stable. What has happened?" I asked, concerned.

"Pneumonia. He knows that it is usually fatal. He wishes to legally recognize you as his daughter, Emilia. It is the man's dying wish," he informed me.

"Oh! I'm afraid that cannot be, Mr. Williams. Francisco Claro is my father," I explained.

"How's that?"

"My Papo, my stepfather, that is. He raised me; he is my true father," I told him.

"Will you not please consider our unfortunate Gonzalo Andrés's request, so that he may die in peace? It would change nothing for you, since you do not even live in this country. Also, as you must surely suspect, it is not a matter of money, but of honor. Your father does not possess any material goods to bequeath you. All he can do is lift the stigma of being a bastard."

"That stigma does not concern me in the slightest. And I find it curious that you should tell me all of this behind doña Paulina del Valle's back," I said.

"Paulina's nephew has asked her to serve as witness to his testimony before the law, but she has refused. She calls it a crackpot scheme planted in the ailing man's head by Father Restrepo. I know my wife well, however, and I know she will change her mind. If you will only give your consent, I will arrange the details," he suggested.

TWO DAYS LATER, Paulina del Valle, Fredrick Williams, and I arrived at the Argentine consulate. Paulina was dressed entirely in black, with a fur cape that gave her the appearance of an enormous furry animal, a showy hat with a thick veil, and the fluffy dog in her arms. Fredrick was also dressed quite formally. Paulina did not return my greeting and I had no way of knowing whether she had even glanced in my direction, hidden as she was under the veil, but her posture made it clear that she was displeased. Williams must exert some mysterious power over that imposing woman to have been able to drag her there against her will.

The Argentine ambassador welcomed us somberly, as was fitting for the occasion, and he summoned Rufina to show us to the ailing man's room. Waiting there was a notary with the document at the ready and the sinister Father Restrepo murmuring prayers in Latin near the bed. The gloom, the stench, and the staleness were the same as always, but something had shifted; I could clearly detect the foul wind of death in the air. One glance was enough to understand that Williams had not been exaggerating; my father was truly dying. He sat propped up on a pile of pillows, eyes closed, bluish hands clutching the sheets.

The loyal Rufina dabbed his brow with a damp cloth and asked him to open his eyes because his daughter had come to see him. There was no response.

"My nephew is in no condition to sign anything," Paulina said to the notary, a little man who seemed terrified of her.

"Don Gonzalo Andrés has delegated the signing of the document to you, Señora del Valle," Father Restrepo interrupted.

"I do not plan on signing anything. I was asked to come as a witness, nothing more. And let the record state that I am opposed to this last-minute hoodwink. I do not understand why you waste your time here, Father, my nephew has nothing to leave the church," she spat.

"You insult me, madam. I am not here out of greed, but to save the soul of this man, a servant of God," the priest replied.

"I have made myself clear: I do not plan to sign any document drafted by some pettifogger," she repeated.

"In recent days, don Gonzalo Andrés has taken a turn for the worse. He named you, madam, to act in his stead while he was still in full use of his faculties," the priest insisted firmly.

"Is there anyone else who has heard this and confirms it?" Paulina asked in an insolent tone.

"Our Almighty God, who art in heaven and is present in all places," the priest replied in the same manner.

"How convenient! Otherwise, only you heard him, correct?" she responded.

"Pardon me, señora, but I also heard Mr. Gonzalo say this," said Rufina timidly.

"There you have it, doña Paulina. It falls to you to clear your godson's good name and save his soul. As a Catholic, you cannot refuse," the priest concluded with all the weight of his investiture.

Paulina del Valle lifted the veil from her face, and from her expression, I feared she would spit at the priest. But her husband placed an arm around her shoulders, pulled her toward him, and whispered who-knows-what into her ear.

She tilted her head toward him, making the extravagant bows and feathers of her hat tremble. "So be it, then," she spat.

"By means of the present document, don Gonzalo Andrés del Valle certifies, in full use of his faculties and of his own free will, that Miss Emilia del Valle, daughter of Molly Walsh, is his biological daughter. He recognizes her as such before God and the Law, with all the rights and privileges that shall correspond to her therein," the notary read, standing a prudent distance from Paulina.

"Let the record state that this is a vile ruse," she muttered, throwing the priest a furious glance.

Fredrick Williams dipped a quill into a pot of ink, placed it in his wife's hand, and watched as she signed two copies of the document.

Suddenly, the powerful matriarch released a choked sob, followed by another and another, as tears ran down her face. She dropped the dog, which landed with a whimper, and leaned over the bed to kiss the dying man's face and hands.

"Go in peace, my boy, your sins were all nonsense. You were not the first man to squander an inheritance or leave his mother and sisters in indigence. You were nothing but a brainless boy at the time; it was not your fault, it was your friends, those scoundrels. But nothing is all bad, you saw that I took care of them, they have never wanted for anything. And now your sisters, whom God favors, ugly as they are, have wealthy husbands and packs of children, whereas you have not so much as a dog to bark at you, poor dear. You have paid for your mistakes in life and shall have good credit now in heaven. I have always loved you, despite your many misdeeds, or maybe because of them. You were my most entertaining relation before you fell to the vice of confession and lost all your joy. Do not listen to Father Restrepo, he is not in the business of sending Satan new clients; these priests simply fill people's heads with fears to get money out of them, and I am saying that as someone who sorely regrets all the money I have given to the church. Believe me, my boy, when I say that hell does not exist, it is a lie peddled by the Vatican. All that exists is heaven, where you will soar like a condor, up there where we will all be reunited, the good like you and the bad like me, together again.

"While I do not approve of this Emilia person," Paulina went on, "a stranger who was rained down upon us, if you say that she is your daughter, I have no choice but to accept her into the family. I must warn you, however, that I do so only grudgingly because I do not know anything about her and she has no references here. She could be a gadabout who has come from California to take advantage of us, or worse." And on and on her monologue continued in this way for a good while.

At one point the sick man opened his eyes and looked at me, but I do not think he knew who I was. After that, the notary handed a copy of the document over to me and gave another to Fredrick Williams. Then everyone else exited the room, and I was left alone to accompany my father on his final journey.

Rufina brought me a bowl of soup and sat beside me with a rosary in her hands to pray in silence. Every once in a while, the sick man would stop breathing for a few eternal seconds, but just when we thought he was gone he would suck in a desperate breath of air. This went on for hours, I do not know how many, but I fell asleep in the chair and dreamed of my mother, a dream so clear that it was like a visitation. She was calm and smiling, with nothing of her usual bitterness, in the black dress she reserved for mass and her good shoes, hair styled fashionably and wearing the garnet earrings my Papo had gifted her years before, her only jewels. I like to think Molly Walsh came all that way to say goodbye to her first love.

At dawn, Rufina shook me awake to let me know that it was time for the final goodbye. I found it difficult to stand, my bones made of lead. We approached the bed, and I was able to hold my father as he took his final gasping breath and then fell still. I held him in my arms for a few long minutes, giving his soul time to say goodbye to the world and take its leave. I felt an infinite sadness for this poor man who had wasted so much time plagued by fear, with no enduring love or children to fill his life, only me, whom he had met just a few weeks prior. I want to believe that he left contented, finally free from that worm of regret.

AFTER MY FATHER'S death, I returned to the canteen girls at the army camp in Valparaíso. I had kept in touch with Angelita Ayalef through brief missives. Hers were often difficult to decipher, because she had learned only the rudiments of writing among the soldiers, and Mapuzugun, the language of the Mapuche, was her mother tongue. But in spite of the obstacles to communication, we managed to establish a tentative friendship, which, as I later learned, was not common between whites and indigenous people. In Chile, where the majority of the population have mestizo heritage, there is just as much racism as in the United States.

My admiration for Angelita only grew as I got to know her. She tried to dissuade me from returning to the military encampment, because she predicted that they would soon be called to fight. She knew I was not prepared. But once she accepted that I would not desist, she welcomed me back with the same warm hospitality.

Eric Whelan had alerted me by telegram that the Congressionalist fleet was sailing southward. He estimated that they would make landfall some few kilometers from Valparaíso, although he did not know where, precisely. This was no secret, since Balmaceda's spies had already communicated the same information and General Barbosa was busily preparing to meet the enemy. Eric was emphatic that I should take refuge in Santiago, at the United States consulate if possible, until the conflict was resolved. He said that, during skirmishes in the north, he had watched as entire army detachments had defected to the side of the rebels, led by their officers, and he was certain that this would happen again. His words confirmed something I had perceived, something no one wanted to talk about: President Balmaceda had not earned the loyalty of his troops. The soldiers fought not out of political conviction or patriotism, they were simply following the orders that misfortune had dealt them.

Ignoring Eric's instructions, I decided I could not miss the battle about to be waged for control of Chile. Locking myself up in a consulate in Santiago would prove my editor correct for having doubted my abilities as a reporter simply because I am a woman. *Remember, princess, that you will have to work twice as hard as any man for half the recognition* was one of the lessons my Papo had taught me. Also, I imagined that there would be many human interest stories to come out of the battlefield, which is what Chamberlain wanted.

All around me, no one dared to openly doubt the army's triumph; the official version was that the upcoming conflict would put an end to the war once and for all. That is what was voiced aloud anyway. In whispers, the opposite was feared. I told Rodolfo of the rumor that some of Balmaceda's officers secretly sympathized with the enemy and only remained in the army so as to bring it down from the inside.

"I imagine Balmaceda's generals would have heard that talk as well," I told him.

"That is all part of the campaign of demoralization orchestrated by the rebels. I would advise you not to spread that idle gossip, Emilia. You could be arrested," he warned me.

"As a correspondent, I have to investigate all angles."

"The Chilean Army is an invincible monolith, loyal to the government in defense of the constitution," he said with the fieriness of a preacher, as if he were trying to convince himself. He was emphatic that such betrayal would not occur.

"Until it does occur," I responded, thinking of the troops who had already deserted to join the rebels.

Although he may have harbored some private doubts, Rodolfo had to project full confidence of victory in the newspaper. He published an editorial on the intentions of a victorious Balmaceda to call for a national reconciliation and extend an amnesty agreement that would permit the rebels to maintain their dignity. "Forgive, unify, pacify, and rebuild Chile"—these were his words.

PART THREE

9

I WALKED FOR AN ENTIRE DAY IN THE REAR OF GENERAL Barbosa's troops wearing the uniform that Angelita had obtained for me so that I would be less conspicuous. The pants and skirt were too short, but they afforded me more freedom of movement than my city attire, with all that gathered fabric cinched at the waist.

We were accompanied by Covadonga, the regiment's yellow mutt, who owed her name to a schooner that had participated heroically in a naval battle against Peru and Bolivia. Escaping an armored battleship, the *Covadonga* darted into a zone of submerged rocks where the enemy vessel was run aground. The dog was small, brave, and clever, just like that schooner.

I can't calculate how far we walked, but by dusk we had reached Concón. It was a small fishing village north of Valparaíso at the mouth of a fast-flowing river that reached the sea swollen with the waters of the numerous tributaries that joined its course down the mountainside. It was common knowledge that the battle would be waged in the coming days, because the rebels had made landfall in the area, just as Eric had said they would. General Barbosa, in his attempt to rally the troops, declared that it would be a cruel battle, but a swift one.

Rodolfo León had told me that the president sat before the telegraph in Santiago awaiting confirmation of victory. His confidence in General Barbosa and General Alcérreca was so absolute that he decided not to call in the rest of the troops stationed in the south—he believed the enemy would be dispatched with a fraction of the contingent. Rodolfo commented that Balmaceda's habitual calm had given way to a strange self-absorption, an almost hypnotic state in which he did not express any emotion. In recent weeks, his mind seemed to wander and his heart was closed. In these decisive days he would remain isolated among the few people he trusted, refusing to hear any bad news. He had said that he preferred not to know the extreme decisions his commanders might take, as if he wished to wash his hands of so much bloodshed. That legendary calm, which he had cultivated from the start of his career, belied an almost romantic sensibility that contrasted with his political ambitions. He dreaded the upcoming conflict between his army and the mutinous navy, which would inevitably leave victims by the hundreds, if not thousands. He was a man of profound moral rectitude, unable to free himself of the painful responsibility he felt to each one of those victims. He must have asked himself, in the silence of his somber palace, in the immense isolation of power, if all that sacrifice was worth it.

THE CANTEEN GIRLS, with Angelita as leader, camped on the riverbank alongside a third of the troops, while the rest were divided into two groups to defend our positions in the surrounding foothills. More than an actual encampment, the soldiers were simply lined up in rows, fully exposed to the elements. We kept to the improvised field hospital a certain distance away with the sanitary staff and two medics. The men were hungry and rations were delayed, not due to lack of resources, but because of general disorganization and poor road conditions. It had recently rained and the carts and mules became repeatedly stuck in the mud. The soldiers were given orders to set down their rucksacks, in which they carried a blanket and provisions, and form into combat lines. Angelita explained that the veterans of the war with Peru were accustomed to going hungry, because on several occasions the military leaders had mismanaged the campaign, not bothering to study the desert conditions ahead of time. Many soldiers in that war had died of dysentery because of spoiled food; others perished due to dehydration. But complaining about rations was a punishable offense.

"Do you know what these men fear most? That their bones will be bleached by the sun without a proper grave, and without anyone to remember their names," Angelita concluded.

THAT NIGHT IN Concón, the hunger, damp, and cold were exacerbated by a silent sense of terror, evident on the faces of many soldiers. Some were very young, practically boys; some, recruited by force in the rural areas of the south, had never held a gun before. I knew that they were going to have to face a brave, determined enemy. During my stay in the north, I had seen the strong miners, tempered like steel by hard work and a harsh climate. Many of them had fought previously in the Peruvian war and had joined the rebel forces voluntarily. The government repression they had endured during the strikes made Balmaceda their enemy. I supposed that given the choice between endlessly breaking rocks and shoveling white gold or fighting and killing, they preferred the latter. There were no reports of any of these men having deserted.

For the young recruits and the veteran soldiers alike, the long wait before the battle was excruciating. They gripped their weapons, teeth chattering, eyes red with fatigue, knees weak as wool, hearts pounding in their chests. Throughout that prolonged pause, a sneaking suspicion settled in that they were going to die for nothing, that neither country nor God mattered, that they had been ordered to kill compatriots and die for an uncertain cause, and that if they tried to flee they would be shot dead. What went through their minds during those endless hours? I imagine they recalled their humble homes so far away, their mothers leaning over the fire, the kiss of a girl, a friendly dog, a ball game. And I imagine they were tortured by the inevitable fear that they would never again set eyes on any of those things; all they would see was the black eye of a rifle or the gleam of a bloodied bayonet.

According to what I had been told, there were nearly eight thousand men distributed among the army's three brigades: one on the beach, the other two in the foothills. I do not have any military knowledge to speak of, but it seemed to me that the troops were ill-prepared, many wearing sandals or rags tied around their feet because they lacked proper boots or had never worn shoes. Their weapons were antiquated rifles that fired only a few shots, and after that the bayonet tips could be used as spears; the cannons looked like pachyderms that had seen better days in previous wars. The officers paced the ranks on horseback trying to keep morale up, but they seemed disheartened themselves.

The soldiers received meager wages and any man who had a family saw a portion sent home to his wife and children. What was left over was just enough to buy alcohol, tobacco, and prostitutes. Punishments were severe, life was harsh, and death was never far away. They knew that, if wounded, medical attention would be minimal and likely come too late; many saw the hospital as merely a place to die. The troops contracted venereal diseases, typhus, dysentery, tuberculosis, smallpox. They were also at risk of infections of all kinds, such as the one caused by a much-feared insect that burrowed under the toenail and bore through the skin. It could be treated only by cutting away the rotten flesh with a knife and plugging the hole with ash and tobacco. All amputees would receive a half pension and a prosthetic limb; widows and legitimate children were allotted a fraction of the man's already insufficient salary.

"This is the way it goes in Chile, *gringa*. Haven't you seen the many men missing arms and legs out begging for alms in the street? Well, those are our war veterans," Angelita told me.

"If conditions are so terrible, why do they enlist?" I asked.

"The army offers meals and wages, even if they often come late or sometimes not at all. Some of the boys are simply captured. The army has been known to raid rural villages, hunting men down with dogs. They even recruit criminals and delinquents if necessary. It is better to die fighting than to dry up in prison, don't you agree?" she answered.

"I suppose there are some volunteers as well, Angelita."

"Yes, there are those brainless boys who have caught the patriotic fever. Well, that's what motivated them against Bolivia and Peru anyway, but, in this civil war, we are all fighting for the same nation. They don't know why they're here and I don't either, *gringa;* no matter who wins, nothing is going to change for us, the poor," she said, echoing what I had heard voiced in the mines up north.

THE NIGHT SEEMED endless, with the rebels on one side of the river and the government troops on the other. Was Eric Whelan over there, as worried as I was on this side? Or had he joined the foreign correspondents observing everything from high in the hills? Darkness, the whistle of the wind, the incessant clamor of the sea, the collective sigh of thousands of men huddled together, horses whinnying, voices whispering, coughs. The fog and clouds obscured the moon; there was no light save for a few lanterns, braziers, and small bonfires. News and rumors reached us in hushed tones, it was whispered that the sentries were reporting regularly on the enemy's movements, but the officers were vacillating. When would they give the order to cross the river? Why didn't they attack? Angelita informed me that we couldn't move before dawn, visibility was too poor, no battle could be waged at night. We learned that Barbosa had decided to wait for the other side to make the first move; the longer it took for combat to commence, the more time the other regiments would have to arrive from Santiago and the south and fill in the ranks. Balmaceda had finally decided to confront the enemy with all his regiments.

The women spent those long hours circulating among the soldiers with our canteens and rucksacks, accompanied by Covadonga, who fulfilled her duty of lifting spirits. The men called her over to pet her and she licked their hands in response. There were two chaplains who also spent the night among the ranks hearing confessions and handing out scapulars of the Virgen del Carmen. According to Angelita, very few of those men were religious and almost none of them went to mass, but when death loomed, they all clung to that little cloth image of the patron saint of Chile, believing it would protect them against bullets like a shield.

"The enemies have the same scapulars with the same little virgin, though. We'll have to see which of the two sides she favors," Angelita commented.

Before our arrival, I imagined, this spot had been a peaceful shoreline, with its beach, dunes, brush, fishermen's shacks, boats, and seagulls. But the presence of the battalions, animals, and artillery had transformed the terrain into a mud pit laden with obstacles. Before the battle had even begun, that bucolic landscape was in ruin. My boots and pants were soaked through. I had tucked the edge of my skirt into my waist, like the other canteen girls, but my jacket was so tight that I couldn't button it, and I had lost my cap, leaving my hair a tangled mess tousled by the damp wind. How had I reached this state? I had left San Francisco as a respectable journalist, packing an evening gown and a pair of fashionable hats without ever dreaming I would find myself in a filthy borrowed uniform in the middle of a battlefield thousands of miles from my home and family. I could die there, and my body would simply decompose alongside so many others at the bottom of a pit.

Angelita Ayalef gave instructions to the women: First we would pass out chicory coffee with plenty of sugar and rum to warm the boys and bolster their courage. Then, later, after combat began, we would supply them with water. According to military regulation, liquor should be strictly rationed since no amount of discipline could make up for inebriated troops. In practice, however, alcohol was spilled out for everything, from killing lice to cleaning wounds. On the men's free days, aguardiente, rum, and *chicha* circulated freely among them. In previous wars, the Chilean soldiers had committed superhuman acts of courage drugged on *chupilca del diablo,* a mixture of alcohol and gunpowder, but I didn't see Angelita placing any powder in the canteens.

We also distributed small pieces of hard bread to keep hunger at bay, but there was not enough of it to go around. There were only a few of us women to attend thousands of soldiers. We took more time with the younger ones, the most frightened, asking them where they were from, if they had families or a girl waiting for them at home, what they were going to do when they got back, and generally trying to distract them a bit. "Remember my name, miss," some of them said to me. Others handed me letters for their loved ones with the request to mail them if they didn't survive, or asked me in a whisper to pray with them. They didn't want to appear weak in front of their comrades, but machismo was not enough to stave off so much uncertainty—they needed the comfort of religion. There were also veterans seasoned by many years in the army, men accustomed to risk and the exaltation of fighting and killing, silent, impenetrable, hostile, with hardened gazes and indifferent expressions. These men did not require the attentions of the canteen girls.

In the darkness, only the gleam of the eye distinguished soldier from shadow. They stank of sweat and damp clothes. No one slept during those long hours in wait.

·　　·　　·

LITTLE BY LITTLE the night receded and in the first light of dawn I was able to make out the haggard faces of those men gripping their weapons, fearful of what would come, praying to heaven that death would pass them by. Some had dug trenches in the sand, others were halfway protected by makeshift barricades. I felt infected by that mood of desolation, that foreshadowing of defeat.

At seven o'clock in the morning on August 21, 1891, with the sky lightening but still hung with fog, I heard the start of the Congressionalist cannon fire from the opposite bank of the river. It was followed by more blasts from their ships anchored along the shore. Soon the army responded and the cannon fire from both sides was deafening, as flashes and explosions kicked up sand and rocks, shaking the world like some cataclysmic earthquake. Angelita assured me that at that distance the cannons would not cause too many causalities, but the effect on the morale of the youngest soldiers was devastating. Some dropped their weapons and tried to scurry away, but they were halted by their comrades before the officers could catch them. Desertion was a crime punishable by death, a shot to the forehead. Unless, that is, it occurred en masse.

The fog began to dissipate, and the rebels came into view on the opposite bank, ready to advance. We received news that they were already charging the army's second brigade in the hills, attacking on two flanks at once. The white of their uniforms seemed to disappear into the sand, smoke, and fog, whereas the army's bright reds and blues offered a sure target.

The wide river, swollen from winter rains, carried stones and rubble in its current, but the Congressionalist infantry, spurred on by their officers, threw themselves into the rushing water, even though the majority of the men did not know how to swim. The soldiers advanced with difficulty, the water up to their chests and their rifles held high to keep them dry. The current took many men, and others fell to the enemy fire that they were unable to return, but by eleven o'clock that morning the bulk of the Congressionalist troops had crossed the river. The Battle of Concón had begun.

IT IS IMPOSSIBLE to describe the horror of war. Nothing I can write will come close to the reality of it, and I can only describe it from my limited perspective on the ground. Perhaps the officers from the height of their mounts or the press correspondents in the nearby hills were able to discern what was happening, but those of us in the thick of it were moving blindly. The idea that I could have been more or less safe if I had joined the other journalists did cross my mind, but I immediately discarded the notion, because none of them, from that distance, would have been able to experience what I felt there among the soldiers. Every man was his own story and thousands would never get to tell theirs. It was my job to collect the dispersed fragments of those tales.

The commanders had ordered the small group of canteen girls to remain in the ambulance tent, as the field hospital was referred to, until we were called into action. From there, we were unable to help. It was immediately evident that the enemy had an immense advantage: new weapons we had never seen before, rifles that could fire repeatedly from a long range, capable of shooting several bullets in a row. The army, by contrast, had to reload after each shot, their bullets had a much shorter range, and the rifles overheated after a few firings, rendering them useless. No matter how skilled the soldier, the loading of weapons wasted precious seconds that could mean the difference between life and death.

The rebels' repeating rifles wreaked havoc as one in every four soldiers fell to the ground riddled with bullets. Line after line of combat was swept with a hailstorm of projectiles. It was a bloodbath. The ranks soon broke, the enemies jumped the barricades that the soldiers had improvised with rocks from the beach, and hand-to-hand combat commenced. The deafening roar of bullets, cannon blasts, shouted orders, howls of pain, wails of dying men, the whinnying of terrified horses. The smell of smoke filled the air, we coughed, suffocating, and some vomited a thick foam. General Barbosa, like an emaciated phantom, went riding by with his saber held high, trying to rally the men, but his weak voice was lost to the chaos. After that, I did not see him again. I supposed that he followed the remainder of the battle from higher ground.

I was terrified, trembling from fear and cold, hunched down with my head in my hands, trying to make myself invisible. I cursed my decision to stay instead of returning to Santiago as Eric had asked me to, muttering prayers, imagining my body mortally wounded by bullets, sabers, or bayonets, limbs amputated, eyes blinded, paralyzed, disfigured. *No, my God, no, if I cannot survive whole, please send me a mercy shot to the heart.*

Just then, two hands lifted me by the shoulders and shook me roughly. It was Angelita Ayalef, leaning over me, muttering words I could not hear over the roar of gunfire, but I understood her intention. I watched as she marched decisively toward the lines of combat and I, without thinking, followed her. As we advanced, I felt a wave of heat and fury rise up from my guts, a superhuman force came over me, a war cry formed in my throat, and I forgot all my doubts and fears as I became invincible, immortal, protected by some magical armor.

ANGELITA AND I moved around the battlefield, crouched or sometimes dragging ourselves along. Other canteen girls followed us, and I later learned that some of those women fell alongside the soldiers. I slipped in the mud and stumbled into brambles that scratched my face and clothes. I was drenched in sweat, but blazing with emotion, I no longer felt the cold. Soon my canteen was empty and I dedicated myself to lifting the spirits of the fallen, even if the help I could offer was minimal.

The bravery of the orderlies astounded me, one at each end of a stretcher, forced to march upright across a battlefield as bullets and bayonets flew. They took the wounded to a small forest of scrub brush bent by the wind where doctors and nurses, under canvas awnings, administered first aid. For each soldier that might survive, another would die, if not then and there, later, from trauma, blood loss, infection, gangrene. There were not enough bandages for so many wounds, not enough laudanum or morphine for so much pain. The blood was soaked up by the sand.

A very young soldier fell at my feet and I watched as a red rose bloomed from his face: A bullet had entered through his eye but he was still alive. I had the urge to summon the stretcher-bearers, but Angelita, who was near, gestured for me to leave him, that it was too late. She was applying a tourniquet to another soldier's leg as he writhed in pain. I sat down beside the boy and placed his head on my lap as I murmured the lullaby that my Papo always sang to me: *Duérmete mi niño, duérmete mi sol, duérmete pedaço de mi corazón . . .* And when he fell asleep forever, I rested his head on the ground and dragged myself to the next wounded man, my clothes and hands stained with blood, my stomach shuddering and my eyes clouded with tears and smoke. I learned to leave the most gravely wounded—they were not going to survive no matter what I did—and focus on those who could be saved.

On that field of death, we tripped over the bodies of inert horses, their glassy eyes staring, and others, still alive, who could not stand up because their legs were broken or their bellies ripped open by the swipe of a saber. If I'd had a weapon, I would have put them out of their misery, the poor beasts. Some hungry dogs paced nearby, attracted by the smell of viscera, but they did not dare come too close. I did not see Covadonga anywhere. I lost count of the men I saw die, lost count of the men I was able to help, lost count of the hours that passed.

Hand-to-hand combat was much more brutal than gunfire, because the men had to look each other in the eye, locked in embrace as they killed or died. Our boys fell by the dozens, by the hundreds. With some demented sense of valor, brandishing their fixed bayonets and their Chilean corvos, the soldiers launched themselves against the repeating rifles, chests bared. A man in a white uniform spotted me amidst the dusty commotion and had just aimed his weapon when one of our blue-coated boys slit his throat with his knife. I thought I saw Angelita, out of the corner of my eye, wielding her corvo, but it could have been a mirage.

I no longer know what I actually witnessed and how much I only imagined; it is all a jumbled confusion of horror in my memory. I had never seen violence and death up close—nothing in my twenty-five years of existence had prepared me for so much barbarism, so much suffering. As the bullets whistled all around me and men fell broken and disarticulated like marionettes with cut strings, I numbly carried out the duties that Angelita had assigned me. My head echoed with the certainty, like a strident bell, that so much cruelty and death was unjustifiable, absurd, a senseless waste of life, a sinister game played by the men in power. How is it possible that, from the dawn of their presence on earth, men have systematically set out to murder one another? What fatal madness do we carry in our soul? That propensity toward destruction is the original sin.

ANGELITA HAD TOLD me that the most difficult part of a battle came after, when the survivors would walk the battlefield to collect the wounded, close the eyes of the dead, and pray over the pit of bodies piled atop the others, all equal in the same woeful world filled with black birds of ill omen and the stench of rot and the smoke of the bonfires built to burn the carcasses of the dead horses and mules. This time, we would not have to face any of that. Angelita had been present for several battles, all victorious, but in Concón the army was forced to retreat. The bodies strewn across the battlefield would be left in the hands of the enemy.

How long did that battle last? I cannot know for sure. It felt like an entire day, or a week, or forever, but, as I was later told, it was just over four hours before Balmaceda's troops disbanded. I watched as some soldiers turned their jackets inside out to mimic the white enemy uniform and donned red armbands ripped away from the fallen Congressionalist soldiers. I did not hear the trumpet call to retreat, nor do I believe that anyone gave the order. Those who had not passed over to the enemy side simply dropped their useless weapons and ran off in all directions, every man for himself—first the cavalry, followed by the foot soldiers, the officers, the infantry, and us, the canteen girls.

Angelita Ayalef was among the first to understand that we had been defeated, and she immediately sought me out amidst the chaos. She took me by the hand and dragged me along behind her; if we were captured we would be shown no mercy, she said. We ran and ran and ran, uphill, panting, spurred on by a desperate fear, covered in mud and blood. We ripped off the skirts of our uniforms, sticky with blood from the wounded soldiers, and we continued on wearing only our shirts and pants. The enemy cavalry pursued us for a stretch and some men fell, shot in the back or sliced through by sabers.

I learned that soon afterward came the madness of triumph, the "second pass," as they called the inhuman task of giving death to the wounded.

The rebels' victory was resounding. So was the government's defeat.

THE SURVIVING SOLDIERS retreated in complete disorder to Valparaíso, where General Barbosa was reorganizing the miserable men. Not all of them made it—dozens of wounded fell along the road and many others simply disappeared, having stripped off their uniforms and deserted, I suppose, fleeing as far away as possible.

Night fell as Angelita Ayalef and I huddled in the scrub brush along a ravine. I do not know what happened to the other women. We had climbed into the foothills over rough terrain, clutching at the dense vegetation, tripping and falling, our strength drained. We had not eaten anything since the previous day, but we found a pool of water left by the rain and quenched our thirst with no concern for the smell of stagnation. Angelita wet her handkerchief and cleaned my face, then she pulled disinfectant from the bag she wore at her waist and applied it to my forehead. I had not noticed the deep scratches and the open wound above my right brow; I also had blood on my hands, but I did not know whether it belonged to me or to the fallen men.

"I will need to stitch that cut so that it heals properly, but we will wait till daylight," she told me.

"Stitches?"

"It won't be the first time I've done it, *gringa*. It's like sewing a button. That's what the needle and thread are for, among other uses," she explained, pointing toward her bag.

She bandaged my forehead with the same damp cloth and then we curled up between two boulders, covering ourselves with branches, shivering. At first the silence of the night seemed absolute compared to the clamor of battle that still rang in our ears, but once we had caught our breath and calmed down, we were able to differentiate the sounds of nature from the echo of voices, sporadic gunshots, and the crackle of flames. We saw a gleam of bonfires in the distance and detected the unmistakable smell of burning wood. Angelita deduced that the soldiers who had fled were setting fire to the forests to mark a path for those who came behind, but she thought it too risky to venture out into the darkness without knowing the terrain. We spent several hours huddled together for warmth, unable to sleep even though we were dead tired and had not rested at all the night before. The damp coastal air, the cold, and the terror of being discovered kept us alert. Our clothes were wet, our feet numb, and we had a painful emptiness in our stomachs.

"What I wouldn't give for a piece of bread!" I said to Angelita.

"Don't think about that. As long as we have water, we're fine. Hunger can be endured," she told me.

"For how long?" I asked.

"In the hills of Peru I learned to chew coca leaves, like the *cholos*. That helped pass several days without eating or sleeping. But it does not grow here."

"You have had a very hard life, Angelita. War is a torment," I said.

Angelita then told me of how she had joined the army in the last year of the war against Peru and Bolivia, unaware of what she was getting into, merely wanting to be near Manuel, her husband. They had been married only four months when he was drafted into the army. As soon as the opportunity presented itself, she joined the canteen girls.

"But you can't choose anything in the army, you simply obey orders, and I never got to be near Manuel," she told me.

"Tell me about him," I asked.

"He was a good man and a good soldier. He died in the battle of Huamachuco. I could not be with him, I could not bury him, I do not know what happened to his body, it surely ended up in a common grave like thousands of other Chilean and Peruvian men. I can only hope that God took mercy on him and let him pass quickly. Maybe there was a woman at his side, as I have been beside other dying men."

"I am terribly sorry, Angelita! Why did you continue on with the army after you were widowed?"

"Where would I go? This is all I have left," she answered.

"This life is very dangerous. You could be shot or stabbed with a bayonet. You yourself have said that female prisoners are raped and murdered."

"That's why we have to run like rabbits. Never let them catch you alive," she replied.

"Aren't you ever afraid, Angelita?" I asked her.

"All the time, but I don't think about it. I want to die with my boots on my feet," she answered.

A short while later we heard a rustling of foliage made by something much larger than a rodent or rabbit. Angelita gestured for me to keep silent, and she placed a hand on her corvo, ready to defend us in case it was an enemy, although it was unlikely they would have followed us that far. We waited a few moments frozen in the darkness, barely breathing, until a short bark rang out and the ever-loyal Covadonga jumped up to greet us. It is impossible to describe the relief we felt as we embraced her. The poor dog was as scared and hungry as we were.

Finally, in the early hours, we managed to doze off with Covadonga between us for warmth. That night I learned that I am stronger and more resilient than I ever imagined. Whenever I felt that I could not bear another minute of the cold, hunger, and fear, I closed my eyes and thought of my Papo showing me a map of the world, of my mother kneading bread for the poor, of Eric Whelan, my best friend, with a pencil tucked behind his ear, commenting on some news story. I did not know who I truly was until circumstances put me to the test.

AT DAWN THE air hung with the smell of smoke and an almost supernatural calm. We woke to a peaceful world, the chirping of birds and the whisper of rodents rushing between the brush, the murmur of the wind between the trees, the soothing presence of the dog. The sky cleared early and a timid August sun emerged, not strong enough to warm us, but sufficient to raise our spirits.

"Thank goodness you don't have a mirror, *gringa*. You look horrible," Angelita said, laughing.

She removed the improvised bandage and cleaned my wound, which was now bleeding very little, and she set about sewing it up. I could not open the affected eye, my head hurt, and I was so disoriented and hungry that I couldn't think about anything else. Angelita cut my complaints short, ordering me to thank the heavens I was still alive with at least one good eye. *Better to have one eye than to be blind* were her words of consolation as she sewed me up with several stitches. We drank water from the same pool as the night before, and in the light of day we could see that it contained tadpoles, a sign that it was not poisoned. Swallowing a tadpole or two would not harm us.

Angelita remembered or guessed the route by which we'd reached Concón two days prior, and she assured me that we would arrive to Valparaíso in a matter of hours. We started out cautiously at first until we understood that the rebels had not set about hunting down the defeated troops; they had most likely remained on the battlefield picking up their wounded and burying their dead, or had once again boarded their ships. Out of precaution, we avoided the road and continued through the countryside without losing sight of the sea, which served as a compass. The terrain was familiar, despite the stretches of burnt forest. A few hours later we ran into a handful of army soldiers who had managed to come out of the battle unscathed or with only minor wounds and were headed south, where General Barbosa was camped.

Just as Angelita had calculated, we reached Valparaíso before nightfall, and there we parted ways. She and Covadonga would return to meet up with the troops. I supposed that the better part of the civilian population had fled to the nearby villages or Santiago, as the city had been overrun by military apparatus, soldiers, horses, supplies, and vehicles. The hospitals were overwhelmed by the hundreds of victims from Concón, and schools and inns were being used as makeshift clinics. Volunteer groups formed to go out in search of those who were wounded or killed in the retreat. The charity carts passed at regular intervals loaded down with their sad cargo en route to the cemetery, trailed by a cloud of flies.

I TRIED TO return to the same hotel where I had stayed before and where the military command and other journalists were housed, but I was informed that there were no rooms available. I believe that my appearance terrified the hotel manager; I looked like a beggar, with my face scratched, one eye covered by a bloody bandage, wearing men's trousers and a filthy blouse, a far cry from the impeccable young foreign woman who had been there mere days prior. He wouldn't even return my luggage, despite the identification that I always carry with me. As I was pleading with that immovable man, who threatened to remove me from the premises by force, Rodolfo León, bless him, came to my rescue, although it took him a moment to recognize me and intercede on my behalf.

"You cannot stay here alone, Emilia. You need to see a doctor and have someone take care of you. You are wounded!" he exclaimed.

"I am fine, Rodolfo. All I need is some food and a bed."

"Let me help you. Come to my house," he offered.

"I wouldn't think of it! I could never impose on your family . . ." I responded. I had learned that in Chile you should never accept a favor without first refusing a few times.

"It is no imposition, quite the contrary," he replied, in accordance with the habitual protocol.

"These are terrible times, Rodolfo, you have enough to worry about," I insisted, even as I wanted with all my heart to accept his invitation.

This exchange went on for a few moments, as was proper, and then I let myself be led to his home, much more modest than I had imagined but perched on a hill with a panoramic view of the port. I was welcomed by Sara, his wife, a kind and efficient young woman, mother of a child, who did not express shock at my appearance.

Finally finding myself in a safe place, I suddenly felt that I was about to faint. My legs bent and I fell to my knees as I placed my head in my hands and began to sob uncontrollably. I was back in Concón, trapped on the battlefield with the dead and wounded and the blood and the gunpowder, with those poor boys howling in agony, the bodies run through with bayonets and the beach sown with human limbs blown off by cannon blasts. So many men left suffering and dying, so many women left sobbing, so many children left fatherless.

Sara was wise beyond her years. She knelt down without touching me and sat silently by my side until I was so overcome by exhaustion that I curled up like a newborn babe on the floor, bathed in tears.

"Cry, Emilia, it will do you good," Sara stammered.

"The dead men . . . those poor boys bleeding out on the ground . . . they will never leave me," I murmured.

"You will learn to live with their memory, Emilia. You are shattered, poor dear, let me help you."

Sara lifted me off the floor and helped me into the kitchen, where she prepared me a cup of warm wine with cinnamon, orange peel, and sugar, which helped to calm me.

"Now I shall clean your face and check your wound," she announced.

Without giving me the chance to object, she carefully removed the rag that Angelita had used to bandage my face and proceeded to wash my injuries with warm soapy water. She explained that the eye seemed to be fine, but that I would not be able to open it for a few days, until the inflammation subsided.

"Who gave you these stitches?" she asked, surprised.

"A friend of mine, a canteen girl."

"Nice work. It is not a deep wound, but it will take a few weeks to heal. You shall have to keep it clean so that it does not get infected," she told me, applying gauze with phenol diluted in water.

The liquid stung, but it was less painful than Angelita's stitches had been, and I was able to endure the discomfort without complaint, recalling all the wounded men I had seen in Concón—my suffering was nothing by comparison.

"You need to eat something to get your strength back. If I had known you were coming, I would have prepared a nicer meal," Sara said as she placed a plate of hearty potato-and-vegetable stew in front of me.

In the effort to get back to Valparaíso and my argument with the hotel manager, I had all but forgotten my hunger, but as soon as I smelled that food I felt the painful emptiness in my stomach like a punch to the gut. I devoured the delicious stew with the desperation of a castaway.

After eating I asked Sara to cut my hair; untangling that rat's nest would have been an eternal task, but she refused to chop it as short as I requested, which she felt would be akin to mutilation. We compromised on a shoulder-length cut, then she prepared me a bath, helped me to wash my hair, and combed it with infinite patience. Oh, what a pleasure to be submerged in that warm, soothing water! I felt I had been reborn. Sara lent me a skirt, which only reached down to my calves, a blouse, and undergarments. I looked at myself in the mirror for the first time in days: My face looked like a bruised melon.

I REMAINED IN my friends' home the following day, as Rodolfo recovered my luggage and tried to find me a room to rent. I slept so much that their child asked Sara if I was dead. The family cat had just passed a few days prior and the little one thought that death was contagious. That long rest helped me to recover from my fatigue and brought clarity to my mind. I had traveled to cover the war in Chile in total ignorance, planning to observe it from a prudent distance, but the war had swallowed me up into its dragonlike jaws. The human interest stories that my editor had wanted for the entertainment of his indifferent readers six thousand miles away seemed ridiculous and offensive in the face of the reality I had witnessed in Concón. I would never again write on frivolous topics. Nothing could possibly compare to what I had witnessed on that beach. There, I was introduced to true, visceral fear, the kind that settles into your bones and remains coiled there, ready to strike at the slightest provocation. After seeing that violence up close, I understood that I would never be free of it. Sara and Rodolfo's peaceful home, filled with the noise of their kid and the smell of cooking, was nothing more than a brief, illusory respite from the turbulence of the world.

FROM THAT HOUSE on the hill, I was able to witness as Congressionalist ships tried to take the city. The powerful army cannons at the Valparaíso fort quickly dissuaded the vessels, which retreated into open waters without taking damage. From that distance they looked like toys on the immense horizon. Meanwhile thousands of soldiers arrived to the city by train, reinforcements for the battalions stationed there, almost all very young. General Barbosa and General Alcérreca were preparing to confront the rebels with fresh troops, as Rodolfo informed me, and I found that term quite jarring. Faceless, nameless men, all disposable, fresh meat destined for the slaughterhouse.

I later learned of the tremendous losses that the army had suffered at Concón and the savage reprisal that followed the battle. The victors had murdered wounded men, razed the field hospital to the ground, captured a thousand prisoners, seized the army's artillery—thousands of guns and boxes of ammunition—and fattened their ranks with hundreds of deserters. Angelita Ayalef had been right in forcing me to escape with her; if the other side had captured us, they would have shown no mercy.

After a few days, I left the León home, where I had been welcomed so warmly, and checked in to a boardinghouse near the port, which Rodolfo had managed to reserve for me thanks to his extensive connections. There were no free rooms in the entire city.

10

DURING THE DAYS THAT FOLLOWED THE DEFEAT AT CON-
cón, the international press descended on Valparaíso, where the army
was preparing to wage the decisive battle for power. There were correspondents from Europe, Argentina, and the United States. Among
them was Eric Whelan. We'd had limited contact through a few letters and telegrams since June, always using the ridiculous code we'd
invented. Spotting him from a distance, with his red mane and his
disheveled appearance, my heart flipped in my chest. I realized in that
moment that, in those two months apart, I had missed him terribly.
Eric saw me at the same time and we ran to embrace with a rare urgency. Emilia! Eric! We repeated each other's names, our faces moving closer until, suddenly, we were locked in a passionate kiss. It was
an endless kiss, or maybe infinite kisses in a row.

What is certain is that it was enough for both of us to comprehend
that we were in love. I cannot say if it was a feeling that sprang forth
in that moment or if it was something that had been latently brewing
for years. Our relationship had been so solid, so practical and easy,
that neither one of us had ever interpreted it as romance. But there, in
that foreign land, in that foreign war, we had both doubted whether

we would ever see each other again. And that possibility was unbearable.

The original plan of separating to cover more ground now seemed absurd; either of us could have died without getting to say goodbye, without having discovered our shared love. This is what Eric said when the heat of our reunion had subsided and we were sitting in a pastry shop over cups of tea, bringing each other up to speed on everything that had occurred in recent weeks. I felt the same.

"What's happened to you?" he asked, delicately caressing my face.

"I don't know exactly. I think I was grazed by a bullet or perhaps I fell as I fled in Concón—I didn't feel it. My eye is better than it was, I can at least open it a bit now."

"To think you could've gotten yourself killed, Emilia, and our love would've never had a chance to blossom," he said, choking up.

"But that didn't happen, Eric. Here I am, alive and well for many years to come," I responded, kissing him, quickly, so that the other patrons wouldn't see.

"I hope you'll let me stay by your side. And that you'll learn to listen to me every once in a while. I begged you to seek refuge at the American consulate."

"Is that what you would have done? Right here is where the action is, Eric. Do not ask me to do something you wouldn't do yourself," I replied.

I TOLD ERIC everything I'd experienced in Concón, about the defeat and the rebels' barbaric reprisal, how they'd cruelly murdered the doctors, nurses, and orderlies, running everyone through with their sabers, even the women.

He, on the other hand, had been on a navy ship at the time of the battle. He had not yet witnessed the sight of such conflict firsthand.

"How can there be so much hatred among countrymen, Eric?"

"That's how it was in the United States; more men died in our Civil War than in all the other wars we've had. The country was left deeply wounded and I'm not certain it will ever heal," he said.

"Do you think the Chileans will hate each other forever?" I asked.

"Hate often lies dormant under the surface only to sprout back up when given the correct circumstances. That is how it has happened in the United States—we are still very much a divided country."

Eric then told me the story of what had happened in Lo Cañas the day I marched with Barbosa's troops to Concón. Lo Cañas was an estate a few miles outside of Santiago, whose owner, one of the most powerful aristocrats in the country, had taken refuge in a foreign consulate and was a leader of the Revolutionary Committee of Santiago. This group comprised mostly young men from wealthy families, fierce enemies of Balmaceda and inflamed by the conflict that had divided Chile. They lacked military experience but enjoyed the thrill of insurgency, safeguarded as they had always been by the impunity afforded them due to their social position. The young men had decided to meet at the Lo Cañas estate, where they would plot a way to cut off telegraph services and destroy the bridges leading into Santiago. Their aim was to impede the army from concentrating its defenses in the city. It was an idea as bold as it was absurd, given that the president had ordered his men to shoot anyone who even approached the bridges without due authorization.

"The details of what occurred are horrifying, Emilia. The government got word of the gathering of the Committee, and perpetrated as brutal a bloodbath as the one carried out by the rebels in Concón. They tortured all of them before they were massacred. There is great cruelty on both sides," Eric told me.

"Who are these monsters? None of the people I've met would be capable of committing such atrocities," I said.

"You are mistaken, Emilia. The very men who make the sign of the cross at mass become bloodthirsty at the slightest excuse, especially when gathered in a group. One of the Ten Commandments is thou shalt not kill . . . except in war. Cruelty feeds more cruelty."

"Not even wild beasts behave in such a way. Animals only kill out of hunger and to defend their young," I said.

"The males of almost every species fight. Humanity is no different. There will never be peace, Emilia. Violence is man's principal vice."

Eric added that the Lo Cañas massacre horrified the entire nation. Even the most fanatical government supporters denounced the crimes as acts of inconceivable barbarism, while the opposition joined in a single voice to demand justice. The former are weakened by shame, the latter, strengthened by rage.

August 18 marks an unforgettable date. It is the day that President Balmaceda loses the war. No military victory could ever erase this devastating moral defeat.

I TOOK ERIC back to my room the very day we were reunited. Under normal circumstances, we would have perhaps behaved more decorously, but, in war, time is condensed and everything takes on urgency. One feels they cannot waste today because tomorrow may never arrive, social conventions fall to the wayside, and the world's opinion ceases to matter.

Thanks to my Papo's infinite tolerance, I have enjoyed unusual freedoms for a single woman; I may have inspired a bit of gossip here and there, but I have never caused a scandal. That August day in Valparaíso, however, as two armies prepared for a final confrontation and the din of battle reverberated on the air, I gave no consideration to my reputation. I thought only of making love to Eric before violence once again ripped us apart. I took him by the hand and led him to my room, audaciously staring down the proprietress, an ill-humored widow, who attempted to stand in our way, asserting that hers was a respectable home, before finally stepping aside, intimidated.

The hotels of the city were all occupied by the military, politicians, and the press. My boardinghouse was one step above the unsanitary taverns reserved for sailors, which were rented out by the hour and often harbored women for hire. In Valparaíso, a city of steep hills, a few funiculars had been installed some ten years prior, but my boardinghouse could only be accessed via a worn-out staircase between two lines of houses. It was an aging wooden structure perched precariously on a hill, dilapidated and ravaged by inhospitable winds, in sharp contrast to my impeccable lodgings with the French sisters in Santiago. The rooms were normally shared between three people, but Rodolfo had negotiated one for me alone. In the letter I had sent home to my parents I had nicknamed the place the Flea-bitten Inn.

By five-thirty in the evening it was already dark out and a constant, depressing winter wind blew in from the sea. Oil lamp in hand, I guided Eric, one hand on my waist, up to my room. I was thankful that the weak light obscured some of the poverty and grime. The room was small, with a ceiling so low that I had to duck to keep from hitting my forehead on the beams, and it was freezing since there was no coal for the brazier. It also smelled of fish, and I suspected that rodents hid in the cracks in the wood. I had a pitcher of water, washbasin, and small chamber pot for my personal hygiene. The horsehair mattress was worn so thin that the springs of the cot stuck into my sides. Amidst that sordid scene, Eric and I would have to invent the perfect love.

Owen Whelan had been a good instructor in the possibilities of pleasure, teaching me to understand my body and his, to overcome prudishness, to ask for what I wanted, to give as much as I received, and to participate in lovemaking with an innocent, childlike delight. Those lessons, however, had proved to be a hindrance in other romantic situations, because they had made me seem spoiled and demanding by normal standards. I had allowed only a few suitors into my intimacy, nothing to brag about, and compared to Owen, they had all come up short. In that sense, I can say that Eric was an exception, perhaps because my love for him bathed everything in a golden glow. I had been in love with his brother as well, it's true, but that had been like trying to pluck a fish from the water with my bare hands. Owen had let me know from the outset that our romance would be merely a brief fling, although I hadn't believed him and had felt something much deeper than mere infatuation. It took me several months to get over that heartbreak and I had since been distrusting of love. Until Eric and I kissed on the street.

When I first met Owen, I had been struck by the fact that he was so different from Eric in appearance and personality. The explanation he had given was that his brother was an improved version of him thanks to an indiscretion on his mother's part; there was no way the two men could possibly have the same father. The brothers' differences also carried over into lovemaking. Owen was a master in the art, light and free as a bird, whereas Eric was inexperienced, intense, and sentimental.

For Eric, our relationship implied from the start a formal commitment. I helped him get to know my body as I explored his. I could guide him, but slowly and with care, because men have very fragile self-esteem. Omene, the brash exotic dancer, had taught me that: Men need to believe that they know more, especially in bed.

I HAD GROWN up surrounded by women: my mother, her friends, our neighbors, the baking assistants, and other ladies who would visit our home, where the door was always open. They would drop in to rest awhile after completing their chores, sitting in a circle to sew, knit, and chat. Sometimes they would pray for some ailing person who needed their request for divine clemency or to celebrate some important saint. Other times they would listen silently as my mother read chapters of Brandon J. Price's novels of revenge and heartache. In general, however, they took advantage of that brief interlude from their effortful existence to share confidences. As a little girl, I would crouch in a corner to eavesdrop; later on, I was allowed to join the circle. These women shared everything, laughed in unison, sometimes cried, but they always offered some piece of advice and, if the situation warranted, would take action as a group. There were several violent men in the Mission who would sometimes overdo it with the tequila and lash out at their wives and children. On more than one occasion, the warrior women from that circle went out in defense of the victims, armed with rolling pins and ladles. But, in all those years, I had never heard a single one of them mention carnal relations. The word "sex" was never uttered. Out of modesty, all reference to the topic was veiled in complex euphemism. If it hadn't been for my Papo's frank scientific talks, I surely would have reached age twenty with some understanding of the reproductive cycle of chickens, but without the foggiest notion of how humans managed the process. My mother raised me as the nuns had raised her: The soul belonged to God, the body was of the Devil, and one had to be very careful with the mind. So when my body began to change in puberty, I had turned to my Papo in search of answers. Whenever he was too embarrassed to explain something out loud, he would reach for his scientific textbooks. From the pollination of flowers, we moved through several chapters before reaching the mammals. But before meeting Owen I had been limited to anatomical drawings of skinless men with muscles and bones exposed, wearing underwear.

I am better informed than most decent women, whose virtue is measured by the size of their ignorance, but I am still embarrassed by the topic. The things I cannot say out loud, I may be able to put down in writing.

. . .

I DRAGGED ERIC to the Flea-bitten Inn with the obvious objective of making love, but once there I suddenly lost all vestiges of audacity and found myself shivering with cold, gripping the oil lamp. Eric seemed as bewildered as I was, and after closing the door behind us, he waited a few eternal minutes before taking the lamp from my hand and the heavy cape from my shoulders. Finally, he wrapped me in an embrace and began to kiss me. His voracity was flattering but would have contributed very little to awakening my passion had I not been yearning for it, moist with anticipation and so dizzy with love that I felt a furious fluttering in my stomach as my knees turned to rubber. Hurry is an enemy to pleasure, but Eric and I had too much pent-up passion to practice that first lesson, which consists of drawing out caresses for as long as possible before proceeding to the final act. The greater delight is in the preambles, which clear the mind of distractions. My mind is constantly distracted, and my Papo says that I always have a stew of ideas simmering in my head. On that occasion it was also filled with the horrible memory of the recent bloodbath I had witnessed in Concón.

Eric had no difficulty undressing me, because I did not wear a corset and my blouse did not have twenty tiny buttons, as was the fashion, but merely five large ones. I also did not wear lace-up boots or a tower of hair with extra curls pinned in. By simply removing three hairpins, my hair fell to my shoulders; Sara had chopped the waist-length mane that my mother had insisted I grow from childhood as a sign of femininity. I let Eric lead me to the bed, where he embraced me and pulled my clothes off. He smelled of tobacco and the sweet sweat of a young man. Despite the dim light I was able to admire his delicate skin and soft chest hair. What did he discover in seeing me? I cannot know, because I have never seen myself naked in the mirror. Other men have enjoyed my body; I have to hope that it did not disappoint him, despite the fact that I am far from the feminine ideal, with few curves and too many long lines, strong hands, and feet made for walking. My Papo assures me that I am as lovely as my mother, but his opinion does not count for much since he would find me beautiful even if I had the face of a toad.

My mind was a jumble of terrifying images and I could not close my eyes without seeing myself once again covered in blood, choking on smoke, shaken by the thunder of the gunshots and the wails of pain. For several nights, I had been startled awake by images of mutilated men and horses in agony. I did not know then that my nights would be haunted by these scenes for a long time to come. I had been lucky to come out of the battle physically unscathed, but the wounds of the mind would take much longer to heal. No one who has experienced war is ever the same again; something fundamental changes inside upon witnessing the systematic cruelty and brutality of so much death. Innocence is forever lost. Nevertheless, love can be more powerful than horror, and despite the trauma of Concón, I was able to join in Eric's passionate, youthful ardor.

Ours was a desperate, rushed embrace that concluded moments later with his long groan. I felt the weight of Eric's body collapse onto me and his breath on my neck murmuring words of love and apologies for so much urgency. But it was still early, we had many hours ahead before the light of day would deliver us back to reality.

ERIC SLEPT FOR a few minutes and as I calmed down I realized that, in the vertigo of desire, I had acted imprudently, exactly as Owen had warned me not to. The fear of pregnancy or one of those disgusting diseases that no one dares to name is often completely forgotten in the whirlwind of passionate love. The dreadful danger of sensuality was something my mother had drilled into me from the time my breasts first sprouted at age fourteen.

"Do not ever let a man lay a finger on you, Emilia. It starts with hand-holding and ends up in the gutter. A woman's ruin lies in abandoning herself to the shamelessness of the flesh," Saint Molly preached, surely recalling her own experience with her Chilean Romeo.

I knew how to look after myself using the rubber half-lemon given to me by that doctor, but it was in my bag and I did not have a private moment to insert it until my companion fell asleep. When he awoke, Eric placed the oil lamp on a chair beside the bed, to see me better, he said. Then he began caressing me, delighted by the smoothness of my skin, my firm breasts, flat stomach, and long legs. These are all normal attributes for a woman of my age, but to him they seemed exceptional, as he eloquently described each of my body parts, reciting them like a chant. He kissed me on the neck, nipples, belly button, and on my sex, panting, transmitting his desire and his willingness to give me the pleasure that had been previously overlooked. But he must have sensed my reservations, because he stopped short of penetration.

"Don't worry, I'll take care of you, I'll pull out in time. Sorry that I didn't do it before," he murmured between kisses.

"It's not necessary, I will not fall with child. But I have no way to protect myself from any disease . . ." I told him.

"I've never had anything like that!" he exclaimed, offended.

"I have to ask, Eric."

"I see you have experience," he replied, deflated.

"I'm not a virgin and I'm no fool. I don't suppose you are either," I answered, covering his mouth with mine to keep such prosaic matters from ruining the moment.

All of us have some private garden where we cultivate secrets, regrets, shameful resentments, and precious memories that we wish to conserve, because, once shared, they dissolve like bread in soup. I have never tried to invade another person's garden, because I jealously guard my own. It did not feel like an opportune moment to tell Eric of my adventure with Owen Whelan. I wanted to start from scratch and build an enduring love with Eric, so I knew that I would have to tell him about my relationship with his brother sooner rather than later; an omission of that magnitude would constitute a deep crack in the foundation of our trust. Even though it had occurred long before the idea of love wafted on the air between us, it would pain him to hear about it, which is why I kept it to myself that night. We had such little time, we could not waste it on jealousy or misunderstanding, and I didn't want to hurt him.

I'd thought that I knew Eric well, his intelligence, his integrity, his touch of cynicism, but as a lover, he revealed other sides to me, such as his delicate soul and his lonely heart. His broad shoulders and broken nose gave him the look of a hard man, but belied a great vulnerability.

"I never realized it, Emilia, but I have been waiting for you all my life. I remember the first time I saw you in Chamberlain's office, so pretty, serious, and dignified, with that horrible dead bird on your hat. You won me over when I saw you pour your glass of brandy into the spittoon," he told me.

"Golly! I thought you were angry because you were going to have to share the Arnold Cole story," I reminded him.

"I liked everything about you, your self-assurance, your intelligence. I thought we would make good colleagues."

"And lovers, perhaps?" I asked.

"No. I was so used to being alone, my bachelor routines—the idea of sharing my existence with a woman terrified me. I never thought I could be so lucky. How did I live so long without love?" he said.

"It wasn't that long, Eric. You're only thirty-six. I think you have a ways to go before you're elderly and decrepit," I replied.

"I am being serious, don't make fun of me. Now that I've got you, I won't ever let you go. Marry me," he begged.

"When?" I asked, laughing.

"Tomorrow. Say yes."

"We're in the middle of a war, Eric!" I reminded him.

"That's precisely why we can't wait," he argued.

"Fear of death is no reason to get married," I said.

"It's the best reason of all," he insisted.

"Look, if we survive this, you can propose again. But I should warn you that I won't leave my work and I don't like children; they are nothing but a nuisance."

"Children? Isn't it a bit early to talk about that?" he asked, surprised.

"I'm letting you know now because I had to help my mother raise my three brothers and it taught me that motherhood demands great sacrifice and offers little in return," I explained.

"You may change your mind, Emilia. Wouldn't you like to have some little redheaded babies?" he asked with a sly wink.

"No."

"Well, why bother making such long-term plans? Life surprises us at every turn," he said.

"And death can surprise us at any moment as well," I added.

My mother would have said that we made love like bunnies, but that would be an exaggeration. We enjoyed each other like any new couple in their first chance to express their love in private and with hours to do so. Around midnight, we finally fell asleep under the rough blankets that smelled of wet dog, so tightly embraced that I did not know where my body ended and his began, whose arms and legs were whose, if I was dreaming my own dream or one we shared. That newly minted love kept away the specters of Concón, waiting their turn to torment me in the dark corners of the room.

ERIC AND I had three glorious days together in which the winter and the war both receded to give us a brief truce. While the other correspondents spent day and night waiting beside the telegraph for news from the capital, interviewing officers and reporting back to their newspapers and magazines, we avoided the places frequented by the foreign press. Without discussing it, neither of us had been in contact with the *Examiner,* and we did not know about the many frantic messages sent by Chamberlain, who imagined, since he hadn't heard from us, that we had both perished in the revolution. The entire city was on red alert preparing for the next battle as we were navigating new love.

The first day we awoke surprised to feel a total intimacy that neither of us had experienced before, like an elderly couple who had spent a lifetime together. That sensation of familiar trust contrasted with the newly awakened physical passion that we'd experienced hours prior, when we'd been naked together for the first time. In the milky daylight filtering through the blinds rattled by the wind, I examined Eric with curiosity, his wavy hair, the constellations of golden freckles on his face, which from afar made him look eternally sun-kissed, his sleepy hazelnut eyes, dark lashes, his broken bandit's nose, his perfectly drawn, almost feminine lips, his strong jaw. Lying there, defenseless to my scrutiny, he looked young and vulnerable, so different from the self-assured man I thought I knew. He examined me, in turn, with the intensity of a portrait painter.

"I am so afraid of losing you!" he murmured, lightly touching my bandage, still in place despite the madness of the night before.

Huddled under the blankets, we were safeguarded from the pervasive cold, but hunger eventually spurred us into action. Eric got out of bed first and quickly put on his pants and boots, shivering. He had to break through a crust of frost on the pitcher of water to wash his hands and face. Then he helped me into my stockings, shirt, and petticoat, draped in the blanket for warmth. I splashed some freezing water on my face and pinned my hair up into a messy bun.

Eric needed to get a change of clothes from his hotel, where he was sharing a room with two British journalists. We agreed that as uncomfortable as my accommodation might be, it was the only place we could be together in private. It would be improper for us to be seen together; Eric was more concerned with my reputation than I was. I was reminded of Molly Walsh and I thought how scandalized she would be to see me openly giving myself over to love—her daughter had truly become a bad woman. My Papo, on the other hand, would understand that the circumstances did not allow for a moment of hesitation. In any event, we avoided the city center and stuck to the more remote neighborhoods where we could walk arm in arm.

At the foot of the long staircase that led up the hill to the boardinghouse was El Condorito, a hole in the wall that sold fresh-baked bread at all hours. We breakfasted on tea, cheese, and that fragrant bread; for dinner we ate fresh food at the tables in the market. Eric hadn't tried a bite of fish since adolescence, when it was all he and his brother had to eat, and the very idea of seafood repulsed him, but in that local market he discovered the difference between the spoiled fish of his memory and a fresh catch from the sea, all shining scales fried in oil with peppers and onion.

Eric, tasked with reporting on the rebels, was supposed to be on one of the navy's vessels. He had disembarked in Valparaíso by small boat, cloaked in darkness. He confessed that he had done so with the singular objective of finding me, because it had been several weeks since our last communication and he feared, with good reason, that I had not heeded his instructions to find safe refuge. He had just registered with the foreign press when he saw me on the street. Since then, he had all but abandoned his duties to dedicate his time exclusively to me. The light of day after our first night together, however, restored his sense of responsibility.

"I've spent these months reporting to Chamberlain on the rebels. I need to speak with Balmaceda's soldiers to get a more complete picture of what is happening on the front line. But access is quite limited," he told me.

"The press has access," I reminded him.

"They are suspicious of me because I've spent so much time with the rebels. They don't like what I have published in the *Examiner*. I'm on the blacklist as an enemy of the state."

"If that were the case, you would already be locked up," I said.

"I'm a journalist from the United States with a letter of safe conduct; I suppose that's why they haven't gotten their hands on me yet," he explained.

"I have an idea," I announced.

WHILE ERIC WENT to get his luggage, I went to see Angelita Ayalef, who was easy to find because everyone knew her. She was not camped with Barbosa and Alcérreca's troops, as I had expected, but helping out in the hospital where the men defeated at Concón had been taken. She had managed to get a new uniform and had cleaned herself up. She wasn't the only canteen girl there; I saw several circulating among the hundreds of wounded that spilled out into the hallways. The majority of men lay on pallets on the floor, many of them still in their ripped and bloodied uniforms, shivering with fevers and cold.

"Hello, *gringa*, looks like you won't lose that eye after all. Next week I'll remove those stitches and that scar will be embroidered on your face like a cross-stitch," my friend said.

"What a horror, Angelita!" I exclaimed, gesturing to the men on the floor all around us.

"There's some hope for these boys at least. The ones that didn't manage to escape and the ones still lying along the side of the road have no hope at all," she said.

"It has been several days since then, there can't be anyone left alive . . ."

"Death can take its time," she said flatly.

"Do you know how many losses there were at Concón, Angelita?"

"Not yet. It's hard to calculate. Several hundred died then and there and the seriously injured were not counted, but they will soon die as well. The other side took many prisoners and there were also soldiers and officers who deserted. That hasn't been mentioned, so as not to sow panic, but everyone knows it. I suppose you'll have come to help," she said.

"I can't, Angelita, forgive me."

"Why?"

"I have discovered love," I blubbered, blushing with embarrassment.

"With who? Barbosa?" she asked, laughing.

"It's a friend I have known for some time. He's a reporter from California, like me. His name is Eric. I want to be with him now because we don't know what will happen," I told her.

"What's going to happen is another battle and it will be worse than Concón, but this time we are going to win," she assured me.

Angelita agreed to speak with Eric and an hour later the three of us were sitting in a tavern near the port over plates of *chorrillana*. It was a typical Valparaíso dish, rich enough for a magnate, which consisted of sausage and beef on a bed of fried potatoes and onion crowned with a pair of fried eggs. We washed it all down with a table wine that scratched our throats and according to Angelita would dissolve the fat in our guts.

I served as interpreter, because although in those months among the Chileans Eric had learned a few words of Spanish, enough to communicate his essential needs, he had a very hard time understanding the local accent. Angelita told us the reinforcements arriving by train were very young and inexperienced soldiers who had not yet been christened by combat, but that they would increase the troops to numbers that surpassed the enemy, and that General Barbosa had chosen an unassailable battle site at Placilla, a few kilometers from Valparaíso. There, the army had already posted their artillery and raised barricades.

AT NIGHTFALL ANGELITA took us to where one of the battalions was quartered. Troops were continuously arriving, and there was so much movement of people and supplies that hardly anyone noticed our presence. We were able to spend a few hours interviewing the soldiers, their recent defeat weighing on them like a gravestone. We found out that the army troops numbered around nine thousand five hundred men.

"Their belief in their numerical superiority is inaccurate; the rebels have more than eleven thousand men. Also, they are better armed, with GebirgsKanone cannons," Eric informed me after we'd parted ways with Angelita.

"Cannons? How are they going to get those up the hill?" I asked.

"These are special weapons designed to be used in mountainous regions. They can be completely taken apart and transported by mule then easily reassembled at the proper location. It is going to be a massacre, Emilia," he told me.

"We cannot know what will happen. Perhaps the generals shall come to an agreement . . ." I said with little conviction.

"Battle is inevitable, it's only a matter of when it will happen. I cannot miss the action, Emilia, this is the reason I came to Chile," he told me.

"I don't think I am capable of witnessing another battle, Eric. You have no idea what it's like. Please, stay with me . . ." I begged him.

"I can't. You need to keep out of harm's way, but I have to rejoin the rebel troops when the time comes," he said.

"That's mad, Eric! Your place is with the press. You are an impartial observer, that is your only role," I insisted.

"Let's not argue, Emilia. We have such little time, we have to take advantage of it," he said.

11

I WAS NOT PRESENT AT THE BATTLE OF PLACILLA, WHICH I've been told was the bloodiest, most cruel of all the conflicts Chile had seen. Former comrades who had fought side by side in the previous war and the Araucanía campaign were now forced to confront each other, Chileans against Chileans, brother against brother. A short while later, when an inventory of the horror was finally taken, they calculated that the civil war had seen more men fall in a few months than in the four years of war with Peru and Bolivia.

On the night of August 27, Angelita visited the boardinghouse to let us know that the moment of truth had arrived—the two armies were positioned such a short distance apart that they could hear each other's conversations and smell the smoke of each other's tobacco. She hugged me briefly and then rushed off to rejoin the other canteen girls. Eric was prepared to leave, having awaited this moment for days, vacillating between enthusiasm for lovemaking and bouts of impatience. He was eager to experience the insanity of war once and for all. He proclaimed himself to be a rational pacifist, but he had succumbed like all the other men to the thrill of violence. At five o'clock the next morning we said goodbye, after having spent the better part of the night making love at regular intervals and discussing this foreign war. And all night he'd had one foot out the door, while I argued that if he truly cared for me he would stay.

"Promise me that you will take care of yourself and come back to me in one piece," I begged him, gripping his jacket, understanding that it was useless to continue arguing.

"I will take care of myself, don't worry. And you promise me that you will lock the door and stay in this room until I return."

"Sure, sure," I said.

"Promise me, Emilia! You must wait for me here. I will come back as soon as I can and then we shall be married, do you hear me?" he said, extracting himself from my embrace.

I bid him farewell in the doorway with a final kiss and watched as he walked down the stairway in the hillside. His backpack was slung over a shoulder and he held a lantern in his hand. When the night finally swallowed him up, I felt his absence like a blow of icy wind to the chest.

ERIC WHELAN WAS one of the few correspondents who did not observe the Battle of Placilla from the location assigned to the press, safe from the bullets but close enough to witness what occurred. He was still young and thought himself immortal. He had not lived enough to be able to imagine death. He easily assimilated with the ranks of rebel soldiers because he had made several friends in the north among the officers, including the captains of all the ships and General del Canto, who commanded the entire navy. He felt that after having spent weeks drinking and betting on games of cards as they awaited battle, his place as a reporter was there beside them, where he'd always said he would be, where he could experience the conflict firsthand. He drafted in his mind the reports he would send back to the *Examiner*.

He said goodbye to me with the certainty that he would soon return to the Flea-bitten Inn, where I would be waiting to marry him.

We had agreed, half joking and half serious, that I would be his guide in bed as he admitted that he knew nothing of romance and little of sex, since he had not had the opportunity to learn much about it. I did not count vast experience either, but I outpaced him in imagination and willingness to experiment.

Eric had told me that at age seventeen, in New York, he worked by day and attended night school, where he fell in love with a young teacher, not aware that she was dating his brother. A short while later she was with child and she married Owen, to Eric's chagrin. He decided to go as far away as possible from New York and from his sister-in-law so that he would not have to witness his brother's good fortune.

In California, he began earning a living writing publicity ads, as he had done before, until he got a job with Mr. Chamberlain and quickly became the *Examiner*'s top reporter. The pleasure he took in his work and the frenetic pace of San Francisco cured him of his heartbreak in due time. In the city, the gold dust had not yet settled and an impatient disorder reigned, fed by greedy businessmen, corrupt politicians and police, immigrants and sailors of all races, good-time gals, and apocalyptic preachers. It was the perfect place for a young journalist. He soon forgave his brother and extracted the young teacher from his heart, but he'd never gotten over his shyness with women. He assured me that if I hadn't crossed his path at the right moment, he would've remained an inveterate bachelor for the rest of his existence.

Perhaps the most honest thing on my part would've been to confess then and there what had happened with his brother. But our fortune felt so fragile and precious that I did not want to risk it simply to ease my conscience. I felt guilty for not having told him about it from the outset, and with each day that passed, that omission seemed more a lie and a heavier burden. Eric went away to Placilla with my last kiss on his lips and I was left with an empty pit in my stomach and a fluttering of foreboding in my heart.

The battlefield was nothing like Eric had imagined from the drunken descriptions he had heard in the north among the sailors of the insurgent navy. Up to that moment he'd had no idea what it meant to mobilize troops, thousands and thousands of soldiers, ambulances, armaments, mules and horses, food for the men and animals, field tents, and even drinking water.

And my descriptions of my experience had clearly not captured it fully either.

The rebels' battalions had marched from their camp near Concón and taken formation at the foot of the Placilla hills, each man alert, gripping their rifles, faces anxious, eager for the action to commence. The German mountain cannons, hastily assembled, were positioned at the proper distance. Eric's gaze was lost to the sea of uniforms, the infantrymen and the cavalry. They were very close to the position held by the government troops, strategically placed by Generals Barbosa and Alcérreca on a plateau protected by hills on three sides, blocking the way to Valparaíso, with a rise in the middle to shelter the cavalry and natural terraces for the artillery. Cliffs that dropped off almost in parallel like a fan, steep and very dangerous for the enemy infantry, which was left exposed on all sides to gunfire from above.

Before this abrupt topography, which seemed impossible to scale, Eric wondered in horror what General del Canto could've possibly been thinking. He was sending his men to the slaughter, and he recalled the conclusion we had reached on one occasion while discussing that war we were tasked with witnessing: hate and more hate, thousands of victims, heartbroken mothers, wives, and orphans, all for political rivalry, for the illusory distribution of power, for nothing. It was pure insanity.

AS THE SKY was just beginning to brighten on the twenty-eighth, shortly after saying goodbye to Eric I went to the hospital to offer my services. I left word with the owner of the boardinghouse to tell Eric where I had gone in case he came back for me before I returned.

The entire city was on alert, because the two armies had opened fire and dull cannon blasts could be heard in the distance. The first light of a timid August sun illuminated the horizon but the damp and cold of the night persisted, settling into my bones. I needed a cup of tea and a bite to eat, but El Condorito was closed and surely would not open that day. The baker, like the rest of the city's inhabitants, was locked away behind closed doors. After what I had experienced in Concón, I was not certain I could again witness all the pain and death I had glimpsed only briefly in the hospital, but they were going to need all the help they could get when the victims of Placilla began to arrive. The least I could do given the circumstances was offer to assist with cleaning or any other hard labor they might assign me. That seemed preferable to remaining locked inside waiting for news, as I had promised Eric. I would not have been able to bear the anxiety.

The hospital was over a hundred years old, an ancient brick-and-masonry construction with peeling paint and walls stained by a century of suffering. It was divided up into one main area, which occupied the better part of the building, a women's pavilion, and a section for the insane. For the past week, however, the entirety of the facility had been designated for those wounded in battle. There was a morgue in the basement, also overwhelmed by the war, with bodies piled up wherever they could find space for them. In the hospital courtyard, I encountered other women with the same intention to help, some of them clearly wealthier ladies, judging by their fashion sense and the air of superiority that set them apart from the rest. I saw Sara León and ran to greet her.

A tall nun with the broad back of a stevedore stood on a bench and introduced herself as Sister Gerda, head nurse, then proceeded to dole out basic instructions in a military tone with a slight foreign accent.

"Anyone frightened by blood or startled by screams may leave now. You are not here to observe or to sit and pray, only to work. We need strong arms. All of the doctors and nurses of Valparaíso have been summoned, even the dentists and veterinarians. They are tasked with operating and amputating, treating wounds; you are simply here to obey orders, scrub floors, sop up blood, vomit, and human waste. Is that understood? May the grandmothers take a step forward."

The older women among us obeyed.

"You are going to help in the kitchen or to arrange the bodies so that they may be dispatched with dignity to the next world," she informed them. "Raise a hand, anyone who can obtain pallets, pillows, blankets, cloth for bandages, and tobacco. Sometimes the only thing a dying man wants is a cigarette. Who can provide hot food? Transportation?"

Several women went off in search of the necessities, and the rest of us were told where to leave our hats and coats as they passed out long-sleeved aprons to protect our clothes and sent us marching off to the different pavilions. The rooms were dark and poorly ventilated, with small windows that let in very little light, but everything was clean. Some twenty years prior, hospitals in Europe and the United States had begun requiring careful hygiene for surgeons and instruments, sterilized gauze, and phenol spray to eliminate airborne bacteria. These measures had dramatically reduced infections and gangrene, which in the past had killed the majority of patients with open wounds. The nauseating stench of pus and putrefaction had been replaced by the medicinal odor of disinfectant.

In that old and impoverished Valparaíso clinic, asepsis was as rigorous as in the best hospitals of France and England. The beds were metal cots with worn horsehair mattresses but the sheets were clean, although gray and almost transparent from so many washes. I suppose that in normal times there was as much attention placed on order as on cleanliness, but the war had turned the hospital upside down in a whirlwind of chaos and suffering. I could not imagine where they would possibly accommodate any new victims of the battle being waged a short distance away. Sara León informed me that they were setting up military tents in the hospital courtyards.

THE NIGHT BEFORE, several foreign doctors had arrived at the hospital from the ships in the port. They had rolled up their sleeves to work alongside their Chilean counterparts and organized transportation to attend some of the patients on board. By seven-thirty in the morning we began to receive news, which came in every ten or fifteen minutes. At Placilla, the rebel forces had launched a frontal attack with all its brigades and reserves. General Barbosa was putting up a tenacious resistance. The acrid stench of gunpowder, cannon fire, and smoke was carried on the breeze.

The first of the wounded government troops began to arrive, adding to those injured in Concón. The triage process began with the selection of the most serious cases that could still be saved, often taken immediately to the operating tables; the rest had to wait. The nuns and nurses applied tourniquets, washed and disinfected wounds, set broken bones, and sewed stitches. Everything was in short supply: beds, ether, chloroform, morphine, disinfectant, clean bandages. The wounded wailed in pain and the relief we were able to offer was limited to laudanum and hard liquor. Despite the urgency and haste, every person dutifully carried out their role. I seemed to be the only one pacing around disoriented. Sara León was placed in charge of administering the alcohol, stored in barrels, which she poured into canteens to be distributed among the patients, often the only relief for their indescribable misery.

Among the first soldiers I was tasked with inebriating was a boy with a splinted arm. He had been treated by the veterinarian who worked at the equestrian club, the city's most famous bonesetter, who had also extracted a bullet, all with the skill of a magician. But the patient awoke from the ether in brutal pain. I was giving him sips from the canteen when the imposing figure of Sister Gerda appeared before me.

"I have been told that you speak English. Come with me," she ordered, handing me a piece of lye soap. "Wash your hands up to your elbows. You're going to assist Dr. Whitaker; he doesn't speak Spanish."

Sister Gerda watched as I carefully scrubbed up and then she led me behind a heavy curtain of waxed canvas that separated one of the improvised operating rooms.

I SUDDENLY FOUND myself before a Dantean scene, illuminated by the pallid light that filtered in through two narrow windows. On a wooden table with a metal top lay the patient, pinned down by two strapping orderlies. His pants had been cut from his body so that he was barely covered by a shirt, and I could see that the lower part of his right leg had been destroyed. A thick layer of sawdust covered the floor but did little to absorb the blood dripping down the side of the table, which had evidently been used to operate on other unfortunate souls.

Whitaker, the English surgeon, his sleeves rolled up and wearing a stained apron, looked a little like Eric might in another fifteen years: tall, strong, reddish hair peppered with gray, and bushy sideburns that covered the better part of his cheeks. He had tied a handkerchief around his forehead like a pirate to keep the sweat from dripping into his eyes. I immediately noticed his muscular arms and enormous red hands, like a butcher. His assistant, a Chilean doctor by the last name of Tobar, so young and thin that he looked like a student, was disinfecting the area above the patient's knee.

"Administer the chloroform," he ordered me in English without raising his eyes.

"I've never done that before," I blubbered.

"Then what are you doing here!" he shouted.

Sister Gerda picked up a mask and explained the procedure. I had to give the wounded soldier enough chloroform to put him to sleep and administer more during surgery if necessary. Gerda warned me that an excessive dose could cause serious damage to the heart or lungs.

"Take a deep breath, my boy. Relax. Don't be afraid, you won't feel any pain, everything is going to be all right," she said to the soldier on the table in a sweet, motherly tone, very different from the way she spoke to the rest of the world.

In a few moments the man was unconscious, and she gave me a final set of instructions. "Check his pulse and watch the color of his skin," she told me, but I had no idea how to do that.

She rushed away, leaving me so scared that my hands shook. The young doctor gave me an encouraging wink.

"I don't know how to take a pulse. I came to mop the floor," I murmured in a thread of a voice.

"Don't worry, miss. I will remain attentive to the vital signs. You take care of the chloroform, that's it," he told me, as he placed a tourniquet around the thigh of the boy on the table.

Fortunately, the English doctor did not understand and so was unaware of my continued clumsiness. I dutifully translated the few phrases that the doctors exchanged. Witnessing the amputation, I felt a spasm in my stomach and waves of nausea. It took an immense effort to remain standing and complete the task that had been assigned to me.

The surgeon made a deep circular cut in the flesh, quickly separated the skin and muscles, pushing them back to expose the femur. The wound flooded with blood in spite of the tourniquet, and Dr. Tobar proceeded to close the blood vessels with clips and sop up the blood with sponges. The patient was still unconscious, but I thought I heard him moan, and without hesitation I administered more chloroform.

"Saw," the Englishman said, and I did not know how to translate it, because I couldn't remember that word in Spanish, but Dr. Tobar knew what to do.

Then I watched as the Englishman's strong arms and hands maneuvered the saw to slice through the bone in three confident movements. Decisiveness, cold-bloodedness, and speed—the marks of a good surgeon. One of the orderlies retrieved the discarded limb and threw it into a washing pan containing other body parts, as flies buzzed around. The Chilean doctor proceeded to suture the tissue and bandage the stump, leaving a drainage.

"Nine minutes," said the Englishman, glancing at the clock on the wall.

"Well done, Dr. Whitaker," his colleague said approvingly, and I translated.

"No, Doctor. Before the invention of anesthesia it was done in three minutes. There is no reason why we should take longer with it now."

"Before anesthesia speed was essential. Now we can be more careful."

"Does it seem to you that I have not been careful?" the English doctor asked brusquely.

"I didn't say that! I meant that before, many people died of the trauma, in addition to the infections."

"They still die on us. But this boy is strong and he will live," the surgeon concluded.

"I think he's waking up," I said.

They checked that the patient's pulse was normal and the orderlies carried him away on a stretcher. Soon the young man would suffer a fit of vomiting produced by the chloroform and feel excruciating pain.

"Could you get us a cup of tea?" the English surgeon asked me, as he washed his hands in a basin of water with bleach, preparing for the next operation.

· · ·

IN THE HOURS that followed, the Battle of Placilla came to an end. At ten-thirty in the morning the government troops retreated en masse and the enemy initiated a fierce pursuit that left the field sown with new corpses and wounded. In this final phase of battle, both General Barbosa and General Alcérreca were killed. I did not hear the details, but there were rumors that the generals had been cruelly mutilated and that all soldiers of the defeated army were systematically executed.

Victims flooded into the hospital by the hundreds, quickly filling the campaign tents, the improvised ambulances, and even the homes of some families who had agreed to receive the wounded. We learned that the Congressionalist field hospital, which had acted with exemplary efficiency in the Battle of Concón and counted a well-trained team of six surgeons, ten assistants, and thirty orderlies, in addition to over two hundred stretchers and who knows how many mules, were treating the most urgent cases at Placilla but had arranged to transport most of their wounded to Valparaíso. I would estimate that, in those first hours, some four hundred rebel wounded came to us. I do not know how many wounded the government tallied.

Upon learning of the defeat, Sara León bid me farewell and rushed to where her child was waiting. She did not have any news of her husband, who had been in Placilla along with other members of the press. She feared for him, because there was little hope that the journalists who supported Balmaceda would be spared. Rodolfo had founded his newspaper to defend liberal democracy, exalt the government, and spread news of the president's accomplishments. During the months that the war had lasted, the newspaper had criticized the Congressionalist insurgents on every page; they would not forgive Rodolfo León any of that.

I thought of Eric, but did not worry too much because he was on the side of the victors. I was so busy trying to help in the hospital that I did not have time to think about anything else. Up to that point, we had been indiscriminately treating the wounded from both bands alike. The color of the patient's uniform was irrelevant, everyone received the same care according to the gravity of their situation.

But around noon on August 28, everything changed. The orderlies began to bring in wounded from the Congressionalist troops alone, their white uniforms in bloody shreds. They were clearly leaving behind the survivors of the defeated army, who would not be picked up until much later. The victorious soldiers removed patients from beds to make room for their own men; many who could have been saved were left to die without receiving medical attention.

NO ONE NOTIFIED us that the government had lost the war, it was not necessary. At eleven o'clock in the morning we heard the church bells ring out, accompanied by a thundering of salutes and triumphant cannon fire. The better part of the population supported the Congressionalists and so the people took to the streets waving Chilean flags, the women in festive garb mingling with the hordes of soldiers intoxicated on victory and violence.

I heard explosions in the distance, shots fired into the air, the whinnying of horses, sounds of broken glass, shouting. Immediately, the shops and homes of Balmaceda supporters began to burn. Dense black smoke filled the air outside. I didn't have time to be alarmed, because I was too occupied with the wounded that came in, one after another, and because I felt that the hospital was a safe place. Since the rebel wounded were already receiving priority attention, I concentrated on the men in blue-and-red uniforms dumped unceremoniously in the courtyards and hallways. This is where I found Angelita Ayalef.

I first spotted Covadonga by her side in the midst of that nightmare of human suffering. My friend was lying on the ground with her back resting against the wall, the only woman among so many men brought in over all those hours. She was still wearing her red-and-blue uniform with the little barrel that the canteen girls carried and her bag of medical instruments, but she had lost her cap and her braids were encrusted with blood.

I moved closer calling and calling to her, but she did not lift her head, which was resting on her chest. With a scream trapped in my guts, I crouched beside her repeating her name, "Angelita, Angelita," but she did not stir. Her soul was already moving away. I lifted her head and saw her gray bloodless face, eyes closed, her mouth hanging open with a pinkish foam sliding down her chin, but she was still breathing. I gently pushed aside the dog, who was licking her face, and I opened her jacket searching for her wound, but I could not find any.

As I held her, it was as if the tenuous structure that supported her finally gave way and her body collapsed like an inert rag doll. I rocked her in my arms, gushing false promises, that they would see to her soon, to keep breathing, that the doctor was about to arrive, that she was going to be all right, please don't leave me, for the love of God please don't die, Angelita.

She never recovered consciousness, and a few minutes later, Angelita died in my arms. I didn't realize it immediately, because I was crying, rocking her, calling to her, repeating those senseless words. Who knows how much time went by until I finally felt Sister Gerda's firm hand shaking me.

"Let her go. You cannot do anything for her now, and we need you in surgery," she told me.

I ripped myself away from Angelita's body, laying her gently on her side. It was then I saw that the back of her jacket was slit from top to bottom and covered in blood. She had been run through with a saber from behind.

"Change your apron, wash your hands, and get back to work," the nun ordered. Then, after a brief pause, she added, in the maternal tone reserved for patients, that she deeply regretted the loss of my friend.

What destiny befell the other canteen girls? I never learned if any of them survived the massacre. I felt that I had betrayed them, that I had abandoned them like a coward because I did not want to again experience the horrors I'd seen in Concón. I was only alive because Angelita had taken my hand and forced me to run and run, not simply fleeing on her own, but taking me with her. If we had been together at Placilla, perhaps she would have done the same, and in the attempt to save me, she would have been spared that murderous saber. Angelita Ayalef had not been afraid of death, but neither did she go in search of it.

She had fulfilled her wish to die with her boots on her feet, but that was little consolation for me.

ERIC KNEW THAT Balmaceda's army had been reinforced with troops from the south and from Santiago, but they had seen their morale destroyed by the defeat at Concón and by fear of the enemy's new German repeating rifles, the devastating effects of which they had already suffered. The men had several days to regroup and rest, but also to count their losses, their wounded, and the deserters who had fled or joined the enemy ranks. General Barbosa was not able to imbue them with the confidence they had lost. The Congressionalist soldiers, in contrast, buoyed by their recent victory, seemed indifferent to the tremendous obstacles presented by the terrain at Placilla.

As soon as day broke, the rebel general gave the order to attack on two flanks. The infantry, howling at the top of their lungs, launched themselves, chests bared, into the dense artillery of the government troops, as they began to climb the plateau. Eric tripped along behind them, grabbing on to anything he could get ahold of, staying close to the ground to avoid the bullets that whizzed over his head. He followed the men ahead of him, but he could not understand the orders being shouted over the thunderous noise. The stampede of boots soon churned the ground into a mud pit as he moved, slipping and falling down the abrupt throat of the hill. He had the advantage of not carrying a weapon, affording him greater mobility than the others, but that did not make up for his lack of training, a grave disadvantage. He had not paid any mind to his physical state for many years, and he no longer counted the strength and flexibility he'd had when his brother had forced him to box so that he could learn to defend himself.

In a matter of minutes, the government artillery had brought down the first lines and Eric found himself in an inferno surrounded by wounded men begging for help, falling to the ground, or rolling off the cliffs, many of their bodies ruined or inert wearing surprised expressions because they did not yet know that they were dead. But more men came immediately rushing in from behind, climbing the hill and jumping over the fallen, their eyes fixed forward, blind and deaf to the clamor of their comrades, with a suicidal determination to take control of the enemy artillery and put an end to that slaughter. Eric's good sense ordered him to seek shelter—this was not his war, he was only there to report on it—but he seemed to have been infected by the other men's blind rage, feeling a violent comradery that he was willing to kill and die for, the warrior or hunter's instinct. He ripped the rifle from the hands of a dead soldier and continued advancing alongside the other men.

Eric was not able to witness the rebel cavalry's audacious attack, in which three hundred horsemen galloped up the only access to the plateau, straight into Barbosa's artillerymen. Shortly before that, he had been thrown through the air by a detonated grenade. First had come the flash, the blast, then a formidable shove that forced all the air from his chest. Finally, a white incandescent light flashed, followed by a phantasmal silence. The explosion caught him on one of the peaks referred to as knife blades due to their sawlike shape. From there he rolled downhill into a deep ravine that broke his fall. It was a quarter past nine in the morning. At noon, thanks to the cavalry-men's demented courage, General del Canto's troops would occupy the Placilla plateau and Barbosa's men would scatter in retreat. President Balmaceda's army had disintegrated.

The civil war was over.

THE DETONATED GRENADE launched Eric downhill and left him lying among the rocks, bruised and unconscious. That providential blast distanced him from the center of battle and saved his life, because those who remained in the line of artillery fire met a worse fate. He managed to sit up at intervals and tried in vain to stand, only to stumble and fall, disoriented.

The entire morning passed before he had fully regained consciousness and was able to move. He patted himself down and saw that he was covered in scrapes and cuts; a strip of skin had been torn from his left hand and the scratches on his knees bled between the rips in his pants. He looked up to the top of the hillside trying to calculate how many meters he had rolled down the ravine, thankful for the miracle of being alive. He had lost his rifle, his backpack, and his pocket watch, ripped from its chain. He stared for a moment at the red rag he wore tied around his arm, trying to remember what it meant. He was surprised by the quiet around him, a muted, cottony silence, like being submerged in a snowy landscape; the thunder of the battle still rumbled inside him. The only sound he could hear was the buzzing of bees—or maybe it was the wind whispering in the distant pines.

He sat up, one joint at a time, dizzy, and tried again to stand, but his legs failed him. He felt a sharp pain in his left ankle, but found that he was able to put weight on it. He made two more attempts before finally managing to stand, leaning against a nearby boulder.

He glanced around, stunned at having reached those craggy rocks at the foot of the mountain without breaking his spine. He felt a sense of vertigo, as if he were balancing over an abyss; he closed his eyes and inhaled deeply trying to recover his balance. Long minutes passed before the images of the battle began to sprout in his mind's eye, as confusing as scenes from a nightmare. Only the caustic smell of gunpowder and ash indicated that it had not been a dream, that something had happened or was happening, something terrible that slipped his memory, but that he knew he must try to recall. He made an effort to give some order to those fleeting images so that he could determine what to do next. He took a few vacillating steps, wailing with the torment of each muscle, rigid and cramped from the hours lying immobile on the frozen terrain.

Suddenly he felt a sharp pain in his head, as if he had been clubbed, which briefly blinded him and almost brought him to his knees, but he was able to remain standing and slowly advance a few meters. He realized that the sea was not far off, he could see it like a brilliant black band down below, but he could not hear it. He had spent months on the water, in Iquique, on the navy ships, and at the ports, and his veins now pulsed with the unmistakable roar of the Pacific Ocean breaking in enormous waves, eternal, powerful, indefatigable, all foam and fury. Why had it suddenly fallen silent? Impossible. That is when he began to suspect that something was impeding him from hearing and that the whistling of the wind was in reality a persistent murmur in his mind.

Suddenly panicked by the abysmal silence, he shouted several times. He could feel the exhalation of each scream, but nothing more, not a single sound. My God, I am deaf! he exclaimed, feeling the words in his mouth, but unable to hear them. Calm down, he murmured to himself, try to think, you have to get out of here. Seeing that the ocean was his only reference point, he hoped that he would be able to get his bearings if he could only reach the shore.

The slope of the terrain aided his cautious descent, step by step. He swallowed back nausea, overcoming dizziness. A stretch of ground that would have normally taken half an hour to cover was an endless march, until, finally, he reached a path that ran along the coast, very near the sea.

He began walking northward, in the direction of Valparaíso, limping from the pain in his ankle. He did not have to wonder at the outcome of the Battle of Placilla, because along the way he saw many men rushing between the trees, stripped of their jackets and fleeing in shirtsleeves. From their red pants, he could tell they were defeated government soldiers.

HOURS LATER, ERIC reached the outskirts of Valparaíso. The sun was sinking into the horizon and the cloudy sky was tinged with orange. It was the golden hour, when the light begins to fade and the world is as delicate as a watercolor. He could see the outline of several ships at sea, the complete navy squadron, and the glimmer of the tiny lights from the houses sparkling on the hillside.

As he made his way into the city, he began to vaguely recognize the main streets, the plazas, the customs house, the tavern he had frequented, the twisting lanes, the English tearoom, the stairs and funiculars. Emilia! Emilia! he blubbered, suddenly desperate to be reunited. He increased his pace, despite his dizziness and the pain of his swollen ankle, and soon found himself near the port.

The city was lit up by bonfires and torches, it smelled of smoke, and everywhere people were running, jumping, fighting, in total silence, a nightmare of deaf confusion. He grabbed a man by the arm and asked him in English what was going on, but he could not hear his own voice and the man responded with a hard shove that knocked Eric to the ground before running off to join the other men ahead of him.

The city was a grotesque carnival of violence, frenzied euphoria, and unchecked animal instinct, the magnetic mob mentality that enabled destruction with impunity and anonymity. Groups of soldiers in tattered or incomplete uniforms and civilians armed with clubs and torches attacked shops and residences, looting, breaking windows, beating the men they were able to apprehend, dragging women by the hair, shooting stray dogs for the sheer pleasure of cruelty. The white uniforms of the aggressors confirmed what Eric already knew. Scenes of the war assailed him with absolute clarity, the Congressionalist troops, the march to Placilla. Emilia! He conjured my image as he had seen me for the last time, our parting kiss. He was unable to get his bearings, he did not recognize the streets, and the roving hordes pushed him from side to side. He noticed they were all wearing armbands or carrying red rags. He understood that this was what saved him from being attacked: The red band he bore placed him on the side of the victors.

SOMETIME AROUND MIDNIGHT, Eric Whelan found himself lost in a labyrinth of alleyways looking for the Flea-bitten Inn, whose address he did not know, because previously I had led him there. Reeling with vertigo, he tried to ask others for help, but no one stopped to aid him, lost to the euphoria of pillaging, as groups circulated, brandishing rifles and flags, shouting, singing, and terrorizing innocent bystanders. Eric tripped several times, picked himself back up, and continued on, not knowing where he was going, until, in one of his falls he hit the ground a few paces from a miserable hole in the wall, a rough clapboard tavern. He lay there for a moment, in good company, the streets sown with men sleeping off drunkenness or recovering from a beating.

He had set out before dawn that day in a hurried march to Placilla, and as he waited with the soldiers at the foot of the plateau they would soon conquer, he had been served a half cup of watery chicory coffee and a hunk of the brown bread allotted to the troops. Curled up on the ground that night, he did not think of hunger, but he was overcome by thirst, something he had not had time to think about in all those hours; he knew that the pounding in his head and his increasing dizziness were caused by the fact that he was so dry inside. He managed to crawl into the tavern, still busy with patrons, and he stumbled to the bar to ask for water. He remembered the word in Spanish. Agua, agua. A large sweaty woman passed him a pitcher and he drank it in huge gulps, thirsty as a camel. The barmaid said something that he was not able to hear, but he could guess her meaning: He needed to pay up. He searched in his jacket and found that his money and his documents were still there, he had not lost them in the fall. He gave her a coin and she placed a glass of red wine before him, but Eric needed to get something into his stomach or he would faint right then and there. He made the universal gesture for eating. The value of the coin was more than enough to purchase him a hearty meal, but at that late hour there was nothing left in the kitchen, and he had to make do with the bitter wine.

The large woman behind the bar could tell at a simple glance that this man who could hardly stand was a *gringo*, like so many others in Valparaíso, and that he had a good sum of money on him. She walked around the bar, approached him solicitously, and guided him falteringly to a shed at the back of the tavern. The woodshed housed a goat, a sleeping horse with his legs folded under him, a haystack, and a few tons of logs. The woman, convinced that this customer was either deaf or dumb, gripped him by the clothes and pushed him into a corner. She told him in gestures to rest and left him alone. Exhausted, Eric nestled in between the horse and the goat for warmth and shelter from the freezing air that blew in between the boards. He fell instantly into a sleep so heavy that he did not even notice when they emptied his pockets.

12

~

I WAS ARRESTED AT THE HOSPITAL JUST AS NIGHT FELL on that unforgettable day of the last battle. I had spent over twelve hours working without a moment's pause and with no sustenance beyond two cups of tea, but I did not feel tiredness or hunger, numbed as I was by so much suffering, by Angelita's death, by the avalanche of victims that piled up by the minute and by some terrifying scenes briefly witnessed from the door of the hospital, such as the naked, defiled bodies of the two defeated generals being paraded through the streets. I did not know the other man, but I recognized the elderly General Barbosa immediately, a bundle of bones slung over the back of a mule, bloodied, jeered at and insulted, spat upon, garbage launched in his direction.

I will never know who turned me in. I suppose it could have been any one of the people who had met me and knew of my friendship with Ambassador Patrick Egan and other supporters of the Balmaceda government, such as Rodolfo León. Or it could have been that my column in the *Examiner* circulated in Chile, leading to my downfall.

They found me in the operating room assisting Dr. Whitaker, who had only been able to rest one hour before returning to his post.

If I was tired, it is easy to imagine how exhausted he must have been, with the lives of so many poor souls in his hands. Watching him operate that day, I had developed affection and admiration for him; despite his brusque manners and the hardened haste of his profession, he seemed to be a good man. Once we'd gotten into a rhythm and I was able to translate without hesitation, he treated me with respect, explaining the procedures to me like a professor. When the soldiers came in to arrest me, I was confidently administering chloroform and the doctor was sewing up the scalp of a boy who had come in with metal shrapnel embedded in his skull.

Whitaker was sure that he could save him, but at what cost he was still uncertain. He told me that this question still plagued him after twenty-three years performing surgery. If he were to awaken from anesthesia to find he had the brain of a rabbit, he would prefer a thousand times over never to wake again.

It was three men, two in uniform and another who looked like a bureaucrat, the first two carrying rifles and the third holding a list upon which my name apparently figured.

"Emilia del Valle? Come with us!" they ordered.

They gripped me by the arms, but Dr. Whitaker, scalpel in one hand and the other wiping his forehead, damp in spite of the handkerchief, stood in front of them with all the tremendous authority of his height, booming voice, and bloodied apron. In English, he demanded that they release me. But, even if they had understood his words, they would not have heeded them.

"Stay out of this, mister! You don't want to get involved," the man with the list warned him. I had to translate what he'd said.

"This young lady is a U.S. citizen! Can't you see we are performing surgery here?" the doctor bellowed.

"We don't give a damn. Step aside," the other replied.

"Emilia! Tell these animals that I need you here and that they cannot take you away without a judicial order," Whitaker insisted.

I knew it was useless to continue translating. The Englishman had not yet realized that the war had dispensed with all semblance of legality, and that violence was the only law for the moment. I assured the doctor that it was all a misunderstanding and asked him to please send a telegram to the United States consulate notifying them of what was happening to me. I doubted whether Patrick Egan would be able to do anything, occupied as he must have been in defending his diplomatic immunity, since the new rulers of Chile detested him, but it was essential to send word. People had been known to disappear entirely after being arrested. I would have liked to send a message to Eric, but I did not know how to tell Whitaker to contact him.

They dragged me from the clinic, pushing and pulling me along. Crossing the courtyard, I caught a glimpse of Covadonga, who was still in the same position beside Angelita's corpse. Sister Gerda rushed hurriedly past, and I called out to her with the ludicrous notion that the authoritative German nun could somehow rescue me, but she was too far away and did not hear me. The dog, however, perked up when she recognized my voice.

"Shut up, whore!" one of the soldiers barked, slapping me hard across the face.

Blinded by pain, my legs gave way and my mouth filled with blood, but their claws trapped my arms, keeping me upright. They led me in this way for several blocks to the Valparaíso prison, followed closely by Covadonga. All along the route I witnessed pillage and plunder.

The rebel troops, soaked in alcohol, had occupied the city and began to exact their revenge with impunity. Many civilians joined in the destruction, robberies, rape, and murder, as the deserters from the government troops took advantage of the chaos to get lost in the crowd. I supposed that most of Balmaceda's supporters would have fled terrified into the hills or hunkered down wherever they could find refuge. I imagine that many of them mingled with the victorious horde in order to avoid being singled out, but many others were captured. I saw a pair of men dragged out into the street and beaten brutally, as an officer on horseback looked on in amusement. Several women participated in this exercise of cruelty, kicking the fallen men with a demented joy; these were most likely ordinary women who hours prior had been going about their lives as wives and mothers.

DAY DAWNED ON August 29 and the victory celebration in Valparaíso began to dissipate as the triumphant troops prepared to leave for Santiago, where the Revolutionary Junta was going to occupy the post that President Balmaceda had left in the wee hours of that very morning. Little by little, some decorum was restored to the streets of Valparaíso as the citizens undertook the Herculean task of putting out the last fires, sifting through the rubble, collecting the garbage, treating the wounded, burying the dead, and reestablishing a semblance of order. Healthcare workers and groups of volunteers set out to gather the wounded soldiers who had remained at Placilla. The charity mule carts rumbled through the streets with their sad cargo of decimated men, the volunteer Congressionalist soldiers from the north lumped in with the fresh government troops from the south, the boys who had been hunted down with dogs to be used as cannon fodder. The poor souls whom no one could identify and no one came to claim were laid to rest in mass graves, one atop the other, piled up like cordwood, sprinkled with raw lime, and covered with soil. The stench of putrefaction came in waves mingled with the smell of charred flesh from the carcasses of the animals burnt in huge pyres.

In Santiago, President Balmaceda followed the events by telegraph and messages that came in as the hours passed. The evening of the twenty-eighth, he had celebrated his wife's name day with a dinner attended by his children, some friends, and cabinet ministers in an atmosphere of forced calm. Given the lack of heartening news, everyone began to suspect the ominous outcome at Placilla. They had just served the soup when he received a telegram, which he read unblinkingly, folded up, and placed beside his plate. The missive announced the total annihilation, as well as the deaths of his two generals, Barbosa and Alcérreca. He took only a few seconds to pick up his spoon and return to the soup with his characteristic calm, which in recent months had become so extreme that Rodolfo León classified it as a hypnotic state. Nothing in his aristocratic semblance revealed any emotion upon learning that his ambitious dream for Chile had ended hours prior in a total bloodbath. At his wife's inquiry into the contents of the telegram, he responded that there was no news, and he moved on to the second course, chatting with his guests, showing no signs of concern.

But before dessert, he retired to his study to give his final instructions.

What did he think in those moments? What did he feel? He had the profound conviction that he had fulfilled his duty, having faithfully served Chile throughout his long political career. He had also exercised his presidential authority with integrity, which he believed fundamental to leading an orderly nation with a vision for the future. His political enemies' project of establishing a parliamentary regime, on the other hand, would bring chaos and corruption, and benefit only foreign capital. But the civil war had ended badly for him, and he understood that in order to avoid a greater rift across his broken nation, he must resign from power that very night. He was too proud to flee. If he had any thoughts of turning himself in, he quickly discarded them; he had already heard the rumors of the violent revenge exacted in Valparaíso and he knew that his enemies would show him no mercy. He had to preserve the dignity of the presidency; he could not offer himself up to ridicule and humiliation. Above all, he had to ensure his family's safety.

JUST PAST MIDNIGHT, five of his children set out for the United States consulate, where Patrick Egan would offer them asylum; his wife joined them shortly thereafter. The woman bid her husband a tearful farewell, never imagining it would be the last time she saw him. She and her children slept in beds that, the night before, had been occupied by fierce critics of the president.

Meanwhile, Balmaceda carefully drafted his resignation from the presidency in his elegant calligraphy and without a single correction, as if he had prepared it ahead of time. He delegated command to a heroic general from previous wars, with the hope that his prestige would facilitate the transition of power between his government and the Revolutionary Junta. He believed that Chile needed a firm military hand; a civilian would not inspire the respect required to restore calm, impose order, and prevent further violence.

The general tried to shirk the responsibility that Balmaceda wished to bestow on him, but the president insisted that there were certain duties that an honorable man could not shy away from. The general had finally given his vow of honor to protect the lives and properties of government supporters and bureaucrats along with the military men who had carried out his orders. Balmaceda reminded the general that his was the legitimate, constitutionally elected government, and that the Revolutionary Junta had illegally taken power by force.

Balmaceda erred greatly in his selection of successor. The general, who had demonstrated so much courage on the battlefield, displayed a shocking weakness of character when faced with the task delegated to him by the president that night. He all but dozed off in the presidential chair as chaos ensued. He was not the right man under any circumstances, but perhaps no one would have been able to prevent what followed.

Before dawn, the bells of the cathedral rang out celebrating the Congressionalist triumph, echoed by the bells of the firehouse. The Catholic church detested the president. Just as the clang of the bells began reverberating through the silence of the night, the president exited La Moneda Palace and walked calmly to the Argentine consulate, wearing his black cloak and riding boots, armed with a revolver, and escorted by a few of his closest friends. As soon as he'd learned of the outcome at Placilla, Ambassador Uriburu had sent a message offering asylum, and Balmaceda accepted. Patrick Egan had extended the same offer but the president declined, supposing that his family would be safer at the United States consulate if he was not with them. The Argentine ambassador personally admitted the president, extended a whispered welcome, and led him to a room on the second floor where a bed had been prepared for him.

By one of those strange coincidences, President Balmaceda occupied the same room where, shortly before, my father had died.

ERIC WHELAN WAS awakened by the rough lick of a goat's tongue against his cheek. He pushed the animal aside and sat up, disoriented. It took him a few moments to recall what had happened the day before and to recognize the shed behind the tavern where he'd spent part of the night. His mind was now clearer and he could make out some sounds of the world, filtered through the noise of bumblebees buzzing in his ears. *At least I won't be deaf forever,* he thought. He patted his head, which felt like it was gripped by an iron vise, and he discovered a lump the size of an egg at the base of his skull. He deduced that it was a concussion and knew that the best thing would be to move as little as possible, but he did not have time for that, he needed to find me.

He stood up and saw that his ankle was badly swollen as he brushed the straw from his hair and clothes. He splashed water from the horse trough on his face. He still wore the red band around his arm that would allow him to go out on the street without being attacked. He needed to eat something.

At that time of day, the tavern was nearly empty except for a few clients snoring off their drunkenness and a girl who was cleaning the floor and collecting cups and plates. Eric indicated that he wanted food, put his hand in his jacket pocket, and let out a curse upon realizing that all of his coins had vanished. Luckily, his documents were still there. The girl looked at him with large, terrified eyes, holding the broom in front of her like a weapon to fend off this ragged beggar, blubbering foreign gibberish. Eric lamented more than ever his incurable clumsiness with languages. He tried to calm the girl, using hand gestures and maintaining distance. Finally understanding that the eccentric *gringo* did not represent a threat, she lowered the broom and attempted to understand what he was communicating. She gestured for him to wait, disappeared for a few minutes, and returned with a piece of hard cheese and an onion. She placed the food on one of the rough tables and brought out a ceramic pitcher of water. Eric explained in mime that he could not pay her but she simply shrugged and returned to the task of sweeping the floor, as Eric took gulps of water and devoured the rustic meal, which tasted delicious. He said goodbye to the girl with a kiss on the hand and a blessing in English. She laughed heartily; this *gringo* was mad.

Eric limped down the street. The city was less threatening in the clear light of day, but it had not returned to normal. The bloody scenes from the night before would have seemed like the monstrous imaginings of his battered brain if it hadn't been for all the rubble and ash, the broken glass, doors hanging from their hinges, and dead animals strewn over the ground. He walked toward the Iglesia de la Matriz, orienting himself by the church bell tower that stood out above the surrounding buildings. The bells, which had rung out joyfully announcing triumph for twenty-four hours, now sounded every half hour, calling the faithful to give thanks to the Lord for saving their homeland.

The church was in the heart of the port neighborhood, where it had stood since the mid-sixteenth century, having been reconstructed several times after earthquakes and pirate attacks. Eric easily located the basilica, its doors thrown wide as, inside, several priests presided over a mass, and, outside, a crowd of worshipers were huddled on the steps, many of them without having slept the previous night, given over as they were to violent revelry. Eric stood there, trying to get his bearings, when a gentleman wearing a top hat and fur-collared coat placed a coin in his hand. Eric decided that the first thing he should do was get more money, since he didn't have a single peso on him, and then find a telegraph to send word to the *Examiner* that the war was over. He believed me to be safe and sound at the Flea-bitten Inn and trusted that we would soon be reunited.

He headed toward the Plaza de la Intendencia, which he recalled as being close to the church, and soon found himself before the elegant Bank of Valparaíso. He looked like someone who had survived a shipwreck, but he had papers proving his identity and he believed, with the blind confidence of an American who has never traveled abroad, that he should not have any trouble getting an advance on the money that the *Examiner* could wire to the bank. As a United States citizen and a press correspondent, this should be simple, but he found the bank closed, boarded up in the chaos of the war, and, furthermore, because it was Saturday.

There were several English soldiers posted in the plaza and a few armed American marines, easily identifiable by their uniforms and by the bewildered look of men who had landed there from another planet. Finally among his compatriots, Eric was able to explain in his own language that he was in dire straits. The soldiers loaned him some pesos and explained that they were there to guard the foreign-owned businesses and residences; they did not know the city well, but they were able to give him directions to the hotel where the press was housed. Eric took down the name of the man who had lent him the money so that he could pay him back.

At the hotel, Eric ran across several colleagues who, upon seeing him hungry and in such a state, invited him to breakfast and filled him in on the details of the battle. The causalities on both sides had been catastrophic. Added to the losses at Concón and previous conflicts, they calculated that the few months of that civil war had cost Chile thousands and thousands of men. The telegraph system was supposed to be reserved for military use, but the hotel had installed one for the foreign press, and he was able to send an initial wire to Chamberlain providing the information he'd been able to verify. He then followed up with a second cable assuring the editor that both he and Emilia del Valle were safe and would be in contact again once communications were normalized.

IN THAT CITY of hills, twisting lanes, endless staircases, and funiculars, it was easy for someone who had not lived there a long time to get turned around. Eric did not have any way to ask for directions, but he was saved by chance. After wandering for a long while, he suddenly found himself near El Condorito, the small bakery at the foot of the staircase where we had purchased breakfast during the three days he'd spent with me. He let out a cry of relief as he breathed in the aroma of fresh-baked bread. Each step on the staircase echoed through his head, as he winced in pain over his swollen ankle and rubbed the lump at the base of his skull.

The landlady of the Flea-bitten Inn opened the door with a red rag around her arm and another around her neck. She had seen Eric a few times during the short while he stayed with me, and had little love for either of us. On the morning that Eric had left for Placilla, I had overheard her say that we were immoral *gringos* who had invaded her house to roll around like pigs in a sty as if her respectable inn were some house of ill repute, that Americans were all arrogant and vulgar, and to top it off, we were on Balmaceda's side. The comment was made to the servant girl, but her voice was loud enough to be heard from inside my room. This surprised me, because I had always treated her with respect and Eric had even left her a generous tip. She would not have dared to kick us out before, but since the victory of the previous day, the situation had changed. The months of civil war had threatened her business and complicated her existence; it did not matter to her which side won as long as the mayhem ceased. She tried to keep Eric from going up to the second floor, but the widow was no match for him, a strong, desperate man. Also, since the *gringo* wore a red armband, the woman was forced to swallow her displeasure and step aside.

Eric rushed up to the room we had shared. Upon finding it empty he went back down to question the landlady. "Emilia? Emilia?" he shouted.

The woman responded with an expression of contempt, shrugging her shoulders, but he had been through too much and was not going to let this witch mock him. He felt the blood pound in his temples and the lump on his head swell up like a bubble about to burst. He grabbed the woman by her clothes, lifted her a few inches off the floor, shaking her, red with fury. Finally, terrified, she blubbered the word "hospital," which sounded almost the same in English.

Of course I would have marched straight off to volunteer at the hospital, Eric thought angrily. He had made me promise I would stay in the room with the door locked until the conflict was resolved and he returned, but he realized now that I had never intended to do anything of the sort. It was not the first time I had ignored his advice. He concluded that I would do as I pleased and was not to be trusted, but at least I was safe. He decided to wash, shave, and change his clothes before going in search of me so as to avoid being offered alms again like some beggar.

EVERYONE KNEW WHERE the hospital was, and Eric was able to get directions when he pronounced that magic word. The relative calm of the streets began to deteriorate as he neared the clinic, where a permanent state of emergency had been in effect ever since the Battle of Concón. The wounded rebels had been transported there from Placilla and they took up the main wing, while the rest of the patients were housed in other buildings or field tents. Victims continued to arrive, many of them hauled to the clinic on improvised stretchers by well-meaning citizens, as the healthcare workers from both sides joined forces to treat them. A day after the battle, no one in the hospital distinguished between friend or foe, all the wounded were treated equally. The janitorial team endlessly mopped up blood, disposed of amputated limbs, boiled used bandages, and moved the cadavers to the morgue.

Amidst all that commotion, no one had time to attend to the *gringo* wandering around pestering them, unable to articulate his questions in Spanish. After searching for me, unsuccessfully, for a good while, Eric finally crossed paths with a haughty nun who ordered him to get out; he was not allowed to be there. Seeing that he did not understand her, she repeated herself in German, but Eric was as stubborn as she was and remained rooted to the spot repeating "Emilia, Emilia, Emilia." Finally Sister Gerda understood that he was looking for the American translator, and she told him to see Dr. Whitaker.

The surgeon had worked ceaselessly for thirty hours before fatigue finally got the better of him. He had to be dragged against his will to a field cot inside a small broom closet adjacent to the operating room. There, he collapsed and began snoring before they could even throw a blanket on top of him. He had been deep in slumber for a good while when Eric Whelan managed to ascertain his whereabouts. He found the doctor face down on a cot that was much too short for him, his feet in the air and his arms hanging off, surrounded by brooms, scrub brushes, and buckets. It took Eric a few minutes to wake the man and explain that he was looking for Emilia del Valle. Whitaker took another two minutes to shake off slumber enough to respond.

"They arrested her," he said.

"What do you mean they arrested her? Who? Why?"

"It happened last night. They pulled her away in the middle of an operation. She asked me to notify the United States ambassador in Santiago, but I have not had the chance to do so, nor is it possible to access the telegraph," he explained.

"Where did they take her?"

"I do not know. It was a pair of uniformed guards. I suppose they should have released her by now; they wouldn't dare to detain a citizen of the United States," Whitaker said.

"I have to find her!" Eric exclaimed.

"I would ask at the prison if I were you," the surgeon advised him before collapsing back onto the cot.

A SERGEANT WITH his coat unbuttoned and his eyes glassy from fatigue or from alcohol greeted Eric Whelan at the front desk at the Valparaíso prison. Eric was asked to wait, watching as prisoners, almost all of them badly beaten, were brought in and swallowed up by the metal gate leading into that sinister facility. Imagining that I could be behind that door, Eric felt a ball of fire in the pit of his stomach, his hands shook. He once again cursed the fact that he could not communicate in the local language and that he did not have enough money to bribe the guard. The sergeant did not react to my name, repeated over and over, but just when Eric was about to explode, another man in uniform appeared, who seemingly had more authority. He handed Eric a pencil and gestured for him to write the name in a notebook on the counter. Eric obeyed and also showed the man the credentials identifying him as a member of the foreign press. The officer examined the documents, asked Eric to wait, and left.

Two hours passed, or perhaps even three or four. Eric could no longer calculate the time, desperate, sitting on the floor because there were no chairs, observing that macabre parade of prisoners, guards, and soldiers. Finally the man returned and, using unmistakable gestures, indicated that the person Eric was looking for was not there.

"You arrested her! She cannot have simply disappeared! Tell me where she is!" Eric shouted, but the other man did not understand him or did not care to.

Eric was brusquely escorted out onto the street and he was certain that if he had not had the red armband and his documentation, he would have been arrested as well.

PART
FOUR

13

ᢣᢧᡒ

I GRADUALLY REGAINED CONSCIOUSNESS IN A CELL. I could only vaguely remember the beating that had happened, the kicks, the blows, the insults; I could hardly breathe through the pain in my chest and stomach. The wound on my forehead had reopened and my hair was sticky with dried blood. It took me a moment to understand where I was, a small, square space, empty, dark, all cement walls and filthy floor. I suppose I had lain there semiconscious for a while, hours, perhaps, because a thread of light filtered through a crack along the ceiling, indicating that day had dawned. I could hear shouted orders, slamming doors, the sound of something heavy being dragged across the floor. The walls were thin.

I sat up little by little and confirmed that I was still wearing my hospital apron, stiff with filth and stained with blood, my skirt and blouse beneath it, as well as my underwear and slip, damp with urine, and my boots. The Virgen de Guadalupe medallion was still pinned to my brassiere. I deduced that I had not been robbed and, given that I was fully dressed, I had not been raped, either. This was such a relief that I began to weep, and every sob was like a knife to the chest. I was certain that a few of my ribs were broken. What happened? Why had I been arrested? What crime was I being accused of? These questions flashed through my mind, but I was too frightened to think clearly. I curled up on the floor and closed my eyes.

Perhaps I slept or perhaps I simply fainted, but when I awoke again it was brighter, now daytime. I looked at the cracked wall, names carved roughly into it, speckled with mildew. The only door was wooden and crooked, threads of light filtered through the cracks. A small but bold mouse scurried between my feet and disappeared through a hole. I called out to him to keep me company, and he soon returned to run a few reconnaissance circles around me.

That day, August 29, a day of total terror, was one of the worst of my life. I had a vague sense of the passage of time thanks to the changes in the meager light that entered the cell. I was quaking from fear and cold, thirsty, driven mad by the howls of people being whipped and beaten nearby and the shots of the firing squad. The horror of what was occurring on the other side of those walls never left me for an instant, I felt the other prisoners' agony in my own body, and I repeated like a litany the prayers my mother had taught me in childhood. I had distanced myself from religion years prior, agnostic, like my Papo, but in my anguish, I pleaded with the Virgen de Guadalupe, *Sacred Mother of Jesus, rescue me from this terrifying cell, please do not abandon me now and if I must die, oh Mother of God, please do not abandon me in the hour of my death . . .*

Only once did the door open. I knew it would be futile to beg for release or ask questions, so I remained curled up with my eyes shut tight. The footfalls across the cement floor were the slow, heavy steps of boots.

"We got carried away with this one," said a man's voice from the door.

I felt a light kick to the legs and I could not repress a shudder as I imagined what was about to occur.

"Is she alive?" asked the same voice.

"Fainted or dopey," responded the man beside me.

They left the cell, bolting the lock, and I breathed a sigh of relief.

They had left me alone, for the moment. I saw that they had deposited a tin plate and cup beside the door, and that's when I felt the riot of hunger that the pain of the beating had suppressed. And the unquenchable thirst. I dragged myself over to the cup and drank the water in long gulps, desperate, then I picked up the wooden spoon and devoured the grayish maize pudding. Minutes later, I vomited it all up.

I WAS SO exhausted during the second endless night that I fell into a kind of trancelike state for short bursts, something between unconsciousness and sleep, which freed me momentarily from the nightmare of my punishment and the suffering taking place in the other cells. These were a very brief respite, a few blessed seconds in which I became deaf to the world, as if I were submerged in deep water.

It was hard to breathe, each inhalation painful, so I swallowed air in short sips, almost suffocating. Crouched in a corner I urinated a reddish liquid, and I did not know if I was bleeding from the womb or the bladder.

The dawn came on the second day of my captivity. The men returned, one a guard or low-ranking soldier with half his face disfigured by burn scars and the other a man who appeared to have more authority, perhaps an officer. They found me curled up in the same corner as before. The first man stood in the doorway, the second moved toward me and I braced myself for what would come.

"Do you know Rodolfo León?" he demanded.

I shook my head because I was unable to utter a single word, my mouth and throat felt as if I had swallowed sand.

"You want water, don't you? Then answer!"

"No," I murmured.

"I can't hear you! Speak up and don't lie to me, *gringa de mierda*! Do you know him?"

"No," I said again.

"We'll see if that's true. We have him in the next cell and we'll pull the names of all the dictator's spies out of him," he said.

"I am a journalist . . ."

"A spy! That's what you are, you filthy whore!" he spat.

They stood for an unending minute observing me before they finally left without touching me. A few minutes later the burned guard returned with a cup of water, which I swallowed in huge gulps.

"More, please," I begged him.

"I can't," he said, but he picked up the cup, left, and returned with more water. I did not dare to ask again.

Shortly thereafter, Rodolfo León's torture began. Through the wall, I could clearly hear the insults, the accusations, the beatings, the hate and violence, the most atrocious cruelty. They were not trying to get information out of him, they did not ask him any questions, not a single name. It was merely a punishment, revenge for his newspaper, for his career in the Chamber of Deputies, for his progressive ideas, for his loyalty to the president. His wails of pain were drowned out by the shouting of his tormentors, but Rodolfo did not break. During a pause in the torture, he told them that he had defended the legitimate government and the constitution, that he was an honorable Chilean, a husband and father. They did not allow him to say any more. I heard a dull thud, like a clay pot being broken, then a pause, a sinister silence, and finally a gunshot followed by two more.

"Take him away and clean up this blood," someone ordered.

I HAD VERY little time to mourn Rodolfo León and give thought to the fate of Sara and her child. Soon I was escorted from the cell by two guards and seated before three uniformed men who would try me for my crimes. I imagined that these were the very men who had fought at Placilla, sacked Valparaíso, spent the last two days torturing prisoners, and recently murdered my friend. They were dirty and looked as if they had not slept, strung out on the rapture of violence.

My appearance was much worse, and I reeked of urine, vomit, and sweat—filthy, disgusting. Fearing I might faint before they finished trying me, they brought in a chair and gave me water. I had been attempting to escape reality, holding tight to the memory of Eric and our nights of love, but when the interrogation began, my only thought was to maintain calm and not allow terror to get the better of me.

"Emilia del Valle, do you know what a war council is?"

"Yes," I responded, trying to control the trembling in my voice.

"Speak up!" my interrogator barked.

"A war council is a tribunal presided over by a general and other high-ranking officers," I said, remembering that I had used that information in one of the dime novels written by Brandon J. Price.

"Exactly!"

"They are set up to try military crimes . . ." I added.

"We are at war," one of the men interrupted.

"This is not my war. I am not a soldier."

"You are being tried as an enemy combatant. You participated in the Battle of Concón wearing the army's uniform. Any immunity you had as a member of the foreign press, you lost," he told me.

"I am a journalist from the United States. I have papers," I insisted.

"You came to Chile on the *Charleston* to confiscate weapons legally acquired by the Revolutionary Junta."

"I traveled here as a journalist," I repeated.

"We know that you collaborated with the dictator and you published articles about him in the United States."

"I interviewed President Balmaceda once for my newspaper," I replied.

"You also collaborated with the traitor Barbosa."

"I spent three minutes in the general's presence. I needed his authorization to interview the troops. All the other journalists did the same," I explained.

"You turned in the young men of the Revolutionary Committee

at Lo Cañas and, because of you, those men were all cruelly murdered."

"I did not know anything about that! How could I? I was in Valparaíso!" I exclaimed, despite knowing that any defense would be futile. These men had already condemned me.

"You are accused of espionage and high treason. This is a summary trial and your sentence is death. You will be executed by firing squad tomorrow at dawn. Do you understand?"

"No. And I do not understand this farce of a trial. You are going to kill me anyway, why bother whitewashing it with legality?" I managed to stammer. Then they gripped me by the arms and dragged me out of the room.

They returned me to the same cell I had occupied before. A few hours later the guard brought me a jug of water, a plate of soup, and a piece of bread, which I shared with my friend the mouse.

"They told me to ask you if you wanted a priest," the guard told me.

"Have them bring me a bishop," I responded defiantly, with the last spark of courage I had left.

THE HOURS PASSED slowly on my final night, giving me time to release the heavy burden of fear. I was not alone, the brave little mouse stayed with me, staring out from the shadows with its shining black eyes like glass beads.

Death was also with me, silently waiting its turn. It did not materialize as a repulsive skeleton with a scythe, but as a patient older woman dressed in white who inspired a strange sense of acceptance—a feeling that the story of my life had been written this way from birth and nothing could change it. I forgot the cold, hunger, and thirst that had tortured me since being imprisoned. I detached from my body and floated in midair, looking from above with a certain curiosity at the miserable woman lying on the floor. No, she was not on the floor, she was held in the arms of a red-haired man.

Eric appeared in the cell beside me exactly as I had seen him for the last time when we said goodbye in the doorway of the Flea-bitten Inn. I invoked him with all the formidable force of my desperation, and he materialized just as I needed him to, as a friend, a lover, a protector. I imagined the warmth of his body, the smell of his clothes, his breath on my neck, his firm chest and arms supporting me. He felt so real that I feared it was not some illusion created by my feverish mind but his spirit, venturing over from the Great Beyond to console me. No! Eric was alive! I had to hold on to that certainty and not even consider that he could have died at Placilla. Soon thereafter my parents also appeared to bid me farewell, and their presence calmed me, because I understood that Eric was like them, a vision, not a ghost. My mother knelt down to pray the rosary. My Papo sat beside me and repeated his most essential teachings: *Hold your head high, remember that everyone else is more afraid than you are, love and honor are the only things that matter.*

Rodolfo León and Angelita Ayalef, intact, without any signs of war or torture, came to welcome me over to the other side, along with Gonzalo Andrés del Valle, as young and handsome as when he'd seduced Molly Walsh. I was anguished to have to join them at only twenty-five years old, but they insisted that there was nothing to lament, because I had fulfilled my destiny, an existence complete with family, friends, adventure, love, and war. It was true, but I did not want to say goodbye to Eric so soon; we had only just fallen in love, we had not had time to get to know each other on a deeper level or create stories together, everything happened to us in a flash. *Oh! If I could stay forever curled up in your arms,* I told Eric. *And why shouldn't you?* he asked. My Papo says that we invent the afterlife because we can't bear the notion of vanishing into nothing, but my mother believes in heaven and in the eternal happiness of good souls. If she was right, Eric and I would be reunited someday, because he is a good soul and so am I; the thing about me being a bad woman was merely a family joke. I could do nothing but smile at the glorious idea of eternal life; it is very hard to remain agnostic on death's doorstep.

The memories came to me like elves, jumping and skipping into my mind without rhyme or reason: the swing that my Papo hung for me in the yard behind Aztec Pride, kind Rufina praying beside my father's deathbed, my first dime novel smelling of fresh ink and paper, the third-class passengers on the train from New York, the mate passed from hand to hand between the women of the mines, a golden sunset on the infinite ocean from the deck of the *Charleston*, my naughty brothers cackling as they fled my mother's thrown sandals, the marvelous intimacy of making love with Eric on a dilapidated bed. Other, more terrifying images slipped in as well, from Concón and the hospital, but I banished them, cursing. Get out, damn you, leave me in peace! And they were swept away like kites on the wind.

Since childhood, I have viewed everything that happens to me like a story narrated to a mute listener, and in that exercise of narrating, I am able to organize my thoughts and give meaning to my existence. That night, I longed for a pencil and a piece of paper to put down my memories, since, in a short while, rifle fire would erase my story completely. I knew that my life would not matter to anyone, it would be pure vanity to try to preserve it for posterity, but the pencil and paper would help me reconstruct the chain of events that had led me to that cell and perhaps accept the injustice of my sentence. I understood that the life of each and every soldier in that war was worth the same as mine, that all our souls were precious and all of us were at the mercy of forces beyond our control. I was going to die for nothing, just like those men, all of us disposable, anonymous, numbers tallied up by generals and politicians on the balance sheet of history.

I once again asked the Virgen de Guadalupe to keep me from faltering, that the dawn would bring me valor and dignity. And She responded that She would stay with me, that there was nothing to fear, that it would be quick. She said there would be only noise, that I would feel no pain, that it would not be a terrible end like Rodolfo's, like so many others tortured in that prison, or the poor soldiers left to bleed out on the battleground.

I suppose exhaustion eventually overcame me and I dozed off at brief intervals, accompanied by Eric and other spirits dead and alive. When the darkness began to dissipate and the first orangey light peeked through the cracks in the door, two guards entered my cell and shook me awake.

THE EXECUTION WALL was at the end of the prison's back courtyard. I imagine the neighbors—if there were any—heard the wails of the tortured and shots of the firing squad day and night. It had rained, and puddles shone out of the dirt like black mirrors. I took a deep breath of cold air, which still smelled of smoke and gunpowder; the piercing pain between my broken ribs was almost a pleasure, a sign that I was alive. The birds had returned. I heard them nearby and imagined that they were chirping just for me. A dog barked on the other side of the wall and I thought of Covadonga, wondering what had become of her. I felt the damp ground moving up through the soles of my boots, I was shivering with cold and fright; I clenched my jaw to stop my teeth from chattering.

The men had tied my hands behind my back, but I did not allow them to drag me along.

"Let me go. I do not need your help," I said. They heeded me, surprised, perhaps unaccustomed to executing women.

It was a long courtyard and in the center was a thick column tinged red with blood, the punishment post. Three days prior Balmaceda's detractors had been whipped there, and it now served to torture his supporters. I walked past trying not to picture any of that, I needed to imagine only Eric at my side, my Papo on the other, and my mother ahead of us praying, as well as the Virgen de Guadalupe and Her promise that I would die without pain. I slipped a few times in the mud, but the men who led me did not try to hold me up, staying a few steps behind.

I walked to the end of the yard, where the firing squad was waiting for me, five soldiers and an officer, and I stopped before the wall splattered with fresh blood. I was trembling, gripped by a visceral terror, drenched in an icy sweat. During the night I had resigned myself to my fate, but in those final instants, my courage waned. I murmured my Papo's words like a prayer: *Head high, princess, always held high.*

At an order from the officer, one of the guards approached with a rag to cover my eyes.

"Don't touch me, soldier," I told him. I was surprised by the firmness of my voice even as my body felt boneless, watery, ready to dissolve.

"Are you certain?" the officer asked.

"Quite certain," I responded.

The officer in charge hesitated before nodding and the guard stepped back with the blindfold in his hands. They placed me against the wall.

"Aim!" the officer exclaimed with a sword held high and I watched as the five rifles rose up in unison, five black holes. I closed my eyes.

"Fire!" the officer shouted.

The last thing I heard before falling to the ground was the thunder of the rifles. Nothing else, no pain, only darkness, emptiness.

14

∽

NO ONE COULD PREVENT THE REPRISALS THAT OCCURRED in Santiago. To the tolling of bells that announced the end of the civil war, the population took to the streets en masse to celebrate the fall of the tyrant. Chanting and shouting insults at the top of their lungs, they were a threatening clamor of hundreds and hundreds of voices demanding Balmaceda's head.

The indecisive general who had been designated by the deposed president to safeguard order and assure a peaceful transition of power was unable to do so. He was weak of character and did not have help; everyone, down to the guards of the presidential palace, had fled. He counted only a few police officers who did not dare to go out, because the mob threw stones at them. The city center and the main plaza outside La Moneda were flooded with a feverish horde from the slums, modest neighborhoods, and mansions alike, pouring into the adjacent streets like a sea of red flags, ponchos, conical straw hats, capes and rags, nuns in their black habits and exultant priests, top hats and ties, all mixed together, many of them brandishing clubs, canes, and knives. The revelry increased without any authority to curb emotions until it bubbled over into a lust for violence, a desire to beat, harass, burn, and destroy. Balmaceda's political prisoners were released and the cells were filled instead with enemies of the junta. Common criminals walked out the front gate to join the chaos.

Finally that tragic night began to recede and by midmorning it was sunny. That is when the well-organized plunder began. They traveled in bands, ironically called commissions, with a leader on horseback ringing a bell to announce their presence and carrying a list of homes, businesses, and offices owned by government supporters. These bands were made up of members of the Brotherhood of San José, as well as henchmen hired by the clergy and other conservatives, common criminals, miscreants, volunteers who figured as "decent people" and "guardians of order." Some firemen also joined in, along with a few priests interested in seizing works of fine art for their churches. They used carts and carriages to transport their spoils through the city. It was said that the aristocratic women and the priests had helped to build those lists, the same people who toasted the government's defeat with champagne. Precise instructions were given to leave all individual homes uninhabitable: Here, take whatever but do not burn it down; here, burn everything except the documents; here, break everything and take whatever; here, burn it to the ground. Residents were to be humiliated and terrorized but left alive, some arrested. The houses of those who had recently been in power were singled out and stormed, hatchets and clubs held high. Fine furnishings were tossed out onto the street and pulled apart, statues decapitated, priceless artworks sliced through, houses set ablaze. Everything that had been spared the hatchet was thrown onto pyres, including rare books from the personal libraries.

The victims were not exclusively upper class, plundering occurred at all social levels out of miserly revenge, resentment, and jealousy; all it took was an accusation of having collaborated with the government and no proof was necessary, mere suspicion was enough. Paulina del Valle's coachman had to hide as a mob destroyed his modest home and killed his dog. He had been singled out by his brother-in-law, with whom he had quarreled over a minor debt.

A commission reached the United States consulate to cries of "Death to Balmaceda!" Patrick Egan felt the Irish fighter reawaken inside him and he rushed outside, red with fury, accompanied by two of his sons. Unarmed, he addressed the exalted crowd in his broken Spanish.

"Balmaceda is not here! Even if he were, I would never turn him over to you! Get out, you swine! This is a diplomatic consulate! You will have to go through me to get in! That day will be the end of Chile!" Faced with that furious foreigner, the assailants retreated.

The rebels who had sheltered for months in the foreign consulates were reunited with their families, and the ones in hiding far from the capital announced their return, while the newly persecuted government supporters requested asylum in the same rooms, occupying the still-warm beds of their political adversaries.

The triumphant troops made their entrance into the capital amidst a delirious chorus of cheers and fireworks, military parades, and church bells announcing the fall of the Anti-Christ, the tyrant who had imposed civil matrimony, equality among *huachos* and legitimate children, and promiscuous cemeteries where Catholic and heretical souls were jumbled together as one. The junta set about occupying the presidential palace.

By nightfall, some order was restored as the exhausted crowds began to return to their homes, vandals and frenzied drunks having had their fill. That evening, a sad waning moon rose in the sky, obscured by the smoke that filled the air. The firemen gave themselves over to the task of stamping out the flames, and the newly recruited police force set about patrolling the streets. The looting of loan offices, liquor stores, and grocery shops, however, would continue for days to come.

Finally, when the fatigue was greater than the rage, the city began to recover some degree of normalcy. Civilians began to emerge timidly from their dens to evaluate the immense destruction, sweep up the rubble, rinse the blood from the streets, burn the animal carcasses, and bury the dead. The prevailing emotion was now a vague sense of shame over so much inexplicable hatred.

PAULINA DEL VALLE, who had been holed up in her mansion for months, tossed an opulent fur cape over her shoulders and went out on her husband's arm to measure the magnitude of the chaos and extend her hospitality to Balmaceda's mother. She found her friend's home with the doors and windows thrown wide, every corner stripped bare, with the fine French furnishings and the grand piano in splinters out on the street, and the marble bust of her son strung up from a lantern. A terrified servant informed her that the lady of the house had sought asylum at a foreign consulate, as had the rest of the president's family, but she did not know which one.

"Something must be done, Fredrick," said Paulina, thinking how it could have been herself who suffered that same fate in all the confusion and violence of recent months.

"What do you propose, my dear?" he asked.

"For starters, someone has to clean up this house, repair the doors and windows, make an inventory of the furnishings that were spared. I don't know, just figure out how to help my friend."

Fredrick Williams, imperturbable and efficient as always, carried out his wife's instructions. I imagined that the house would have to stay boarded up for years until the owner or her descendants were free to occupy it once again. By then, the echo of the civil war would be a vague recollection in our poor collective memory, Balmaceda commemorated with a statue on the main square, and his supporters returned from exile to participate once again in politics. I suspected that, if Balmaceda was correct, the parliamentary regime would fail and the ten thousand deaths would be but a footnote to the story of what occurred in this fateful year, 1891.

. . .

I WAS NOT executed by the firing squad. It is possible that my heart stopped and I was dead for a few brief instants—I do not know. The first indication that I was still in this world was the echo of faraway laughter, the joyless laughter of ridicule. I opened my eyes to see the line of the firing squad, laughing hysterically at me.

"Not today, *gringa de mierda*. Prepare to die tomorrow," the officer said.

Their rifles had been loaded with blanks.

I was not the only one forced to endure that senseless suffering. The brutal murder of Rodolfo León produced a chain reaction among the foreign correspondents who sent the news back to their countries. The rebels proceeded to destroy printing presses and publishing houses, arresting all journalists who had supported the previous government. Less than twenty-four hours after the gruesome details of Rodolfo León's death were published in Europe and the United States, the ambassadors of several nations appealed to the Revolutionary Junta and the general temporarily occupying the presidential seat. The junta was determined to shut down all of the opposition press in Chile, but they needed to establish legitimacy before the eyes of the world; it would not do to make enemies with foreign correspondents and see their image abroad deteriorate.

At this, several journalists who had been arrested and were waiting to be executed were set free, after first receiving punishment, and with the warning that they would receive no such preferential treatment in the future. Others, like me, were escorted before the firing squad only to be shot with blanks for cruel diversion.

They did not set me free, because I was unpresentable. They could not allow me to appear outside the prison walls, filthy, beaten, encrusted with dried blood, hunched over like an elderly woman, and breathing in tiny sips of air because of my broken ribs. I was one of the few women in the press and also a *gringa,* and I would have drawn too much attention. I suppose they were unsure what to do with me, and were awaiting instructions. They returned me to the same cell, and the soldier with the scarred face brought me a blanket, food, and a cup of black tea.

"Don't be frightened. I heard that they aren't going to shoot you tomorrow either," he said in a whisper.

But I did not have to wait that long to find out; they came for me that evening. The same officer I'd faced that morning before the execution wall entered my cell accompanied by another man carrying a pitcher of water and a bundle of clothes. He spoke to me in a formal, respectful tone, as if nothing of the previous mistreatment had occurred.

"We have brought you water and soap to bathe, señorita. We did not have a dress in your size, but you can change your underclothes and take off that apron," he informed me.

"You want to dress me up before you kill me? Then bring me a feathered hat," I responded. I'd been emboldened by what the guard had told me, that I was not to be killed.

"You have visitors," he responded dryly.

After I washed, they led me down a hallway and through a metal door. Waiting on the other side was Eric, tired and haggard, his jacket wrinkled as if he had slept in it. I couldn't move, but he stepped forward and wrapped me in his arms murmuring my name. I think he was crying. At his side was Paulina's husband, Fredrick Williams, impeccable in his tweed traveling suit with leather elbow pads and matching tweed hat. The two of them helped me out of the prison and into a waiting coach. Then I heard a sharp bark and noticed that Covadonga was in the street and had followed us. The faithful dog had been waiting for me all that time—perhaps without food or water for days.

"What about this dog?" Fredrick asked.

"She is mine," I murmured in a barely audible voice.

Without another word, Fredrick—a lover of dogs—invited Covadonga, who was skin and bones and covered in fleas, into the coach. She curled at my feet, exhausted, panting from thirst as we rode to the train station.

．　　　　．　　　　．

DURING MY INCARCERATION, time was distorted, minutes seemed hours, and I felt as if I had been in the cell with the mouse for several months.

Eric had been able to locate me after planting himself outside the prison with a lover's determination. Someone had finally confirmed that there was a tall, ragged *gringa* in one of the cells. Eric described the man as short with a disfigured face, and I knew that it was the same guard who had taken pity on me.

Understanding that he would not get anywhere without some influence, Eric sent a telegram to Ambassador Patrick Egan explaining my situation, and then sought out the navy captain with whom he had played so many hands of cards in the north. The Revolutionary Junta had put the man in charge of the maritime government of Valparaíso. Eric argued that I was a citizen of the United States, a journalist, and more important, a member of the del Valle family.

I estimate that just as Eric was making my case to his friend, I was being tried by the war council that condemned me to death. Without that captain's providential intervention, the firing squad would have most likely employed real bullets. Also thanks to that captain, who wrote a letter with clear instructions, they let me go when Eric came to get me.

I was so shattered that I let myself be guided onto the train without asking any questions. For several weeks, the trains had been exclusively designated for military use, but the war was now over, and Fredrick Williams somehow persuaded them to add on a first-class car so that we could travel in comfort. How did he accomplish that? I do not know if it was through mysterious connections with the new authorities or bribery, plain and simple. Inside, the car was wood-paneled and carpeted, with gas lamps, tasseled curtains, and seats covered in quilted green velvet, like a smoking lounge in some English gentlemen's club. We were the only three passengers, plus the dog, attended by a waiter who, per Fredrick's instructions, put a bowl of water in front of Covadonga. She drank and drank interminably. The waiter then covered the table with a long cloth and served us a three-course meal that included wine and dessert. I gobbled up the food, voracious, sharing it with Covadonga, and then began to weep from fatigue and relief. Eric tried to soothe me with embraces and a ballad of consoling words, as Fredrick Williams sat impassively smoking his pipe until I ran out of tears.

"Where are we going?" I asked, when my voice finally returned to me.

"To Santiago. I implore you to accept our hospitality, Emilia. What you need now is rest and care," the Englishman kindly replied.

Fredrick informed me that Ambassador Patrick Egan, upon receiving Eric's telegram, had contacted Paulina del Valle. Just as I had supposed, the ambassador was overwhelmed with a new round of refugees and negotiations with the Revolutionary Junta, who considered him a clear enemy. He could not personally remedy my situation, but he offered me asylum at the United States consulate as soon as I was freed from prison. Paulina del Valle had rejected his suggestion out of hand; that was what family was for and she had her own connections. I was no longer a *huacha;* I was the legally recognized daughter of Gonzalo Andrés del Valle. My place was in her home.

"The political situation is still quite unstable, Mr. Williams. I believe Emilia would be safer at the consulate," Eric said.

"No one would dare to touch Miss Emilia in our home, Mr. Whelan. Even when we were in opposition to the government, we were never harassed by the president's fearsome security apparatus. Now Paulina enjoys a position of privilege among the rebels," Fredrick Williams explained.

"I am very grateful," I said.

"Of course, the invitation extends to you as well, Mr. Whelan," the Englishman added.

.   .   .

I WAS QUITE ill for two weeks, urinating blood, and each breath felt like a tiger roaring in my chest. But I was very well cared for by the staff at Paulina and Fredrick's mansion. When I first arrived, they drew me a bath and saw that my body was covered in purple bruises that would take weeks to heal; I also had lice. They soaked my hair in vinegar and wrapped my head in a towel for a few hours, and then one of the patient maids removed all of the dead insects with a special comb. They also had to bathe Covadonga, who refused to leave my side and slept on my bed. Fredrick's mastiff and Paulina's lap dog did not take well all the attention she was receiving.

The family doctor, who had taken refuge in a foreign consulate at the start of the civil war in January, was finally free and paid me daily visits. He prescribed the same home remedies that my mother used— hot poultices of medicinal herbs, lemonade with rum, willow bark tea—and he ordered bed rest until my ribs healed. They assigned me a room with a view of the Andes Mountains from the four-poster bed with a fringed brocade canopy. Paulina wanted to hire a nurse for me, but they were all busy with those injured in the war, dying daily of gangrene, so I had to make do with the services of a nun.

Eric was given a room at the opposite end of the mansion, slightly less luxurious than mine, but quite comfortable. We were not married, and it would be improper for us to openly behave like lovers; the nun was present whenever he came to see me. We were almost never alone in that house, but it did not matter much because I was in no condition to commit the sin of lust. Eric was busy reporting on the transition of power in Chile for the *Examiner*. He had the generosity to sign his articles with his name and mine to remind Chamberlain that I was his correspondent as well. In his free time, he found an ideal companion in Fredrick Williams, who took him duck hunting and to sip whiskey with the gentlemen of high birth at his club. They discovered that they had a lot in common.

At first, Paulina del Valle would only occasionally look into my room to ask after my health, but once my fever subsided, she came in to sit with me, often accompanied by her granddaughter Aurora. The girl would pretend to read or draw, but she did not miss a word of our conversations. She was much sharper than her grandmother gave her credit for.

The visits became long and frequent, as she interrogated me over tea and pastries. She wanted to know all about my mother, my Papo, my life in San Francisco, even the few conversations I'd had with Gonzalo Andrés del Valle. I believe she might have been trying to ensure that I was not an impostor, that her nephew was truly my father.

As soon as I felt stronger, I began asking questions of my own, and it was like opening Pandora's box. That foul-tempered, distrusting woman told me about her family, her life, her first marriage to the man with whom she'd shared a runaway passion, as she called it, about how she made her fortune with ice in California and how she was doubling it now with her vineyards.

"I wanted Gonzalo Andrés to take over my wine business, but he was an idle loaf, like all the men in my family who don't even know how to clean their own asses," she informed me.

In Chilean aristocratic families, the unbreakable rule is that dirty laundry must never be aired. Paulina had finally accepted me as another del Valle, sharing with me the secrets of her extensive clan. I learned, for example, that I was not the only *huacha* in the family; several del Valle men had sown illegitimate children whom they did not recognize and whose unlucky mothers they refused to help. On one occasion, when we were alone, she confided that Aurora was the daughter of her oldest son. Just as her nephew had done with Molly Walsh, he had seduced a girl in San Francisco only to abandon her.

"But Aurora is no *huacha*, because one of my nephews put out his neck for the family. He married the mother and gave the girl our last name."

"Why does the girl live with you?" I asked.

"Her mother died in childbirth and her father, my son, died of a rare illness. The maternal grandparents kept her for a time in California, and then they turned her over to me. I am raising her."

"And what happened to your nephew, the one who married Aurora's mother?"

"I convinced him that the child was better off with me. He remarried, had several children, and continues to grow his brood. His wife is perpetually pregnant, but that doesn't stop her from being the most interesting person in the family. She has her husband and those children wrapped around her little finger, but she manages them with a sweet sense of humor. She has a clear mind and a generous heart, very much like me." Paulina said this without a hint of modesty.

IN ADDITION TO the broken ribs and bruised kidneys, I also had pneumonia, which is usually fatal, but I had been raised in the backyard of Aztec Pride with the hens and dogs, making me immune to the ills that often kill those of weaker constitution. I recovered more quickly than expected, stopped coughing up blood like a consumptive, and was soon able to get out of bed and take short walks in the garden with Covadonga. But I had to admit that I was not feeling strong.

"In light of the fact that you are not going to die, Emilia, the time has come to inform you of the inheritance your father left you," Paulina announced.

"Inheritance?" I asked, surprised.

"Do not get your hopes up, it is pitiful. As you know, Gonzalo Andrés squandered the fortune he received from his father."

She explained that Gonzalo Andrés del Valle's only possession had been a landholding. It was a tract of forest in the south of the country, in a valley of the Andes Mountains. Very remote, there were no roads leading there, only mule paths, and it was in native territory. The only whites who lived in those parts were Austro-Hungarian settlers who had arrived in Chile along with the German and French some forty years prior through a selective immigration law. The idea had been to populate the south with foreign craftsmen who would bring civilization and progress to the areas that the Chileans were still reluctant to settle. Reading between the lines, it had also been an attempt to whiten the race.

The plan had worked, according to Paulina. The immigrants were granted land that the Mapuche had called home for several centuries, and the settlers further expanded their plots through bribes of alcohol and fraudulent purchases at deeply unfair prices. When all else failed, they would simply find an excuse to shoot the natives.

"The Mapuche attack the settlers' farms, burn their crops, and kill their animals," she told me.

"With good reason, don't you think? It's their form of obtaining justice," I argued.

"Whoever told you that there was justice in this world? The stronger always win and the weaker are screwed," Paulina concluded.

She added that my father's land was not settled, because of its isolation and because it was useless for crops or livestock. He had been unable to sell it and had all but forgotten about it. Fredrick Williams had discovered the property title while going through Gonzalo Andrés's papers. As his only recognized descendant and therefore his only heir, I now owned fifty hectares near Lake Pirihueico, in the province of Valdivia.

"I imagine it would be of little interest to you, Emilia, but it is yours and if it ever acquires any value, which I highly doubt, you can sell it. Fifty hectares of wilderness is as good as nothing, so no one in this family will dispute your claim to it. They do not even know of its existence, and I will not be the one to alert them to it," Paulina added.

The first thing that came to my mind was my mother's obsession with the matter of the inheritance I should receive from my father. This news would delight her: Her daughter was a legitimate aristocratic landholder in Chile. The vicissitudes of the war, the beatings, the broken bones, the sinister joke of execution by firing squad—it would all be worth it to her mind.

That very night I wrote to tell her about it, leaving out the fact that it was a worthless strip of land deep in the south, almost at the end of the world. That unexpected twist of fate would finally allow my mother to free herself of the bitterness of her first love.

I DID NOT think again on that remote land until mid-September, when the doctor determined that I had recovered sufficiently to take a stroll in the park. It would do me good to be out in the pure spring-time air, with its court of bees and buds in bloom celebrating the new Chile, free now from the long winter of dictatorship and civil war, as that doctor declaimed in an emotional tone. He had a lyrical manner of expressing himself that did not seem out of place in that country full of poets. This was something difficult to reconcile, since the same Chileans who so loved the beauty of poetry were also quite bloody-minded. When I commented on this to Paulina del Valle, she answered that the Russians were the same.

"I knew several Russians in San Francisco. They were initially there to sell furs, but then they came for the gold. I am telling you, Emilia, they were true barbarians capable of the greatest brutality, but they would cry over romantic songs."

As soon as she began to suspect that I would not die, Paulina mobilized her relatives to build me a wardrobe appropriate for the changing season, since I had arrived at her home with nothing but the clothes on my back. As I shivered like a chicken in bed, the women of the del Valle clan paraded through with gifts of clothes. Paulina brought in a seamstress to lengthen the skirts and sleeves, but she was unable to find women's shoes in my size. When I had recovered enough to dress myself, I donned exquisite suits of organdy, gay straw hats, and my beaten-up boots, while a shoemaker fabricated more presentable footwear.

"Fix yourself up, Emilia. We are going to have your portrait done by the maestro Juan Ribero. He is quite famous. Those boots won't show, we will hide them under your skirts," the matriarch announced.

"You want a portrait of me?" I asked, surprised.

"It is not out of affection. You have not yet won that. It is so that I may remember your face once you leave and become the only member of the family outside of my orbit," she replied.

"You won't be able to tell me what to do," I commented jokingly.

"Exactly, California is too far for that," she responded solemnly.

Photography had not progressed much since my first experience posing with a dusty harp at the Dutchman's studio in San Francisco. In Chile, the images of the recent battles were already circulating, taken after the shooting had quieted down and there were only dead men left to pose immobile for all eternity. Desolate, smoking fields, corpses of men and animals, abandoned weapons, rubble and ruin. Perhaps one day the camera would be able to capture the action. Eric brought some photographs home and Paulina made sure they did not fall into Aurora's hands, because she was not of age to see such things, but nothing escaped that child's curiosity and cleverness. She insisted on accompanying me to the photography studio, where Juan Ribero immortalized us posing hand in hand, with almost identical dresses and frightened eyes.

ON SEPTEMBER 18, the anniversary of Chile's independence, the city awoke early with a riot of church bells calling the faithful to mass amidst a festive mood of patriotic celebration. Chilean flags and the red banners of the junta waved from windows of homes and public buildings, the plazas filled with improvised stalls selling alcohol and food. Rodeos were organized along with greyhound races, and the population dressed in their finest and took to the streets to drink and dance the cueca to the rhythm of guitars. Early on, the main streets were cordoned off for the military parade, and the soldiers who were not mutilated or dying goose-stepped down the street in an imitation of the Prussian army, trailed by bedraggled children and stray dogs.

All the "good people," as the members of the upper classes referred to themselves, attended the Te Deums presided over by bishops, dressed in gala attire, to hear the children's choirs and celebrate God's triumph over the liberals. The diplomatic corps and all the people of important surnames attended, along with generals of the junta, their chests covered in medals they had bestowed upon themselves. Father Restrepo was expected to grace the audience with one of his apocalyptic sermons known to leave the faithful sweating in terror—he was a great enthusiast of hell—but fortunately he fell sick with a stomach bug and was unable to attend.

"They say he drank bad chicken broth, and he is voiding his guts from both ends. He deserves it, the cursed priest," was Paulina's comment.

The matriarch indulged in the luxury of skipping the mass, but Fredrick, who declared himself a member of the Anglican Church, attended in the family's name. To anyone who asked, he said that his wife was indisposed. Two hours later she was seen unabashedly riding through the streets in her carriage.

Paulina and her retinue—which is to say Eric, her husband, her lapdog, Covadonga, and I—took the coach out to visit the stalls selling adulterated red wine and empanadas, which according to Paulina were filled with the meat of stray cats. They were delicious and she ate two. Then we watched the military parade. From a place of honor, the president of the junta extolled patriotic values and his victory in war, but the megaphone distorted his voice, and we could hardly understand a word. All that furious activity left me exhausted and I happily returned to Paulina's home and crawled into bed. Eric came to visit me while the nun sat in the corner knitting socks for the orphans, one eye fixed on us.

"I am thinking of going to the south," I told Eric. It was an idea that had been brewing in my mind the past few days.

"Where, exactly?" he asked.

"To a place near a lake called Pirihueico. That is where my farm is located, and I want to see it. Well, it isn't a farm, it is merely a tract of land. I have never owned anything, and it turns out that now there's this. How could I not go see it?"

"Why? And how are you planning to get there?" he asked.

"I still need to work that out. As I have no sense of direction to speak of, nor experience in exploration, we shall have to seek assistance," I told him.

"You speak in the plural, but I have no desire to face off with angry Indians and pumas."

"In that case I will have to go alone," I said.

I believe that he was just as curious as I was to see the south. Despite the brutal war we had witnessed, Chile had captivated both of us. That very night, we spoke with Fredrick Williams in the mansion's library, where the walls were lined in bound tomes that no one had ever read, and we planned our journey to where the Devil lost his poncho, as Paulina called that remote region. Fredrick was able to point out the exact location of the land that now belonged to me, marking it with a red circle on the map.

The following day, as we were having our breakfast of hot chocolate in the bird gallery, a rumor reached us. Eric and Fredrick went out to verify it and returned with tragic news. President Balmaceda had committed suicide in his room at the Argentine consulate.

SEPTEMBER 19, 1891
SACRIFICE
By Emilia del Valle

This morning at dawn the president of Chile, José Manuel Balmaceda, died of a gunshot to the temple. The president had been deposed by the Revolutionary Junta that emerged victorious from the civil war after the final battle waged near the port of Valparaíso on August 28. It ended a conflict that tore the country apart for eight months, leaving a balance of ten thousand dead.

After ensuring that his family was safe, Balmaceda sought asylum at the Argentine consulate on the very night of the army's defeat. His friend Ambassador José Evaristo Uriburu offered him refuge, never imagining what would come next. From a small room on the second floor, his guest watches as furious mobs demand his head and pillage the city of Santiago, including his mother's home. He is suspected to be hiding in the city, but his exact whereabouts are unknown. The Argentine foreign ambassador guards the secret, but the situation becomes untenable, as he fears that the rabble will storm the diplomatic seat just as they attempted to raid the United States consulate, where Ambassador Patrick Egan faced down the angry crowd and risked his own life to impede their entrance.

Days of anxious waiting follow, with no honorable exit in sight for the refugee, who spends his hours writing letters, drafting his political legacy, and reading articles threatening his life, calling him out as a traitor and a dictator, and blaming him for every ill that afflicts Chile. His initial intention is to turn himself in to be tried, and have the opportunity to defend his government and his person, but he changes his thinking when he sees the merciless revenge exacted by the victors. He learns of friends being imprisoned and tortured; he hears the faraway sounds of the firing squads. He cannot submit himself to be humiliated by those who clamor for his head, eager to wipe his government's achievements from the annals of history.

Ambassador Uriburu does not attempt to obtain a letter of safe conduct for Balmaceda, who will not consider fleeing like a cowardly fugitive. But the secret of his location is an uncontainable rumor, and the new authorities pressure the diplomat to turn over his guest. Refusal could provoke a grave international incident.

Isolated, disillusioned, the president is fully aware that his very presence puts his host at risk. There is no honorable exit. His only choice is to sacrifice himself, which is what he decides to do on September 18, the day that his term as president comes to an end.

Ambassador Uriburu returns from the theater, stops in to say good night to his guest, and finds the man at peace, almost jovial. It is past midnight, and the president prepares for his final act with the calm care that he puts into everything. He leaves letters of farewell for his wife, his children, and his closest friends. He dresses in his finest, unlocks the door, lies on the bed, presses the revolver to his right temple, and pulls the trigger. The bullet penetrates his skull.

The sound of the gunshot awakens Ambassador Uriburu, who enters the room to find the president's body sprawled across the bed and a thick envelope on the table. This is Balmaceda's political testament, written in a firm hand, in which he defends his government and accuses the Revolutionary Junta of imposing an arbitrary regime in violation of the law and the constitution. He concludes by calling for faith in democracy: "If our flag, incarnation of our truly democratic government by the people, has fallen rumpled and bloodied on the fields of battle, it will be hoisted again in a not-too-distant future by more numerous and more fortunate defenders than ourselves, to fly again in honor of all Chilean institutions and for the benefit of my nation, which I have loved above all things."

The president's sacrifice facilitates reconciliation among Chileans. A clandestine pamphlet is already circulating calling Balmaceda a martyr for the nation. Perhaps this is how he will be remembered by history.

I learned the details of the president's death from Rufina, the woman who cared for my father in his final days and with whom I had become friends. When she found out that I was convalescing at the home of Paulina del Valle, she came to visit several times, never empty-handed. She would show up covered in her black mantle, with a basket under her arm, arriving through the service entrance and humbly asking for permission to sit at my side to pray. Then she would fill me in on the latest gossip. There were no secrets among the servants of the prominent families. As much as they might try to protect their vices and errors from view, it was all common knowledge one rung down the social ladder. Rufina brought me sweets prepared by the cook at the Argentine consulate, natural remedies as efficient as the poultices and infusions prescribed by the doctor, images of saints said to work miracles, woolen socks, and other gifts that I was unable to reciprocate.

"I promised your papá that I would look after you, niña Emilia, and promises made to the dead are sacred. I am not able to look after you myself, but please accept these pastries, at least," she said.

I never dared to openly ask about the rumors of Balmaceda being harbored in the consulate, because I did not want to oblige her to lie in the case that they were true. But after his suicide, Rufina was able to speak freely. By then the news had caught fire like gunpowder at dawn and spread through Santiago via the infallible gossip mill, while the rest of the country was informed by telegraph. Immediately, there was a shift in the mood of the nation. The very same persons who only a day prior had called for Balmaceda's head now seemed embarrassed and repentant. Even the most radical Congressionalist newspapers measured their words. Balmaceda had redeemed himself in death.

Ambassador Uriburu had assigned Rufina the task of attending to the president, just as she had cared for my father before him. She had brought Balmaceda his meals, prepared his baths, washed his clothes, and even cut his hair and trimmed his mustache. She saw him writing away incessantly, marveling at the fact that he could put his thoughts to paper unwaveringly, never needing to make a single correction. The day prior to his death, he asked Rufina to iron his frock coat and most elegant shirt, as if he were planning to go out. He mentioned that at dawn, his mandate would expire and he would no longer be president. Then he bade her a kind good night, as he always did.

Rufina slept close by, separated from his room by a thin partition wall, and was the first to arrive on the scene when the sound of the gunshot echoed through the walls of the consulate. Minutes later the ambassador burst in. Rufina told me, sobbing, that the president was found lying on his back, left leg folded under the right, the revolver in his hand beside his head on the pillow, the bullet lodged in the wall behind him.

"The ambassador did not allow anyone besides me into the room until the doctor arrived and then the coroner, who presumed him dead, they said. I don't know what they meant since they did not need to presume anything, the man was dead as a doornail," she told me.

A crowd gathered in the streets surrounding the consulate, but this time no one shouted hate-filled slogans; instead, a respectful silence reigned. The people waited all day. At seven o'clock that evening a modest hearse pulled through the gates, stopped for a while before the front door, and then set off in the direction of the cemetery. A chaplain came out to announce that the president was no longer there, and to ask that the crowd disperse. A short while later, when the streets had emptied, a hired coach drove away with the remains of the president wrapped in a blanket, accompanied by two officers.

Police were posted along the way to prevent any possible attack, but nothing happened; the hatred had dissolved like salt in water. At the cemetery, the body was placed in a coffin and deposited in a tomb provided by one of Balmaceda's supporters. It was eight o'clock at night.

The president's political testament did not fall into the hands of the junta, who surely would have destroyed it. The original was safeguarded in a secret location by one of Balmaceda's friends, but copies of the document began to circulate from hand to hand that very day, allowing me to write my column.

Peace and prosperity were all but assured for the victors of the civil war and their supporters. The rest of the population would have to wait several more years.

15

ERIC AND I TALKED OF MARRYING SOON, MAYBE IN EARLY October at the San Francisco colonial church, the oldest in Santiago. In Chile, only civil matrimony was valid before the law, but the religious ceremony was what counted for most people. No one was considered truly wed without receiving the sacrament; the clergy and the women made sure of that. There were nonbelievers—no one used the term "atheist," which was an insult.

In our case, no one knew us, meaning that the religious ceremony would be intimate and simple, but Paulina del Valle decided to officially announce our engagement with a "ring ceremony," as it was called, celebrated with a large party. She purchased two gold bands without asking our opinion and invited the crème de la crème of her social circle along with the entirety of the del Valle clan. She had been cooped up inside for months, and she jumped at the excuse to throw her doors wide and remind the world who she was.

It was also a chance to introduce everyone to her great-niece, daughter of her nephew Gonzalo Andrés, may he rest in peace. No one needed to know that the charming *gringa* had been accused of spying for Balmaceda and had been freed from a prison cell just in time to avoid being executed. I was accepted without too many questions; it was enough to merely carry the last name del Valle.

Behind the matriarch's back swirled a hurricane of malicious gossip. Her wayward nephew's religious conversion and his decision to recognize an illegitimate foreign daughter on his deathbed were delicious morsels savored by all the gossips, additional condiments sprinkled on with each new retelling.

Fredrick tried to dissuade his wife from the party; he thought it poor taste to throw such an extravagant event while so many families still mourned. But Paulina silenced him with the reasoning that society had returned to normal. With this, she was referring to her social class alone—the rest of the population was not counted as "society." For the aristocracy, all that had changed was that gatherings now often included séances and Ouija boards to converse with spirits of the departed, in spite of the ecclesiastical prohibition of such activities, since every family counted one or more victims of the civil war.

A dazzling spring had settled in, lifting the veil of hatred that had darkened the mood of the nation. The junta's repression was not felt among people of Paulina's class, but I was aware of what went on beyond those circles thanks to Eric, who investigated broadly for his articles in the *Examiner*. I do not know how he managed to get his information with his serious linguistic limitations.

THE NOTION OF a wedding made me uncomfortable, because my parents would never forgive me for marrying so far away from home, to a man they hardly knew. Also, in all my twenty-five years, I had never felt the temptation to become a wife and mother. The world was too full of possibilities, and I wanted to experience freedom a while longer.

Eric was as enthusiastic about the wedding as Paulina, but I finally was able to convince him that we needed time to get to know each

other better. We could not make a decision of this magnitude motivated solely by passion, we should first give our love room to grow.

"We have known each other for almost three years, by my calcula-
tions, and friendship is a solid foundation for marriage. Also, the
word of a Chilean priest has no validity in the United States. You can
try me out, and if you find me to be a satisfactory husband we can
marry at home. It is no crime or sin to marry the same person twice.
If, on the other hand, you regret it, we won't have another ceremony.
You'll be free," Eric suggested.

"No. I don't think so. This cannot be a farce. Whether we marry
here or in any other corner of the planet, it's the same to me. Our
intention is what counts."

"I intend to love you forever," he said.

"Forever is a long time," I replied.

"Look, Emilia, this is important to doña Paulina. It would be dis-
courteous to deny her this; she has been very kind to you."

"We cannot marry simply to please her!" I exclaimed.

"Let us marry to please me, then," he insisted, smiling.

And we went on arguing about all kinds of things. Where would
we live? What would become of my column for the *Examiner*? They
would surely fire me, because they did not allow married couples, and
it was always the woman who lost out. And if we had children, would
he continue living his life while I would be forever bound by motherhood and domestic chores, no more travels or adventures for me, my
world reduced to four walls?

Around and around we went like this until I finally understood
that the emptiness in the pit of my stomach was not a consequence of
the beating I took in the Valparaíso prison or the bloody scenes of
battles and hospitals that tormented me each night. It was the crush-
ing weight of so much uncertainty. I was tempted by the notion of
having that kindhearted redhead as a husband, but I was not ready
yet. I was in love, but that was not enough to silence the internal

voice whispering a litany of doubts. I agreed to exchange rings with Eric at Paulina's engagement party, but we would put off the wedding until we returned to California.

Together, we drafted a letter to my parents. Eric formally requested my hand in marriage, and I asked them to begin organizing a wedding at the local Mission District chapel, where I would walk down the aisle on my Papo's arm, trailed by my mother and my three rascally brothers. My Papo could invite the entire neighborhood, just as he'd wanted to when we published the first dime novel under the name of Brandon J. Price.

PAULINA'S PARTY WAS a simple Chilean soirée—no imitating Versailles with a French chef, as she would have liked, because that would have been considered poor taste. Patriotism was in fashion. Instead, they filled the mansion on Avenida Ejército Libertador with bouquets of flowers, hung tricolor banners, and hired musicians to play popular songs. There was dancing and a banquet: a profusion of grilled meats, fresh shellfish, corn stew, cheeses, sweets, fruit, and red wine from Paulina's vineyards, served by her domestic staff and extra waiters hired for the occasion. Fredrick Williams organized the evening to perfection. It was definitively Chilean, but without too much false patriotic fanfare, abundant without being scandalous, refined yet unpretentious. This confirmed my belief that, in another life, he had been a butler.

The guests filled the mansion's reception halls and two dining rooms. Paulina had obtained tables of different shapes and sizes and had linen cloths tailor-made for each. Eric and I had to walk from table to table greeting each person as if we knew them, while Paulina presided over the evening from a magnificent seat, said to be a faithful copy of the throne of the queen of Hungary. Half of those in attendance were there because they owed the hostess some favor and the other half because they were afraid of her. A kind, pudgy priest submitted us to a mercifully brief sermon on a couple's duty to the family, society, the poor, and the church. Then he blessed the rings presented on a silver platter by little Aurora, and he blessed Eric and me. We were now officially engaged, and all that remained was to set a date for the wedding. In the meantime, we were expected to live in chastity and project an image of virtue and decency. At that part of the sermon Eric winked an eye at me, and trying to stifle a laugh, I let out a kind of bark that was echoed by Covadonga.

The guests drank, ate, danced, and sang until midnight, in light of the fact that the curfew had been lifted, and when they finally said their goodbyes, Paulina, feet swollen, collapsed exhausted into bed. The future bride and groom each went to our own rooms, as was proper, but an hour later, Eric tiptoed through the vast mansion and slid into bed with me. The nun had finally returned to her convent and we were at liberty to embrace in privacy. The contrast between that regal bed and the cot at the Flea-bitten Inn was dramatic, but we did not need feather pillows to indulge in pleasure; being together was all that mattered. We had gone several weeks without touching, but our unbridled passion was curbed by the fact that I was still quite weak.

And there, between Paulina's embroidered sheets, as we made love with the delicacy of an elderly couple, I finally told Eric about my affair with his brother Owen. Naturally, he was taken aback but I reminded him that at the time I had been unattached. I didn't give him any details and he did not ask for them. It was ancient history.

THE COUNTRY WAS a profusion of flags, military marches, and solemn acts of homage to the fallen. That is to say, the fallen among the victors—the others did not count. Spring in Santiago was traditionally a time for debutante balls, weddings, flower shows, horse races, rodeos, and traveling circuses, but, that year, all celebration was tempered by the tremendous weight of the war, a secret collective shame over the atrocities committed. The souls of the dead had not yet moved on, still wandering the earth in search of their scattered bones.

By late September, Eric and I had run out of excuses to prolong our stay in Chile. Back in San Francisco, Mr. Chamberlain was beginning to lose his patience with us—readers were no longer interested in the Chilean Civil War. My column on Balmaceda's death was the last piece published about Chile. Chamberlain sent me a telegram demanding I return immediately if I wanted to continue contributing to the *Examiner*. Eric was not threatened so directly, but was also encouraged to return, because his job as war correspondent had concluded. Peace was of no interest to anyone.

Eric learned that the next passenger vessel bound for San Francisco would set out from Valparaíso in five days and yes, we could travel with a dog; we had just enough time to prepare for the voyage and say our goodbyes to the del Valle clan. Eric had already mentally returned to California, and made his preparations.

But me? Of course my home in the Mission beckoned. After all I had been through, the idea of seeing my parents and my brothers was the sweetest prospect. I missed them. Not a day had gone by without thinking of home. And yet, something held me back. I was pulled between nostalgia for my life in San Francisco and something else that I couldn't name, something stronger than my usual curiosity, a kind of urgent calling. I felt like I had unfinished business in Chile: I had to see that parcel of land left to me by my father. I knew that it didn't make any sense, and that it would be almost impossible to convince Eric.

In the scant four months I had spent in Chile, I had aged. I had become physically more fragile and vulnerable, as if my skin could no longer protect me. The horrors I had witnessed and the proximity to death had made me sensitive to noise and tumult. What had before inspired me now left me overwhelmed. I did not feel capable of writing columns designed to entertain frivolous readers, like the one about the murder of Senator Cole or the indecent curves of the divine Omene. I needed solitude and silence. I needed time to absorb the new outline of the world as I now understood it, after looking death straight in the eye. It was an unknown world and I had to find my place in this strange new landscape. Somehow, I believed that the answers I was looking for were in that mysterious region in the south of the continent. I knew nothing of that territory—I could not even imagine it—but I hoped that there I would overcome my nightmares and recover my strength. I would never again be my old self, but maybe in the south I would become a new and stronger version of the woman I had been.

Eric assured me that we would return to Chile in the future and travel south together, but I knew that this was a journey I had to make on my own. I suggested that he return to San Francisco to appease Mr. Chamberlain and I would soon follow; we would spend Christmas together with my parents in the Mission District.

"No, Emilia, I don't think that's a good idea. One makes plans and then life spoils them. Why risk being separated? It would be tempting fate. I hope this isn't some excuse to put off the wedding. Or some way to get rid of me. You needn't be evasive. Tell me the truth, I can take it," he replied, angry.

"Of course I am not trying to get rid of you! How can you think that? I love you. I will always love you, Eric. I want us to be together forever; I even want to have those redheaded kids that you dream of," I said.

"Then I don't see what's preventing you from going back home with me."

"I will go home, but not right now. I need to find myself. I know that's a cliché, but there's no other way of explaining this feeling of being incomplete. There's something for me in the south. It's not a fantasy, Eric. It's a certainty," I told him.

"In that case I will go with you," he replied.

"No. You have to return to your work. I have thought this over carefully, Eric, and I know that I have to go alone. This is a journey to find my soul. Please, please, try to understand," I begged him.

"I can't understand, but I have to trust you, Emilia. I love the fierce person that you are. I will respect your decision even if it worries me terribly and it breaks my heart," he replied, holding me in his arms.

I felt his choked sob, the beating of his heart, the strength of his embrace, his smell of tobacco and wool, my own tears on his shirt.

We spent the little time we had left making plans during the day and making love at night. I suspect that by then everybody in the house, including Paulina, knew about those passionate nights but they pretended that it was not happening.

Finally, the time came to part. I saw Eric off at the train station with a knot in my chest and a feeling of foreboding in my heart. What if he was right, and this separation was tempting fate? Just before he left, I handed him a letter to my parents and a copy of my portrait taken by the photographer Juan Ribero. I told my parents that I missed them and how much I loved Eric and was looking forward to our wedding . . . but that in fact I might not be home immediately after all.

Eric would travel to Valparaíso and from there sail to California on an American ship, as I prepared to journey south in a few days' time. Why did I do it? Because, with a flutter in my gut, I felt a visceral, irresistible yearning.

Paulina del Valle whipped herself into a frenzy when she learned of my plans, which she considered to be absolutely ludicrous for many reasons but especially because I had not fully recovered my health. It's true that the illness had taken a toll, but that didn't change my decision to leave. In the end I had to leave without her blessing.

I estimated that I could make the trip in less than three weeks and fulfill my promise to Eric that we would spend Christmas together in San Francisco. I packed minimal luggage and went to the port, where

I obtained passage on a weathered two-masted Chilean schooner. Of course, Covadonga came with me, I could not leave her behind.

SEA AND MORE sea, short days and long nights, the sun winking out on the horizon, golden twilights, the moon gliding across the black sky, crimson sunrises, radiant noonday clarity, sepulchral clouds. On clear nights, Captain Janus would point out the Southern Cross and Sirius, the brightest, whitest star in the firmament. He was a gaunt man who claimed to have descended from Dutch pirates, with deep wrinkles and a white beard, surely not as old as he looked. He had made this voyage more times than he could count and was capable of reading the celestial map like the alphabet of the stars. The rhythmic lapping of the waves against the sides of the ship and the flapping of the sails in the wind cut through the silence of the ocean. Dolphins escorted us for long stretches and sometimes monumental whales as well.

The schooner, sweetly named the *Niña Juanita,* had traveled that same route for many years, with its yellowed sails like the wings of some prehistoric bird. It had six crew members in addition to the Peruvian cook and Captain Janus, who also acted as ship medic if need be, because in his youth he had taken a first aid course in the navy. On one stormy evening he distributed among the passengers a bitter tea that he assured us was nature's remedy for seasickness. By the smell of camphor I was able to identify it as laudanum, which I had administered in the Valparaíso hospital. We slept numbly for twelve hours, dreaming of thunder and lightning.

"Tell me, Captain Janus, have any of your passengers ever suffered a bad reaction to your natural remedy?" I asked him the next day, still a bit sluggish from the drug.

"Like what, for example?"

"Like a heart attack," I suggested.

"No, never anything as serious as all that. Just a bit of chest pain and cold sweats maybe. Vomiting their guts out would be worse, don't you agree, miss?" he replied.

The *Niña Juanita* was a cargo vessel with four simple berths for passengers. I was assigned to the smallest because I was the only woman on board, the others slept two to a cabin. Above my bunk was a canopy of tarred canvas to catch the water that filtered between the boards of the deck when the waves raged; whenever it became too swollen, one of the crew would empty it with a bucket. On more than one occasion, however, Covadonga and I were awoken by a shower of seawater.

I spent the better part of the voyage on the deck, in spite of the cold and sea spray, because my tiny cabin lacked any ventilation. Captain Janus supplied me with a board to place over my lap as a table, and in this way I could continue writing in the notebook I had started while staying with Paulina del Valle. My objective was to narrate everything I had experienced in Chile so that it would not be swept away by any gust of oblivion, but I unwittingly began eighteen years earlier with one of my most vivid memories from childhood, when my mother took me to see the decapitated head of Joaquín Murieta. From that moment on I had been unable to imagine my biological father any other way. Until three months prior, when I met Gonzalo Andrés del Valle on his deathbed, I had pictured him as that unfortunate soul with his eyes sewn shut and teeth bared in a horrific smile.

There was nothing to do aboard the ship. While the other passengers passed the time playing cards, discussing politics, and planning business ventures, I wrote. It never occurred to them to invite me to the card table since they considered gambling an improper activity for a young lady. They were wise, because I would have cleaned them out, just as I'd done with the officers on the *Charleston,* who would have lost the shirts off their backs if we had been playing for dollars instead of matches.

"I see that your notebook is almost finished, Miss Emilia," the captain commented.

"I have two new ones. I never run out of paper, Captain."

"What are you writing about?" he asked me.

"About my life," I said.

"Isn't that a bit premature? Your life has hardly begun. I, on the other hand, have a lot to tell and I would like to write it, but I don't know how. Could you help me?"

"If we meet again and we have the time, maybe I will, Captain Janus. For the moment, start taking notes on what you remember; that is how you begin to write a life's story," I told him.

MY EXPERIENCE ABOARD the *Charleston* traveling from California had been all empty ocean with no sight of land for days on end, but the *Niña Juanita* was a modest coastal trade ship and we were never far from shore. We would approach tiny inlets, tenuous and blurry, which looked as if they had been unpopulated since the dawn of time. But, as soon as we disembarked on the beaches of endless rocks to the clamor of marine birds and the barking of seals, the inhabitants would materialize as if by work of enchantment. They weren't many, barely a handful of tired yet curious men and women wearing heavy ponchos and wool caps, their skin tanned from sun and salt, children with black eyes full of wonder and cheeks chapped red from the wind. The *Niña Juanita* delivered mail and outdated newspapers and supplied the emporiums. As our crew stretched their legs and had a drink at the local tavern, generally nothing more than a small shack, Captain Janus distributed disinfectant; cod liver oil to strengthen the children; Dr. Ross's pills, which could cure anything except epilepsy; and condoms, handed out discreetly.

I would attempt to make friends with the womenfolk. We talked about their children, their work, the men who had left, never to return, and others lost to alcohol, bad weather, rain, and cold, the summer that always took its time in coming. They asked me what the capital was like and if it was true that the streets were lit with lamps, or if I had gotten the chance to try iced cream. No one mentioned the civil war, as if it were something that had happened in another time and place.

On a few occasions we stopped before a coastline of ancient boulders that seemed to have been carved by blows of some telluric axe. Only a few tenacious crew members would go ashore by rowboat, fighting the whipping waves. I went with them, the only passenger who dared to climb into that small vessel jostled by the ocean. The others were all serious men, a hydraulic engineer, a dentist, two entrepreneurs, a Protestant missionary aiming to compete with the Jesuits, and a Belgian scientist studying the virtues of the soil and climate for a banana company. Captain Janus advised him not to waste his time; Chile would never become a banana republic.

I MET FOREIGN families who lived isolated for months at a time, surviving on resourcefulness and hard work in much harsher conditions than those immigrants who had settled in towns and cities. Some had arrived thirty years prior, and had had children and grandchildren born in Chile, yet they still spoke only their mother tongue. The children were sent off to austere religious boarding schools in the north where they studied for nine months of the year, and spent the summers with their parents getting their fill of fruit and sunshine. These were people who had come under the auspices of the Chilean government, in many cases settling on lands that had been snatched away from the indigenous peoples who had resided there for centuries. With their homes handed over to the Europeans, they were condemned to poverty. This dispossession inevitably led to violence, but despite the constant threat and harsh living conditions, those foreigners loved Chile and would not trade it for any of the comforts of

Europe. For them, Chile was magnificent natural beauty, the scent of forest and sea, crystal clear air, hard silence. The rest of the country did not exist.

Those days I spent aboard the *Niña Juanita* were dedicated entirely to compiling memories in my notebook. I needed to write down everything I had experienced before I forgot. Suddenly I would think of something I had left out and have to slip a page or two in between the previous ones, or I might cut out a paragraph and paste it in somewhere else. My notebook was full of scribbles in the margins and extra annotations added in here and there. I was only able to read it because I had lived every word of its contents.

From time to time, when Captain Janus handed the wheel over to his skipper, he would sit beside me and we would talk about the memoir that he wanted to write. He said that remembering was important, that one had to look to the past to be able to understand the present and face the future.

"My life has been marked by change. I have always been restless— you and I are similar in that way. I start something and I am already thinking of finishing it to start something new. I suppose that's why I've had so many adventures, drawn as I am to the border of the unknown. I have done it all, even spent some time as a smuggler," he told me.

"But you've been captaining the *Niña Juanita* for many years, haven't you?"

"Yes, but I only sail for eight months of the year, when the climate is good. In winter, I go inland."

"Where do you go?" I asked.

"Before, I used to travel to other lands, that is how I saw America. But now I prefer the mountains, forests, and lakes of Chile. Why go off somewhere far away if the best of Creation is right here? Although it's true that you have to know how to get around in winter, study the land, weather the storms, trudge through snow, sleep under the rain," he explained.

"Fortunately, the weather is good. But they have warned me to be wary of the natives," I said.

"If you don't bother them, I don't imagine they will bother you. What you need to watch out for are the pumas and the bandits. The Mapuche are a warrior people, and they are hostile toward the whites with good reason. They call us *huincas,* which means thieves and liars, but they won't harm you merely because you dare to travel alone. They respect courage. Also, you will be entrusted to them."

"What does it mean that I will be entrusted to them?" I asked.

"I have some acquaintances among them. They accept me because I am a brother in name of the toqui Aliwenkura. He was a great warrior, but his tribe was defeated in the occupation campaigns against the Araucanía, and his spirit never fully recovered. I visit him almost every year. I will let them know about you. You will be protected," he responded.

AFTER SEVERAL DAYS of sailing we reached Valdivia, the first major port I had seen on that voyage. Here, I would disembark from the schooner. We entered a wide bay where a city rose up. The soul of Chile lies on the sea, the Pacific Ocean, which spans its entire length from the northern border down to the Patagonia. Sea, blue lakes, raging rivers, waterfalls, springs, persistent rains, snow, and tears, water everywhere, save for that tremendous desert of nitrate.

The city was marked by a clear German presence, with many settlers having built prosperous businesses in cured meats, leather, or dairy products, as well as in the sawmills and in commerce. There was a German club, two German schools, and a German hospital, in addition to several taverns that competed over homebrewed ale. Captain Janus invited me for tea and apple strudel, and later that night we tried the famous sausages with sauerkraut made from red cabbage. Everywhere we went, people greeted Janus; that man knew everyone. He advised me to rest for a few days and stock up on whatever

I might need for the remainder of my journey. I took the opportunity to have all of my clothes washed by a woman who earned her modest living with a bucket and Marsella soap. She patiently counted every article of clothing and returned them to me clean and smelling of the coal from the brazier she had dried them on.

In the United States and in Europe, some modern women wore trousers for horseback riding or biking, but I did not dare to dress that way in Chile. I'd learned from the canteen girls, however, the advantage of wearing pants beneath my petticoats, so I purchased two pairs from a gentlemen's tailor. I was not able to try them on in the shop, of course, that would have been scandalous. On the advice of the captain, who in the brief time we'd spent together had taken me under his protective wing and treated me with a brusque kindness, I traded my boots, which were quite worn, for some wide explorer's boots made in Germany that I could wear with thick woolen socks. I had told the captain of my plan to reach Lake Pirihueico and the tract of land that had been left to me.

"As long as you keep your feet dry and warm, you'll be able to walk far," he told me, examining my new shoes with his expert eye.

"I am going to have to walk a great distance, Captain," I said, showing him the map on which Fredrick Williams had marked my destination in red ink.

"That's true. It is quite far. How are you planning to get there? And what will you do if you make it?" he asked.

"I do not yet know. I shall have to see how I get along as the obstacles present themselves, Captain."

"That is very brave of you, Emilia. I can't imagine a woman alone on an adventure of this sort."

"Why not, Captain? I recognize that it must be much easier to be a man, but I am not going to let that hold me back. And I will not be alone, my dog will be with me. There is so much to see in the world!" I said.

"I noticed that you wear a ring on your finger. Are you married?"

"Only engaged, but we are planning to get married soon. I miss him," I responded.

"And why didn't your fiancé come with you?" he asked, surprised.

"He had to return to his job in California. Also, the truth is that I needed to come here alone," I explained.

"Too bad. He should not have left you. If you were my daughter, I would never let you travel alone through these parts," he replied.

"If you were my father, I would ask you to accompany me. Do you have children, Captain?" I asked.

"I had a daughter. She would be almost forty years old by now . . ." he said.

"What happened to her?"

"She went away with a saint at age sixteen."

"With a saint, you say?"

"He was a holy man from Brazil who came to announce the arrival of a new Messiah, like Saint John the Baptist. He worked miracles, or so his disciples said, but no one around here ever saw one. A charlatan, is what I think he was. My daughter followed him and I never heard from her again," he told me.

"Have you gone in search of her?"

"I am always searching for her, but I believe that if she was alive, she would have contacted me by now. She would know where to find me. A woman on her own runs a great risk. I would tell you not to go any farther," Captain Janus insisted.

"I have to do it. The risk does not overly concern me, Captain. You told me that you were a trekker and adventurer before becoming a sailor, so you must understand better than anyone the thrill of pushing onward," I responded.

"Yes, Emilia, but I am a man. However, if you won't listen to reason, what can I do? My daughter was as stubborn as a guanaco, too. You will need a warm poncho and a gun. I can get you a revolver."

"Thank you, Captain, but please don't trouble yourself. I wouldn't know how to use one and it would be a burden."

·   ·   ·

I DO NOT know when or why Captain Janus decided to accompany me, but he did not announce his intention to do so until it came time to say goodbye. When I went to pay the bill at the little hotel where I'd been staying, with my backpack and the canvas bag that contained my few belongings—the elegant clothes Paulina del Valle gifted me had stayed behind in Santiago—the captain was there waiting for me. He had traded his blue jacket and sailor's cap for a coat lined with sheepskin and a black beret that gave him the look of a Basque shepherd. He had trimmed his beard and he looked younger. At his feet were a sailor's sack and a large basket. He stood leaning on a shotgun.

"From here on out the journey will not be very comfortable. We will go by boat for a stretch and the rest on horseback or by foot," he explained.

"*We* will, did you say?" I asked, surprised.

"The *Niña Juanita* needs repairs. She is taking in water through several cracks. We'll have her fixed up here, which gives me time to guide you for part of the way."

"How could you think of it? You should not waste your time on me, Captain!" I exclaimed.

"I am not doing it for you, Emilia, I am doing it because I like to explore. I have been around those parts before, and I would enjoy seeing the lake again," he responded.

And so we went back and forth in this way for a few minutes, as Chilean courtesy demands, the captain offering to do me this favor, which I refused, to avoid being a bother. Finally, I was allowed to pretend that he had persuaded me with his arguments, and he pretended that I had agreed to keep from disappointing him.

We bid farewell to the crew, who would take care of the ship's repairs until the captain returned. Then we made our way to the river port, where the boatman Janus had hired waited for us. He was a large, dark man, square as a wardrobe, with a kind, mostly toothless smile, wearing tall fisherman's boots. He was the owner of the vessel, simple but in good condition, complete with an awning to protect us from sun and rain. He arranged our scant luggage, and before I had time to protest, he lifted me and effortlessly deposited me inside the boat. He did the same with Covadonga, who after sailing on the ocean was no longer afraid of water. Janus sat in front to balance out the weight.

16

THE BOATMAN HAD GROWN UP NAVIGATING THE CALLE-
Calle River in both directions, he knew every bend, every obstacle,
where to double his effort and where to let the current aid our advance. He rowed hour after hour until the sun set, singing all the
while. We stopped three times, twice to stretch our legs and once to
eat. The captain opened his basket and presented us with an unexpected spread of provisions: grilled chicken, cold cuts, cheeses, fresh
bread, fruit, sweets, and two bottles of red wine that were received
like a blessing. I was dizzy, despite the fact that the boat rocked very
little, and I supposed I was still feeling the final traces of the beating
I'd suffered in prison and the fevers that had plagued me during my
recovery at the home of Paulina del Valle.

Water, lakes, rivers, swamps, forests, hills, far-off peaks of mountains and volcanoes; the proud spectacle of nature greeted us as we
ventured deeper into the country with each new slap of the oar. The
captain explained that there were hundreds of volcanoes in Chile,
which is why no one was frightened by a little tremor; they reserved
their panic for the true earthquakes, the ones that toppled everything
to the ground within seconds, ripped cracks in the earth, filled the air

with dust and the ground with rubble, killing humans and animals alike.

It is impossible to describe that majestic landscape with only a pencil and paper, it would take a poet to even attempt it. The vast expanse of millenary trees, the coigüe, canelo, araucaria, hazelnut, and cypresses of the Andes Mountains. Green—a hundred shades of it—and, sometimes, from on high, the blaze of a red copihue, the national flower of Chile. Birds of all varieties, choruses of boisterous song and suddenly the silent flight of an Andean condor. The pure, crisp air like crystal that seeps into every corner of the body and soul, rinsing clean the secret pathways of the veins and thoughts. I sucked in that air, my heart open and my eyes brimming with tears, my gratitude so deep that I could not find the words to express it, constantly murmuring private prayers, *Thank you, thank you, thank you, thank you for not letting them kill me, thank you for letting me live to make it here to this original paradise, this virgin landscape, thank you, a thousand times thank you.* Captain Janus openly observed me and I think he understood my emotion over so much sacred beauty. Perhaps he even shared it.

"I never imagined a place like this existed, Captain," I confessed, my voice breaking.

"Wait, Emilia. You have not yet laid your eyes on Lake Pirihueico. It is the most beautiful place there is, I can assure you, and I've seen most of the world," he responded.

"I feel like I've been here before, Captain. In another time, in another life. I wish I could stay here forever," I told him.

"What about your fiancé?" he asked, winking an eye.

I realized then that my memory of Eric had not been lost to that enchanted landscape, and I felt his absence with a pang of anxiety. He would still be on his way to California, making plans for our life together, while I was drifting farther and farther away.

.   .   .

THE SUN SET late in those latitudes and evening was just settling in when the boatman left us at a rotting wooden dock. He bid us farewell with the enigmatic advice to watch out for *wekufes*. Janus explained that, according to local lore, these were maleficent spirits.

There was no human in sight, no trail, nothing. There, in that vast solitude, the last leg of my adventure would commence. Janus carried my pack as he began to cut a path through the brush, and twenty minutes later we found ourselves in a clearing in the vegetation with a grouping of four or five shacks made of mud and straw. Weak columns of smoke escaped from a hole in the roof of two of the dwellings. Several horses, hens, and a hog occupied the central space, a common patio where most of daily life was surely carried out, as indicated by the glowing coals. The barking of the dogs alerted the inhabitants to our presence.

The children peeked out first, followed by the mothers, pure Mapuche women in their traditional garb. Janus greeted them in their language, and we stood waiting as they silently observed us and their dogs continued growling and barking. Finally, after what seemed like a long while, two men stepped out of one of the *rucas*. They were advanced in age, their skin crisscrossed with wrinkles and their black hair peppered with gray. One held an old double-barreled shotgun and the other a short axe. But their distrusting attitude faded when they recognized the captain.

Just as Janus had said, his friendship with the toqui Aliwenkura served as a letter of safe conduct, allowing us to overcome the hatred of whites that dated back to the Spanish conquest in the sixteenth century, and had been exacerbated by the Chilean government's recent war for the control and exploitation of Araucanía lands. These elderly men were relatives of the toqui, part of the intricate nexus of family ties connecting all the tribes of that territory. We were invited into one of the *rucas,* a round, dark, windowless hut with a small fire built on a bed of stones in the center. It smelled of herbs and manure, which was used as fuel.

Janus sat down with the men on sheep hides and the women seated themselves on the pressed dirt floor. The men shared *muday* and the offer was extended to me as well, as a guest and a foreigner, but not to the other women. This was an alcoholic drink made of fermented maize or grain served in a clay cup. I found the taste repugnant, but I swallowed it down without wincing, because Janus had warned me that rejecting an offer of food or drink was considered an insult. I later learned that the women chewed the grains of maize and spit them into a clay jar as a step in the fermentation process. The culture of hospitality, a common trait of rich and poor alike, was alive even there, among people who did not consider themselves Chilean, but children of the land.

This was a small clan made up of grandparents, women, and children. I did not understand a word they said, but Janus later told me that they were going through hard times; the winter had been one of the worst in memory. The young men that survived the military roundup had gone into the mountains to keep from being captured. They had heard that the war was over, but they did not yet dare to return, remembering all too well the cruel abuses of the pacification campaigns that had taken everything from them. They feared the government.

In the evening, the women cooked a maize pudding with strips of jerky and squash, unappealing in appearance, but tasty. When the sun set, the temperature dropped and as the men continued drinking *muday,* so inebriated they could no longer speak, the women curled up with the children, covered by heavy woolen blankets. On that hard ground, with my backpack as a pillow and my dog at my side, I slept deeply for seven hours.

AT DAWN, JANUS was waiting for me fully dressed, his hair wet after bathing in freezing water. He showed no signs of a *muday* hangover; he must've had guts of steel. He had persuaded the men to lend

us two horses with the promise to return them in good condition—
old, hardy animals apt for any terrain and capable of withstanding the
cold. He informed me that the horses could only take us so far, and
from there we would have to walk. I knew that I would not be capable
of carrying weight for long stretches, so I placed only the essentials
in my backpack and left the rest with the Mapuche family. I had been
told that the indigenous people were accustomed to sharing everything they had and for this reason they did not respect private property, but most of the things I had brought no longer felt truly
necessary. One can survive on very little.

An hour later we set out single file. Janus marked the way as I followed behind him, hypnotized by the landscape. A girl of about
twelve years rode behind me on the rump of my horse. She would
take the animals back to her family.

For several hours we followed a trail that was invisible to me, but
evident to Janus and the horses. Large native trees flanked our passage, so tall and leafy that the sunlight barely filtered through their
canopies. We did not pass a single person in that vast, infinite solitude. We traveled in respectful silence, listening to the life all around:
the trilling of birds, the murmur of foliage, the babbling of brooks
and springs, the tromping of the horses. We rode all day, followed by
Covadonga, and at a certain point Janus let us know that we would
have to pick up our pace, because night would soon fall and we could
not continue on in the dark.

We finally arrived at a primitive cabin made of log and stone, windowless, with a door disproportionately tall and wide, that seemed to
rise up out of the vegetation by an act of enchantment. It was an old
smugglers' outpost known only by the men of that trade. The interior
contained a wooden platform that served as a bunk, a rustic table, a
cookstove, a woodpile, and a metal drum of water; enough to spend
a few nights. It had been several years since Janus had traveled that
unmarked trail that did not figure on any map, existing only in the
memory of those who used it, but he remembered it perfectly. He

explained that, in recent times, in addition to the goods and animals that had always been smuggled over the border, deserters from the army crossed clandestinely, along with people escaping political persecution in Chile, just as in other times fugitives from Argentina had fled in the other direction. I thought of Rodolfo León and his cruel death—if he could have reached these secret trails through the mountains, he might have been saved.

We ate jerky, bread, and hard cheese that we carried in our bags, washing the frugal supper down with mate and sips of hard liquor to warm our bones. My horse turned out to be quite capricious, digging in his heels or taking off at a trot of his own accord. He once whipped his head around angrily and I thought he was going to bite me. I am not accustomed to riding, since my family could not afford the luxury of horses. All we'd had was Alberto, a lame mule that my mother saved from the slaughterhouse to become our pet. Alberto spent his old age well attended to among the hens, dogs, and cats; no one ever would have thought to ride him.

The result of so many hours straddled on horseback with only a blanket for a saddle left me with my backside bruised and my thighs chafed raw. In addition, my ribs had not fully healed. The girl, who had not said a single word since we set out, burst into laughter when she saw me waddling around like a duck. She gave the animals hay and water, as she animatedly conversed with them in her language, and then she led them into the cabin. That's when I understood the reason for the tall, wide door. The smugglers had to hide out with their horses.

"So they don't get stolen," she said.

There was no one around, however, and I think she simply wanted to protect them from the cold. With the animals inside, the space was reduced by at least half, but I felt warmed by our large travel companions, with their sweet musky scent. The girl and I squeezed together on the bunk and the captain lay down on the floor next to Covadonga. I fell asleep to the sound of the man's snoring and the horses' deep sighs. The girl, curled beside me, smelled of smoke and she talked in her sleep.

THE DAY DAWNED cloudy, the light filtering down through a foamy bride's veil. The girl was the first to awaken, and when she took the horses out I saw her stop in the doorway and murmur something that seemed like a prayer, as if she were greeting the day. She and Janus went to fetch water and cut firewood, because the rule was to leave the shelter for the next traveler just as one had found it. Meanwhile, I cleaned up the manure. After a breakfast of mate and the rest of the bread, the girl prepared the horses. I was unsure as to whether I would be able to stand another day like the one before; the night's rest had done little to ameliorate the pain in my bones and the irritation on my skin. I was afraid I might turn out to be sickly like my mother, who jotted down her daily ills in the notebook she also used to keep track of our accounts.

That second day we rode slowly for many hours, always followed closely by Covadonga, who was much stronger than she looked. The clouds dispersed early and we were gently warmed by the rays of sunlight that passed through the foliage. The ground was strewn with obstacles, the forest so impenetrable in some parts that we had to forge a new path, the faint trail having been swallowed by the vegetation. I felt like we were walking in circles, but the girl and the captain seemed confident of the direction. We bordered river basins and swampy wetlands flooded by winter rains. I came to a truce with my horse. Perhaps he took pity on me, but, whatever the reason, he adopted a smoother gait and did not give me any more trouble.

I calculated that it was around three or four in the afternoon when we began to approach a volcano, its sides black with dried lava and peak glimmering with snow. The captain explained that it was actually twin volcanoes, both dormant for the last twenty-five years. The girl announced that this was as far as she would go, she had to return with the horses. She said that the volcanoes were grumpy and angered over any little thing, one never knew when they would spit fire from their mouths. She added that one of the volcanoes did not have a tip because it had lost it in a fight with another mountain and she warned us that *pillañes* roamed the area, magical spirits of thunder, lightning, and burning lava. It would be wise to make them an offering.

Janus decided that we would camp right there, and he tried to convince the girl to stay with us, but she said that she had relatives she could stay with less than an hour's ride away. She was frightened of the *pillañes,* but undaunted by riding alone through the forest.

CAPTAIN JANUS SET up a basic campsite with a shelter of branches and a small bonfire, where he heated water for mate. The aching in my body had increased, I felt worse than the day before; every movement was an effort, each inhalation ricocheted through my ribs. Although I tried to hide it, Janus divined my discomfort. He gave me a sip of liquor and had me chew tobacco to relax my muscles. He also offered me sheep fat to rub on my skin and muscles. He walked away to give me privacy, with the excuse of setting some traps, and I took off my pants and rubbed myself down with the thick pomade that smelled of cheese.

For dinner, we ate most of the food we'd brought from Valdivia, jerky, hard bread, and a handful of walnuts, but Janus did not want to touch the four potatoes we still had left. He didn't seem worried, confident he would be able to trap more food. He told me that during his travels he had walked for months with no luggage besides a blanket, a hatchet, a knife, and the clothes on his back. That was enough to survive, he assured me.

We spent the rest of the night huddled under the improvised shelter of branches, back to back, covered only by my poncho and the clothes we wore. Something seemed to give way inside me, and I entered a strange state of mind in which habitual rules did not apply. I fell asleep leaning against a man I had met only ten days prior, warmed up by the dog on the other side, remembering those wonderful nights of love and confidences with Eric in the Flea-bitten Inn and thinking of my parents, my mother baking bread at dawn, my Papo with his smell of cigarettes and his large hands braiding my hair and telling me about comets and asteroids. The captain was a calming presence, solid and warm. With him I almost felt as if I were back in the safety of my home in the Mission District.

As soon as the day began to dawn, the captain got up to check his traps and returned with a wild hare. As he stoked the fire, I removed the hide and guts, as Angelita Ayalef had taught me in the army camp, and sprinkled it with salt to cook it on the coals. It was a small animal, and once skinned and grilled it was reduced to almost nothing, but we were hungry and found it delicious. Before leaving, Janus made sure that we stamped out the fire. He told me that each year forests caught fire because of lightning storms, this was a natural and necessary process, but that it was a sin for a human to start a forest fire. We set out at an unhurried pace, because, as the captain said, he who goes slow, goes far.

The captain's care eased my pain. As we advanced step-by-step I stopped thinking about my discomfort and was able to appreciate the supernatural beauty of that landscape, untouched since the dawn of the world. I don't know how many hours we walked through that vegetation so dense that the horses would not have been able to pass, but it must not have been as many hours as it seemed, because the sun was still high when suddenly, around a bend, Lake Pirihueico appeared. It lay at our feet, long and narrow, undulating, crystalline, calm, a deep blue framed in the distance by the tall mountains and forest reaching right down to its shores. Janus explained that it was a glacier lake, one of seven such in the region, more beautiful than all the rest and the most remote. Its name meant snow lake.

"Very few travelers venture this far," he commented.

"I hope there is never a road that will allow them to," I added.

"Exactly, Emilia. That way they cannot come and cut down the trees to raise animals, as they have done in other parts."

It took us another two hours to descend the slope and advance through the tangle of trees to a small inlet. The captain announced that, according to Fredrick Williams's map, I would have to travel all the way across the lake to the extreme southern shore, and from there walk to the base of the Andes to reach my land.

"Now we wait," he added, and he set about gathering wood for a fire.

"What are we waiting for?" I asked.

"For the boatman."

"How do you plan to notify the boatman that we are here?" I wanted to know.

"Do not be impatient, Emilia. Here, clocks and haste will do us no good, time cannot be measured and plans cannot be made, we just live. It might be several days, depending. Sooner or later someone will let the boatman know that we are waiting. Where there is no mail and no radio, news travels by word of mouth," he responded.

"That may be so, but I don't see anyone around at all, Captain."

"There are very few people here, it is true. Not counting the *sumpalles,* the tribe of mythological creatures that live inside the lake and look after the waters, according to legend."

We bathed in the lake wearing our underwear to wash off the dirt and sweat. The first blow of cold water took my breath away, but once I had fully submerged myself I felt cleansed inside and out, purged of the war and the nightmares that still plagued me, reconciled with life, and with my memories. Suddenly the idea of claiming the land bequeathed to me by my father seemed as absurd as trying to take possession of the air or water. My objective was ridiculous; that pristine nature belonged only to the gods and spirits. I did not own anything, I was merely a visitor.

I asked the *sumpalles* in the lake to let me stay with them awhile longer, floating weightlessly, with a wig of reeds, a petticoat of foam, and a vest of fish scales. That is what death must be like: silent, cold, peaceful.

WRAPPED IN MY poncho I warmed up by the fire that Janus had built to dry our clothes. He also improvised a few fishing rods and planted them on the shore. The day was spent building a roof of branches, like the one that had sheltered us the night before, drinking mate, and conversing. We did not catch a single fish and had to make do with potatoes cooked on the coals because the little jerky we had left was for Covadonga. The captain taught me to eat very slowly to fool my hunger. Later, as he smoked his pipe with tranquil delight, I chewed some tobacco to ease the pain in my legs. He had ridden and walked as far as I had and was at least forty years older, but he seemed immune to fatigue.

We spent a long while talking around the campfire, the only hint of light in the absolute darkness that enveloped us. If there was a moon, it must have been hidden by the clouds. I told Janus about the civil war, and he recounted tales of other wars he had participated in as a young man. I asked him about his travels and he told me of the legends and magic he had seen. He said that there were many realities and parallel worlds, which our senses were not sharp enough to de-tect, but that sometimes it was possible to cross the veil that blinds us and briefly glimpse other dimensions. Seeking out that experience, he had tried strong drugs, ceremonies, and ancient rites, extreme fast-ing, hypnosis, and meditation, pushing his body and mind to the lim-its of resistance.

"But I have never had a true revelation. That is something that cannot be found by searching for it, it must come like a gift," he con-cluded.

I confessed my strange experience in the cell of the Valparaíso prison, that night when I waited to be executed at dawn, when the specters of the living and the dead came to bid me farewell, and the Virgen de Guadalupe appeared to console me.

"The fear drove me mad, Captain," I said.

"Do not try to understand what happened, my friend. It is an enigma. Guard that moment in your memory like a treasure," he replied.

Just as we had done the previous night, we slept fully clothed down to our boots, huddled as close together as possible for warmth. The captain rested very little, because he got up several times to stoke the fire that offered us a bit of heat and enough light to keep the pumas away. I was also unable to sleep due to the cold and pervasive humidity that penetrated my very bones.

I anxiously anticipated sunrise, but at dawn we saw that a fog dense as meringue had settled in. The mountains and the forest had all but disappeared and the lakeshore was but a line of steely gray. I imagined that no one would come for us under those conditions and resigned myself to wait an unspecified period of time—the possibility no longer seemed so grave. There was no hurry, as the captain had said.

IT WOULD APPEAR that the fog has settled in to stay. I am becoming accustomed to the hunger. At times I feel nauseous and if I weren't so certain that it was impossible, I would suspect that I was with child. All it takes is a moment of carelessness, which Eric and I had in August, and a woman's life is forever changed. I am also becoming accustomed to the pain in my legs, which has extended to the rest of my body, but it wanes when I become distracted. Pain is only pain, it can only be endured, as Angelita Ayalef taught me.

The captain let me know that this was as far as he could take me, to this threshold, beyond this point I will continue on my own until I find what I am looking for. He must return to the *Niña Juanita*, to his crew and his life. But he assured me that I will not be alone because the boatman will take me to the southern edge of the lake, where someone will be waiting for me.

Thanks to this notebook, which keeps me occupied, the hours slip by easily and the morning has soon been spent. I write and write although I can barely make out the letters through the cottony gloom. My notebook is full, and when I reach the foot of this final page, I will not be able to add a single word more. But I will continue writing my life in another until I run out of memories.

The captain has a habit of quietude, which I suppose is necessary in his life on the sea. Aboard the schooner he spent the better part of his days at the wheel, his eyes lost to the horizon, immobile and silent. This is how he has been all morning. He has excellent vision, despite his age, and it was he who first divined the presence of the boat, barely a pinpoint in the fog.

"Here comes the boatman, little Emilia. It is not too late to return to civilization. I have been observing you, and I believe you are unwell. What's wrong?" he asked.

"Nothing serious, I think I just caught a touch of cold, that's all," I replied, but truth be told I felt weak and feverish.

"You should not continue on," he told me.

"It will only be a few days, Captain, don't worry."

"How do you plan to get back? Do you feel capable of retracing the route that we have just followed?" he asked.

"No," I admitted.

"You have bathed in Lake Pirihueico, what more do you want? The other side is identical to this one. Come back with me," he said again.

"I want to finish this Chilean odyssey of mine properly, Captain. I can't give up at the last moment, don't you agree?" I responded.

"There is nothing to see there, your property is an illusion. It is not marked and even if it were, what good would it do to reach it?" he insisted.

"You're right, Captain Janus. I own nothing, but I have to go on a little farther so that I may tell my mother that I was here. It doesn't matter that I will never see this lake again," I said.

Nevertheless, I know that one day in the far future I will return, because I belong to this landscape. I imagine living out my final years here—dying here and letting my body disintegrate into fertilizer for the soil. But for as long as my mother and Papo live, I want to be near them. And what about Eric? I pray that he will come here with me, that he too will grow old and die here. This magical place in the south of Chile holds my most ancient roots, the roots of my indigenous, Spanish, and mestizo ancestors, running much deeper than my mother's connection to Ireland or mine to California. This is the only explanation that occurs to me to describe my irresistible attraction to this faraway land at the foot of the volcanoes. My father's legacy is much more than fifty hectares of land, it is my roots.

Epilogue

ᘓᘓᘓ

ERIC WHELAN

IT WAS ONE OF THE HARDEST THINGS I'VE EVER HAD TO do to leave Emilia and return home to San Francisco. It felt risky, even dangerous, that we should be putting more and more miles between us, as she traveled south and I traveled north. The thread that connected us unspooled farther and farther, though I always felt it there, binding us together.

Emilia's parents welcomed me warmly when I turned up with the last letter she had written them. They began to plan our wedding, just as she had asked. We awaited news from her for months, growing anxious, because she normally wrote to her family at least once a week. I communicated with Paulina del Valle and with Ambassador Patrick Egan in Chile, but neither of them had heard from Emilia either. Although they promised to attempt to locate her, I never obtained any response.

Emilia did not return to California before Christmas, as we had agreed.

It was not possible that my future wife had simply vanished from the face of the earth. In February 1892, having suffered more sleepless nights than I can describe, I could wait no longer. I bid farewell to Mr. Chamberlain and my colleagues at the newspaper and prepared to return to Chile in search of her.

Shortly before my departure, an envelope with Chilean stamps arrived for me at the *Examiner.* It contained a letter written in Spanish and dated five weeks prior. Emilia's parents translated it for me. This is what it said:

Esteemed Mr. Eric Whelan,

Please excuse me for writing to you without a proper introduction. This letter might seem like a serious intrusion in your private affairs, but be assured that I have taken this initiative in good faith and with great respect.

I am the owner of the *Niña Juanita,* a commercial sailboat. I had the honor of meeting Miss Emilia del Valle recently, when she booked passage on my ship to travel to the province of Valdivia in southern Chile. On the way, we became better acquainted, and she told me about you.

As you know, she wished to visit a piece of land belonging to her near Lake Pirihueico. The lake is quite extensive, irregular in shape with innumerable bends and curves, but she had a fairly clear idea of her property's location. I accompanied her as far as the northern shore of the lake, where we parted ways on October 20, when I had to return to my obligations.

The day she continued on without me was one of oppressive fog, something common to those latitudes. We waited on the shore of the lake until about two in the afternoon, when a boatman arrived, having received word that his services were required. I know him as a man of utmost integrity and trusted him with Miss del Valle's care. I was reassured by the fact that the lady traveled with her dog, who was never far from her side.

I am not a sentimental man, but I must confess that it was an emotional goodbye for me, and I believe that she felt the same. Miss del Valle bid me farewell with a warm embrace and told me that we would meet again in a few weeks. She expected me to take her back to Valparaíso where she would board a ship to California. I understood that she planned to get married soon.

The last glimpse I had of her was her silhouette inside the boat, fading into the fog until it disappeared completely.

I have not been able to get Miss Emilia out of my mind. When weeks went by without news from her, I made some inquiries. Thanks to my contacts in the region, I learned that she had become gravely ill. That prompted my decision to write to you. You have the right to know what has happened to your bride. I have sent this letter to your newspaper in San Francisco with the hope that it reaches your hands without delay.

Miss Emilia del Valle made a lasting impression on me through her sensitivity, her determination, and her courage. In the event that you should wish to journey to Chile in search of her, I place myself entirely at your disposal, ready and willing to aid you in that objective.

Your ever attentive and faithful servant,
Captain Martín Janus

When Emilia's stepfather had finished translating the letter, his eyes met mine. We didn't really have to speak; we both feared the worst. Emilia's mother covered her face with her hands and prayed aloud. Over the years, they'd necessarily grown accustomed to their daughter's sense of adventure and tendency to set out for farther and farther shores, but this was the first time she'd seemingly sailed over the horizon.

I sent a telegram to Captain Janus announcing my plans and boarded a steamship bound for Chile. The journey seemed eternal; each day could be the last of Emilia in this world. I prayed to heaven that I would reach her in time to help her, to save her if that was possible.

·　　·　　·

I REACHED VALPARAÍSO in mid-March and Captain Janus was waiting for me on the dock. We had never met but we recognized each other instinctively. I boarded the *Niña Juanita* and the captain led me along the same route he had followed with Emilia the year prior to the shores of Lake Pirihueico. There, the same boatman picked us up.

The boatman had known Captain Janus when they were young and they had both smuggled silver across the border with Bolivia. He told us that he had ferried Emilia to the extreme southern tip of the lake. She had been met by a native woman who had had word of her arrival through an inexplicable conduit, and had agreed to accompany her. He was not able to tell us anything else.

He navigated his boat along the contours of the lake, which snaked like a fabulous blue ribbon between hillsides dotted with majestic trees, and eventually deposited us on a narrow beach. Janus knew the location of a Mapuche settlement, and from there we set out on foot, trusting in our fate and in the captain's compass.

Captain Janus and I spoke very little, because I know only enough Spanish to communicate basic necessities and he does not speak English, but he managed to express that he felt he should not have allowed her to continue her journey alone, and that he was responsible for her being in possible danger now. I assured him that if anyone was responsible, it was me. We walked for many hours, the captain insisting that if we did not find the Mapuche, they would find us. That is ultimately what happened. At dusk, when I was beginning to assume that we would have to spend the night in the open air, we were approached by two women who appeared out of the dense trees. Janus was able to communicate with them in their language, and we followed them to a small settlement of a few *rucas* that housed an extended family: an elderly man, two teenagers, several women, and half a dozen children of varying ages. I think they only had a few llamas, chickens, and a vegetable garden.

I was overwhelmed by fatigue. After offering the old man some

liquor and tobacco, the captain sat down to smoke, drink, and converse unhurriedly. They spoke with eternal pauses, and it seemed to
me that they repeated the same words or ideas, as if they were talking
in circles. After a long while, the captain translated for me. Some time
back, the family had taken in a foreigner, a *newen ʒomo,* a strong
woman who dared to travel alone.

I showed them Emilia's photograph, which her parents had given
me and I always carry next to my heart, but if they recognized her,
they didn't say so. According to Janus, he would not have recognized
her either. The rigid woman in fancy clothes, with an elaborate
hairdo, staring forward with a startled expression—she didn't look
like the Emilia he knew.

They told him that the woman had been quite ill, reaching the
very edge of death and even peering over onto the other side, but that
a *machi* had arrived from far away to heal her with herbs, rituals, and
chants. Even though their guest was white, the ceremonies were effective in curing her body and when she returned to life, she had
transformed. They were all able to see that light that she had inside,
which is why they gave her a new name: Ailen, meaning luminous
and transparent. Many days later, once she had recovered the desire
to speak and eat, Ailen announced that the time had come for her to
continue on. She gifted them with her only possession of value as a
token by which to remember her. Then she picked up her backpack
and walked into the trees with her dog.

AILEN, THE *NEWEN ʒumo,* had been chosen by Ñuke Mapu, the
Mother Earth, who had brought her back from the abyss and com-
missioned the spirits of air, water, and soil to protect her. They
showed me what Ailen had given them: It was the gold medallion that
Emilia had always worn pinned to her brassiere. Seeing it, I had the
horrible fear that she had died, had perhaps even been murdered, but
Janus assured me that they spoke the truth.

"Return to your country, Mr. Whelan. You will not find one who does not want to be found. Emilia has the soul of a nomad, no one will be able to tie her down," the captain told me.

"It is true that she was made to explore, and that she would have been restless until she found this land, this place where she feels her roots are planted. But she was also made to love, and she would only want a life where both things are possible," I told him.

Still, I understood what the captain was trying to tell me. I felt, as undoubtedly Emilia had felt too, that I was in an enchanted world, a Garden of Eden that persists like an eternal dream in humanity's collective memory. In spite of the anguish that spurred me onward, I was captivated by the extraordinary beauty of that landscape. For months I had lived with a knot in my stomach imagining the worst reasons for the absence and silence of the woman I love—a thousand accidents, a thousand deaths. Now it occurred to me that she had simply wished to continue walking, pulled ever forward. Maybe she needed to exorcize her terrible memories of the war or maybe she was looking for God. I don't know. But at some point, the calling of Emilia's family and our love would be more powerful than the magnetic attraction of this paradise. I decided that when that happened, I would be at her side to take her by the hand and help her find her way back to the life she had before.

I explained to Captain Janus that if I had gotten so far, I had to continue. If Emilia was able to go alone into the immensity of those dark woods and to those high mountains shrouded in mist, I could too.

"Prepare for the possibility that Miss Emilia might not have survived," the captain warned me.

He added that neither the long arm of the government nor the rural police reached there, and that no foreign settlers lived around; the Mapuche inhabitants hated white people and I didn't even speak their language. He told me that he had tried to explain to our elderly host that I was not like other *huincas*—I had not come to offend Ñuke Mapu or steal—I had come only to look for my woman.

"I have to return to my ship now, but you can stay here. When the husbands of these women return, they may be willing to guide you."

"When will that be, Captain?"

"I cannot say," he answered. "Time is relative here, and impatience is useless."

We embraced, and when I saw him walk away, I felt the oppressive weight of my solitude. That good man was my only link to the outside world. I was in the hands of some Indians, and without their help I would never find Emilia. Every hour that passed, she was getting farther and farther away. I could only wait.

AT DUSK ON the third day—three days that felt like three years—two men on horseback arrived. They wore woolen ponchos and red bandanas on their foreheads, they were solid, as if sculpted from dark stone, with long raven-black hair and severe features. One of them had a spear and the other an old rifle. They raised their weapons when they saw me, but the old man calmed them with a gesture and proceeded to explain something at length. They listened with a hostile expression but finally they dismounted. The women unpacked the saddlebags. They contained big pieces of smoked meat; they had hunted a puma.

That night even the dogs ate until they were full and the men got drunk on *muday*. They were astonished at my capacity for alcohol, inherited from my Irish ancestors. It was considered proof of my manhood. After that, they became more friendly and with gestures they let me know that they would help me. But the next morning, I realized we would have to wait another day until they got over the effects of too much *muday*.

Finally, the day after, we left early. One of the hunters accompanied me, pulling a horse by the reins. I was surprised that we would go on foot but I had no way of asking him any questions, so I simply followed him in silence. We walked until it was dark and we couldn't continue. We spent the night near a creek, taking turns feeding a small fire to keep away wild animals. My guide didn't show signs of fatigue, but I was exhausted and hungry; we had brought only some jerky and dry cornbread to eat. It was a long and cold night.

At the crack of dawn, we went onward.

Several hours later we reached the foot of a steep hill and we started climbing. The man and the horse knew the terrain and avoided the obstacles easily, but I hurt my hands with sharp rocks. We had climbed halfway when I heard some furious barking. My guide answered with a long whistle and very soon I saw a yellow dog running toward us. With an uncontrollable cry of relief, I greeted Covadonga.

A few minutes later, Emilia appeared at the top of the slope. After I climbed the last few feet, I opened my arms, repeating her name, and she pressed herself against my chest. She was so thin! Holding her I felt a wave of love and compassion for this woman who smelled of smoke, so different from the Emilia I remembered. But we were together: I had her in my arms and I would never let her go. She lifted her face, touched my tears, kissed me on the lips, and then she was again as before, my indomitable bride.

"I was waiting for you!" she announced.

The news that I was on my way had reached her when Janus and I were at the Mapuche settlement—that is to say, six days prior. I will never know how words travel in those solitudes.

"Why didn't you come home, Emilia? I have been in hell thinking that I would never see you again . . ." I reproached her.

"I wanted you to see where I have lived the past few months," she replied.

We turned to look out over a wide expanse of landscape that was visible from the hill: forest, mountains, and far away the shining outline of the lake. She took me to a cave on the side of the hill that, according to her, had been used by smugglers and Indians who didn't acknowledge the existence of borders and went back and forth between Argentina and Chile. The entrance was protected by rocks and branches so it was invisible for anybody who didn't know its exact location.

The Mapuche called her Ailen and they treated each other with a kind of rough affection; I understood that they saw each other frequently. The refuge contained the minimum needed for survival, including some fodder for horses and chopped wood. Two sheepskins and some blankets served as a bed; I saw some clay pots and garlic and onions hanging from hooks. The table was a board on a couple of stones. It was wet and cold, a dangerous place for someone who had been so ill. She told me that she had probably had a relapse of pneumonia, but she had healed completely, and although she had lost a lot of weight, she now felt strong.

"For God's sake, Emilia, what are you doing here!" I exclaimed, shocked.

"Writing. Don't panic—I have not lost my mind," she said, guessing what I was thinking.

She explained that once she had reached her father's land, she had known that the other thing she needed to do was complete the story she'd begun. In her retreat she had been safe and at peace. Covadonga was her loyal companion and the Mapuche protected and fed her, they brought her corn, yam, potatoes, smoked meat, and dry fruit. No one had bothered her. She had dedicated the summer months to writing.

But now the weather was turning, and she would have to abandon her dwelling before the frost of autumn truly set in. She showed me three notebooks filled to the margins in diminutive handwriting and explained that it was a memoir of her experiences, but also the novel she always wanted to write. I expect it was only the first of many; she was always meant to be a writer.

Emilia is a wild and bright spirit. I will never be able to hold her, I can only hope to accompany her and that love will keep us always together.

"I finished my story. I am ready to go home," Emilia said.

Acknowledgments

Juan Allende, my brother, for his invaluable research skills.

Johanna Castillo, my fierce agent and loving friend.

Jennifer Hershey, for her meticulous and inspiring editing.

David Trías, my editor in Spain.

Elizabeth Subercaseaux, my literary friend and patient reader.

My little family, Roger, Nico, and Lori, for putting up with me.

ABOUT THE AUTHOR

ISABEL ALLENDE, born in Peru and raised in Chile, is a novelist, feminist, and philanthropist. She is one of the most widely read authors in the world, having sold more than eighty million copies of her books across forty-two languages. She is the author of many bestselling and critically acclaimed books, including *The Wind Knows My Name, Violeta, A Long Petal of the Sea, The House of the Spirits, Of Love and Shadows, Eva Luna,* and *Paula.* In addition to her work as a writer, Allende devotes much of her time to human rights causes. She has received fifteen honorary doctorates, has been inducted into the California Hall of Fame, and received the PEN Center USA's Lifetime Achievement Award and the Anisfield-Wolf Book Award for Lifetime Achievement. In 2014, President Barack Obama awarded her the Presidential Medal of Freedom, the nation's highest civilian honor, and in 2018, she received the Medal for Distinguished Contribution to American Letters from the National Book Foundation. Allende lives in California with her husband and dogs.

IsabelAllende.com

Facebook.com/IsabelAllende

Instagram: @allendeisabel